About the Author

A linguist and political scientist by academic background, Robert Ramsay was for many years a senior official at the heart of government in Belfast, London and Brussels. He witnessed at close quarters many of the situations and personalities described in this book and he has maintained contacts right across the political and security spectrum

His interest in the theme of terrorism and governance inspired his first book, 'The Corsican Time Bomb' (ISBN -10-071900893X) and he has also written a memoir of his own career in the UK and EU, entitled 'Ringside Seats' (ISBN 9780 7165 3020 6).

He is now an international consultant on administrative affairs, dividing his time, when not on foreign assignment, between the coast of County Down and the south of Spain.

Dedication

To James, Jonathan, Carl and Brian; and all theirs.

Robert Ramsay

CALLING THE SHOTS

A CIP catalogue record for this title is available from the British Library.

ISBN 978 1 78554 084 4 (Paperback)
ISBN 978 1 78554 085 1 (Hardback)

www.austinmacauley.com

First Published (2015)
Austin Macauley Publishers Ltd.
25 Canada Square
Canary Wharf
London
E14 5LQ

Printed and bound in Great Britain

Acknowledgments

My sincere thanks go to a great number of friends, colleagues and sources, in both high and low places, whose co-operation made the writing of this book possible.

They are too numerous to mention – and many of them would, in any case, prefer to remain in the shadows, which is their natural habitat.

They know who they are and that I am grateful to them. May their recompense be a certain satisfaction that this side of the story has at last been told.

DECLARATION

This book is partly a work of fiction, based on unpalatable facts. Where actual events are described, background details and names have been changed in order to protect the innocent ... and the guilty.

ABBREVIATIONS

ACC Assistant Chief Constable

ASU Active Service Unit, of the (Provisional) IRA

BOTDR Brillouin Optical Time Domain Reflectometry

CASTLE Stormont Castle, administrative seat of the SoS (NI)

CC Chief Constable of the RUC

CID Criminal Investigation Division of the RUC

CLF Commander Land Forces (British Army)

CRUM Short for Crumlin Road Prison

DIY Do it yourself

DST Direction de la Surveillance du Territoire, the French equivalent of MI5

FCO Foreign and Commonwealth Office

GCMG Grand Cross of the Order of St Michael and St George

GFA Good Friday Agreement (also known as the Belfast Agreement)

GOC General Officer Commanding

HMG Her Majesty's Government

HSB Head of the RUC's Special Branch. These initials were used as a form of address to the officer.

HUMINTEL Intelligence from human resources

JCB Heavy mechanical digger, manufactured by J. C. Bamford Excavators Limited

JSC Joint Security Committee

JSC (INTEL) Intelligence subcommittee of the JSC

KCMG Knight Commander of the Order of St Michael and St George

NIO Northern Ireland Office

OC Officer Commanding in the British Army; (used also by some of the paramilitary organisations)

ODCs 'Ordinary decent criminals' (i.e. not paramilitaries)

PIRA Provisional Irish Republican Army (a title often abbreviated to 'IRA', or to 'the 'RA'

PPE Philosophy, Politics and Economics, Oxbridge degree course

PUS Permanent Undersecretary of State, the most senior civil servant in any department; he/she is addressed as such.

RHC Red Hand Commandos, a Loyalist paramilitary organisation

RPG Rocket-propelled grenade

RUC Royal Ulster Constabulary

SAS Special Air Services

SB Special Branch (of RUC)

SoS (NI) Secretary of State for Northern Ireland. He /she is addressed as such

TECHNITEL Intelligence acquired through technical devices

UDA Ulster Defence Association, a Loyalist organisation which was originally legal, but later banned

UDR Ulster Defence Regiment (of the British Army)

UFF Ulster Freedom Fighters, an offshoot of the UDA and banned organisation

UVF Ulster Volunteer Force, a Loyalist paramilitary organisation

WBG West Belfast Growth A government – sponsored organisation aimed at improving employment opportunities in the area

GLOSSARY

Albornoz: Spanish for bathrobe

An Phoblacht: Irish for 'The Republic', a publication sympathetic to the 'armed struggle'

Ard fheisanna: annual conferences of Sinn Fein

Balneario: Spanish for thermal spa

Bateau-mouche: tourist pleasure boat on the Seine

Billy Sanderson: name deliberately distorted by Loyalists, of IRA hunger striker, Bobby Sands

Brick: a small police foot patrol, guarded by soldiers

Cisteoir: Irish for 'treasurer'

Ceili: Irish party with music

Claudia: Gunrunning ship arrested by the Irish navy in 1973

Garda Siochana: Irish for 'Civic Guard', the Republic's police force

Green-booked: IRA slang for 'sworn in'.

Hallion: Ulster Scots dialect word for 'scamp, scoundrel'

Maze: Prison (formerly called 'Long Kesh') in which most paramilitary prisoners were held

Mozo: Spanish for 'porter / bell hop'

Oglaigh na hEireann: Irish for 'Irish Army', the self-appointed name of the IRA

PANORAMA: Computerised databank used by the security forces to build up information on suspects

Ruby Murray: Belfast-born singer. Ulster slang rhymes her name with 'curry'

Shebeen: An illegal drinking den

Sunningdale: British Government administrative complex near London, where a failed power-sharing agreement was signed between NI political parties in 1973

Taoiseach: Irish Prime Minister

Teague: Pejorative nickname for a 'nationalist / Roman Catholic'

Tiocfaidh ar lá: Irish for 'Our day will come', a slogan of the IRA

VELLUM: A surveillance programme based on the bugging of suspects' vehicles
Woodbine: a brand of cheap cigarettes

Chapter 1

The sphincter-slackening moment of decision could be delayed no longer. This bomb was 'old' and Major Tomkins knew it could explode within minutes, perhaps seconds. He had already worked on it for well over an hour, huddled in a corner of the Ford Transit van, in which the business end of the device, a mass of wires and soldering, had been wedged against the panel which divided the cargo area from the driver's cab. There was no way 'Robbie the Robot' could be used to winkle this bomb out. Each bomb was now more difficult to deal with than its predecessor; the war of wits between bomb designer and bomb disposal officer had become an ever more lethal struggle.

Tomkins' temples throbbed from the effort of working in an almost upside-down position, but the sustained adrenaline flow through his body deadened the pain in his limbs. He had at once recognized in the layout of the device the signature handiwork of the PIRA bomb-brain he and his colleagues referred to as 'Colin' – so called because the first device of this particular signature retrieved intact had been in Colin Glen, a small parkland area of West Belfast.

Tomkins had already discovered two tilt switches in the mechanism, which if interfered with would have at once set off the bomb. But had Colin invented a third anti-handling device and hidden it in the jumble of the wiring which had been inserted to cause confusion? And what if the electronic jamming equipment being used by his colleagues from their operational command vehicle down the road to prevent the bomb being detonated by remote control could have been circumvented by some new gadget in PIRA's armoury?

You're sliding towards defeatism, Tomkins, old man. Pull yourself together. Think positively.

He must review the situation one more time, then back his knowledge, experience and judgement against the devious skills of that bastard Colin.

As he gently manipulated the wires, he looked for the first time in a long while at the back of his own hands. Not a tremble: he was still 'Steady Eddy', the revered head of the squad, with dozens of 'dismantles' to his credit, and authorship of an Operational Manual which had become the standard reference work in several armies and police forces around the world. But for how much longer could he lead this sort of life? He noticed, almost with a start, a brown liver spot, half the size of the nail of his little finger, in the middle of his left hand. The first real reminder in his own body, of age and mortality.

But look on the bright side.

Age would carry him to retirement in less than two years; then the cottage in Cumbria with Valery. That's if he could keep ahead of Colin.

He thought through the wiring layout one last time, and remained convinced that to cut wire 'K', as he had christened it in his mind, was to break the link between detonator and explosive charge.

'I'm going to slice', he whispered coolly into the mouthpiece of his communications unit, buttoned into the top of his shirt. That was heard not only by his colleagues in the van down the road, but by the crisis team assembled in the operations room at Castlereagh RUC Holding Centre, some five miles away in the east of the city. As he took the wire cutters from his belt and carefully placed them round 'K', he received, superimposed on what he was concentrating on, an image of Valery and the girls, sitting in a sunlit meadow, laughing as they enjoyed a picnic. It was an image which always came to him at the moment of truth. He did not know where the meadow was, and the girls were but lentiginous-faced children, not their adult selves, but he knew this was literally 'the picture of happiness', which he suspected his subconscious had constructed for him, lest this thought prove to be his last. He wore no protective clothing – *I can't work as a watchmaker, dressed as an ice hockey goalkeeper* – and his colleagues could not gainsay his calculation that if a 1000 kilo device exploded at close quarters the wearing of the most sophisticated protective gear available would have the effect of reducing the number of body parts to be picked up from four hundred to four – an advantage of no interest to him whatsoever.

With a firm grip he squeezed the cutters. Snick. Nothing. The ache in his limbs, rather than relief, flooded his consciousness. He moved to the back of the van and gave a 'thumbs-up' sign in the direction of the command vehicle.

In the crisis management room at Castlereagh the radio crackled. 'Number One dealt with, contact.'

Despite the tension of the past hours, there was no celebratory outburst from those gathered round the table, just a mild 'Hah' from the CLF, who said 'Good boy, Eddy' and slapped the table with the palm of his hand. HSB and the Security Co-Ordinator smiled nervously at one another, and the supporting staff in the room went about their business. They had all been there for three days, monitoring the crisis and its potential consequences, sleeping on camp beds in the offices along the corridor on the second floor, and eating the artery–clogging Ulster breakfasts brought up from the canteen. A monastic life, focused, not on the raising of the Eucharist, but on the quasi-mystical act of dismantlement performed by Major Tomkins.

The bomb had been aimed at one of two targets, perhaps both. Firstly, an Orange Order parade was due to pass down part of that road late on Saturday morning; and a battalion of a Scottish regiment was to follow much the same route on their way to the docks at the end of a tour of duty. Either would have presented a choice target for the Provisional IRA, even at the risk of collateral damage in the form of death or injury suffered by innocent bystanders.

The security forces were on crisis alert, following a tip-off from an RUC informant, Seamus Toner, codename 'Harry-the-hound', whose Volunteer role in PIRA was as a 'runner', which gave him access to important, but inevitably fragmentary, information relating to terrorist operations, as he carried messages to and fro between local commanders, finance officers, bomb makers, drivers and, sometimes, 'higher authorities'. He had warned his handler earlier in the week that two new mega-bombs would be planted at the weekend. He knew one of them was destined for the Springfield Road area; he did not know the planned location, even generally, of the second, but would keep his ear to the ground and report back by Friday at the latest. Then he had simply vanished.

'What are we doing to find him?' asked Jeremy Granville, the Security Services Director and Co-ordinator of Intelligence.

'His handler, Sgt. Bob McKinney, and five undercover constables are scouring all his known haunts – most of them pubs – but so far there's no sign of him,' replied HSB.

'How sure are we of him?'

'As sure as we can be of any of our touts and agents ...which means up to a point, based on our past positive experience of them, but not all the way. They're not reliable people by nature.' He had almost said 'by profession', but thought the MI5 man might take that amiss.

'"Harry-the-hound "is in fact, a strange one, even by the standards of "the business". He was a walk-in several years ago. His family is solidly Republican on both sides, all the way back to the 1920s, so we were naturally suspicious of his motives at first. McKinney thinks his man felt – still feels indeed – undervalued by the higher-ups in the movement. Then there was something vague about an uncle of his not having received proper assistance after he came out from a stretch in the Maze. But probably more important, nowadays, is that our man values not only our subsidization of his "wee weakness", as they say in Belfast, but, strangely, his relationship with McKinney. A sort of father-and-son thing. And I think it's mutual. We have to watch that, it could be very dangerous. But up to now, we've done very well out of friend Harry.'

'Up to now,' repeated Granville, drily.

'Yes. God alone knows where either he or bomb number two are. We'll just have to keep looking.'

HSB picked up a scrambler phone and dialled home.

'It's me. Shall we go over?'

He pressed the scrambler button.

'Still here. Business only half over. Tell Eric I'm sorry to spoil his birthday. The round of golf will have to wait. Yes, I know he's disappointed. So am I. But at least he can have a drink, now he's of age. Don't hold up the celebrations on my account. I've no idea when I'll be home. I'll ring. You too. Bye.'

Tomkins sat, grey faced, in the front seat of a service car, still at the scene of his triumph. Two of his assistants and a forensic officer were still at work on the bomb-carrying vehicle.

'If I can't have a beer until I've dealt with number two, I'm at least going to have a fag,' he said, reaching into the glove compartment for his Dunhills.

'Well done, sir,' said the young lieutenant who was acting as his deputy that day. It was said sincerely; only those who worked and lived close-up to bombs and their handling could appreciate just how tough the job could be. The amazing thing was that bomb disposal units had traditionally far more applicant volunteers than there were places on the teams. Selecting new members was a delicate task: one didn't want to bring on board 'excitement junkies' – Tomkins personally called them 'the Russian Roulette Rabble' – 'who simply craved danger in their hitherto drab little lives', as he put it. Yet, at the same time, the ideal operator had to be able to channel the excitement of danger into a heightened awareness of all aspects of every tense situation; a totally calm individual might not be able to produce the extraordinarily high level of concentration required to do the job ... and to stay alive. Tomkins smiled to himself, as he concluded his reverie with the thought that the ideal operator had to be a well-balanced, but alert, personality – like himself. He knew how Valery would tease him, if he were to say that out loud in front of her.

'Yes, and modest with it,' she would certainly say.

He had been extremely fortunate in his life, particularly as regards Valery. All army wives have their hours, their days, of anxiety whenever their husbands are 'in theatre'. It is only natural if the heart missed a beat whenever the doorbell or telephone rang, especially at night. But the successful wives do not transmit that angst to their husbands, or complain to them about the stress under which they are living.

Valery and he had been married when he was just out of Sandhurst and she had always been not only his life's partner, but his greatest supporter in his career. She had, without complaint, followed him to various overseas postings, in Cyprus and Germany; and had moved more times than she cared to number round accommodation in army bases in England, while he was serving in places as far away as Oman and Hong Kong. None of these 'homes', as she emphatically and doggedly called them, was anything better than 'comfortable'; several had been decidedly substandard, reflecting the Government's priorities within the defence budget. They were, in terms of her upbringing as a surgeon's only daughter, a sacrifice. Army life also imposed on the Tomkins what they felt was a far greater sacrifice, in that their two daughters had been obliged to go to boarding school from an early age.

All these hardships Valery had accepted as part of her lot in life, and were more than compensated for by sharing her life with as interesting and amusing a man as Eddy. Nevertheless, as his retirement appeared on the horizon – and why did his last posting have to be in Northern Ireland, instead of a cushy number at Staff College – she had started to talk increasingly about 'pay-back time'. This referred to where they would set up their post-army home. Some years before, when posted to the Ministry of Defence in Whitehall, Tomkins had had the wisdom, or the luck, to buy a substantial house in Putney. Its present value would ensure that the existing mortgage could be easily paid off, with enough over to buy a modest house in a region removed from the insane housing market of the South East. Eddy had at first suggested the South Coast, or even France, but she had not considered those possibilities for a moment. 'No. I've rattled around with you in foreign parts long enough, Eddy Tomkins. This time I'm going to MY home, in MY country.'

'But Bournemouth's hardly foreign, is it?'

'To me it is. Home to me is Cumbria.' She could scarcely believe her own daring and outspokenness.

'Cumbria! For God's sake, woman. It never stops raining there.'

'I don't care. In Cumbria I am back to my roots. You know, roots aren't only for the descendants of black African slaves. I want to be where I went to school, where my parents and grandparents are buried, where I can look out every morning at a lake I knew as a child, and where I'll meet old friends down the street or in the pub.'

'I'm all for peace and quiet,' replied Tomkins, 'but isn't Cumbria just a tad out of the way?'

Then she put in her challenge: 'Where would you rather be?'

Tomkins was cornered. He had been on the move for such a long time that he didn't look outside the army for any concept of 'home': he had no alternative to put forward. Besides, he knew that he owed Valery – big time. So Cumbria, with the highest bloody rainfall in the British Isles, it had to be. Cumbria was the first time bomb he had failed to dismantle. But the more he thought about it, the more he liked the idea. He promised to go house hunting there during his next leave. Meanwhile, there was bomb number two to think about – if the police and army could find it in time.

The dual mysteries of the whereabouts of bomb number two and Harry-the-hound were solved within the next hour. Firstly, a huge explosion rocked West Belfast, as a builder's lorry – stolen in the housing estate of Poleglass earlier in the week, it later transpired – flew several metres into the air on the Horseshoe Road on the slopes outside the city, at the entrance to a field. No one was injured, as the road was deserted at the time, no thanks to the bombers, as no warnings had been given. It was surmised by those at Castlereagh that the driver of the bomb-lorry had been 'disturbed' on his way to a designated target, perhaps by the sight of one of the many police and army checkpoints which had been hastily put in place on the basis of Harry-the-hound's intelligence, and had aborted his mission according to PIRA procedures, by simply driving into open country and abandoning his vehicle and its lethal load, which was already primed by the bomb handler. To 'deal with' the explosive device was far beyond the remit, or capabilities, of the Volunteer driver, whose role in, and knowledge of, the operation was limited strictly to driving from 'A' (pick-up point) to 'B' (target). 'C' (point of mission abortion) was at his discretion, and governed by the circumstances he found himself in. He would, however, have to justify the abandonment of his mission in great detail, during a post-operation de-briefing with his local commander and a senior figure from the disciplinary and security unit.

As for Harry-the-hound, Sgt. McKinney had used trusted contacts within the administrative offices of the main Belfast hospitals. It was a delicate matter, as the IRA also had sympathizers in most of them and any speculative enquiry about a patient could easily arouse suspicions. McKinney struck gold with the Royal Victoria Hospital: a Mr Seamus Patrick Toner was indeed a patient, having been admitted by ambulance last Wednesday, with suspected kidney failure. He was recovering, after treatment, in Ward 13 (Men's Surgical).

The poor guy. Kidneys and liver in a terrible state. Partly – indeed mostly, to tell the truth – self-inflicted wounds. But getting out of alcohol dependency is never easy for anyone, particularly for a man under stress. But thank God he's safe and not unmasked. I'll have to look after him.

The daily situation report mentioned the two bombs, an arms find in the Creggan in Londonderry, and some brief 'recreational rioting' at Unity Flats, Belfast. Northern Ireland had seen many worse days, but would it see better ones in the foreseeable future, wondered a tired Granville, as his car accelerated out of the narrow vehicle entrance of the Holding Centre into the traffic in Ladas Drive. It would take more than the successes of the Bomb Disposal Unit to achieve that. The challenge for him, more than for anyone else, was to move 'the situation' into a new dimension.

Chapter 2

Noleen Cassidy's curiosity didn't kill her, but it did bring about what she would later call her 'Eve moment'. She bit into the fruit of the Tree of Knowledge – knowledge of good and evil – by yielding, for the first time in her marriage, to the temptation to be curious and prying about her husband's behaviour. And, as things turned out, it did indeed change her life.

Aidan's voluminous briefcase lay on the bed, a modern version of a Gladstone bag, with a clasp at the top. The zip was pulled fully to the side, leaving an inviting gap of a couple of inches. She had never seen Aidan carry a case like that and as she now watched him outside in the driveway, talking to Ernie, the gardener, she smiled at her own temerity in not pulling aside the lips of the bag – he could not possibly come back into the house and be up the stairs in less than twenty seconds; he might well even stay outside for several more minutes. Yet she hesitated. To pry did not come naturally or easily to her. And despite the fact that she might have admitted to a certain loss of intimacy in recent years, she felt a pang of guilt – or was it apprehension – as she tentatively opened the bag another few inches, as carefully as a bomb disposal officer.

She caught her breath and her hands froze on the lips of the bag. Inside were stacked, in neat bundles, twenty pound sterling notes, along with US dollars and Irish punts in various denominations. Hurriedly, she returned the bag to its original state and irrationally tiptoed out of the bedroom, across the landing to the bathroom, where she locked the door and, turning on the taps, sat down, panting and out of breath, on the mock Roman stool by the bath. She didn't know whether to be relieved or horrified; she was certainly disturbed. She had noticed for some time that Aidan had some part of his life he was no longer sharing with her. Was there another woman? Possibly. She shuddered at the thought. They had been so close, ever since her teenage years. He was not what she or her girl friends would have called exciting, but instinctively she admired his steadiness and had relied on his supportive strength. He had helped her over two great traumas in her life – the potential disgrace of her youthful 'indiscretions' and the unexpected death of her mother. He had always been her confidant. They knew one another's innermost thoughts and she had once been sure that he had no secrets from her.

There was only one faint shadow in their relationship, and it was on her account. It wasn't, strictly speaking a secret, as she felt sure that Aidan knew about it, or at least harboured strong suspicions, but it was the only taboo subject between them. In their circles it was almost certain that he would have heard a rumour of her brief fling, at the age of eighteen, with Sean Byrne, who had been a classmate of Aidan's at St Mary's College.

Men, she reflected, were always prone to stray, as her mother had never tired of saying, but now she felt sure that the more likely explanation of Aidan's withdrawal from their former complete intimacy lay in another direction, almost equally alarming – 'the movement'. They were both from Catholic families in West Belfast, which meant more or less automatically that they were nationalists. The world outside tended to look on that community as united and homogeneous. But within even 'Catholic West Belfast', not to mention the Catholic population at large, were many contrasting, as well as overlapping, groups. Her father, John-Joe McManus, had inherited two public houses, which he had developed into a thriving business, opening three other bars within a decade. He had visibly prospered despite the 'Troubles'. His nationalism shaded subtly towards republicanism and support for 'the armed struggle'. He was publicly identified with various local protest movements – notably about prison conditions for IRA men at the Maze –

organized by Sinn Fein – and it was generally known that he was a generous donor to many republican causes. Beyond that, who knew how far, in practical terms, his support would reach? That would depend on what he was asked to do and, so far, the security forces had him marked down merely as a 'supporter', with no direct links to acts of violence. He would joke with his wife, a Dubliner who had no interest in politics of any sort, that his position was the only sensible one to take for a man who wished to preserve both his business and his own skin. Noleen had heard that family conversation repeated many times since her childhood but had never been sure whether her father's refrain was the truth, or whether he was indeed 'dedicated to the cause', as many of his neighbours and customers would have said of him. She shared her mother's indifference to political matters, particularly the lethal Irish variety, though her schooling and upbringing had imbued her with an almost automatic antipathy to all things British, to whom most of the woes of Ireland were ritually ascribed. She had also inherited her mother's love of the pictorial arts and looked on her collection of books on European paintings and her frequent visits to the great continental galleries as the core of her personal version of the Good Life – never a birthday or wedding anniversary went by without such a treat. Aidan would from time to time tease her that she was 'high artistic maintenance', but, like her mother before her, she took these privileges for granted, whilst regarding them as something to be enjoyed discreetly.

Aidan's family were standard issue 'Lower Falls': a two-up, two-down house in a side street; father a maintenance mechanic in the Royal Victoria Hospital ; mother a cleaner. He had been a conscientious pupil, a plodder rather than an academic high flyer at St. Mary's and had had difficulty in gaining his B.Sc. (Commerce) at Queen's University, where he had been obliged to repeat his final year. He persevered with studies bringing him post-graduate professional qualifications and, thanks to financial backing from his father-in-law, was able, within a short time, to set up his own business as an insurance broker, in prestigious premises on the top floor of the Scottish Provident Building, overlooking Belfast City Hall, the hub of the city. That upward social and financial mobility had isolated him to some extent from his three older brothers, who had remained rooted in what they were happy to call the working class, though it was rare for all three of them to be working, in any sort of employment, at any given moment. He was also separated from them by a large age gap, his nearest brother being seven years older, and he could sense their resentment at the fact that he was the only son to have had an education which opened doors to a higher standard of living. 'But I've worked for it, while they played billiards', was his self-justification, whenever he thought about their attitude towards him. He was still in touch with them, but not closely, and when his parents had both died within a year of one another, his involvement with his brothers and the wider family circle shrank to the essentials of funerals, weddings and christenings. It was happier for all that way.

Chapter 3

'Any cigars in the SitReps?' asked the Head of Special Branch, putting his head round the door of the Operations Room. (*En clair*: any significant arrests in the Situation Reports?).

"One here that might be. An Executive Officer, no less, of the Northern Ireland Office, drunk and disorderly in Shaftesbury Square. Mixed up with Glasgow Rangers' supporters coming out of their club after the Old Firm match. Apparently blitzed out of his skull, fighting with all and sundry, including one of our uniformed brethren. Now contrite as a repentant sinner, not to mention shit-scared for the consequences for his job."

"What is his job exactly?"

"Apparently he's the chief cipher clerk in Communications at Stormont Castle."

"Really? Sounds promising. Is he at Castlereagh?"

"No, but I can have him sent there if you think he's a suitable case for treatment."

"Do NIO know about this yet?"

"No."

"Good. Keep it that way. Let's see what we can do. I'll brief Austin and Niblock before they give our man the once over."

An hour or so later John Archibald McCune arrives at the RUC's Holding Centre in Ladas Drive, Castlereagh, on the eastern outskirts of Belfast. This is where terrorist suspects are customarily grilled; ODCs – ordinary decent criminals – rarely appear there, but McCune is a special case. He knows, of course, as do the public at large, what 'Castlereagh' is for and is puzzled, though not yet alarmed, as to why he is there.

He cuts a sorry figure as he is 'administratively processed' by a bored constable prior to his interrogation. Personal details are taken with the same disinterest as his fingerprints. Ditto his account of what happened to him in Shaftesbury Square.

"But I've already told all that to the police where they took me."

"Well tell it again, sunshine, I've got my job to do."

He suspects they are looking for contradictions in his two versions of the events; in reality his first statement doesn't look like a Castlereagh document, so the police are starting from scratch.

Files in a recognisable format look better. Just in case. You never know with tribunals of inquiry these days.

Does he want to be seen by a doctor? Does he want his solicitor alerted? He gives a puzzled look.

"Just asking," says the constable. "Must make sure all your tender human rights are respected."

"No."

"Good. Much better that way."

Incongruously for a football supporter out on the town, he is wearing a dark, three-piece suit and tie, as he had gone to the club direct from a Saturday morning spell of duty at Stormont Castle. A bruise on his left cheek and some blood stains on the collar of his white shirt were glaring indications that his Saturday had not gone well. Firstly, 'Gers' had lost 2-1 to the ancient enemy, Celtic, and would now almost certainly lose the league championship to them. To a fan such as McCune, a Rangers supporter since birth, if not indeed conception, that was tragedy enough for one Saturday, but the circumstances of the defeat made things worse: a disputed penalty in injury time.

"Definitely not a hand ball – it struck the full back when he put up his hand to shield his face."

Discussion of the sad end to the game prolonged his planned post-match stay in the club. His fellow supporters shared his outrage: *Fuckin' ref. is probably a Teague* summed up the general sentiment. McCune's unchanging weekend drinking practice was to hoover up pints of stout at a steady pace, with no intermissions, so that his longer-than-usual stay in the club meant that even his capacity to hold his drink, which had gradually been expanded over the years to an impressive degree, had been overcome by the sheer volume which flowed down his throat that afternoon. Once out in the fresh air, which hit him like a hammer to the head, he struggled to find his bearings and to set his course for Oxford Street bus station and his way home to Comber.

He had no idea how, or why, the fight had started in Shaftesbury Square. He only knew that, suddenly, the four or five others who had left the club with him were under attack from a much larger group of teenagers, who kicked and punched and swore and yelled, all at the same time. McCune had been in such scenes before and reacted automatically, swinging punches and kicking wildly at anyone who came into his blurred field of vision. He had not taken on board the fact that the police had arrived until, flat on his back on the pavement, he managed to locate and straighten his thick horn-rimmed glasses and make out the new key fact in his predicament, namely that the man who had pinned him to the ground was a uniformed constable of the RUC. As he re- told the story, it became ever more unreal to himself. Would he awake and find it was all a hangover-fuelled nightmare? Instead, he now lapsed into sleep and slid slightly along the wall.

He was awakened roughly by Constable Report Maker, who yanked him to his feet and half led, half dragged him along a long corridor. Now he was ushered into one of the state-of-the-black-art interrogation rooms, complete with sound system, monitoring TV camera and observation window/mirror. He felt nauseous and was glad to be able to crouch forward over the table that stood between him and his Special Branch inquisitors. There were two of them. Gradually he focused on the older man, who seemed to have an extraordinarily large, round, sad face, in which stood out little squiggles of broken purple veins on both sides of his nose, like a marginal warning note.

'Well, well, what a tragedy,' began Bill Austin with a deep sigh, peering closely at McCune through thick glasses. 'Just look at you. As the Good Book says "strong drink mocketh a man." And, boy, did it make a monkey out of you. What a pity!'

He paused for a moment, shaking his head, as though struggling to come to terms with the enormity of the pity of it all, as he studied the pangolin figure before him.

'It's your poor old Mammy in Motherwell I feel sorry for,', he went on mournfully, thus deliberately revealing that he had already run a check on McCune with his Scottish opposite number.

'There she was, widowed at forty, bringing up four hallions all on her lonesome. And thinking she at least had you off her hands, with honour, no less: through high school, an established civil servant with special skills, and an index-linked pension; could go all over the world on Her Majesty's business. Now over here with great perks – free housing, allowances for this and that, trips home twice a month...sure, you couldn't beat it with a big stick. On the pig's back. The life of Riley in spades.'

He spread his hands wide, to indicate the abundance of McCune's personal cornucopia.

'And now this.'

Much shaking of earnest jowls. 'Now this. Drunk and disorderly. Breach of the peace. And grievous bodily harm to a policeman. That alone's bound to be two years in the Crumlin. Ever been in our wee jail, son? Not a good place to be, "the Crum". And, of course, you'll be unemployed and unemployable when you come out – dishonourably discharged from the Service, with not a friend in the world, believe you me. What a tragedy!'

To the outside observer it would have been clear that Austin adored just such a tragedy, since it chimed perfectly with his personal vision of lost humanity. His enjoyment in this particular tragedy was, however, tempered by the professional knowledge that his role in it was intended to be but the first of two very different acts. They were known as 'Bill and Ben, the statements men.'

'If you've nothing to say – and what could you say? – I'll get the papers ready for the DPP and the court.'

Muttering "Strong drink, strong drink... dear, oh dear..." he packed up his file and left the room.

Ben Niblock waited a while before taking up the running. He did not try to rouse McCune, who remained slumped forward, his face almost touching the tabletop. McCune at last stirred, removed his glasses and wiped them on his blue tie. He peered at Niblock, who smiled at him. This was still a copper's face, but sharp and alert. McCune could now see that his interrogator was dressed in a track suit – a fitness fanatic, was he?

'Would you like a cigarette, Jimmy?'

"My name is John," said McCune, with just a hint of defiance.

''Course it is, 'course it is. Look, I'm only trying to help. Here, have a Benson and Hedges,' he said, flicking a cigarette across the table.

"Tipped OK for you? You see, Jimmy, I'm your man's superior,' (thumb jerked in the direction of the departed Austin), 'and I could overrule all that. I mean the court case and so on. But I'd need your help. Couldn't do it at all without your help."

McCune's head remained down. He said nothing.

'You see, Jimmy, I'd really like to help, personally. Between you, me and the gatepost, I'm a 'Gers supporter myself...and all that. Know what I mean? Not that we're allowed to say that too openly nowadays. A bit of a taboo in our line of work, you might say. But, of course, our common interests – yours and mine– can't get you off the hook. There has to be, what do you call it, a *quid pro quo*. Right?'

McCune remained silent.

'Well, John, I'll lay it out for you: I'll mark your get-out-of-jail card.'

He lit his own cigarette and reached over the table with the lighter in his hand. McCune sat up almost straight, sucked on the cigarette till it glowed brightly. After a deep breath, he exhaled a long stream of smoke.

'You're housed in Comber, right?' McCune nodded.

'Do you share a house or flat?'

'No, I have a small house to myself, off High Street.'

'That's nice, so it is. Comber's a good place. Convenient wee town. Loyal wee town. Peaceful. Not bad shopping. One or two reasonable pubs. Regular bus service to Belfast.'

He paused. *Were there any other jewels in Comber's crown?*

'Suppose you know McDade's on the Square?'

McCune appeared to come partly to life at the mention. 'Aye, I do.'

'Grand pub. I was once stationed up the street from there. Always a friendly crowd in. Salt of the earth. The food's pretty good in the restaurant upstairs, I'm told. Especially their Sunday roasts. Ever tried it?'

'Not really,' replied McCune, for whom food held no particular pleasure, beyond its essential uses as fuel and blotting paper. Which explained why he was, as colleagues said, as thin as a pipe cleaner, despite his weekly intake of alcohol.

'So, here's the deal, John. You're a bright young man, I'm sure, when you're not rolling about in Shaftsbury Square, but instead handling the day-to-day documents between London and Stormont Castle. The day job. Encrypting and decrypting and all that technical stuff. You could do an extra copy of anything that struck you as being likely to be of interest to us. You know the sort of thing – policy papers, papers on the political situation, the security assessments, relations with the army and police....what the mandarins are thinking. I'm sure you could make a good selection of the important ones.'

'No, no, I couldn't do that. That's criminal. That's the sack for sure.'

His Security Training Course (Advanced) would have been proud of his reaction, however ephemeral.

'But my dear John, at this moment dismissal and jail are precisely what you are facing. And I am offering to get you out of all that trouble. It's a no-brainer. Play my game and, OK, there are risks, but you can control them yourself. Don't play for me and all those risks are already a reality.'

Niblock paused to let the proposition sink in.

'But we're friends, John, so I can do better than that. My man will see you in McDade's every Saturday, or some other day, by arrangement, at lunch time. If you have something for nhim, you can slip out to the gents' to hand it over. I don't expect "product", as we call it in the trade, every week, but one never knows. And here's the good bit ...' Niblock paused and smiled broadly at his soon-to-be recruit.

'Whatever the week may bring or hold, my man will have a wee packet for you – enough for your Saturday's entertainment and a bit more. A few pints of heavy (here Niblock attempted a Glaswegian accent), a flutter on the nags, a Ruby Murray at Raji's and a bevy or two more before bedtime. Now, I can't say fairer than that, can I?'

McCune did not look overjoyed, but as he drew on his cigarette, he visibly relaxed.

'Shall I stop the file?' asked Niblock.

'OK,' came the weak reply, after some hesitation.

'Done!' cried Niblock, reaching over to clap his now-fully-fledged-recruit on the shoulder.

Thus began OPERATION GILLESPIE, 'a window into the murky soul of London', as HSB would come to describe it.

Chapter 4

Sir Julian Beardsley KCMG, sat back in the vast armchair by the window of his club and gazed down at the swift-flowing traffic in St James's Street. He had the contented air of a man for whom the important things in life (to him at any rate) had turned out well: his Foreign Office career, boosted by an early spell in MI6, with which he had retained 'an association', had so far taken him to within one step from the very top; the shrewd investments he had made with the inheritance from his father and the property in Marbella, bought before Spanish prices had joined those of the rest of Europe, had already assured him of a comfortable retirement; and, not least, his golf was still the source of enjoyment, rather than frustration, and he found it socially rewarding in both Spain and Surrey and, at a steadfastly maintained handicap of four, it was in his eyes an admirable accomplishment for a man of his age.

The one box which an analyst of the Beardsleyan *vita* would have hesitated to tick was 'sex and marriage'. Of the latter there was not the slightest sign; of the former scarcely a discernible trace. At Magdalen, where he had read PPE, he had been far too busy working on his First (duly acquired, along with a couple of the Glittering Prizes) to go partying or playing the field. Then it was straight into the FCO, where he had plunged headlong into the project of building 'The Career', as he termed it whenever confiding in his mother, his greatest fan.

There had been, it is true, the one 'incident', early in his career, when posted to the embassy in Copenhagen. One of the locally recruited staff, a stocky, short-haired nymphomaniac, Lottie Pedersen, was renowned for her conquests among her colleagues, both British and Danish. Her directness and availability often trumped her basic unattractiveness. She was also a notorious gossip, even – indeed especially – about herself. It was generally accepted that she had succeeded, after an Aalborg-fuelled office party to celebrate the Queen's birthday, in getting Beardsley into bed, but claimed subsequently to her friends that 'he hadn't been able to raise the mortgage'.

Was he perhaps a homosexual? The question arose officially every three years or so, whenever he underwent his Positive Vetting procedure. The little Scotsman, ex-police by the look and sound of him, who put the question in a slightly embarrassed way, did not probe further in the interview once he had received the firm, simple answer 'No'. But he had had enough experience of senior mandarins, who were, he assumed, by definition and way of life, practised professional liars one and all, to make his own extensive enquiries. The point was not whether Beardsley was gay or not – God knows there were enough of them in the FCO out of the closet to form a medium-sized Gay Parade all by themselves – but, if he had falsely denied homosexuality he would, in the eyes of Security, be potentially open to blackmail. Big black marks all round; indeed loss of top security clearance, therefore end of career.

Scottish Positive Vetter failed to turn up anything faintly incriminating in the voluminous evidence he amassed from his sniffing around Beardsley's colleagues, neighbours, golf partners and even the regulars at his local gastropub, where he took his mother to Sunday lunch as a family ritual. Nevertheless, tongues were bound to wag from time to time. Bizarrely, his moustache, broad as Stalin's but thinner and turned down slightly at the ends, was occasionally the focus of slanderous speculation amongst some of the more irreverent juniors in the staff canteen whenever he put in an appearance there.

'Can't you see him, with that moustache, dark sunglasses and a leather jacket, mincing along the *paseo* in Tossa del Mar hand in hand with some Scandinavian bum-chum in pink?'

'You're sure he'd be the daddy?'

'Of course, always in control. That's our Beardy.'

In reality, no one had ever seen Beardsley, except on a golf course, in anything other than a double-breasted suit, which simultaneously spoke of expense and a lack of female oversight. In the words of one of his contemporaries, he had brought crumpled elegance to a new peak as an art form. Indeed he seemed to have a double-breasted personality, perhaps even wore double-breasted pyjamas, suggested one joker. More charitable observers, that is to say his protégés, such as Granville, thought that, on the balance of evidence, Beardsley was probably one of life's non-combatants as far as sex was concerned. Power was more his thing – power exercised in the service of his confident personal view of what should be. As one of his colleagues, whom Beardsley had overtaken on the career ladder, had once remarked, in a phrase which gained common currency in the Office, 'If Julian had been Jehovah, the universe would have been organised differently.'

On the threshold of the drawing room, Granville paused to straighten his tie before strolling over to where the great man was sitting. He shook hands formally with Sir Julian (despite their long-standing familiarity. Granville was always careful to include the 'Sir', at least on first meeting) and was at once offered a drink .

'A double Bombay gin and tonic, with a slice of lime, please.'

'Thank you for coming, Jeremy,' Beardsley began. 'I thought we had better have our little chat extramurally, so to speak, with no minutes, watchers etcetera. I have no doubt we are entering a very delicate phase in Ireland, which will require *especially* delicate handling. *Especially* by you. So I thought we two should compare notes.'

Granville knew that meant: 'I'll now tell you what to do'.

Beardsley sipped his Scotch and soda, set down his glass and put his hands into church-steeple mode – his favourite pontifical posture.

'We have done very well – you, Jeremy, have done very well – out there in recent months. It was a stroke of genius on your part to draft "clarifications of government policies" to feed out under the table as a way of opening up talks-about-talks with the other side.'

Granville almost purred at this expression of praise; Sir Julian was usually swifter to chide. He was emboldened to interrupt the flow of wisdom to make an ambitious claim, 'I'm convinced that will eventually lure the top people in SF/IRA into asking for direct, substantive talks.'

'Yes, but we must not be seen as the "demandeurs" in this. But if we can manoeuvre them into asking for talks, we're in business. Super. And so far, I emphasise *so far*, we haven't had to pay a price in relation to any of our other customers: the army, the RUC, the NIO and ministers and MPs here, not to mention the local politicos, who don't seem to have cottoned on just yet.'

'I wouldn't *entirely* agree with all of that,' ventured Grenville.

'I sense that James Wheeler and I are regarded with some suspicion in many quarters, especially by the police and army, even by the NIO. The deeper in we get with this ploy, the more those suspicions risk developing into opposition, through obstruction, reduced co-operation and so on.

And we mustn't forget that the media have been docile only because they haven't worked out where these "clarifications" are intended to lead. Once they put two and two together they will blow our cover story out of the water.'

'I know, I know,' interjected Beardsley with a wave of his hand.

'That is why the matter is now urgent. It will be our job – your job – to push on with the greatest possible speed. Far faster than heretofore. And let's not kid ourselves, it's going to get much harder still, because,' he took a long swig of his whisky, 'because we are now going to go for The Big One, which will call for even more handling skills. But if we pull it off, it will be the greatest prize we have won diplomatically in a generation. And you and I, Jeremy, will have our part in the victory – and the spoils.'

He smiled warmly at Granville, clapped him on the knee and paused to receive a reciprocal sign of willingness.

'I've been through this informally and in total confidence with the Foreign Secretary and the PM. And, just as importantly, with the Leader of the Opposition and his top people, including your friend Crispin Myles. They are all up for it – provided, of course, that we can bring it off.'

'Oh sure – and if it all goes pear-shaped, where will they all be?'

Beardsley ignored this discordant note, resisting the rare temptation to tell the truth, which would have been 'off stage like a shot'. Instead, he resumed his lecture.

'Here's the change and the challenge.'

Sounds like one of his Power Point slides, thought Granville, recalling the many Beardsley performances he had witnessed over the years, as the great man had briefed ministers, military brass hats and closed sessions of the Security and Foreign Affairs Committees on what they should think about the Balkans, the Middle East or North Korea. He revelled in his reputation as the 'Office Thinker'.

'So far, we have been aiming at a slow transition of the Provos from "war" to "peace", keeping them under uncomfortable pressure, but without going for the jugular, as some of our chums would like, and at the same time fostering the idea that a settlement has to be found. Hitherto the general assumption, particularly amongst our stakeholders – Westminster, Dublin, Washington *et al.* – has been that it is HMG's policy to bring Sinn Fein into the democratic process. In return, of course , for a package of goodies – early release of PIRA prisoners, reform of the police, guaranteed respect for the identity and values of the minority community, some sort of Bill of Rights, *enfin, tout le bazar.*'

The use of the French expression recalled their time together in the embassy in Paris; Beardsley liked mood music.

'The further assumption has been that this revived democratic process and its framework will be to the benefit of Hume's SDLP and the Official Unionists. But here's the change...'

He looked round the otherwise empty room, cautiously.

'I can see a truly, once-in-a-lifetime opportunity to go further. We will have it in our power, once we have Sinn Fein firmly on board, to push them ahead of the SDLP, by dealing more or less openly with new-found friends at Provo HQ, and neglecting Hume. In effect making them top dogs.'

Granville looked as though he wished to object, but Beardsley waved away the threatened interruption.

'The penny will soon drop with the nationalists as well as the republicans and political support will flow towards the perceived winners.'

'But that would produce all sorts of trouble from the Prods. Paisley would have a field day.'

'Precisely,' cried Beardsley in triumph,

'And that's the beauty of Part Two of The Big One..... Paisley will, on the back of unionist resentment, wax automatically along with Sinn Fein. And don't tell me he isn't interested in power. He will sell his church, his Orange Order support, his Ballymena Bogtrotters and, if necessary, his blind grandmother, down the river for a whiff of power. He's been after it now for over thirty years and he's seventy in the shade, so it's pretty much "now or never" for him.'

'I can see the ultras on both sides winning in the endgame. And neither of them can be overtaken on the extremes. With that sort of political peace – and the absence of bang-bangs – we shall have delivered something which looks remarkably like a Solution, with capital 'S', to the Irish Question. Until, of course, the bloody Irish change the question. But that's for another era altogether.'

'Of course, our political masters can't see that far ahead – they have to live from day-to-day, but it is our duty to peer into the future for them and to ease them along, step by step.'

Beardsley leaned back in his chair, well pleased with his exposition, and with a circular movement of his index finger indicated to the club steward across the deserted room, 'same again'.

'It is now your job, dear boy, to move the game along in that direction. Without making the first open request for talks, step up the hints in the right quarters that this is HMG's long-term aim. But with the fall-back threat that if we are frigged about, we'll be back to the long haul military solution and a war of attrition which, you would have to convince them, will pain them more than it will pain us. Even if that's not quite true, as more big bombs in GB would certainly hurt us a lot. They know that, militarily, we now have them by the nethers and that if General Chesham is let off the leash, the "shoot-to-kill" controversies of the past will be as a bun fight at a Sunday school picnic. So, we can frighten them with the prospect of a painful 'long war', but hold out the alternative prospect of being our partners in progress.'

Oh God, another Power Point slogan.

'Have I – have you – really got cover for this?' asked Granville instinctively and somewhat too abruptly for his own liking.

'Yes indeed,' came the prompt reply, 'and without wishing to sound pompous (whereupon he cleared his throat and sounded more pompous than usual), I'll be taking over the Office from Roderick some time next year – probably the early part, as his health problems seem to be getting worse – and it will be up to us, with or without a new PM, to see this thing through. We can't go wider than that in the meantime, I'm afraid. Remember what our old friend Machiavelli very nearly said: "No enterprise is more likely to succeed than one concealed from the enemy – or one's allies – until it is ripe for execution". However, the Cabinet and the usual committees can be brought into the game once we've made some significant progress.'

Then, patting Granville on the knee, 'I leave it to you as to how best to shield your hand from all the colleagues and partners in crime in Belfast.'

Beardsley put down his glass and leant forward again, looking Granville steadfastly in the eye.

'I really do need you on this, Jeremy. You're the only one who can make the change, the transition. You have the ability to win the confidence of the other side, which is vital, absolutely vital. I'd say it'll take a maximum of two years, even at the Irish pace of doing things. And then you can have your pick of the embassies which interest you amongst the A-rabs. Out in the light, as Her Britannic Majesty's Ambassador to...wherever. That's still your goal, I take it?'

'I haven't thought about it lately, but yes, you know me, that would be a consummation devoutly to be wished. *Rabat de préférence.*'

'Excellent!' Then, changing tone, to indicate business complete, 'How's Penny? Still seeing her à

deux, so to speak?'

'Yes, fine, thanks. She's a bit fed up with my being out in Ireland, but she's OK.'

Not an entirely re-assuring response.

Beardsley paused to drain his glass.

'Do give her my love, won't you?'

Granville's endgame was underway.

Chapter 5

Within the intelligence community in Northern Ireland, the role of Jeremy Granville was, to say the least, controversial. Since the beginning of OPERATION CHIFFON, MI5 had been given, rather late in the day in the opinion of many analysts, the responsibility for the overall management of intelligence. At first Granville's two predecessors had concentrated on the bureaucratic efficiency side of the business, making sure that the various agencies involved not only co-operated in the sharing of information, but also co-ordinated their activities, day by day. It took some time to overcome territorial jealousies – the so-called 'turf wars' – and to build up mutual trust between the army and police at the top level and between the agencies within both, which could often act as rivals. It was no easy task, which took up a great deal of time and effort and would never be complete. For example, Special Branch, RUC, frequently cut across the activities of the CID, in cases where 'Ordinary Decent Criminals' appeared to have paramilitary connections or where valuable SB informants needed to be shielded from the normal rigours of law enforcement; similarly, the SAS and 14th Brigade caused many headaches for the army leadership whenever they acted 'independently', that is to say, outside normal army control and sometimes at variance with the very law of the land ('in order to get things done', as their defenders were wont to plead).

Gradually, as they built up the number of their own operatives, those predecessors paved the way for a more pro-active role for MI5.The organisation had been engaged in a certain amount of what was known as 'backstairs activity', meaning talking to people in, or close to, hard core republican circles; sounding out opinion, especially as regards how the more realistic terrorist leaders saw an end to the conflict. Those contacts had been fostered by a couple of 'mountain climbers', through intermediaries, but it gradually became clear to Granville, even before his anointment by Sir Julian, that his mission was to take them to an altogether higher level.

His appointment brought with it the grand title of 'Security Service Director and Co-ordinator of Intelligence' and with Beardsley's backing – backing where it really mattered – he intended to be, as he told James Wheeler, the senior Government Press Officer, fellow MI5 member and closest professional confidant – not that he had many of those – 'the determinant catalyst' in the overall situation.

Despite never having set foot in Ireland, North or South, before his appointment, Granville was, in his own eyes at least, ideal for the job. Unusually, he had served in both MI5 and MI6, and thus had experience in both sides of 'the business'. He had been sounded out for recruitment while still at Emmanuel College, Cambridge, where his academic success in Modern Languages, achieved without any great effort on his part, had marked him out as 'suitable material'. The talent spotter from MI6, a friend of the Master of the college, had contacted him during a professional 'milk round' in his last term. He had walked him round the garden pond a few times, chatting about 'government service' generally, before asking him whether he would like 'to be of particular service to your country, in a rather specialised role'. Granville guessed what that meant and was flattered to be considered in that context of 'the business'. He knew of family friends who had reputedly unspecified links to that 'business'. No doubt that had reinforced his attractiveness to the talent scouts. *One of our own.*

On coming down from Cambridge, he passed the entrance examination for the Foreign and Commonwealth Office, (with 'encouragement' from the said scouts) which made possible his double life as a diplomat and an MI6 officer attached to embassies abroad. His career had been boosted early on by his emergence as a star student at the FCO's Arabic Language

School in the Lebanese village of Shemlan, in the hills some twenty miles from Beirut. There he had caught the eye of its director, Donald Maitland. That led to postings in a series of Arab-speaking capitals, as well as spells in Paris and London. In recent years he had been on loan to MI5, which was an arrangement of mutual benefit.

MI5 had precious few Arabic speakers and the need for them was growing. Most of those recruited in haste to meet operational demand were of Middle Eastern ethnicity and it was the unspoken concern of management (unspoken for reasons of political correctness) that there should be a significant number of top flight ethnic Brits (*real Brit*s in non-PC English) involved, 'just to keep an eye on everything'.

Granville's need, at least in the short term, had been for regular orthopaedic monitoring and physiotherapeutic treatment and care, following his accident, the turning point in his life.

How many times had he relived those awful moments?

The sun is shining, the sky is an improbable, electric blue, the motorway traffic is slight and they will be in Alicante in good time for dinner at El Suquet, a highly recommended restaurant to which he has phoned ahead a reservation. He glances at Helena, who smiles at him happily. Pregnancy this time has been good for her. No threat of a miscarriage; no trouble at all. He touches her warm, sun-tanned cheek. It was her excellent idea to drive back on summer leave from North Africa and do a little tourism on the way. She closes her eyes and leans back against the headrest, still smiling. He looks back at the road.

'Christ!'

The giant refrigerator-lorry in front seems to be hurtling towards him. He takes in the red lights and, absurdly, the graffiti scrawled on the back door. Brake! Brake! The moment of collision has been erased from his memory. He can only see metal, he can feel nothing. He is half awake. Spanish voices all around; flashing blue lights.

'Helena!'

No reply. Then a crescendo of pain, then oblivion.

Now this must be hospital. Tubes, machinery, pain, lots of white.

'Helena?' 'Helena?'

Some time later...how much later? a white-coated presence on his left. A low voice in his ear: '*Lo siento muchissimo, señ or*. Your wife, la señora, we could not....'

Granville looked out of the window, over the immaculate green lawns to the glasshouses to the rear of Stormont Castle, as PUS called the meeting to order. As the 'Lord High Co-Ordinator'(as Beardsley had dubbed him), it fell to him to present the overview of the intelligence situation. He began by acknowledging that this topic overlapped with the political situation. He would leave it to PUS to cover the broader picture. PUS nodded agreement; General Chesham visibly scowled, as though pained by indigestion.

There was much progress to report. Penetration of all the paramilitary organisations had continued apace, and at all levels. The computerised version of OPERATION PANORAMA had dramatically increased the ability to discover links between individuals; thus surmounting the hurdle which, particularly in the case of PIRA, the 'small cell structure' had posed in the past. He reeled off the statistics about the number of terrorist operations which had been nipped in the bud, or which, *post facto*, had been followed by good arrests, charges and convictions, thanks to intelligence, rather than normal detective work.

As to the current thinking of the paramilitaries, there was the usual sharp contrast between PIRA on the one hand and the Loyalist 'alphabet soup' organisations– UDA, UVF, UFF, RHC and the rest – on the other. The 'thinking' of the latter was focused largely on the 'fast buck', that is to say the proceeds of criminality, largely within their own community – protection rackets, robberies and burglaries. In general, they had no clear objectives, beyond the perpetuation of their own existence, though one or two had serious political aspirations to take over from the conventional unionist parties in

Protestant working class areas, campaigning on the bandwagon slogan of 'reversing deprivation'. That strain, he opined, might in the long run be susceptible to cultivation, though he doubted it would ever make much general political headway.

As for PIRA, the philosophy of the 'long haul war' appeared to be still generally valid, at least officially, even though the penetration achieved against that organisation and the consequent loss of a certain amount of momentum in their military operations had no doubt dented confidence. Their leadership was also worried about signs of war-weariness in the Catholic population. Moreover, the IRA's obvious inability to shield Catholics from the latest Loyalist tactic of random sectarian assassinations – aimed at destabilising the overall situation and getting brownie points from working class Protestants for 'hitting back' – had somewhat undermined their former reputation as 'Protectors'.

Granville was now getting to the potentially difficult passage. He tried not to look directly at either Chesham or the Chief Constable.

'You will have seen Vincent Glass's piece in the *Tribune* about so-called "talks" with the Provo leadership. A nice bit of sensational journalism, but it's important we all understand the more prosaic reality behind it.'

He paused, in order to underline the importance of what he was about to say.

'It seems that the top Republicans have taken to dissecting every policy statement or speech by the SoS. Ever since the Peter Brooke speech about HMG having "no strategic interest" in Northern Ireland, they keep looking for more crumbs and in my specific sphere of operations the job is to keep explaining, speech after speech, that there ain't any.'

'Oh, I do hope so,' said Chesham loudly and with more than a hint of irony.

'Before I conclude,' went on Granville, tiptoeing away from the backstairs operations, 'there are just two points I wish to make. Firstly, we have to be careful, in expanding our informer network and acting on the intelligence gleaned from it, by way of searches, "taking in for questionings" etc, that we do not lay ourselves open to accusations of "systematic harassment of the ghetto populations", to quote our friend Glass. There are already signs that the human rights lobby are going to make a big issue out of that.'

He could sense the Chief Constable bristling with indignation at his side.

'And secondly, whilst our inter-agency co-operation has clearly improved, we can still do better. I don't think we need another structural review, which would be time-consuming and take our eye off the ball. What I am specifically thinking of is the need to register centrally, for use in PANORAMA, all new informants as soon as any agency has one on board. We have so many now, which is a great success, that we risk stumbling over one another's feet. There have been one or two cases of late insertion of info into PANORAMA, through a lack of overall vision of the field of play and of all the known players.'

'Through you, Mr Chairman, does that apply to MI5 as well?' asked the General, clearly with malice aforethought.

'Of course,' lied Granville, without the slightest hesitation.

It was now PUS's turn to give an overview of relations with, and between, the constitutional political parties. Granville listened with only half an ear: none of this was new; it had all been in the media and besides, James Wheeler sat in on all the meetings with the local parties and briefed him extensively after each one. The present situation was that the parties were all more or less standing on the touchline, shouting various accusations and demands at HMG, and waiting for their own game to start, in some new forum, on the far side of the physical conflict.

Would PUS be a help or a hindrance to his own game, as it developed? Hard to say, mused Granville. On the one hand Pickford was a dyed-in-the-wool civil servant and would implement whatever policy came from on high. Imagination wasn't his strong suit, as far as new policy thinking was concerned – which, again, probably wasn't a bad thing.

Conflicting visions could be a nightmare. But on the other hand, he had been a Home Office official, man and boy, a law and order enthusiast through and through. His instincts were therefore in favour of locking up the 'baddies', be they murderers, rapists, bank robbers or terrorists, and don't expect him to shed any tears if afterwards the key cannot be found. Cutting a deal with the Provos would be his last ever thought, both personally and professionally. He would require careful handling. And this sort of meeting, chaired by PUS, would have to be gradually sidelined and replaced in importance by one under his, Granville's, direct control.

When the meeting was over Granville found his driver and they headed off down the Bangor Road to St Oswald's, the vast, government-owned house which was his residence and alternative HQ. It was set in five acres of glorious, secluded gardens in a bend in the side road which led down from the main road at the Culloden Hotel to the seafront. The profusion of mature trees and shrubs and the winding driveway totally hid the house from the road. In any case, it was discreetly guarded by a unit of the Royal Military Police, who were under strict orders to fraternize with no one. It was as secure as anywhere could be in this life; nevertheless, he had a 'techo team' from London check the grounds, premises and communications equipment on a regular monthly basis.

He chose a Mahler symphony on his hi-fi system, poured himself a more-than-generous gin and tonic and lit his first Gauloise of the day. *Really must give them up.* As he closed his eyes and drew strongly on the cigarette, so that his cheeks hollowed, he might well have added an Augustinian *but not just yet.*

Must ring Penny! As the thought flashed into his mind he also realised that it was the first such thought for a long time – and what was no doubt for her a *very* long time.

Penny and he went back a long way. Her husband, Guy Harbinson, had entered the Foreign Office on the same day as himself and they had studied together at Shemlan. That time in Lebanon had been an idyll for all of them. In retrospect it was the happiest time of his life – and theirs. They were young and vigorous and gliding effortlessly towards a golden future. The country they were living in had everything: Mediterranean beaches, ski resorts in the mountains and the fascinating melting pot of Beirut. There had been enough spare time from study for the Harbinsons and Granvilles to go exploring, picnicking and dining out in the nearby villages. It was the Lebanese cuisine, healthy yet full of flavour, which had first stimulated his interest in cooking, the only domestic or DIY skill he had ever acquired, if one discounted dexterity with a corkscrew.

Without warning, the Lebanese idyll would later collapse into civil war, symbolically in parallel with the happiness of the two couples. Guy was diagnosed with pancreatic cancer and died within six months, just a year before the motorway accident in which Helena had perished. Jeremy and Penny had consoled one another, as old and close friends, and gradually they had grown closer. Their friends began to nod knowingly: there was general agreement that widow and widower would make an ideal pair.

Both appeared to move imperceptibly towards acceptance of the idea. There was not just a growing physical attraction between them, as the taboo of their former relationship faded; there was also the key factor that they recognised they were both creatures from the strange world of security and intelligence. That was a world in which few people could feel at ease, such were the pressures of living a double life, but it was one in which they both felt at home. Their relationship was now at the stage of 'romance'; they were recognized socially as 'an item'. Neither had raised the subject of marriage, but it was becoming what Jeremy's father termed 'a working hypothesis'.

Every time Jeremy thought of it – and he had to admit to himself that recently he had thought of it less frequently – he would end up saying to himself: *Let's get Ireland out of the way first.*

Chapter 6

Since the beginning of the 'troubles', Aidan Cassidy had played an increasingly important back room role in the Provisional IRA. It was a role only a very few knew about. He was never seen at a Sinn Fein, never mind a PIRA, function, rally or protest march. To those amongst whom he had grown up, he appeared to have 'moved on'. He had married money, become a 'business suit' and had long since escaped from – or deserted, depending on your point of view – his former life in the Lower Falls ghetto, for a socially desirable address in Myrtlefield Park, in the affluent Malone district of South Belfast. There he had merged with the background of his professional and mercantile neighbours with the ease of a chameleon in the Amazonian undergrowth. Active membership of the Rotary Club and the Chamber of Industry and Commerce put the seal on his standing as a solid citizen, the sort of middle class Catholic businessman that Protestant moderates wanted to see more of in public life. More like them, less of a threat.

Cassidy was not as he seemed. Over twenty years earlier, when the struggle had started in earnest, he had been 'green-booked' , that is to say initiated, in the upstairs office of one of his father-in-law's public houses on the Andersonstown Road. Old McManus had organized the swearing in and the local battalion commander, Sean Feeney, administered the oath, with all the solemnity of a Clerk to the Privy Council, in the presence of only one other witness, Feeney's son. This was a membership to be kept strictly under wraps. Feeney made clear that the new recruit's role was never to be within an 'Active Service Unit'; on the contrary, he was to insulate himself as far as possible from all contact with all those engaged in the armed struggle.

Cassidy raised his right hand and read from a dog-eared card handed to him by Feeney:

'I, Aidan Patrick Cassidy, promise that I will promote the objects of Oglaigh na hEireann to the best of my knowledge and ability and that I will obey all orders and regulations issued to me by the Army Authority and by my superior officer.'

'Young man,' said Feeney, gripping him by the forearm, 'the part you will play will be even more important than that of those who bear arms, handle propaganda or lead our people. The sinews of war are money ,and it's the money you'll have to take care of. You'll do so on behalf of all of us.' His voice broke slightly as he added with fresh emphasis and piety, 'On behalf of Ireland.'

Organisationally, Cassidy did not feature in the normal hierarchy if the IRA. He had been deputy to the overall *cisteoir,* the elderly Pat McGoldrick, a retired banker from Dungannon, who reported directly to the nine-man Army Council, on which Seamus Tolan had special responsibility for finance. Each battalion had a finance officer, who contributed 'takings' to the centre and distributed monies locally as required, but who, for security reasons, kept no financial records beyond a maximum of seven days. McGoldrick and Cassidy between them ran the overall operation, meeting once a month, usually at McGoldrick's house. He, in turn, presented his figures to the Army Council on a quarterly basis, in one of the six or seven 'safe houses' in North Donegal, just over the border from Derry, or in Dundalk, over the border from Newry.

'Monies in' came from various sources: donations, either locally or through Noraid, the IRA's fund raisers in the United States; profits from illegal shebeens; protection rackets, largely from building sites, but also from small shopkeepers; and straightforward robbery and theft, from bank and post office raids. The American connection had been particularly important in the early years. In the Irish bars of New York and

Boston and on various St Patrick's Day organising committees, the fund raisers' message of 'Help defend the Catholic population from the British in the occupied North' initially produced a generous response. In recent years, thanks to the efforts of the British embassy and consulates with the US media, that simplistic approach had been progressively eroded, but America was still an important element in 'monies in'.

'Monies out' went to support the families of republican prisoners; to pay small amounts of 'bounties' to volunteers for services such as transportation or concealment of weapons; larger amounts for the expenses of more senior members; and, once in a while, to pay for supplies of guns and explosives.

'We are our own auditors,' McGoldrick had told him. 'They trust us. But God help us if ever they suspect we have...' He paused, searching for the right euphemism '...gone wrong in the sums somewhere.'

Was that a hint, a warning? His impression was that McGoldrick had taken less and less specific interest in the details of the finances as his health had deteriorated. Bouts of angina had landed him in hospital for several weeks in the past year. But had some sixth sense in the wily old bruiser told him that something was amiss?

Cassidy had pondered on that question many times since, and now it had become uppermost in his mind when he read his 'summons'. His line of communication with the regular structure of the IRA was through a single, trusted runner; all other means of communication being considered as vulnerable to interception. That runner was Malachy Doyle, cousin of one of the commanders in Belfast city and proprietor of a pizza house and delivery service in Castle Street, a five minute walk from Cassidy's office. Doyle was therefore a frequent visitor to the top floor of the Scottish Provident Building, bearing not only Shamrock pizzas, which mercifully Cassidy liked, but, concealed in his large delivery box, bundles of banknotes, along with notes as to their origin or intended destination.

Today Doyle brought him only a simple note, initialled by someone he knew to be a member of the Army Council. It read: 'Come to meeting, 1 pm, this coming Sunday...'and added an address which he knew to be just outside the village of Rathmelton in Donegal.

Had McGoldrick voiced any doubts to Seamus Tolan before he died last week? Had he even worked again on the accounts themselves? Cassidy had taken the precaution of re-working his own figures, covering the hole of £150,000 by distributing £2000 round various items which would be hard to check on, and marking £ 100,000 to a new 'Contingency Reserve', which did not exist in actual cash fact. When would he have to make his accountancy fiction match reality? And, more importantly, how?

He poured himself a stiff whisky and stared glumly into the depths of the glass, as though the answer might lie therein. Then his fingers dialled, automatically, a number on his desktop phone.

'Hello. Yes, customer number 15047. Good. £150 on *My Hero* in the 2.30 at Newbury. And £100 each way on *Yellow Mellow* in the 3.30 at York. That's correct. Thanks.'

Like most gamblers, he harboured the irrational hope that his luck would be bound to turn, and so he convinced himself, perhaps subconsciously, that he had better continue to bet, lest he miss the benefits of this upturn in his fortunes. It was a habit which had slowly developed from his student days, starting with sweepstakes on the big races, such as the Grand National, and snowballing into a regular weekend pastime. With a few friends he would spend Saturday afternoons drinking in bars on the Falls Road, interrupting the intake of Guinness every so often to nip down the street to a bookmaker's shop to place his bets, before returning to watch many of the races on television in the pub. Some days he was up on the 'investment' game, as he liked to call it, but, with mathematical inevitability, the days on which he was down were more frequent.

Why did he do it? Not being a reflective personality, he generally avoided the question. He would, if pressed, probably have pleaded guilty to greed, but that was hardly the whole story. There was also the depressive masochistic pleasure in the thrill of probable loss and, once he had achieved adult and professional respectability, there was the added subconscious attraction of secrecy. He no longer frequented betting shops, but 'invested' by telephone. Noleen knew, of course, that 'he liked a flutter now and then', but was blissfully ignorant of the extent of his habit. It was a habit which had progressively become a major factor in his life. Access to clients' money through his business had increased the temptations – and the risks of things getting out of hand and ending in bankruptcy. More recently, being entrusted with the IRA's funds, with only a loose control, also increased the temptations and the risks of being unmasked – and ending in a shallow, unmarked grave.

Noleen Cassidy had only been half right when she had concluded her husband's secret related to his active participation in 'the movement'; there was another factor in the equation. Her name was Colette McShane.

Colette was a beautician in one of the department stores in the Castle Court shopping complex in central Belfast. Aidan had met her, inappropriately, two Christmases ago, when buying perfume for his wife. She had flirted with him in a coquettish way, as indeed she did with many male customers – it always, in her experience, helped sales along. While allowing him to sample various products, she lightly touched his forearm and fluttered her long eyelashes, as she tilted her head this way and that, encouraging him to buy the best.

'If I were your girlfriend, I'd be really impressed with the "Caprice"', she said, with an encouraging smile.

On the spur of the moment (how many lives have been impaled on that spur?), whilst following her advice, Aidan asked her for her telephone number, the first time in twenty years he could remember having done such a thing, and certainly not since his marriage.

In his eyes, Colette was a thing of beauty; and she turned out to be a joy for a considerable time, but inevitably only for a time. She was petite, very dark and, unsurprisingly, skilfully *maquillée* at any time of the day or night. Dressed usually in sombre colours which heightened her overall allure, she moved always in a way which blatantly promised an underlying sensuousness.

It was a promise swiftly fulfilled for Aidan on their very first intimate encounter. She had readily responded to his 'phone calls and at the third time of asking, agreed to go with him, on her Monday off, to Dublin, where he had an insurance business meeting. On the return journey that afternoon they stopped at the Ravensdale Forest Hotel, just before the border, and after a meal Aidan booked and paid for a room. The pleasure of the next few hours eclipsed for the first time in months his constant worries about money, security and the future. Nirvana was possible. And could be visited every other week or so with Colette, discretion guaranteed.

She had entered into the relationship with her mascara-rimmed eyes wide open. She knew he was married and before long knew who he was and what he did – or at least knew as much about him as his friends in West Belfast or his neighbours in Myrtlefield Park did.

'You're a naughty boy, Aidan,' she would say. 'But then again,' she went on, with a giggle, as she unzipped her grey pencil skirt, 'I'm a naughty girl.'

This conjuncture of lust seemed for a while to be exquisitely convenient for both parties. Its end came for two reasons. Aidan's ever-increasing familiarity with Colette's charms, wardrobe and seductive tricks began to breed not contempt, but the first twinges of boredom, in all affairs the most lethal element imaginable. Then there was Colette's growing ambition. She felt in Aidan's pleasure her own potential power over him. If he wanted her that much – which was obvious – why couldn't she have him properly, and to herself? She had begun to extract little half promises from him – that they could have a week together in London, that he would help her set up her own beauty salon – but had recently dared to go for broke, telling him that if he really loved her, as he claimed, he should follow his destiny and hers, make a clean break with his wife and build a life together with her. A film star role model of hers had made a similar speech to her lover, as reported in *Cosmopolitan* magazine..

Their bedroom time together now followed an emotionally draining routine: Colette's complaints, ending in tears, about neglect and his lack of resolve; his consoling her, whilst inventing excuses; and, finally, a reconciliatory lovemaking of cathartic proportions. For Aidan each time was just about worth the candle, but his pleasure was further diminished by the realization that it could not indefinitely be repeated. Nirvana had been lost, probably for ever.

He did not wish to sacrifice Colette, but in his calmer moments he knew that he was never going to make real sacrifices *for* her. There leaked into his mind the fear, the growing certainty, that she had become so obsessive that, if thwarted, she could ruin him through the unleashing of a scandal. The consequences of that, in family and 'movement' terms, were too painful to contemplate. One day – soon – he would have to decide to do something which would resolve the situation without damage; but not just yet, he would tell himself, as she snuggled against his chest, her perfume fragrant in his nostrils. As to what that 'something' could be, he had as yet no clear, or even hazy, idea.

Chapter 7

He was glad that it was drizzling – that kept people off the streets. Cassidy parked the car in the main square of the little Co. Donegal town and, after walking about for a few minutes to make sure he was not being followed, he made his way to the designated house. It was small but detached and sat somewhat at an angle to its nearest neighbours, in a straggling side street which petered out soon afterwards into the rocky Donegal countryside. On a good day, the view out over the ocean was stunningly beautiful, but today visibility offshore was scarcely a hundred yards. Not that he was here for the view.

There were no cars parked near the house, but he noticed a keen face peering out from the window of the little pebble-dashed porch. As he approached it, down a short, crazy paved path, the door opened and he was ushered inside. Two obvious minders sat around in the narrow inner hallway and in the front room. One of them in the hall jerked his thumb in the direction of the latter. Cassidy had barely sat down when another minder called him and opened the door for him into the main living room at the back of the house. The curtains were drawn and there was no central light on; two table lamps provided less-than-adequate illumination. Cassidy only recognized his Belfast Army Council man, the head man from Derry and Tolan, the member responsible for finance. These three were seated at a table, along with others and two more sat in armchairs either side of the fireplace, in which a low fire smoked blackly.

Greetings were murmured, but no introductions made.

'Right,' said Tolan, turning to face Cassidy head-on. 'Let's get to the point. Or rather points. Number one, the succession. You are moving up into McGoldrick's place. God rest his soul. And your deputy, your twin, will be Liam McGarrity from Derry. You know him?'

Cassidy nodded negatively.

'Well, he runs a big garage business on the Claudy Road and he's an accountant. Point two and most important: we need another shipment. We've lost a lot of gear recently. Why, is a different matter and security are looking into it. But it has seriously held up operations. We can't let momentum flag any further. It'll be risky bringing in more stuff and we don't want another *Claudia* fiasco on our hands. But we've no choice.'

'How much are we talking about?' ventured Cassidy.

'Anything from a half to three quarters of a million quid. It has to be a big delivery to make a real difference. Our contacts have identified a dealer in Belgium who can set things up.'

'Our shopping list is being worked out by Tomas McGiolla, who can brief you on probable prices,' intervened the Derryman. 'He'll look after the goods angle, you'll handle the finance. It's a joint operation.'

'If it went much over half a million, we'd be hard pressed,' said Cassidy. 'Overheads like total payments to prisoner families are going up and up, as the numbers go up, even though you could argue that each family gets far too little.'

'Too bad,' shot back the Derryman, with a dismissive sweep of his hand. 'This is make or break time. Whatever it takes...Besides, (he smiled thinly), I believe we may be able to, how shall I put it, supplement the coffers significantly within the next few weeks.'

Over the next few hours the details of Cassidy's mission to Belgium were discussed. He declined an offered drink, on the grounds of his driving, though his nerves could have done with a tranquillizer

Back on the road and over the border without being stopped by a British Army patrol, he headed from Derry towards the Glenshane Pass and home. He turned the discussions of the day over and over again in his mind. The most positive thing was that the Council seemed to have confidence in him. At no point had he had the feeling that he was being 'questioned' in any way. He had not even been asked to update his last financial report to Tolan, which would have entailed repeating the myth of the 'Contingency Reserve' and perhaps cross-examination on that all-too-dangerous point. On the other hand, the nomination of McGarrity as his 'twin' was not good news. McGarrity was bound to be close to the Derryman, indeed he was in all probability 'his man'. And the Derry lot were always critical of Belfast, almost as a reflex. Yes, he thought, McGarrity could be a real danger, especially if it turned out that he wanted to immerse himself in the minutiae of the books, as accountants tended to do, as a natural reflex. Danger was also written all over the Belgian operation. Confidentiality and security were becoming an increasing problem within their own organisation, but once outsiders became involved, particularly the sort of outsiders whose stock-in-trade was illegal arms dealing, the risks of betrayal, detection and capture were multiplied. Those who approached such arms dealers were immediately exposed to the risk of being 'shopped'; nowadays government security agents paid good money – and no questions asked – to those who delivered the would-be buyers into their hands. He thought of the score or more of Irish Republicans who were languishing in various continental jails, victims of international operations which had gone wrong – usually through the treachery of outside 'partners'.

Unlike many, if not most, of his comrades-in-arms, Cassidy felt no exhilaration at the prospect of that sort of danger. Merely a dull dread, which he felt as though it were simultaneously a clamp on the back of his head and on his stomach. And in his relationship with Colette, he felt no pleasure in the danger of being discovered – his motivation was essentially lust and escapism. Now his life was becoming dominated by fear – fear of the Colette situation exploding in his face, which would mean the end of his marriage, scandal and public attention focused on him, contrary to the IRA's wishes; fear of being caught with his hand in the movement's till, which could bring any punishment up to a bullet in the head; and fear that his recent neglect of his own business could bring financial ruin in any case.

Special Branch were not fully aware of the extent of Cassidy's perceived problems, but they were beginning to build up what for them was an encouraging picture. HSB was briefed by the Detective Sergeant in charge of the file:

'Since we had the tip-off from that runner fella, Harry-the hound, we've been listening to Cassidy's phones, tracking his car, talking to business colleagues in other firms...all the usual. He's a canny one, doesn't give much away by way of careless talk or action, but he's a baddie for sure, despite the appearances he keeps up. Two bonus points for us: he's into the geegees in a big way, with a running account with a bookmaker in London, and he's got a floozy on the side.'

'You don't say!' chuckled HSB.

'Yip! Sees to her in out-of-town hotels. He recently had a trip to Donegal, the trackers in VELLUM tell me. Probably not for nookie, that one. More likely Provo-related. We think Bunny was there. We are working on that, and we've asked the Gards if they can throw any light on the matter. And that's about it, as regards Mr Aidan Cassidy, so far.'

HSB turned to his deputy, 'What do you think? Is there any advantage in letting the hare sit and seeing what else we might learn?'

'Don't think so. Not in this case. It looks as though he's not operational in the usual sense, so by just watching him, we're not going to be led to any action as such.'

'I agree,' said HSB briskly, 'lift him. He could come in useful.'

Chapter 8

OPERATION GILLESPIE took four weeks to bear its first fruits. HSB now had before him a copy of a minute, classification SECRET, sent from the most senior civil servant in the NIO, the PUS (Permanent Undersecretary of State) to the Secretary of State. It read:

'SoS:

This is to follow up our brief airborne conversation of last week about police expenditure.

You told me the First Secretary of the Treasury had indicated to you informally that there were concerns in that quarter about some aspects of the RUC's accounts; and about the Police Authority's ability, efficiently to monitor and control them.

No doubt these concerns arise from the overall 'Spot Check' financial control initiative and the visit here last month of the Walton team from the Treasury. We had detected some initial borborygmus from that quarter, but I am grateful for your early warning about the detail of their initial findings and concentration on the police.

Having prised detailed statistics from a somewhat reluctant Police Authority, and thanks to considerable lucubration by officials here, my view is that there are three principal areas of vulnerability:

• Police overtime, the cost of which has increased by 46% over the past two years.

• The cost of specialist equipment. (See the attached graph of the increase in these costs over the past three years). The Americans, and indeed Army Logistics, have introduced the RUC to a whole range of new electronic and other gadgetry and for the future there is the danger of "the boy in the toy shop" syndrome.

• Most vulnerable of all are the payments from the slush funds in the Black Boxes, for informants, the protection of witnesses and the re-settlement of ex-terrorists who have turned Queen's evidence. Accounting for these expenses in due course to the Comptroller and Auditor General could present particular difficulties.

I believe the police here have never been used to financial constraints and they tend to take a microptian view of their over-spends. They blithely expect the Police Authority to provide them with whatever funds they feel they need, all in the name of operational requirements. Through the Police Authority, we have been challenging the management side of the RUC to introduce more efficient measures of cost control, but they have constantly perendinated their introduction.

It is true that the Police Authority themselves have not been strong on financial control. It is hard to get financially competent people interested in serving on the Authority. However, new appointments due in two months' time will give us the opportunity to strengthen the PA's capacity to monitor costs. I attach a note on the proposed nominations (which will be formally submitted within a few weeks for your approval, when choices and soundings have been completed).You will see that, with luck, we shall have a stronger team in place before long.

I agree with you that we need a tighter grip on all of this, for political as well as financial reasons, but I must also caution against any excessive restraints being placed on the RUC. I know certain colleagues have sometimes been Laodecean about the role and organisation of the police, but, in an improved partnership with the army, they have been doing rather well recently in the field and it would be most regrettable if our policy of "the primacy of the police" were to be undermined in any way. It has served us well so far, particularly politically, and should remain a key element in our overall strategy.

I will keep you posted.

PUS '

HSB grunted. 'The Chief Constable must see this at once.
No copies.,' he said, handing his senior clerk the document.
'The bloody moneybags are after us.'

QUANTICO , USA

HSB looked on his annual visit to the FBI Academy in
Quantico, Virginia almost as a period of 'rest and relaxation'.
True, he had to work up a programme of three lectures to be
given there on aspects of the Northern Ireland Situation which
were of special interest to the FBI – this year's topics were:
Communal Conflict; Gangsterism and Revolutionary Activity
and Comparative Interrogation Techniques. It was also true
that a week out of the office and its fast-moving action would
take a week or two to catch up on. However, his stay in
Quantico was always a valuable, and indeed enjoyable,
charge-your-batteries-time.

He was always well received by his American
counterparts and felt that he took on their professional
optimism and 'can-do' philosophy by a sort of professional
osmosis. These guys appeared to have resources unlimited, an
unshakeable belief in their own efficiency and they could, as
they say, 'kick ass' with a swagger. By and large the US
politicians of all stripes felt that they had to be seen to be on
their side. Quite a luxury, by UK or NI standards.

For HSB, Quantico was, above all, its surroundings. The
academy, which had originally been a base for the Marine
Corps, was set in almost four hundred acres of scenic
woodland, well outside the town, some thirty-five miles from
Washington. He would get up early every morning and
wander through the grounds, listening to the birdsong and
breathing in the crisp, pine-scented air. The tensions of his
hectic life at Brooklyn RUC Headquarters left him like dew in
the morning sun. No telephones, no Situation Reports of

another overnight atrocity, no files, no inconvenient questions to be answered. Bliss. A special treat were the two or three rounds of golf he managed to squeeze into his week at the nearby Old Hickory Club were his FBI connections brought him temporary membership. Tricky enough courses, despite their benign appearances, but great fun...and totally anxiety-free from the point of view of personal security.

His lectures were, in general, well received.

'You are a real front line operative, with so much to teach us,' said one of the chairmen of his sessions, with that admiring seriousness which only Americans can produce. Occasionally he could detect a subtle hostility in the questions which followed his talk; references to 'the grievances of the persecuted minority', or questions about how long the British presence in Ireland would last, showed the influence of the Irish American lobby in the US. He noticed that those who introduced such notes had names like Quinn or O'Hagan and he could imagine that their views of Ireland had been received down the generations from forebears who had emigrated to the States in the mid-nineteenth century, during or immediately after the Great Famine, with resentment and hatred of Great Britain in their hearts. However, the questioning was always polite and his answers went unchallenged.

He had developed a private 'Special Relationship' with one of the study supervisors, Frank J. Miller, who unofficially was now not only his 'Opposite Number' but chief sympathiser. Life in the academy was comfortable but isolated from the town. One night in his week there Miller would drive him into town to a favourite restaurant, run by an ex-Major in the Marines and a great local character in Quantico.

Miller was proud of the fact that his family, on his father's side, could trace their origins to Dungannon, Co. Tyrone, thereby claiming a 'Scotch Irish' ancestry. There was little documentary proof of this, beyond some vague references contained in old family letters, but the Millers simply 'knew' about their lineage. He was aware of the other strain of Irishness within his organisation and therefore felt a certain protectiveness towards HSB, whose periodic visits constituted a strange link with his own family's past. Neither he, nor as far as he knew, anyone in his family, had ever visited Ireland, and while he had no immediate plans to do so, his contact with HSB fulfilled a vague wish to be associated in some way with the land of his ancestors.

He therefore privately, and bi-laterally with HSB, often went beyond the normal bounds of inter-force co-operation, in the detailed information which he imparted regarding technological advances in the equipment used in surveillance and detection. The RUC had already benefited from his tip-off about BOTDR – Brillouin Optical Time Domain Reflectometry – developed by the Nippon Telegraph and Telephone Corporation – which had enabled the police greatly to improve their rate of detection of tunnels and underground arms caches.

This evening, as they sipped cold beers in a discreet snug towards the back of 'The Major's', Miller began apologetically, 'I have some news for you, but I'm afraid I can't give you all the data upfront. There has been a policy brake put on technological support with non-US police forces, yours included. To be honest, I think the RUC is particularly targeted in that respect. It's a result of political agitation on Capitol Hill about 'shoot- to- kill' and all that. Our bosses feel they have to respond to that. I wouldn't. I despise those pushy little ethnics, but that's the reality we live with.'

HSB wanted to interrupt, in protest, but Miller raised his hand and went on: 'I know. I know. All that stuff about infringements of human rights is ridiculous. But that's the fashion. However, the good news is that I can point you in the right direction about a new ground-penetrating radar system which should be right up your street.'

'Sounds good. Is it a home product?'

'No, developed by the Israelis. By Technicon – their Institute of Technology. It's super-efficient. We've tested it thoroughly and were amazed by the results. It will certainly be what Truman called "a powerful weapon in the arsenal of righteousness". A rabbit couldn't open a new burrow without his home improvement scheme showing up on screen. It can be operated from a helicopter at a height of several hundred feet. And best of all: within a year or eighteen months it will be capable of being used via satellite, either American or one from the European Space Agency, at a fraction of the cost of use by helicopters. I reckon that with a few sweeps you could cover just about all of your territory with it. How many counties did you say you have?'

'Six.'

'Six? – my home state has two hundred and fifty-four!'

'What state is that?'

'Texas,' said Miller, with an exaggerated swelling of a proud chest, 'I'm from Fort Worth.'

'Oh yeah, isn't that "the buckle on the Bible Belt?" teased HSB.

'Don't knock the Bible Belt. Nowadays it's the only thing holding Uncle Sam's pants up.'

'Well, buckle or no buckle, here's to the new weapon,' said HSB, lifting his glass.

'Remember, don't have this traced back to us – and by that I mean me. I'll give you the contact details and you can go directly to the Israelis as innocent shoppers.'

And with that Miller handed over a traditional brown envelope, size A4. HSB was overjoyed, but the joy was not entirely unalloyed: he could envisage a bumper price tag on the equipment. The Chief Constable, already almost on his knees before the Police Authority and the finance wallahs of the NIO and the Treasury, would not be enamoured of the idea of another massive financial commitment. The argument that such expenditure was cost-effective, measured against the cost of a single IRA bomb, was beginning to wear thin through endless repetition. Both the TECHNITEL and HUMINTEL parts of the budget were now accelerating by the month. It could not go on like that for ever. However, HSB recalled one of the great lessons he had learnt as a schoolboy winger on the rugby field – 'run until you're stopped, and always play to the whistle.'

Damn it, he would go on running.

Chapter 9

On Sunday night Aidan Cassidy's week ahead appeared to be pleasantly convenient. Noleen was off to London on Monday morning for a few days' shopping and to take in a special exhibition at the Royal Academy, as well as a number of galleries she frequented on every London visit. He was to join her as soon as possible later in the week and their holiday would include the following weekend – a routine which was repeated every couple of months. He would have the time and opportunity to see some of his insurance contacts on a keeping-in-touch basis and, more importantly, to do business regarding international bank transfers. It also left a large part of Monday free for Colette.

Things went agley from the start. Having previously agreed to his suggestion, Colette refused to stay the night with him in Myrtlefield Park. ('It would make me feel creepy'). Instead, she met him in sombre mood, and insisted that they go for a drive along the North Down coast. Half an hour later, they ended up parked on Seafront Road, Cultra, outside the town of Holywood, as Colette, who had barely said a word, demanded that he stop and have a 'serious talk about us'.

As they watched the lights on the ferry boat to Scotland move slowly down Belfast Lough, Cassidy knew in his bones what would come next.

'You haven't told your wife about us, as you promised me, have you? I just *knew* you wouldn't.'

'It's very difficult, Colette. There hasn't been the right moment. I want to get it right. For all of us.'

'Get it right? The right time? You have had *months* to get it right. But you haven't the guts, have you? It's so unfair!'

'Now *you're* being unfair. It's easier for you. I have so many things to consider and get right. And I will. Because I love you.'

Seafront Road, Cultra, had doubtless been the scene of many such conversations. It wasn't a 'lovers' lane', but the cars parked along its seaside after dark often contained earnest-talking couples of dubious legitimacy. This pair talked on and on, round and round, until long after the last noisy members had left the nearby yacht club and the lights in the bar had gone out.

At last Aiden felt he had persuaded Colette of his enduring love – and bought himself a little more time, though what to do with that time he had no precise idea. Life seemed increasingly to be made up of a series of short-term escapes – from his creditors, from the Army Council, and now from his mistress. Colette, for her part, believed, mainly because she wanted to believe, that she had succeed in stiffening his resolve, if nothing else. She convinced herself, on the basis of the way he had finally embraced her – tightly and with tears in his eyes – that he really did love her.

When he had dropped Colette off near her home, Cassidy felt relieved to be alone, yet with undiminished foreboding.

Mother of God, how did I get myself into this mess?

It was now late, very late to be ringing Noleen in the Cumberland Hotel, but he knew he must, as she would be expecting his call. He also knew she would ring him back five minutes later, under some pretext or other, just to make sure he was at home. She had become a bit snoopy like that of late. He drove the Jaguar into the long driveway, got out and zapped the remote control. He turned towards the house and not until the last second did he see the two men who stepped out swiftly from the shadow of a tall rhododendron bush.

'Jesus! The UVF.'

He had no time to recover from his shock. He felt a sharp pain in his right shoulder, as he was expertly pinned to the pathway in one overwhelming movement of force. But it wasn't the UVF. A voice in his ear said: 'Aidan Patrick

Cassidy, I am arresting you on suspicion of being a member of an illegal organisation.'

All he managed to say was: 'No.' To his surprise, he wasn't taken off to a police car. He realised in retrospect that there had been, in fact, no vehicle within a hundred yards of the house. Instead, he was bundled inside his own house, where already four or five men were moving purposefully about, intent on various tasks. *Forensic investigators? Would they have cracked the safe?* Two more men came in from the garden, where they had been acting as backup.

'To keep things nice and legal, here's my search warrant,' said the policeman, holding up a document, which Cassidy didn't look at. They pushed him roughly into an armchair in the drawing room. One sat in front of him, straddling a chair; the others sat on sofas to the side.

'Right, Mr Cassidy, time for us to have a little talk.'

'I want to see my solicitor,' said he, hoarsely.

'Oh no, you don't, Mr Cassidy. You don't want to see anyone. And I'll tell you why. If I contacted a solicitor of your choice, or simply took you to Castlereagh, as I'm supposed to, your murderous little playmates would inevitably, and soon, know you had been with us. That would mean that whether you were by some miracle released, or whether you ended up on remand in the "Crum", you would have to be de-briefed by said playmates. And your affairs – I use the term in its widest sense – would then come under some inconvenient scrutiny. As we say in our trade, and indeed yours, you would be "thoroughly investigated". And I do mean thoroughly. Need I say more?'

He paused to let the significance of that sink in.

'I should tell you that we have been doing quite a lot of investigating ourselves, here, and in Donegal Square, and elsewhere. And we've come up with lots of interesting items. Some of these are of special interest to us, as they would no doubt be to the courts. But some would be of equal interest to your – how would you put it? – "comrades-in-arms". What is of interest to us could possibly get you ten to fifteen years in clink. On the other hand, what would be of interest to the comrades would definitely get you....' He drew his index finger over his throat.

'So, bearing all that in mind, shall we talk business?'

'I don't know what you're talking about,' said Cassidy, without much conviction.

Niblock sighed. He turned to his companions. 'Could someone get the coffee on the go. This may take some time.'

Cassidy then told them that he was due to make a telephone call to his wife in London. The SB officers looked at one another, thrown by this development. Niblock took his deputy into the kitchen. 'It's probably a ploy,' said Sgt. McQuitty. 'He'll pass a message to her, through an alarm code word.'

'Let's think this through from his side,' countered Niblock. 'Supposing he's shit-scared – as he should be – that his 'RA chums find out he's with us. In that case, he might be afraid that if the wife doesn't hear from him, she'll go ringing round his friends to find out what's going on. He'll want to keep things as normal as possible until he can see a way out.'

'You're an optimist. I say don't let him make the call.'

At that moment, to their professional embarrassment, both of them jumped, startled by the shrill ring of the telephone. They could debate no longer. Rushing back into the other room, they made contradictory thumbs-up, thumbs-down gestures, until Niblock took charge.

'Let him answer it.'

Cassidy got up and crossed the room, to the 'phone which sat on a small side table by the bookcase. As he reached to pick up the receiver, the ringing stopped.

'Telephonus interruptus,' said Niblock.

The logic of his earlier decision determined that Cassidy was allowed to call the Cumberland and be put through to his wife. However, he was given a 'script', in telegraphic form, which Niblock wrote out for him in a police notebook and tore out the page. His captors stood over him, their close presence a warning that he must not go 'off message'.

When he got through to Noleen, Cassidy claimed to have just missed her call of ten minutes earlier and had gone to the bathroom in the meantime. He explained he had had a terrible day (true!), having had to go on business to Derry in the afternoon. Then he had been obliged to stay for dinner with a client. And to crown it all, the Jag had broken down – again! – on the M2. He had got the AA to tow it to a garage and had taken a taxi home. He was knackered and still had a lot of urgent business to attend to, so he wasn't sure when, or if, he could join her in London. Then, dangerously, the conversation went off the script, as Noleen got a word in edgewise.

'Yes, of course, I'm alright. Everything's fine. I'm just clapped out after today. I'll work at home tomorrow and take it easy. Depending on how I get on, I might get over before the end of the week, but I'll have to catch up for today and that won't be easy. But you enjoy yourself. How was the exhibition? And you. Take care...'

And for the second time that night, albeit in different circumstances, he breathed the great classic message: 'I love you. Night-night.'

His watchers looked at one another. The unspoken question hung in the air. Had he sent a message? Eventually Niblock shook his head, seemingly satisfied.

'OK, let's get back to business. Where were we?'

Answering his own question, he went on: 'Nowhere! Nowhere, all because, dear Cassidy, you don't face up to where *you* are, which is up Shit Creek, without the proverbial paddle.'

Cassidy knew what the IRA 'Green Book' golden rule was: 'Whatever you say, say nothing'. He clung to that line, sometimes merely shaking his head, sometimes saying, 'No comment', more often than not claiming total ignorance of the subject of the questioning. He was convinced that they already knew a lot – but exactly how much? He must not fall into the trap of confirming things they suspected but were not sure of. Occasionally he would vary his stonewall defence with a show of indignant defiance.

'This is illegal. You can't hold me here. You have either to release me or charge me.'

Niblock laughed, glad to have provoked a reaction, however hostile.

'Nothing illegal about it. We are talking to a suspect at the scene of a crime.'

There was no use arguing that that was nonsense: they had the upper hand; he didn't have witnesses; so much for 'due process'.

Niblock kept pounding away, threatening, cajoling, probing – and getting nowhere. Shortly after dawn one of the support team appeared from the kitchen with plates of egg and bacon. Cassidy refused to eat.

'We're not going to have a hunger strike on our hands as well, are we?' joked Niblock.

Tucking into his 'fry', he went on: 'Well, here's to Billy Sanderson. We'll never forget him.'

Cassidy found Niblock's provocations less irritating than the sermonising of his alter ego, Austin, who arrived in mid-morning. As an interrogator, he seemed more interested in achieving a religious conversion than in extracting information. He didn't seem frustrated by Cassidy's non-co-operation; rather , he gave the impression of enjoying the opportunity of pouring out an uninterruptible flow of admonitions. Guilt, God, punishment, repentance, forgiveness were at the core of his vocabulary.

'You may, by your silence, defy the judgment of the court that awaits you here on earth. You may refuse to recognise it. But there is another judgment to which you must surely be subjected: "For it is appointed unto man once to die, but after this the judgment". Mark you, God's own judgment. What will you plead then, my friend, if you have not forsaken your evil ways?'

Cassidy asked to be allowed to shave. No way! When he fell asleep they shook him awake. On and on went the questioning. Who were his contacts and seniors? What were the international banker's drafts in his safe for? He again declined to eat. Was it evening or already night? Thank God, Niblock was back, replacing Austin. Cassidy's vision was becoming distorted, as though he were seeing the world through a series of mirrors in a funfair.

'Mr Cassidy, I am a man with a problem. So are you. I am soon going to have to take you off to Castlereagh, where you'll be processed. And once you are charged, you'll be out of my hands. No more use to me, apart from the material we have already gathered. That would be a big disappointment to me.'

Niblock shook his head sadly, as though already experiencing that deep disappointment.

'And what about your future? Not martyred for the cause, but, sure as eggs is eggs, executed in disgrace – a trusted member who put his hand in the till and cheated his comrades, not to mention his devoted wife.'

Cassidy had slumped sideways; Niblock leaned forward and pushed him into the vertical again.

'Look, Cassidy, I know about most, if not yet all, of your problems. If you play ball with me, I can solve them for you. The big new overdraft, the old one, the debts to William Hill – all of that. Plus an ongoing – what shall I call it? – "consultancy fee". And most important of all, my protection, now and in the future, when the going gets really rough and dirty, as it will.'

Cassidy swayed again in his chair, eyes closed, saying nothing. Niblock leaned forward again, and almost whispered, in confidential tone, in his ear, 'I may even be able to help with the little Colette problem. Think about it, and give me your answer very soon. We're both running out of time. If it's "yes", we can work out the details.'

(A weary thought: *I've done more of these bloody deals in two years than my old man ever did in the cattle market in Enniskillen in a lifetime).* Then with undisguised menace: 'If it's "No", you're off to Castlereagh. Forthwith. In a tumbril. And bugger you.'

It was late on Thursday before Cassidy broke.

Chapter 10

Canon Murray had been a big name in West Belfast for over two decades, first as a parish priest in the outer suburb of Twinbrook, then as a canon, serving in St Peter's Pro-cathedral in the Lower Falls. In many ways he was the archetypical Irish priest of an earlier era – authoritarian, outgoing, energetic, sport-loving, interfering and a man instinctively looked up to by his parishioners. Over six feet tall, with broad shoulders and a great cliff of snowy white hair, he cut an impressive figure as he moved about the district – his district – usually on foot, greeting members of his flock at every turn and taking an intimate interest in their affairs. In his youth he had studied at the Irish College in Rome – normally a sign that the fledgling priest had been identified as a high flyer. At one period of his ministry he had been administrative assistant to the Bishop of Down and Connor, another sign of hierarchal approval. Many had thought of him as a likely bishop, perhaps even an archbishop, in waiting. However, he was already middle aged before he became a canon and it now looked as though he was not going to rise any higher, despite all the earlier promise.

'Why?' asked James Wheeler, with the simplicity of his Balliol directness.

'Oh, God knows – and I suppose a few of his Little Helpers,' replied Vincent Glass, 'but it certainly surprised me; he's a big man in every way. Could be he became too much of a "hearty", as you guys say, with all his GAA and boxing clubs activities. Or maybe his nationalist politics were a bit too up-front. The hierarchy like to keep a low profile in that regard. It could also be that his social welfare work had a tinge of liberation theology about it, which has always been a big "No-no" with the cardinal.'

'You don't seem convinced by your own reasons,' said Wheeler.

'You could be right. Perhaps he just ran across someone who got up the tree faster and made damn sure your man didn't. You know, it's like a reporter who gets shafted by a future editor, or I suppose a civil servant who has his career blighted by some bastard who took a dislike to him.'

'Tell me about it!' said Wheeler, and they both laughed loudly.

Glass was Northern editor of a major Dublin newspaper, who had made his career reporting on the 'Troubles', thanks in no small part to the excellent contacts he had with the republican leadership, thanks, in turn, to the role played by a clutch of his uncles in 'the movement', in an earlier generation. Glass had skilfully supplemented these contacts 'on the other side of the ditch', by cultivating government official spokesmen, who had come to welcome his interest, despite the strident anti-government nature of many of his articles. From their point of view, he could often help interpret the moods and attitudes of the nationalist community. Besides, he was great company and the purveyor of the sort of gossip beloved of newsmen everywhere. He was particularly close to James Wheeler ('Wheela-deala' to his friends), who had been brought by the Secretary of State, on the recommendation of Granville, from the Press Office of the FCO to be Head of Information Services at Stormont Castle. His colleagues suspected, rightly, that he had an MI6 or MI5 past and that his real master was Granville, rather than the politicians.

Apart from official press conferences and briefings, Glass and Wheeler would meet once or twice a month, to chew the fat, as they called it. They avoided places such as the Europa Hotel in Belfast, the main hangout of the press corps, and instead favoured the offbeat location of some of Bangor's better pubs, twelve miles away along the shores of Belfast Lough. Often there was nothing very serious or new to discuss about the political or security situation and the two of them would simply enjoy a convivial evening, poking fun at politicians in Belfast, Dublin and London, and exchanging ribald stories, of which both had an inexhaustible stock.

Occasionally, however, there would be a little nugget of information to be passed on by either side: that HMG was about to seek the extradition of a Sinn Fein fund-raiser from the USA, on charges related to explosions in Great Britain five years previously; or that a PIRA OC on the run in the Republic was dying of cancer in a Dundalk hospital, under an assumed name. Glass and Wheeler knew that such nuggets would be passed on and would make their appearance, suitably veiled, in the former's newspaper, or in Granville's next security report. Information was, they recognised, a trade in its own right, and trade was a two-way street. Wheeler's off-the-record relationship had the blessing of Granville, though with the warning, 'Always remember, diplomats tell lies to journalists and then believe what they read.'

'Is that a pearl of Beardsley wisdom?' asked Wheeler.

'No, it's from Karl Kraus. You won't have heard of him, you were at Oxford.' *Sometimes Master Wheeler needed to be put in his place.*

Today's info-trading, carried out in a snug alcove of the Windsor Bar, beside Bangor's marina, was focused on a major message Glass said he had been asked to pass on. He put down his glass, made sure no one was in earshot, and, to underline the importance of what he was about to say, tapped Wheeler on the chest with his index finger.

'I have been asked to convey to you the following.' He paused to pull a piece of paper from his breast pocket, from which he read rather stiffly, 'to which you have one week to reply, through me: the leadership of the Irish Republican Army is keen to have serious talks with British Government representatives. But, unlike earlier attempts at dialogue, such talks have to be carefully prepared and move along a mutually agreed path.' He paused for effect. 'Canon Murray is their chosen man for first contacts. He will not in any sense negotiate. He will merely explore with you the possibility of establishing initial ground rules, on which further, direct talks could be held.'

Wheeler remained silent for several moments. He was sure Glass was to be taken seriously, but he was momentarily off-balance.

'I must say, I don't quite know what to make of the proposed contacts, via you, then friend Murray, then somebody else. Why so many layers to the onion?'

'Don't let that put you off. It's about a paranoid security fear. A fear about internal security, to be precise. You've no idea how nervous the top guys are about this. They think they now have a reasonable majority in favour of a move to political negotiation, but if anything should go wrong, or leak out prematurely, then there'd be hell to pay. So, take my advice: don't turn your back on this one. Or try to exploit it. Play it straight and see where it will lead.'

'You forget the risks *we* would be running. Can't you see the headlines: "HMG parleys with terrorist leadership"; "Secret negotiations with IRA"? Horrendous! End of Secretary of State.'

'I repeat: don't miss this opportunity. If you do, the hawks will regain the upper hand and the chance for an end to the war will vanish for a decade.'

As they parted, an hour or so later, Glass grasped Wheeler by the hand.

'Tonight could be an historic day for Ireland.'

'You're drunk,' said Wheeler.

And they both laughed, each suspecting that the other was right.

The visitors' reception room in Clonard Monastery was a gloomy, almost uncomfortable place. Sparsely furnished with only two armchairs and a tiny table, it was poorly lit, the brightest light being focused on a small stone sculpture of the Madonna and Child; on another wall hung a print of a garish 'Sacred heart of Jesus', of the series to be seen in half the

Catholic homes in Ireland. Clearly, visitors were not encouraged to stay long.

Canon Murray was already seated in one of the armchairs when Granville was shown in. He rose to greet him, with a firm, more-than-polite handshake.

'Thanks for coming. I thought it best to meet here, rather than at my house. It's more anonymous here; we don't want local questions about strangers. It's vitally important that none of this gets out.'

'Thanks for receiving me. I appreciate the opportunity of meeting you. I fully understand the need for complete confidentiality. And you can assure your contacts that applies to any dealings with them also.'

Murray suddenly smiled. 'We're sounding like two members of the UN Security Council, for God's sake. Let's have a drink. The sun's bound to be over the yardarm by now, if only we could see the damn thing in this foul weather.'

He opened a panel in the low table and produced two glasses, a jug of water and a bottle of Power's whiskey.

'I hope you don't mind the Irish.'

'Not at all,' said Glanville, cheerily. He had, in fact, hated all whiskies since, at the age of ten and in bed with measles, he had been forced by his mother to gulp down two table spoonfuls, 'to bring out the spots'. But.... *always go along with the other side as far as possible, provided the cost to be paid is not too high.*

'I prefer it to scotch,' resumed Murray. 'It's the triple distillation that makes the difference, you know.'

Granville thoughtfully sipped his drink, then said, 'I – that is to say, not only myself but my political masters – were glad to hear that serious links might be renewed with the PIRA leadership. And I am grateful to you for your help. I needn't go over the reasons why earlier contacts failed to come to fruition. That was in any case before my time. This time round, if we can keep in step, things could be different.'

'Yes. I personally sense that both sides now want a way out of the present situation. The recent let-up in harassments has created a space for a new dialogue, which could lead to an end to hostilities. Depending, of course, on what's on offer from your side.'

Granville could scarcely suppress a smile. 'The recent let-up in harassments' he knew had come about as the result of the security forces, almost overwhelmed by the amount of information now flowing in about so many people, being obliged to take stock through the PANORAMA system, of the overall situation in order to determine priorities. He recalled the wording of a recent joint Army / RUC paper on the subject, which foresaw 'a subsequent co-ordinated attack on key operatives, against whom serious charges could be brought, with a reasonable expectation of conviction'.

'I take it that you have a message for me, setting out suggested ground rules and possible pre-conditions?'

'Well, it's simpler than that, really...'

He pulled a sheet of paper from his pocket.

'My instructions come from two members of the Army Council. They will be, what's the diplomatic phrase? Plenipotentiaries. They want a maximum of two British Government representatives, empowered to deal.'

'No problem.'

'We have already touched on confidentiality, but I must re-emphasise it. Complete secrecy. No feed outs to the media. No hints. If challenged on links, talks, negotiations etc., then total denial is to be immediate and automatic.'

'Agreed.'

'Either side can raise any matter – no closed agenda.'

'OK so far.'

'Two small, practical details, but of great importance: the two to be able to carry side arms without fear of prosecution; and the first meeting to be held as soon as possible, in Donegal.'

Granville sucked on his teeth in the time-honoured civil service gesture which indicated 'a problem'.

'Pistols OK. Obviously I can't issue a Firearms Certificate, but you have my word for immunity from prosecution on that score. But Donegal. No. It must be in

Northern Ireland. There are enough remote locations suitable for our purposes.'

'Good,' said Murray. 'I knew you couldn't agree to everything. That would be bad tactical politics.'

'Now you're back at the United Nations,' joked Granville, who was pleased to note that Murray was genuinely amused.

If Murray had the confidence of PIRA behind him, he, Granville, would have to look on him as a valuable asset, who might be brought into play again at some stage in the future. There was nothing on the file about him, as regards 'activity'. It seemed likely that his links with the top of the IRA arose from the fact that the Belfastman (code name in the RUC: 'Bunny') had been his parishioner, involved in sporting clubs run by the church, as well as having been his pupil in religious instruction classes at St Mary's.

Granville decided to explore what was known in his trade as 'Personal Background Factors'.

'I'm very grateful for your help in this matter. You can certainly convey to your contacts our willingness to meet face-to-face to discuss our respective positions. But tell me, I'm curious, how did you come to be involved?'

'You mean what is a man of the cloth doing mixed up with a revolutionary movement?'

'Let's forget about definitions and categories. I am interested in your personal views.'

'Let me ask *you* a question: do you believe in the concept of a just war?'

'If you mean *this* war, I can't accept – and you wouldn't expect me to accept – that it is a just one. There are democratic frameworks within which Sinn Fein and other republicans can pursue their political goals. Terrorism flouts the democratic process and is therefore unjust.'

'But, my friend, the democratic frameworks you refer to were perverted by partition. The Irish people were arbitrarily divided. It is a just war to re-unite them. I regret, of course, the sufferings of war and I'd be the first to acknowledge that mistakes have been made by the IRA, but I look on my

81

modest role as one which can help eliminate the suffering and achieve a lasting peace.'

'Please don't take offence at my personal questions, but do you really believe that role is compatible with your vocation as a priest?'

'Emphatically yes. "Blessed are the peacemakers, for they shall be called sons of God". That's my charter. Indeed I hope peacemaking will save my sacerdotal ministry from failure.'

'Failure?'

Granville theatrically raised his eyebrows. Murray took a deep swig of his whiskey and was silent for a moment. When he started to speak again, it was in a softer, almost sad, voice.

'When I was ordained a priest I gloried in the authority and universality of the Church. I was inspired by the liturgy and I rejoiced in sharing it. All that has been lost. Tell it not in Gath, but Vatican II was a disaster. The present generation, using "modernisation" as a new belief system, no longer recognize the supreme authority of the Church. They have lost the majesty of the Latin Mass. Most of them wouldn't know the Agnus Dei from Mrs Agnes Daly.'

'Agnes Daly?'

'Yes. She runs a sweet shop on the Springfield Road.'

Granville was unsure whether to laugh at that, but Murray beat him to it with a loud guffaw.

'That's awful, isn't it? But you see why I hope my activities of a non-ecclesiastical nature can compensate for my disappointments within the so-called modern church.'

Murray drew deeply again on his Power's. 'But that's a lot about me. Now I have one for you. Are you a man of faith?'

'I wouldn't go so far as to say that. Although my maternal grandfather was a Church of England clergyman – a canon at Warwick Cathedral as it happens. But that didn't seem to get into my DNA. I would hope to qualify as a man of goodwill – isn't that enough when all dogmas are said and done?'

'It all depends on whether you believe in eternity, in the transcendental.'

'I probably don't, in your terms. I mean, for example, belief in an afterlife. I don't have that. What would your reaction be if it could be proved – and I know it can't be, but just suppose – that there was no afterlife?'

'I'd be absolutely delighted. No hell, no retribution, no post-mortem accusations, no purgatorial sufferings. And no boring heaven either, with the righteous congratulating themselves on being in the pound seats for keeps. Instead, all of us tucked up in a snug oblivion, in a never-ending good night's sleep. The sheer eternal luxury of it!'

Murray's enthusiasm for the vision of a future of nothingness did not last long.

'Of course, I couldn't believe in that.'

'Why ever not? Many people do.'

'Because I'm a Catholic. That's all there is to it. My baptism has inoculated me against total unbelief, even if I wanted to stray in that direction. Life is a constant struggle with my own inadequacies and with the temptations of unbelief.'

(*Not to mention the temptations associated with angelic altar boys and the constant fear of denunciation*).

'But definitive unbelief is a place I'll never be in.'

Granville drained his half glass at one go, without flinching. *That should bring out the spots.*

'I'd better be going. We've talked more theology than politics – perhaps it's the setting – but you've been most helpful.'

'Happy to be of use. Here are the contact details.' He passed over a white envelope.

'Whatever your doubts and temptations, pray for success.'

'I will.'

Chapter 11

'To what do I owe the honour of this visit?' said HSB with mock reverence, rising from his desk to greet the GOC. The two men knew one another well, not only from their *ex officio* attendance at the all-too-frequent security meetings in which they represented their respective forces, but from their tussles on the golf course, in which they were evenly matched. They played in a four-ball at Knock Golf Club, close to the Stormont governmental estate, on most Saturday mornings, crises permitting. Occasionally they managed another round on Sunday morning, after which they would entertain their companions to a leisurely lunch, either at Chesham's official residence or chez Campbell, (HSB's family) in a leafy street not far from police HQ at Brooklyn.

The GOC had a senior man based at Brooklyn, but he rarely set foot there himself. HSB had therefore been surprised at the general's discreet request to see him there, 'informally'.

'Thanks. It's not a courtesy call,' he said, unnecessarily. He sat down, looking uncomfortable.

'This is a bit embarrassing, to tell you the truth, but I hope you'll understand. I need your help on this one. I'll owe you one if you can.'

He pulled from his inside pocket a folded A4 sheet and smoothed it out on the desktop. It was a copy of the previous day's RUC list of arrests, which had been circulated to all the usual group of interested parties, as well as being registered on PANORAMA.

Chesham pointed to a name on the list: Francis Fanon.

'That one. He's mine. And I can't afford to lose him.'

HSB could not contain his astonishment.

'Francis Fanon? The Double F-er, as my lads call him? A tout of yours? We have him down as a top notcher and hope this time we have enough forensic on him to nail him good and proper.'

'I heard that was the position. That's why I'm here, on bended knee. You see, I inherited him from my predecessor. I seem to remember he was a "walk-in", offering his services. Which, it must be said, have been invaluable, especially as regards tip-offs about planned ops. To us, he's "Mr Stiletto". My very best asset.'

'And where does he get his info?'

'Well, you were on the button when you called him a top notcher. But you are not going to believe this; he's "head of discipline" for the entire shooting match. No pun intended – but it is a fact that the "discipline" meted out by his kangaroo courts often involve a bullet in the head. He's in on most things, one of the few who know about ops. who aren't directly involved, hands-on.'

Chesham paused to let the full import of his tale sink in.

'He doesn't tell us everything of course, but his carefully abridged version of 'Life in the 'RA' is nonetheless gold dust. Certainly, we are paying him in gold dust, if not indeed gold ingots.'

HSB whistled through his teeth. 'How does he sleep at night?'

'How do any of them sleep at night?'

'Point taken. Do MI5 know about this?'

Chesham coughed. 'That's the thing. They weren't in the game here when Stiletto was first on the scene. And it was all so hush-hush and delicate that we never got round to what dear Jeremy calls "sharing the spoils". Sure you can understand my reluctance to share an asset like Stiletto. It's so delicate, walking on eggshells wouldn't be in it. The more people know on our side, the greater the risk of a leak. Which , if I may mix metaphors, would be to slaughter the goose that lays the golden eggs.'

'That's way out of line with our "sharing-caring" philosophy,' teased HSB.

'This isn't the bloody Co-op. As my old colonel used to say, "information is never shared, it's traded."'

'Well, here's a trading proposition for you. You cut me in, as regards your Stiletto source. And you revise – upwards, of course – the number of "bricks" you can spare the RUC to protect our foot patrols in West and North Belfast. I know four soldiers to one policeman is a heavy manpower ratio, but it's a big deal on our side. The Chief is very keen on it.'

'You mean being seen on the ground?'

'Yes. The more we can do it, the more the mood swings towards thinking the war's nearly over. That's the theory anyway.'

'If only .... but what can you do for me?'

'My proposal is this. I'll put Niblock on the Fanon-Stiletto case. He's our best interrogator, and inventive with it. He'll find a way of releasing your man without arousing suspicions anywhere. Then we'll square things with Jeremy, by dressing up Stiletto as a "re-activated agent" and by overshadowing his case with the sheer joy of our own piece of very good news, which, good boys that we like to think we are, we are about to share with the top of the system.'

And he told him of Cassidy.

'Good God,' cried Chesham. 'We now own the Treasurer and the Head of Discipline! A few more like that and we can launch a take-over bid.'

'Steady on, it's not quite a majority shareholding in Marks & Spencer.'

'Anyway, it's a deal,' said Chesham, holding out his hand as he stood up.

'Care to stay for a spot of lunch?'

Chesham, instantly recalling his last lunch in the Brooklyn canteen, quickly declined.

'Must get back to the ranch.'

Chapter 12

The choreography for Cassidy's new role took some time to be established. The question of who should be the producer was thrashed out at a rather tense meeting of the Joint Intelligence Committee, under Granville's chairmanship.

The first item of business was a statement by the GOC regarding the 'Stiletto' situation. He wished, he said, to be 'crystal clear about this'. His version of the past was, however, distinctly muddy. ('In those days the "need-to-know principle" was paramount'). Nevertheless, that aspect was glossed over, with a rather grovelling acknowledgment on Chesham's part of the present need to share such information, as Granville had so recently emphasised.

There was general euphoria about the RUC's great coup. Congratulations all round. How best to exploit this high-grade asset? The RUC were the players in possession and HSB put up a case for continuing to run what had become *their* man. Granville struck a pensive pose, as though pondering deeply on the issue, before commenting.

'I hear what you say,' (which almost invariably meant 'bollocks to you') 'but I think there are wider considerations here. Cassidy should be able to bring us operational details from time to time – usually *post hoc,* I suspect. That is to say, who has done what, after the event. And , of course, that sort of information can be most appropriately be acted upon by the police. But there is another dimension to this. The *real* potential value of Cassidy – let's call him HERMES, shall we?' (Puzzled looks on several faces). 'You know – the messenger – is that he can throw light on how the top Provos are thinking, particularly as regards strategy.'

.Now for the KO punch.

'That leads us into territory above and beyond law and order pure and simple into the quasi-political field. That is why I feel sure (here he imagined how Sir Julian would put across the point in a way which brooked no return of serve) ...I feel sure MI5 should take over the running. I'll keep a close eye on it myself, for a while at least, to see how it goes. And it goes without saying that whatever we get out of 'HERMES' we'll share with you.'

The others nodded in agreement ... and, in their hearts, disbelief.

'May I take it then that you will be taking over the financial aspects of our ... our obligations?' queried HSB.

'Yes, OK. I think that can be arranged.'

As HSB later reported to the Chief Constable: 'I thought if the buggers were going to nick our best ever tout, they could pay the piper.'

'Just as well, in the light of the pressure we are going to be under as regards our Slush Fund monies. Incidentally, I have been looking at those break-down figures of where your money – *our* money! – is going. A bit worrying. I mean, for example, do you have to have half the hairdressers in North and West Belfast on the payroll?'

'Believe me, Chief, they're very good value, and the individual payments are small. You see, the local women relax when they go there, under those big hoods, whatever they're called. In their everyday lives they have all these pent-up worries, about their sons getting mixed up with the Provos, about violence in their street, and so on. Or they have complaints about what they are expected to do for the cause by the local Republican bullies. They don't normally talk about such things with their neighbours – they're afraid to. But they then confide in the hairdresser, often with useful snippets of information about what is going on, who is doing what and to whom.'

'You mean like the confessional?'

'Yes, only more luxurious and less demanding. The hairdresser doesn't need to say much. She just listens and makes sympathetic – or is it empathetic? – noises from time to time. And there are no "Hail Marys" or "Our Fathers" to be said afterwards, or contributions to church funds to be made. Just the price of a wash and set, plus a modest tip.'

'I am still going through the figures and may need to review policy with you later. But to get back to our prize tout – what are we to call him, HERMES? I thought that was one of my wife's scarves. Anyway, I hope that MI5 will handle him correctly. Above all, not push him too far. He's bound to be under terrific strain. Can you imagine it? And if pushed too far, or too hard, he could go wrong on us. To adapt your bagpipe analogy: "When you've got the piper by the balls, he may play the odd bum note."

'Not to worry. I think Granville will be fine. He's bright and he has tuned into Provo thinking very quickly. Don't forget, he has probably run raghead agents over half the countries of the Middle East. My reservations about him spring from the fact that his ultimate objectives are not always clear. But he's a pro at the handling game.'

HSB thought he should take the opportunity of putting another piece on the chess board.

'About your financial worries, I think I should warn you there's another lot of increased expenditure on the horizon; our Witness Protection Programme. It's wildly expensive in each case – re-housing a whole family, usually. Plus, in all probability, helping with a new identity for the family, or even re-settling in GB, Canada, the States or New Zealand – the whole shebang costs a fortune, but the programme is proving to be a key weapon in our armoury.'

'How do we justify it to NIO, if the costs are spiralling?'

'As you know, after all the cock-ups in the courts, with the original supergrasses, we more or less gave up using our touts as witnesses. But the adaptation of the basic scheme has worked wonderfully well. In reality it is now an "Informers' Protection Programme". We get the touts on board through payments, the promise that we won't use them as witnesses in court and, most important of all, we guarantee "protection", in the widest sense. I need more men to process the candidates in the queue. And more dosh.'

'A request for more money will go down like a lead balloon. Can you work up stats. on the costs/ benefits of that?'

'Sure. The quality of our intelligence has soared since we introduced the policy. The time had come for it. And we are beginning to push at an open door. There are so many Provos around, even in so-called middle management, who are so stressed out and have been at it for so long that they are looking for a way out. We provide that. But we must also do what it takes and pay what it costs, to offer credible protection. If things were to go wrong for some of our clients and they ended up, face down, in the Lagan, our present advances could be just as quickly reversed.'

'I know you are passionate about that. And I'll support you all the way. But get a defensive paper ready for NIO. Most of our war these days seems to be fought on paper.'

Granville arranged for Cassidy to be invited to be a member of 'West Belfast Growth', a voluntary development association set up with the active participation of the Department of Commerce, with the remit to promote the creation of jobs in that area of high deprivation and high unemployment. It was chaired by a junior NIO minister and was staffed by officials from Commerce, under the watchful eye of a NIO official from the Economics Section. On the other side of the table sat a couple of trade unionists, an energetic parish priest, two "community workers" (in reality Provos), two tenant association representatives and a Catholic businessman who had made his money in the wholesale livestock market. The addition of another Catholic businessman would clearly strengthen the team. It would also bring Cassidy into legitimate contact with officialdom, thus simplifying communications enormously.

Cassidy claimed to his security handlers that he would have to clear the appointment with the Army Council, which would entail a delay of nearly three weeks. That was agreed to.

Take him gently. Show him you care.

This time the meeting was in a safe house in Dundalk and Cassidy was relieved when his financial report was accepted with scarcely a query. When he told them of his invitation, there was general laughter.

'The Hillsborough Garden Party will be your next appearance,' said the Derryman. The others looked to the top Belfastman for guidance.

'Don't see why not. Could be useful, getting so close to a Brit minister. You know, we could get Aidan to do a von Stauffenberg.'

Cassidy paled.

'Only joking. Seriously, keep us posted if you get the chance to talk to him off the agenda, so to speak. About the overall situation and how he sees it.'

Head of Operations then took over.

'Aidan ,we have that outing lined up for you – and for the kitty. Now that Her Majesty's post offices have contributed so generously to the cause – more generously than brother Brody in New York, as you have told us, the Belgian operation is now on. McGiolla should be here within the hour and we can set things up for the pair of you.'

Officialdom also underwent an important change at this time, to take account of Cassidy's 'recruitment'; the NIO Principal Officer, Economics Section, was replaced by another NIO Officer, Keith Barrow, recently arrived from London and in reality an MI5 operative. This had caused a little flutter with PUS (NIO), who did not take at all warmly to the idea of MI5 penetrating his domain. However, he was overruled by SoS, thanks to the Granville-Beardsley-Foreign Secretary-PM axis, and he was mollified by the assurance that the post would not come out of his, NIO's, staff complement. Barrow could genuinely – if that adverb had any meaning in this context – look after the 'West Belfast Growth' workload, which represented a freebee for NIO, and there were plenty of other things for him to do in Northern Ireland in his ample spare time. 'Like garrotting passers-by', sniffed PUS.

Cassidy was told that Barrow was to be his own 'little helper' on the board. He also came to know Jeremy Granville, who was to look after his activities more generally. He knew from his 'initiation briefings', that Granville had an 'outside persona', as a senior NIO official, Keith Barrow's boss. But the important relationship was with him as his principal handler, paymaster and, he fervently hoped, protector.

Chapter 13

'Thank you for coming,' began PUS, tapping his teacup with a spoon.

He looked round the large room – formerly the cabinet room, pre-1972, in Stormont Castle – and mentally ticked off the various groups: police, army, NIO, MI5, each with a team of four or five.

'I thought it would be useful to repeat our first joint meeting of some months ago, which I believe was valuable to all of us, in order to have a co-ordinated picture of just where we are, both in security terms and politically. As you know, ministers are keen to see the two fronts go forward together, so it is a good idea, in my view, also to take stock of both in parallel.'

Heads nodded in agreement. But, mused Granville, how much agreement would there be in those heads about the wisdom or otherwise of mutating the underlying policy of their political masters?

'I propose we devote this afternoon's session to security, then take the political situation tomorrow morning. I apologise for having had to cancel this morning's scheduled meeting at such short notice; I could not get away from London last night, as the Northern Ireland Committee in the Commons overran and the SoS wanted to see me afterwards. Now then, where shall we start? With you, Jeremy, or with you, Chief Constable?'

The two made you-go-first gestures to one another, but the Chief Constable took the initiative. Flanked by HSB and his own administrative assistant, he was the only one in the room in uniform, though General Chesham, the GOC, had a taste in clothes which made him look as though he were perpetually in uniform; indeed perpetually taking the salute.

'Thank you, PUS, Mr Chairman,' began the Chief Constable in formal tones. Then, under the careful scrutiny of HSB, who had written most of them, he plunged into a series of notes laid out on top of his slim portfolio. He had a tendency to read at slightly too fast a pace and this was exaggerated whenever he was using material assembled by someone else.

'I am pleased to report that, statistically, there has been a marked improvement on almost all fronts over the past six months, indeed the past year. If I may, I will give you the stats. For the past twelve months, as compared to the preceding twelve months, bombings are down by 60%; shootings by half; the weight of explosives found is 63% greater; the number of serviceable weaponry recovered is up by almost half.'

He paused and looked up from his notes. He judged the meeting to be impressed, if not exactly overwhelmed. Then on he went, like a Tibetan monk rotating his prayer wheel.

'And in terms of people: casualties, excluding terrorists, are down by 15% and on the other side of the balance sheet, our arrest rate has trebled and our charge rate at the DPP is almost double what it was a year ago. It will take some time yet for the conviction rate to improve, but I am confident that will happen, as these new cases move down the pipeline. So, I think we can say with assurance that the policy of "the primacy of the police", propounded by the Bourne Report, has been paying ever better dividends.'

He thought he detected a low growl from Chesham, but as he looked up again, PUS was smiling approvingly.

'Of course, we couldn't do the half of that without the physical backup from the GOC and his forces. And I would like to say a special word of thanks to the Logistical Support Group, for all their technological help, which has literally transformed our intelligence-gathering capacities. The PANORAMA programme and its ongoing development, allows us to monitor a vastly greater number of suspects than was possible only a couple of years ago and, most importantly, that is now done in a co-ordinated way, often even in real time. It's like working with the lights on, instead of in the dark. And we can do better...'

'One thing you haven't mentioned, Chief Constable,' interjected PUS, 'is cost.' He took off his reading glasses and sucked on a stem.

'You are aware, I know, of the new round of expenditure cuts. We're in the throes of juggling with the figures. New savings will be demanded of us. But even before that exercise, I understand from the Police Authority that the RUC was over budget last year and is already seriously over budget this year. We are going to have to enter into special bi-lateral talks with the Treasury about how we get out of *that* particular hole. I will have to don sackcloth and ashes on your behalf. So, I do hope that you are not going to come forward today with any new proposals which would exacerbate the situation.'

The Chief Constable jumped back in at once. 'With respect, PUS,' (in such circles 'with respect' invariably meant the opposite), 'with respect, you cannot simply look at "costs" without at the same time looking at the benefits the investment of those costs have brought and can still bring. You have to look at the situation in the round, with results related to expenditure. Shall I give you an example?'

'Go on, yes, please,' said PUS, with an evident lack of enthusiasm.

'Well, take just one set of outline figures: Criminal Injuries claims: down by over 65%. In gross terms, that is well over treble our overspend in the RUC. And that's only one statistic. Think of the reduced costs in hospital care, in days lost at work, in industrial disruption and so on. Never mind the factor of human lives and suffering spared.'

'I'm not sure we can put all these advances for mankind down to the RUC,' said PUS, with a quick smile which instantly faded. He wondered who had put the CC up to this new cost-benefit defence, but as he was about to follow up his dampener, he could not ignore the firm signal from the GOC that he wanted the floor. As was his wont, Chesham had stretched his right arm out straight before him, almost at shoulder height.

A bit like at Nuremberg, thought Granville.

'I don't wish to get bogged down in the treacle of accountancy. I leave that to my masters in MoD. But I must say I have sympathy with the Chief Constable's point of view. Indeed, in the light of the most recent threat of another round of cuts, I'd go further and challenge ministers head-on.'

The general paused and took a deep breath. The others sensed that a 'Chesham special' was on its way.

'Ministers have got to realize that we're fighting a war here, for God's sake. We're slowly winning, but what we need is a knock-out blow. Something to put Johnnie Terrorist – and by that I mean all of them – to flight once and for all. That is the great lesson taught us by Malaya, the only totally successful anti-insurgency campaign we, or anyone else, have ever fought, anywhere, at any time.'

Oh God, thought Granville, *we're going to get the Field Marshal Templer Memorial Lecture.*

'What we need is a clear and enunciated policy of "victory first, politics later". To be understood by all. No ifs and buts, no nods and winks – just straight down the line. Then a crack- down – I mean a real crackdown – on anything that moves. Police and army together; pressure on all fronts. Flood the difficult areas with personnel. Sit on the buggers. Arrest and interrogate left, right and centre. Inundate the DPP with files. In short, make everybody realise it is wartime and that things won't improve until it's over and the paramilitaries jack it in. Their supporters must be made to yearn for an end to it all and to cry "enough is enough". We can only win that way and we can only win if we can get on with the task without having one hand tied behind our backs.'

Chesham sat back in his chair, slightly red in the face.

'Thank you, General, for those thoughts,' said PUS with exaggerated politeness, 'I must say, however, that they go somewhat beyond the parameters of our current review. And I know you will recognize that they represent a radical departure from what we have hitherto understood to be government policy. And I would add that I have detected no appetite on the part of ministers to take political risks in this sphere. They are already under severe pressure from all quarters – the Opposition at Westminster, the Irish, the Americans, the SDLP, not to mention half the media – about our old friend "Shoot-to-kill" and about the deployment of the SAS. You will say tougher measures have brought significant gains, but it has been at a high political price. My instincts tell me that ministers in this situation will tend to err on the side of caution. And, of course, they will be comforted by the police view, expressed here today, that we are winning.'

'Winning, yes, but when's V-Day? Five, ten, fifteen years from now?' cried Chesham, sitting bolt upright in his place, eyes blazing.

'General,' said PUS quietly, like a schoolmistress calming a promising but unruly pupil, 'we must concentrate today on reviewing where we are. We can, of course, conclude our subsequent paper with recommendations, indeed ministers will expect us to do so. Your views can be incorporated in that section, as one option, but frankly I feel it will be necessary to make clear that your position in that regard is a minority one.'

No one in the other teams moved a muscle.

The meeting then settled down to decide on 'Headings' to be used in their report to the SoS, and to sketch out the contents of each section. The temperature cooled as the participants concentrated on the more bureaucratic aspects of their task. It was remarkable, thought Granville, how the horrible realities of the streets were eventually transformed, as though by alchemy, into the balanced, pellucid arguments of a paper to ministers, logically marshalled and couched in the precise prose of PUS, the ultimate desk jockey.

Immediately after the meeting, PUS and Granville found themselves standing side by side at the urinals of the Gents' lavatory. Granville was a master at such 'chance meetings'.

'Do you think I could have a word with you before tomorrow's session?' he enquired, looking over his shoulder to make sure no one was listening. 'There are one or two things ....'

'Yes, certainly,' was PUS's response, 'that's a good idea. I'm out to dinner this evening, but you could pop up to the flat about half past six for a drink and a chat.'

'Good. See you then.'

Zip, zip.

Granville arrived early, but used the interval to drop by the office of one of his Liaison Staff, where on a secure line he managed a five minute briefing of Sir Julian Beardsley. The office was in the same building, now called 'the Annex', as the small, first-floor flat in which PUS was domestically housed when in Belfast. The red brick building had originally been the official residence of the Speaker of the old Stormont House of Commons, but was now a warren of offices, inhabited mostly by officials whose duties concerned the darker aspects of what came under the title 'security'.

'Lemon or lime?' asked PUS, poised at the cocktail cabinet, a gin and tonic in hand.

'Either, thanks. I must say I think you handled Chesham very well today. He doesn't get any better, does he? I mean, gung-ho is all very well in a military chap, but he is constantly over the top. He may be mostly bluster, but I worry about his influence on others.'

'He could be with us for another eighteen months or so, I'm afraid. I've explored with my oppo. in MoD the possibility of his moving to pastures new at an earlier date, but that's not on – for a funny reason.' He paused to chuckle, then, shaking his head ruefully, 'My man wouldn't agree to it.'

'Your SoS wouldn't agree?'

'That's right. Apparently he likes listening to Chesham, especially when he is arguing with me. Says it gives balance to the picture, presumably meaning he thinks I'm a "wet". But positively, since the GOC's views are, let's say "populist", the SoS hears them expressed all over the place. And when he hears my counter-arguments, he can recycle those whenever tackled on the same lines.'

Both men laughed heartily. PUS was seated in a large high-backed chair, which was out of proportion to the cramped living space. And indeed to PUS himself; Granville could not help noticing that his tiny feet barely touched the carpet.

'About tomorrow,' said Granville, 'this is where I may need some protection from you in the chair. You see, neither police nor army would be enamoured of my intention – which I'll therefore have to disguise somewhat – to push our contacts with Sinn Fein / IRA along significantly, even if they're stalled at the moment. My ideal is to get past the waffle about "giving them explanations of HMG's policies" and to move on to a recognized stage of substantive negotiations. Eventually those negotiations will have to come out into the open, with ministers publicly seen to be involved. At which point I and my colleagues will fade and it will be up to you, in NIO, and no doubt the Foreign Office and Number 10, to manage the end of the endgame.'

'That's an ambitious route map,' said PUS cautiously, pursing his lips. 'And there are a lot of potholes on the route.'

'I know, I know. Including potholes which our own chums can dig for us. That's why I'll have to soft pedal tomorrow on what exactly my links with the paramilitaries are and how I intend to develop them. I'd be grateful if the focus could be firmly on the mainstream political parties and relations with HMG.'

'Certainly, point taken. But, could I say......'

He drew his fingers through the wispy strands of hair over his domed forehead. 'I'd worry slightly about your plan and whether it was watertight. If that were to get out – and Sinn Fein might at some point, for their own reasons, decide to let it get out – then the effect on the overall political situation could be seismic. The Government might even have to disown you.'

'As a rogue elephant ... I mean, a rogue element?' said Granville, laughing off what he recognized as the other's veiled threat. 'Well, excitement was one of the reasons we all joined the Civil Service, was it not?' Then, glancing at his watch, 'Mustn't keep you from your dinner. Anywhere interesting?' *Information gathering can become routinely addictive.*

'Not really. Institute of Directors' Annual, at the Culloden.'

'Ah! I can see it now: prawn cocktail, steak Diane, pavlova, Irish coffee, three boring speeches. A proven formula.'

'Alas, one endlessly repeated in these parts. As will be the calls for firmer security measures.'

'Happy days!'

Chapter 14

Colette McShane didn't usually drink. Bad for the waistline, bad for the complexion. But this evening she had joined some of her friends from work in Kelly's Cellars in the city centre for a brief celebration of the engagement of one of her fellow beauticians. She sipped her vodka and orange half-heartedly and joined in the conversation about rings, wedding venues and dresses without much enthusiasm. Indeed her friend's obvious happiness secretly depressed her further. She seemed to have made little progress with Aidan, despite having pressed him more and more in recent weeks. And yet it could all be so different and so wonderful, if only he could take his courage in his hands and do what he had for such a long time said he wanted to, namely make a fresh start with her.

At the earliest moment in the festivities when she could leave without raising eyebrows, she said her goodbyes to the newly betrothed and made her way to Great Victoria Street railway station, to take the train home to Balmoral. Her home was near Kennedy Way, close to the M1 motorway junction at Stockman's Lane and she preferred the suburban train service to that of the bus, which was less reliable. She had once been on a bus which was hi-jacked and burned out and she had resolved never to be in that position again.

At rush hour the train on her way home was normally crowded, but this evening, over an hour later than usual, there were only a few passengers scattered throughout her carriage. She absentmindedly leafed through a copy of *Cosmopolitan* and daydreamed. As she turned the pages, she became aware that a scruffy-looking man, facing her two seats in front, was taking a more-than-ordinary interest in her. He had long, unkempt hair, an earring in his left ear and a stud to the right of his nose. When they made eye contact, he looked away, but a minute later she noticed he was looking at her again. Colette was used to being the object of male attention, something which did not displease her in the least, but there was something about this man's interest which unnerved her. She was therefore dismayed to find, when she alighted at Balmoral, that the man was the only other passenger on the platform. She walked briskly to Stockman's Lane and was at first relieved to see that he was not keeping pace with her. But as she approached the entrance to a small park on her left, suddenly and silently he was at her side, pushing her roughly into the shadows. She was too startled to cry out. She simply froze; her mind racing. Was he a rapist, a mugger, a mad murderer? To her amazement, he called her by name, as he pressed her brutally against the wall.

'I have a message for you, Colette McShane. One you'd better listen to. Your life depends on it.'

She began to struggle, but at once felt his overpowering strength. She had always heard it said that a woman in such circumstances should make as much noise as possible, but when she opened her mouth, her voice was just a startled whisper.

'Me and my friends know all about you and Aidan Cassidy. He's an important man in our community. And he can't be compromised by a wee whore like you.'

He shook her violently by the shoulders.

'How'd you like to be tied to a lamp post with your knickers round your ankles, all tarred and feathered. Or would you prefer one of these?'

He opened his leather jacket and from its inner pocket pulled out a flick knife which he snapped open with his thumb.

'Say anything about this to anybody – and I mean anybody – and you're dead meat, sweetie. Got that?'

Colette did not reply. She could feel deep sobs swelling up within her and when he released his grip, her knees gave way and she sank to the ground. She was then violently sick on the pathway. When she stopped vomiting and pulled herself to her feet by hanging on to the park gates, her assailant had gone. It was several minutes before she could compose herself and walk the half mile home, conscious of her dishevelled appearance, her laddered tights and her unsteady swaying.

Meanwhile, Detective Sergeant Bill McCullough boarded a train bound for Great Victoria Street, his shift for the day completed.

Chapter 15

The car park at the River Bush end of the village of Portballintrae was virtually deserted when Granville arrived in his Ford Focus shooting brake. His protectors, he knew, were already in place, two in a tall van, two others, sitting close as a couple in the front seat of a family saloon at the other end of the car park, where the narrow path descended to the footbridge over the swirling river. Only one other car was parked there, with a solitary figure behind the steering wheel, munching a sandwich.

Granville had chosen this spot for one principal reason: it was easy to seal off all exit routes from it, should anything go wrong. Not that he thought it would. He could not believe the Provos would mount their elaborate exercise to get into talks simply as a camouflage for a plan to kidnap or assassinate himself. But one never knew.

Don't take a chance you don't need to take.

He was a quarter of an hour early and he knew those fifteen minutes would hang heavily upon him, so he got out of the car, pulled on a parka and turned its hood up against the wind and the half-hearted North Antrim drizzle and set off towards the beach. On the far side of the bridge over the river the sand was deep and heavy and he walked towards the tide to find firmer footing. The waves were booming in, but in a broken line. Not a good surfing day. He still sometimes thought, longingly, of good surfing days, even though the damage done to his legs in the accident at Alicante had put an end to the enjoyment he had derived from that sport since the days of family holidays in North Cornwall.

The beach was deserted; no surfers today and indeed no family bathing parties any day, as a strong east-to-west rip discouraged all but the strongest swimmers. The wind and drizzle had driven away even the dog walkers who favoured the beach in better weather. Except perhaps one. Still several hundred yards away, walking in Granville's direction, was a lone figure, walking close to the seething tide. No, no dog. Granville could see him more clearly now. And as the figure approached he was not surprised to recognize him as one of his designated 'interlocutors', as they said in the trade. It was the Belfastman, reported to be a member of the Army Council (though he was for ever to deny it) and known within security circles as 'Bunny'. No one could now remember how the nickname had arisen. Perhaps it was the anxious, slightly toothy movement of his mouth when he stumbled through the obligatory opening passages in Irish whenever making set piece speeches. Nowadays he sported a full beard and designer glasses, which certainly improved his original image in press and police photographs, which showed a callow youth with heavy, black, horn-rimmed glasses and a wispy, hormone-deficient facial growth.

'You're early,' said Bunny, making the none-too-subtle point that Granville's face was not unknown to him.

'How do you do,' Granville heard himself saying, as he automatically held out his hand in greeting.

Was this really happening to him?

'Let's get back to shelter,' said Bunny. 'I am a nature lover, but this is ridiculous.'

They walked in silence as far as the bridge. As they crossed it, Bunny pointed at the brown flow of the river in flood.

'I'm a teetotaller, but I'm told it's the peaty quality of the water here which gives the special, distinctive characteristic to Bushmills whiskey. Did you know that?'

'No, I didn't.'

'Local knowledge, that. You might call it "an item of intelligence". There's so much the English don't know about Ireland.'

'And vice versa.'

'True, but the difference is this: we are not over there, you are over here.'

'Not entirely true. I could quote you a list of locations in England where you and your friends have visited in recent years, with tragic results.'

'Don't get too serious, too early, we've a long way to go,' rejoined Bunny, with a chuckle.

'I was only teasing you. Now that we're nearly up the hill, your place or mine?'

'Mine,' replied Granville firmly.

'That's OK by me,' said Bunny, soothingly, then added, 'since I assume both it and you are bugged.'

'By that are you accusing me of breaching the terms agreed with Canon Murray?'

'Relax, relax. We know that if you are serious about talks you will sustain them, in agreement with us. If not, then you'll wreck them sooner or later by one means or another. You will have made the same calculation about our thinking. I suggest we both think positively and get on with it and only judge one another against results.'

When they reached Granville's car, Bunny paused and signalled to the lone picnicker, who emerged from his car and came over to join them. Again, no surprise: it was the Derryman, known to the securocrats as 'Butch'.

No prizes for guessing the origins of that nickname.

The three men settled down in Granville's shooting brake (the number plates of which would be changed the following day). Butch had chosen the back seat.

'OK,' said Granville, as though chairing a meeting of the JSC, 'what's on your mind as regards an opening agenda?'

'Not so fast,' replied Bunny. 'We haven't yet established the ground rules.'

'Oh come on – what's the point of using Canon Murray to fix all that, only to start all over again – confidentiality, deniability and all that? My concerns are the same as yours in that respect. Let's get serious. I am offering you the chance, which your, er, movement has never had before, to put forward an agenda which can be the basis of real negotiation.'

'You don't understand the risks we are taking in having any contacts with you. We now have a majority within our community and within our organization for seeking peace, but only for a genuine, lasting peace. I can't over-emphasise that. Any cock-ups and that majority could disappear overnight and the war could go on for ever.'

'Of course, I understand all that. The pressures on my side are the mirror image of yours. We have our own hawks, who want nothing to do with negotiations, and any cock-ups in my dealings with you would play right into their hands.'

Butch stirred in the back seat. 'You asked us for our agenda points. What are yours?'

'Very simple: the Government will want to be convinced about a total and permanent ceasefire, a giving up of all arms and explosives, and will wish to see clear moves towards democratic political activity and away from criminality. In return, we are willing to consider your suggestions as to how that happy outcome can be achieved.'

Bunny took up the running again.

'All that boils down to is that the Brits want us to surrender. That's not on. We need to move in step towards solutions. And we must start with some confidence-building measures and some public indications by ministers of a change of mindset. By that I mean that they accept that republicanism is a valid and acceptable political force, on an equal footing with unionism. The two communities must be viewed and treated as equals.'

He tapped the dashboard for emphasis. 'That is vital to us within our own ranks. And until we get that public sign from on high, we can't even get to first base. And so neither can you.'

'Mind if I smoke?' asked Granville, already pulling out his cigarette case.

'No,' chorused the others without conviction – a lack of enthusiasm which grew as the first billows of Gauloise swirled around them.

'You still haven't given me your agenda points. I can't very well negotiate unilaterally.'

The other two were silent for several seconds, before Bunny spoke again.

'We need a significant sign from your side first, and from the very top, to convince us and our comrades, that you are serious about bringing an end to the present situation and not simply playing silly buggers with us.'

Granville drew heavily on his cigarette.

'It seems to me that we can't go any further today in that case.'

He sensed that this dismissal disappointed them.

'But I will ensure that you have your heavenly sign, publicly, from the mouth of the Secretary of State, within the next few days. And what's good for the goose ...'

'What do you mean?' said Bunny, a hint of anger in his voice.

'I'll be looking for a similar sign from you to match ours. Something in public to indicate you want the conflict to end soon. Then perhaps we can get down to real business. In the meantime, here are my new contact numbers and identification codes.'

Bunny pocketed the envelope without looking at the detail.

'To coin a phrase, where shall we three meet again?' asked Granville.

'I hope somewhere more convenient and sheltered than a beach. We have an open invitation from Canon Murray to use Clonard Monastery, which you already know,' said Butch.

'OK by me,' replied Granville, in neutral voice, remembering the gloom of that place.

'Only one drawback for you,' said Bunny.

'What's that?'

'It's a no smoking area.' And he laughed, faking a wheezing asthmatic cough.

Chapter 16

'I hope you didn't mind my asking to see you here at home this afternoon,' began Granville.

'Since we have such important mutual interests, I thought we should get to know one another better. And exchange views ... that sort of thing'

They were installed in the spacious living room at Myrtlefield Park.

'No, that's alright. Provided you or your ... your colleagues don't crowd me out, or make so many visits that the neighbours start to take notice,' replied Cassidy.

'Good. We can mix it up a bit. I mean, meet in the Department of Commerce downtown in Chichester House, here, or even at Stormont. Now that you have official cover, approved by, well ... all those who matter.'

Cassidy shifted uneasily in his chair.

'I'd like your views on current Republican thinking, based on your contacts. But perhaps we should get some domestic issues out of the way first.'

'Would you like a drink? I should have asked.'

'Thanks, something light. I'm driving. Mustn't get into trouble with the forces of law and order.'

Granville was a shade disappointed that Cassidy did not acknowledge his little joke.

'Something that I don't remember seeing in the file: the exact state of knowledge of your wife.'

Cassidy left the room to fetch drinks and Granville looked around him in the fashion of an interior designer making an initial assessment.

Yes, very tasteful – and expensive.

His eye was drawn to an unusually high pile of coffee table art books, sitting, appropriately enough, on a vast, glass-topped coffee table.

Cassidy returned with two glasses of Coke and a bowl of nibbles on a tray. 'How far is she in the picture as regards me?'

'Just the official version.'

'Excellent. And how about your other life? I don't mean insurance, I mean the IRA.'

'She doesn't know about membership or specific activities. But as regards sympathies and general support, yes, of course. It's a family thing, taken for granted.'

'OK. Now we know where we are. Hope I can meet her soon ...'

His inflexion conveyed a question.

'Sure. She'll probably be back soon. She's exercising a horse over at stables at Purdysburn.'

A pause, then, 'Sorry to have to mention this, but have you heard from Colette recently?'

Cassidy flushed and took a sip of his Coke. 'No. Not a thing. Not for three, four weeks.'

'Good. I don't think you'll have any more trouble from that quarter.'

'You haven't ...'

'Had her bumped off? No, no, no, dear me no.' Granville chuckled in exaggerated fashion.

'But she did receive a rather discouraging message on your behalf.'

He smiled to himself at the thought *allegedly from the IRA*.

A car crunched on the gravel outside.

'That'll be Noleen. She's back early.'

The door to the living room opened.

'Hi, there!' cried a cheery voice, as Noleen, wearing a dark jacket, fawn jodhpurs and polished black riding boots, put her head round the door.

'Be with you in ten minutes. I must just jump in the shower. I'm a mess. See you.'

Granville waved 'hello' and rose half way out of his chair. Then turned back to business.

'Tell me – we must deal with this before your wife comes back – what do you glean ('glean' was a favourite verb in the Granvillian vocabulary) about top Republican thinking. Their public rhetoric seems to me to have gone backwards from our point of view. But perhaps the view from inside is different.'

'What do you mean?'

'Well, now some of the leaders still seem to be encouraging their supporters to dig in for a "long haul war", whereas others talk vaguely of "working for a lasting peace", by joining forces with the SDLP, the Irish government, the Irish-Americans and God knows who-not, in a great pan-Hibernian initiative. I rather like that. It sounds more 'political'. Up to now IRA propaganda has always been consistent, if nothing else. What's going on?'

'They're divided. Pretty much down the middle. The older brigade are mostly "armed struggle" men through and through. They want to "win" (he made inverted comma signs in the air with his fingers), however long that takes. Some areas are very hard line, like South Armagh and East Tyrone. And the "politicos" have had a few bad setbacks recently. Last month's interview in *The Times* with the GOC, in which he talked of "definitively crushing PIRA", was a disaster. And in Belfast, in particular, the Catholic community influences the Provo leadership by loudly complaining to the media about harassment, pointless house searches, the mistreatment of detainees, etc. All that puts politics on the back burner.'

'Interesting. Very interesting indeed. Could you mark my card as to who you think, amongst the important people, are on each side of the argument, starting with the Army Council?' said Granville, producing a small notepad from his pocket.

They had worked through twenty or so names by the time Noleen rejoined them. (PANORAMA would be updated in the morning). Her entrance, Granville would later reflect, made a bigger impression on him than had any woman for years, perhaps decades.

She's so tall! Must be nearly as tall as I am, even without those high heels. And the hair, is that slightly Irish redhead , or is it light blonde?

Introductions. Soft white hand in his. Fair, almost porcelain complexion; playful smile.

What a figure! Have I ever seen such long legs?

A plain dress, understated elegance, minimal jewellery.

The three of them had hardly sat down when the 'phone rang. Cassidy picked up the receiver. After a few seconds he put his hand over the mouthpiece and said: 'This could take a while. I'll go to the study.'

Granville's immediate thought was: *personal security.* But he re-assured himself with the knowledge that his two sets of minders, one in a saloon car, the other in a van marked "TV Repairs", parked at a discreet distance in the thoroughfare outside, would be vigilant on his behalf. Turning to Noleen, Granville said: 'I gather your husband has told you everything about me.'

'Well, not *everything, I'm sure,*' she laughed.

You can say that again, baby.

'You're interested in employment creation in West Belfast, I understand.'

'That's right. Economic and Social Policy overall is my bag. And can I tell you, Mrs Cassidy, how much I admire what your husband is doing, not just in that area but in participating fully in the economic life of the community at large.' He was now well launched on one of his cover set pieces.

'I know it's not easy for someone in the minority community to come forward. They risk suspicion from the other side and often hostility from their own side. But in the long run, it's the only way forward for both sides, don't you think?'

'I'm afraid I'm not really interested in politics as such. But of course I support Aidan. He works very hard. Too hard sometimes. He can often be very tired. But he sticks at it. He has a strong sense of duty.'

Oh yeah?

'Is he interested in art, or is that your thing?' asked Granville, nodding towards the books on the coffee table.

'No, mine, I'm afraid. That's my passion. Always has been. Are you interested in art, Mr Granville?'

'Only peripherally. I think I'm too lazy to develop the expertise necessary for full enjoyment.'

'Too lazy?'

'Yes. I find paintings – or indeed literature, to take another art form – demand a certain amount of intellectual effort; you have to *understand* the significance of the picture and know about the history of the techniques behind it. And with literature, you have to wrestle with the ideas in a good book.'

'And none of that with music?'

She pulled an 'I'm not convinced' face.

'No. With music, knowledge enhances, of course. But it's not initially essential. Music just pours over you (here he stretched his arms in a wide circle) and goes straight into the emotional bloodstream, without the need to be understood.'

She laughed a tinkling, mischievous laugh.

'You make it sound like a life-support intravenous drip in an intensive care ward.'

'Some days, it is almost like that,' he confessed. 'Contrary to popular belief, the Civil Service can work one very hard.'

'Really?' she interjected, in mock astonishment, a twinkle in her eye.

'Yes, believe it or not.' he shot back, smiling as though to say 'touché!'

'And in order to relax, I put on some sublime music and the frustrations and burdens of the day fall away as if by magic. I don't have to *think* about a thing.'

'I can't say I enjoy paintings in quite that way. I have never analysed it – I mean the pleasure of it – but I suppose it's a balance between emotion and intellect. But whatever it is, I love it!'

Cassidy returned.

'Sorry about that. Sure you won't have a real drink?'

'No, thanks. Must be getting along. Your wife and I have been having a pleasant argument about the respective merits of painting and music.'

'Not an argument, surely,' said she. 'More what the critics call "a constructive exchange of views".'

'Anyhow, I'm glad it didn't involve me,' said Cassidy. 'I'm more a figures man myself.'

Yeah, like what you'll bet on the favourite at two-to-one on at Kempton Park.

'Thanks for your hospitality. You'll have to come down to me for supper one of these days. I'll be in London most of next week, but I'll give you a ring after that.'

Chapter 17

Sean Byrne was impatience personified as he sat on a rather threadbare sofa in the tiny front room of a house just off the Falls Road. It was 9th August, anniversary of internment, and he had been given the green light by his battalion OC to carry out a sniper attack on a British Army patrol which was bound to be deployed in the area in response to the protests and disturbances which were the annual ritual. Although it was still early, the sound of metal bin lids being bashed on the ground was already echoing from neighbourhood to neighbourhood. All housewives were expected to take part in the ritual, whilst the local teenagers had carte blanche to hi-jack and burn whatever vehicles were foolish enough to venture 'up the Falls' that day. All but the politically committed housewives looked on this as a chore to be performed, in order to be considered a sound Republican family; the teenagers, on the other hand, played their part with a feral energy and obvious enjoyment.

Byrne was a tall, well-built man, with shoulders so broad that he appeared stocky despite his height. His powerful forearms were the legacy of his sporting youth, when he had been a star amateur boxer of the Holy Family club and the top scorer, year after year, for the water polo team of St Mary's College in the days when they regularly won the inter-schools' Canada Cup. In the light of his later activities, his nickname at that time had unfortunately – but prophetically – been 'The Gun', on account of his strike power with both glove and ball. Sport had dominated his schooldays, to the detriment of his studies, and he had left St Mary's with only a handful of undistinguished qualifications, no tertiary education entitlement and no real job prospects. He had drifted around building sites, doing occasional labouring jobs, like so many of his peers. His life had, however, been transformed by his membership of the IRA, which he joined at the age of nineteen. At training camps in County Cavan and County Louth his marksmanship was outstanding and he revelled in the rigours of the assault course, which was run, incongruously, by a former PT instructor of the Royal Warwickshire Regiment. Above all, the thrill of being 'on operations' gave him his addictive adrenaline rush – the sense of life-threatening danger, the intense concentration on the task in hand, and, ultimately, the satisfaction of the kill, all combined to make him feel supremely alive. Afterwards he would slump both physically and mentally, like a druggie after his trip. But now, in anticipation, he could hear his own heartbeat thudding in his ears. He sat bolt upright on the sofa and stretched his arms out straight in front of him, clenching and unclenching his fists.

When would the runner arrive to tell him the target was heading into the zone selected for his hit? He looked at his watch every two minutes, without ever registering the exact time.

The designated position had been chosen with great care, some days before. It was on the flat roof of a repair garage at the end of a street of houses and from it there was a perfect sniper's view, past a row of houses in the parallel street, to a few square metres of the middle of the road in that street. The view was blocked off by a warehouse to the left and the wall of a school to the right. So, a narrow target area, but it had the safety factor that the sniper could, in turn, only be seen from those few square metres. The position was shielded by a taller building to the north-east from observation from the Army sangar constructed on the roof of a high-rise tower block, but of course all positions were vulnerable to detection from the air; today the usual single patrolling helicopter was joined by two others. Internment Day was a red-letter day in so many different calendars.

Byrne did not carry the rifle or ammunition. That was done by two separate young 'caddies', who, from different depot houses, would bring the component parts of the AK-47 to the firing point. They would then linger, again separately, at street corners nearby until they saw the figure of Byrne leave the garage; retrieving the weapon and returning its parts to the depots was one of the most hazardous phases of the whole game. The value of retaining the rifle, and the evidence which could be obtained from it by Forensics, far outweighed the risk to the freedom of the two 'caddies', who had scarcely any knowledge worth the trouble of extracting by interrogation, should they be caught.

At last, a tap on the front window. The moment had come. Byrne left the house and made his way into the next street and into the garage. He nodded to the proprietor, the deputy of the local OC, who went on with his work, and quickly mounted the steel staircase, which opened out on to the roof. Tight against the parapet lay a large tarpaulin, the dual purpose of which was to hide the now assembled AK47 and, should a helicopter threaten the position, to hide himself. He pulled on the gossamer-thin surgical gloves and, slipping the rifle from under the tarpaulin, peered over the parapet, which was at a convenient height to rest it on. He wished it had been an M60, the great beast of the sniper's armoury, which he had once fired on the secret training ground in County Cavan. That was a mind-boggling experience, allowing him to shatter an armour-plated target piece at a distance of over a kilometre. With that, in the narrower setting of urban Belfast, he could take out several soldiers or policemen at once, as they travelled in an allegedly protected vehicle, with a burst of fire lasting no more than a second. To his disappointment, his battalion OC had told him that a policy decision had been taken 'higher up', not to risk one of the only two M60s in their possession outside South Armagh, where the topography and context gave the operators a better chance of using the weapon without subsequently losing it, or causing unwanted casualties in a built up area.

Peering through the telescopic sight, all he could see was the empty surface of the small and narrow target area. None of the three helicopters hovering over West Belfast posed an immediate threat to him, but if one were to change course and move in his direction he would be in danger within a matter of seconds. If only the facade wall of the garage were a couple of metres higher, he would be shielded on almost 300 degrees. But nothing was ever perfect, not even for the sniper who could choose his position well in advance of his 'hit'.

Where were the bin-lid bangers? He could clearly hear the racket they were making, and as far as he could judge it was coming from the right direction. But there was no movement on the target square. One of the helicopters moved in his direction from Unity Flats, then, just as he was going to retreat to his protective tarpaulin, it veered off to the north. When he focused again on his 'square', he caught a glimpse of a youth in a denim jacket running through it in his direction. He knew several Volunteers had been detailed to lure the security forces along that street; he could only hope Denim Jacket was one of them.

Another helicopter, in the distance, was now on the move, in an easterly direction. A few seconds and it could have him in its sights. Again he lowered himself from the parapet. But when he turned to follow the chopper's flight path, he judged it to be following the line of the M1 motorway into the city. Probably vehicle-spotting.

He returned to his 'square'. Now there were figures, civilians, moving slowly from left to right through it. More figures, some of them throwing stones and the occasional Molotov cocktail. The police and army could only be a hundred metres or so distant. But the movement was agonizingly slow. How long would it take for the confrontation to move those hundred metres? The helicopter which had moved over North Belfast was now heading back towards Unity Flats, and if it stayed on its present course would very soon be in a danger zone as far as he was concerned. He cursed the lookouts who had miscalculated the timing of the operation. If they had to lie on a roof with an AK-47, exposed to British helicopters, like a fledgling to a sparrow hawk ...

His target 'square' went blank; the retreat and advance was underway at last. The helicopter was hovering now, but still drifting slowly towards him. The security forces' line would be a thin one and would probably pass through his target area within seconds, rather than minutes.

Come on, come on, you bastards! Where are you?

He was going to have to crawl back below the tarpaulin if the helicopter came any closer. And the third one had swung from the city centre area out towards the Falls. He was now at risk from two directions.

Still the target 'square' was empty. Then movement, too fast to focus on. Soldiers were coming through, but no realistic target presented itself.

Only take on a certainty – the golden rule.

Then, just as the noise from one of the helicopters noticeably increased, he had in his cross-hairs the upper body of a soldier. In a fraction of a second he took in the fact that he was wearing body armour, but his face was exposed – no visor down. One through the head it had to be. Bryne relaxed momentarily, then squeezed not just his finger but his whole body. As the 'scope sprang up under the force of the blast, he caught a glimpse as of a melon flying apart. He rolled away from the parapet and hurled himself through the door and down the metal stairs into the garage below. It was deserted, with the big outside door closed. Within it there was a smaller door, which he eased open, then stood listening.

The helicopters were no nearer. He closed the door behind him, walked briskly to the corner of the street and fell in alongside stray marchers who were walking away from the direction of the city. Two streets further on he turned off the main road and calmly walked into number sixty-four, the front door of which stood unlocked, awaiting his arrival. As he moved down the narrow hall a small, elderly woman with sparse white hair came out of the kitchen, wiping her hands on a floral apron.

'Sacred Heart, it's yourself, Sean. I'll put the kettle on right away. You'll be wantin' a cup of tea, I'm sure.'

'Aye, right. Thanks. There's a lot goin' on out there.'

Outside, ambulance sirens wailed.

'From early on. What a racket. Honest till God, Sean, my nerves is in ribbons.'

Absent-mindedly clenching and opening his right fist, Byrne muttered, 'I know what y'mean.'

In truth, he did ... and he didn't.

Chapter 18

A van marked 'Roads Service' was in position some hundred yards from the Cassidy home in Myrtlefield Park. The two men in it appeared to be absorbed in paperwork; maps and drawings were unfolded over the dashboard. When Casssidy's Jaguar emerged from his drive one of the men spoke into a microphone: 'Water supply OK in Myrtlefield.' Granville switched on the engine of his car parked in the parallel street and headed for the Cassidy home.

'You've just missed him,' said Noleen, answering the doorbell, 'he left for a meeting two minutes ago.' She was dressed in T-shirt, designer jeans and white trainers.

'Too bad,' said Granville, 'I'll catch up with him later. May I come in for a moment?'

'Yes, of course, sorry.' She stepped back and he brushed past her into the hallway. The door to the kitchen was open and beyond it he could see an easel set up on the sunlit patio outside.

'I should explain that it's nothing too urgent. I just wanted to discuss a draft document he left with me. It's about France; he may have mentioned it to you. It's about the regeneration of depressed areas. I'm not going to today's meeting of the WBG and I thought I would catch him before he left here for that. He's going to be very early at the meeting, is he not?'

'I don't know about the timing, but I do know he often looks into the office downtown before going anywhere else.'

To commune with his turf accountant and/or to receive instructions from his IRA runner?

'Forgive me for being nosey, but I see you are not only a knowledgeable painting buff but a painter yourself? You didn't tell me. May I have a look at what you are working on right now?'

''Fraid not. I'm superstitious about that. When it's finished – that is to say if it ever gets finished, because I sometimes give up the struggle of putting on the canvas what I've seen in my head – I'll invite you to see it then.'

'At the exhibition? I look forward to that.'

'An exhibition would be a fine thing. But don't hold your breath. I don't dream of such things. It's only a hobby, a pastime. Most of my friends have their time taken up with children.'

Granville dared to enter this delicate territory. 'Do you regret not having any?'

'Not really,' said she, automatically, having replied many times to that question. 'Not really', all too clearly meant "yes".

'If you have them then, fine. If not, there are advantages to be found in what the agony aunts call "non-parental freedom". We didn't have any. Simple as that.'

But it is not as simple as that. Like the drowning man who sees his life pass before him in seconds, Noleen has a vivid flashback. She is an Upper Sixth Form boarder in the Dominican Convent School in Portstewart, on the north coast, not far from the Giant's Causeway. Security and discipline is strict and rigid in the convent, overseen by the towering, desiccated Sister Augusta, vigilant as a paranoid meerkat.

Why was it that God only got the women men didn't want?

Despite this regime, the more daring, worldly girls, of whom Noleen is certainly one, occasionally manage to sneak outside the forbidding walls, especially in the summer term, to enjoy the limited fleshpots of the quaint, old-fashioned seaside resort. Boys sometimes feature in these exciting escapades and Noleen is the envy of her friends, for she has a 'steady', who often has a rendezvous with her during the exeat time allowed on Saturdays. Her steady is Sean Byrne. He comes up from Belfast by bus, a large khaki kitbag on his back. Noleen teases him about this 'parachute.' It contains not only his lunch, but a showerproof jacket and a tartan rug. They put the rug to good use as a ground sheet in the secluded hollows in the sand dunes behind the long beach which stretches towards the mouth of the River Bann to the west of the town.

In these far from comfortable surroundings, Noleen loses her virginity. She had never prized it as much as the nuns told her and her classmates they should, and though her over-exercised conscience is wounded, the pain and ultimate ecstasy of Sean's thrustings are somehow unforgettably exciting.

Against the law of probability, she becomes pregnant from this first encounter. She waits for a few panic-stricken days – fortunately it is now the summer holidays – and tells her parents. To her surprise it is her father who is the more distressed – religion, society and self-esteem push him into such a frenzy Noleen fears for her life. On the other hand, her mother, though deeply shocked, soon begins to think of practical ways of getting out of this problem. An abortion is not even considered by any of them. That would be murder. A shotgun marriage to the as yet unsuspecting Byrne is out of the question, says old man McManus.

'No daughter of mine is going to marry a ragamuffin like Sean Byrne.'

So a decision in two parts is taken. First, a discreet birth in England and after that they can decide on whether to put the child up for adoption, or whether Noleen will be willing to play the part of a single mother, far from the family she has disgraced. The cover story is that before going up to university she is going abroad to Florence, to take an Appreciation of Art course. In reality, it is to stay with one of her mother's sisters on the outskirts of Manchester. But again the law of probability plays tricks: her pregnancy is revealed as being ectopic and she needs urgent surgery. While her life is not in immediate danger, the consultant, in his post-operative review, gives her the fateful news.

'The surgical work we have had to carry out makes it highly improbable that you will ever be able to have children.'

When McManus hears this he says, 'It's a punishment from God.' His wife says, 'It could all have been worse.'

Noleen is not keen to return to Belfast, so a real course is organised for her in Florence, and later Venice. She has never told Byrne or Cassidy the truth of her curriculum vitae, though before her marriage she did tell Cassidy that for unspecified 'female reasons' she was unlikely to have children. He had accepted that without further questioning. If Sean Byrne had his suspicions about the sudden departure to Florence, he did not express them to Noleen on the rare occasions their paths crossed in the years ahead, though she often wondered whether the thought had crossed his mind. He had dropped out of her life without drama; when she returned from Italy she discovered that he was being 'consoled' not by one, but several, girls in his neighbourhood. He never sought her out and she made no effort to contact him.

'And how about you?' she asks, almost as a challenge, as she comes back to the present.

Alicante. Lo siento muchissimo, señor...

'My wife had two miscarriages and then died in an accident. I agree with you about the advantages.'

'Yes – but what do you do in your spare time?'

'My job takes up most of my time. Economics and Social Policy is a wide field.'

'I'm sure that's true.'

Does she suspect more?

'But I have my music. If only passively nowadays. I've given up the piano. And then of course there's cooking. I find that relaxing and I enjoy the end result, not to mention the accompanying wine. That's a short and boring list, compared to horse riding, painting, study of art and, obviously, fashion – judging by all the elegant outfits I've seen you in.'

'You know where flattery gets you …'

'That wasn't flattery, it was a sincere comment.'

'Are you a sincere person?'

'Absolutely ... about most things.'

'Your qualification is telling.'

'Perhaps. But I'm not talking about the things I exclude from sincerity. You are not amongst them.'

'Now that *is* flattery!'

Granville, careful not to overplay his hand, took his leave.

'I'll catch up with Aidan later. As I said, nothing urgent.'

'I'll tell him you called.'

'Perhaps best not.'

'Why?'

'Well, I wouldn't want him thinking ... he's got a lot to worry about. He might think there was some sort of emergency.'

He thought her smile held some significance.

'Alright, then ...' said she, knowingly.

Chapter 19

Cassidy's meeting on Belgian soil was to take place in a village outside Brussels and had been arranged by the Belgian arms dealer, Emile Verhagen, who was the fixer for the delivery of arms and explosives all the way from Libya, through Tunisia and France to the Flemish port of Antwerp, and then by the SS St Lucia to Dublin. Verhagen, product of a union between a Brussels father and a Moroccan mother, had made a good living, following his national service in Belgium, as a dealer in arms and armaments; being essentially a well-informed intermediary between shady arms suppliers and even shadier arms buyers in three continents. He was 'known' to the Belgian authorities, but he was always careful to be insulated as much as he could from his actual products, keeping his distance from shipments as far as was organisationally possible and playing a role as background mastermind and go-between. He tried to keep within the rather lax laws of Belgium and he was careful never to annoy gratuitously law enforcement officers who none too subtly kept tabs on him. It would have been an exaggeration to say that he had friends in such places, but it was true that his occasional chats with them took place over a glass or two of kriek, the local cherry beer which was one of his few vices. He liked to think of himself as an 'honest broker', though the Belgian Sureté men would have thought that description was stretching the concept of honesty to the extremity of even a Belgian understanding of the virtue. In the world of arms supplies and the relations between governments and non-governmental (that is to say rebel) agencies, Verhagen paid for the indulgence of his national authorities by providing a certain amount (*not too much, business is business*) of information about what was going on in his occult world.

The present position with the IRA was far from simple, but promised to be extremely fruitful, even if it were to be a one-off. The Irish were obviously very keen to buy, and in large quantities – which pushed up the amount of his 'commission' and he was confident of the efficiency of the three lots of people he was co-ordinating – in North Africa, France and on the high seas. The fact that he spoke fluent Arabic (*merci, Maman*), French and English, as well as his father's Flemish, made things much easier and more secure than they otherwise would have been. He didn't need translators or interpreters, which saved time, avoided misunderstandings and reduced the risk of betrayal.

He had been impressed by the detailed shopping list of arms and explosives which had been prepared by McGiolla – these guys were certainly ambitious about waging their insurrection – and he only hoped that the financial resources were a match for those ambitions.

Verhagen was keen to arrange the vital meeting at which the details of the supply would be finalised – and, most importantly, the part payment for same would be made – in a way which attracted the least attention. Accordingly, McGiolla had flown from Dublin to Paris and had come to Brussels by train, therefore outside the scrutiny of his passport at a Belgian airport. Cassidy flew direct to Zaventem, the international airport of Brussels, as he had a perfect cover story, namely a meeting with officials of the European Commission about the possibility of training grants for setting up businesses in West Belfast.

The three of them were to meet up, as casual visitors to an exhibition of contemporary Flemish art, being staged in the church of Our Lady of the Wood, in the village of Jezus-Eik, just off the motorway to Luxembourg, to the south-east of Brussels. The two Irishmen had arrived separately, by taxi, some two hours before the appointed time and had lunched, extremely well, again separately, in two of the traditional bar-restaurants which lined both sides of the little village street.

Cassidy was surprised at his own nervousness, even though he had tried to console himself with the thought that should the worst happen and the meeting turn out to be a trap, his links with Granville would surely save him from a long jail sentence. He was probably more anxious about McGiolla, he mused to himself over his starter of *moules au vin blanc*.

Tomas Emmet McGiolla was a legend in Republican circles – the ultimate hard man, hardliner from the hard PIRA heartland of South Armagh. Paradoxically, part of his mystique was, that as a young man, he had served five years in the British Army. There was even a legend that he had been in the SAS, which wasn't quite true; he had passed the entrance qualifications for that élite unit, but had been sent back to his regiment after the first month of probation, on the grounds that his 'psychological profile' did not quite fit. Which, of course, had engendered a deep and abiding hatred of the SAS in his Crossmaglen heart. What was, however, even more useful to the IRA – crazy SAS types were not, after all, that rare amongst the Provo volunteers – was the fact that McGiolla had then, by the chance way in which things happen in armies, been transferred to a post where he became specialised in 'Orndnance' – that is to say, weapons of all sorts, for use by all sorts of units, from the infantry and the artillery, to the engineers and sappers. He was immensely proud of his expertise in such matters and in his uncompromising stand on matters political. 'Only the armed struggle can lead us to victory', he would shout to his companions when in his cups. He had become anxious, and even slightly disillusioned, by what he had seen and heard in recent months. Talk of 'political settlements', not only unnerved him; it positively enraged him. 'If those fuckin' politicos are allowed to go cap in hand to the Brits, we'll be sold out once more. When will we learn that we can't just give up, as we did in '62. This time we go all the way. The Brits can't beat us, but if we keep the heat on, we can beat them, through their own public opinion.'

He had therefore been slightly surprised, but greatly encouraged, that this arms importation operation was going ahead. It would, at a stroke, make good all the arms losses of equipment suffered over the past two years and almost double the hit-power of each and every Active Service Unit. That was serious stuff. Perhaps even a turning point in the conflict. He felt better at the thought.

Cassidy also felt better, for a different reason. The *côte à l'os* was the best bit of beef he had had in a long time, and the almost full bottle of *châteauneuf-du-Pape*, with which he washed it down, had certainly relaxed him.

Almost 3.30, time for the art exhibition. The three conspirators found each other easily within the church. Only a few people were moving about looking at the paintings which had been set up on easels every 5 metres or so along the two outer aisles of the mock rococo church. Most of these visitors could be eliminated – women, or members of an obvious family group. The three gravitated to one another, while feigning interest in a particular painting, which was a stylised, Picasso-esque representation of a horse with a split face rearing up on its hind legs.

'Would you gentlemen like a copy of the catalogue?' said Verhagen in his slightly accented English.

'Yes, I would, provided it's not too expensive,' said Cassidy, on script.

'Me too,' said McGiolla 'provided it's in English.'

Verhagen nodded contentedly. 'Follow me.'

He left the church and turned right into the woods, the Foret de Soigne, and walked briskly ahead. The two Irishmen stayed together but did not catch up with their guide. Ten minutes later he led them to a large villa set in several hectares of garden and orchard in Winterendreef. A security gate opened at Verhagen's remote control and he opened the stout oak door of the villa with a large iron key.

Inside, the house was typical of the taste of a self-made Brusselaar: bulbous furniture, lots of regency stripes, heavy chandeliers and a row of pots on the windowsills, containing green and yellow mother-in-law's tongue plants.

Verhagen opened a cocktail cabinet.

'Whisky?'

They both nodded.

'Me too, I've even got Irish for you,' he said, proudly holding up a bottle of Powers.

'So, first of all, agreement on your wish list. I've checked with my suppliers in Libya and all can be supplied, with just three changes – twenty fewer AK-47s, five fewer cases of 7.62mm ammunition, but twenty per cent more semtex.'

'That's OK, provided the price is right,' said McGiolla. 'In fact it's good. I'm in favour of more big bangs. But are you sure about the suppliers? I heard that the Libyans were under severe French surveillance.'

'That's right, your information is correct. But we have another supply route – through Algeria, then in wine, how you say, *camions citernes*, bulk carrier lorries, as far as Paris. There the cargo is safely repacked as agricultural machinery. Last bit is Antwerp and then ship by regular steamer to Dublin. The St Lucia is in and out of Dublin and Antwerp every fortnight or so.'

'Now we come to the interesting bit,' chuckled Verhagen, 'or as we say here, the sorrowful bit – that means, you pay me.' At that he laughed and raised his glass to them. He then slid the mirror at the back of the cocktail cabinet to one side revealing a narrow space from which he retrieved what he referred to as 'the dossier'.

McGiolla pulled out a wad of papers from the vast poacher's pockets in his tweed overcoat and placed them on the low table in front of them. 'Let's see how they match up.'

Verhagen visibly became impatient when McGiolla went slowly through the inventory item by item, price by price, and announced that he thought in broad terms that the price should be reduced by $1100. Cassidy had the feeling he should intervene, as finance was involved, but he subconsciously admitted to himself that McGoilla's overbearing personality would probably drive a better bargain than he could himself. Besides, if the final price had McGiolla's agreement, that would give him, Cassidy, cover, should awkward questions arise later in Belfast.

Verhagen's eyes narrowed, but he controlled his impatience and displeasure. No doubt drawing on that part of his DNA which flowed from his grandfather, *coté feminin*, who had bought and sold camels in Marrakesh in the good old days, he said brightly:

'My friend, I make you a good price. $500 off. You make – how you say – hard bargain for Emile.'

Eventually they settled on a $600 'discount' and were about to move on to payment, when the Irishmen both remembered an important point, pressed upon both of them by the OC of the Operation on the Army Council.

'Can the shipment arrive in Dublin on the 20th instead of the 19th? It's for security reasons at the port – customs and all that.'

'One moment, please,' said Verhagen. He walked to a mock art deco telephone on a side table. He dialled with a bejewelled little finger. When he got through, he spoke in rapid Arabic. There followed a long silence on his part; clearly, the changed date was being checked out at the other end. Finally he said 'Ok' and hung up.

As did Granville at the other end.

Chapter 20

'Brigadier' Blitzer McCann, known to the security forces as the boss of the UDA (and almost certainly of the UVF, its even more sinister wing) in East Belfast, was in a tetchy mood. In other men one might have said a nervous mood, but nervousness was not a condition in which he could easily be imagined. 'McCann can!' was his oft repeated slogan, as he slapped tabletops with the palm of his broad hand in meetings in the realm in which he had chosen to develop his talents, namely gangsterism.

It was a boast well justified. He had grown up in the Willowfield area of Belfast, in a small run-down street which ran between the Cregagh and Castlereagh roads and he was already known as a 'real hard' in the high noon of Teddy boyism. A brief spell in the Royal Irish Rifles had done nothing to smooth his image and he left the army with a dishonourable discharge (following a punch-up with his platoon commander) and a tattoo of the regimental crest on his left forearm. Another tattoo, this time of a royal coat of arms and the UDA motto 'Quis separabit' was to follow later on the right forearm. The political and social turmoil in working class areas of the city in the early 1970s provided the ideal habitat in which the McCanns of this world could flourish. Under the guise of 'protectors' and 'community activists', men like him, by brute force and the threat of more brute force, could impose themselves on whole neighbourhoods, where, largely neglected by the police, they could mightily prosper through extortion rackets, protection schemes and, not infrequently, outright robbery of businesses and individuals. The over-arching organisation for all of this thuggery was allegedly political in nature, the mirror image of the IRA and its political wing, Sinn Fein. The fundamental difference between the two – their methods being chillingly similar – was that while the Republicans had a long-term goal of constitutional change, the Loyalists of the McCann variety wanted no such change; rather, they wished for the perpetuation of the current state of affairs, in which they could continue to prosper. If political power were to come to them, well and good, but for most of them that would be only a bonus.

Blitzer had certainly prospered. He lived with his wife and teenage daughter in a large mock-Tudor house perched on the slope of Ballyhanwood Hill, looking over Dundonald towards Parliament Buildings, perched on Craigantlet Hill on the opposite side of the broad, shallow valley He drove a large red 4X4Land Cruiser, which was a familiar sight outside public houses such as the King Arthur on the Castlereagh Road (his old 'local'), the Great Western on the Newtownards Road and the King's Arms in Knock village. Part of his income came from one-arm bandit gaming machines in these and similar premises, whose owners, knowing what was good for their health, leased him space at 'very reasonable' rates. He also held court daily in the UDA's Information Office above a gents' outfitters on the Newtownards Road. As his associates were wont to say, 'he had it made in the shade'.

Yet today he was indeed tetchy. On the domestic front, the triangular relationships between his wife, Maureen, his daughter, Iris and himself were tense on all three sides. His wife had never really settled in the heights of Ballyhanwood. She yearned for her native urban district, close to her mother and sister, and complained that in Dundonald there wasn't a decent shop, compared to the familiar delights of the 'Cregagh'. Iris, born in 1978 but out of wedlock, nursed not only the teenager's natural antipathy towards, and impatience with, both parents, but also what an educational psychologist might term a socio-sado-narcissist aversion to her circumstances and, ultimately, to herself. Her expensive education – she had been the first child in her wide family circles on both sides to have gone to a private school – had

widened the gulf with her parents and had deepened her
distaste for their attitudes and lifestyle. In an earlier generation
she might have found consolation in religion; in her case,
conviction, and its attendant zealotry, were found in
environmentalism. The publications of 'the bloody buttercups
and daisies brigade', as her father called them, were now her
only reading material. 'Save the planet', was the constant,
indeed almost sole, theme of her conversations, not that these
were very frequent. She lambasted Blitzer for his rape of the
environment, as epitomised by his gas-guzzling vehicle, and
her mother for her no-fewer-than three genuine fur coats, two
mink and one musquash.

As for conjugal relations, the passing passion of youth had
long since passed, secretly to Maureen's relief, and those who
kept an eye on such things would have pointed to the
increasing number of 'lifts home' offered by Blitzer at closing
time, to one of the pretty barmaids at the King Arthur as
circumstantial, yet compelling evidence of where his current
appetites lay. Maureen no longer pleased him; indeed she was
even falling short of the standards of a good Belfast
housekeeper.

'Hey, Maureen, where the hell are my coloured shirts? I
can't see none here at all,' he shouted down the stairs, as he
stood, stripped to the waist, in the dressing room which
opened off the pink master bedroom in the eaves of the house.

'Open your eyes,' came the instant reply.

'Look in the hot press. You've got more coloured shirts in
there than Nelson – fuckin' – Mandela.'

Without a word of thanks, Blitzer duly selected a
patterned blue shirt. Would he go with an open collar, or how
about a yellow silk tie? He regularly took fifteen to twenty
minutes, post- shower and shaving, to kit himself out, such
was the care he took with his appearance. He was proud of his
thick pile of still-black hair, cut by razor in the DA style, a
legacy of his Teddy boy youth. In meetings he would often
pat the nape of his neck with three or four rapid movements of
his hand, to reassure himself that this masterpiece was still in
place. His suits and blazers were always well cut, flattering his

slightly thickening silhouette, which he had managed, by dint of regular weightlifting, to maintain in its essentials, if not in every detail, despite the counterbalance of a heavy weekly intake of alcohol. His large collection of shoes, laid out neatly on their trees in the bottom of his number one wardrobe, ranged from suede, to gleaming black leather, to crocodile skin (his personal favourite and not only because they outraged Iris).

He admired the finished product in the full-length mirror and felt momentarily better, until he remembered the second reason for his own tetchiness: he was due to attend a meeting of 'the Council', as the top of the UDA thuggery was called, with all the reverence which might be accorded a plenary session of NATO. And he did not like one bit how things were developing at HQ.

His unhappiness was due to the influence of his rival, the Supreme Commander, Gordon McVeigh, who spoke for the organisation to the media and who represented its views to 'government' (in reality the latter related to talks with Jeremy Granville, who, from time to time, would flatter him with invitations to St Oswald's for drinks and 'an exchange of views'). Although McVeigh, unlike many in the UDA, had no military background he had many advantages over his fellows and potential rivals. He had been a founder member, had served time in the Maze prison, (or Long Kesh as it was then called), for robbery and illegal possession of a firearm, and was unchallenged within the organisation as the most effective and articulate spokesman. While in prison he had studied for, and obtained, a BA degree in Sociology, which gave him new ideas and a whole new glossary of technical words in his vocabulary, with which he by turns dazzled and infuriated his fellow thugs: words such as 'tranche', 'matrix', 'leverage' and 'fait accompli' were added to his speeches and statements like so many exotic spices. The effect of this enrichment of vocabulary was, however, sometimes undermined by McVeigh's basic grammatical mistakes – 'I done' and 'I have went' being the worst of his howlers.

This also amused Granville who, at the mention of McVeigh's name would say to his secretary: 'Buddy, can you spare a paradigm?' Granville had succeeded nonetheless in influencing McVeigh to the point of manipulation. He encouraged him to look on himself as 'The Political Philosopher' on the Loyalist side, preparing to lead his organisation and community into post-conflict politics, where he could harness the energies and support of the Protestant working class in a genuine left-leaning, progressive political party. But to arrive at that position it would be necessary to turn off the violence and criminality into which the UDA and UVF had quickly sunk after their establishment. He led McVeigh to believe that HMG would assist in such an evolution, by public endorsement and perhaps even financially, through the provision of community development grants which were being planned for the future.

When Sir Julian Beardsley had asked Granville over lunch in his club whether he really believed that such an initiative was necessary, the reply came at once.

'Of course not,' chuckled Granville.

'If we can get the IRA morphed into a genuine political party without an army, the Loyalist paramilitaries will melt like snow. Their only "strength" is in the existence of the IRA and their violence. If that disappears, the traditional unionist parties will take up the running again and there will be no democratic support for any sort of "Loyalist politics". But in the meantime, if we can dangle the prospect of future government support before their greedy little eyes we can have some purchase on them. At worst, our contacts will help sow dissention amongst the leadership, which is to our benefit.'

'Ah, yes,' said Beardsley, 'Isn't their motto *Quis separabit*?'

'Indeed. And my reply is *"Ego ...,with any luck"*. And in any case, in the long run we won't have to deal with them, or worry about them at all.'

'Surely they won't just slip away?'

'You're right, up to a point. The criminal element in the Loyalist paramilitaries will, I am sure, continue their activities without any spurious political cover, but that will be a matter for normal policing and crime prevention. Nothing to do with us. Nothing to do with politics. In the meantime, we must encourage their leadership to get out of criminality and, above all, to put an end to the assassination of random Catholic targets. Those killings help maintain the IRA's fiction of being the defenders of the Catholic population, though I must say that their recent increase in number is beginning to make that protection a bit shaky.'

McVeigh, 'The Political Philosopher', had for some time been arguing with his fellow 'brigadiers' individually and in full 'Council', for a change in policy, towards 'community politics', which warmed Granville's heart when he read the transcripts from the recordings made by the bugging device at UDA headquarters.

The bug was, appropriately enough, concealed in the picture frame of the Queen's portrait which hung on the side wall of the meeting room. (*Your sovereign is listening to you*).

These headquarters premises did not reflect the undoubted financial resources of the UDA, which were known to be substantial, to say the least. Unlike their mirror image, namely the Sinn Fein offices on the Falls Road, they did not convey to the visitor the impression of organisational efficiency. On the contrary, the three upstairs rooms were a jumble of desks and tables, both overflowing with papers, and filing cabinets which seemed to hang open all day. The premises had the virtue of being in the Loyalist heartland and in themselves epitomised the rundown state of that district and its inhabitants. The nearest side street was partially boarded up and the end gable, which featured a striking mural of King Billy on a white horse, crossing the Boyne, was in dire need of refreshment, as were most of the still occupied houses in the street. Many of the walls were defaced with sprayed on graffiti – political and football slogans for the most part, along with the standard sectarian three words, which Vincent Glass had once memorably described, in an atmospheric piece for the *Tribune* as 'a copulatory exhortation with specific reference to the incumbent of the Holy See'.

Blitzer McCann never liked spending much time at HQ. Its untidiness offended his sense of style and the 'handling of relations with the community', which provided some sort of justification for the office, bored him profoundly. He knew he had to be there a reasonable part of the time, if for no other reason than to keep an eye on what was being discussed amongst the other 'brigadiers', but he much preferred to be 'out and about', as he termed it, looking after his own commercial interests and simply enjoying himself. He was deeply unhappy about the proposed change in direction he had heard McVeigh and others talking about. Politics held absolutely no attraction for him. He could not envisage himself begging for votes, instead of telling the locals what to do and think. As for the proposal to have more and better resourced grass roots help centres, he dismissed the idea as one for 'bloody social workers'. He liked things as they were and would argue for that at the meeting. He was already rehearsing in his mind his challenge to McVeigh. He knew that if push came to shove, he could see him off, but the real obstacle to a putsch was Geezer Gifford, perhaps the most brutal of all the 'brigadiers', with several murders already to his name.

Gifford was a great hulk of a man, who dressed in the manner of a 'Hell's Angel' – leather jackets, festooned in metal studs, and with calf-length industrial worker boots. In meetings, regardless of room temperature, he would invariably take off his jacket and roll up his sleeves to reveal bulging biceps and enough tattoos to arouse the envy of a Maori princess. He spent hours every day behind a desk at UDA headquarters, without ever appearing to do anything which could be categorised as 'work'. He spent a large part of the time on the telephone, mostly gossiping with his many cronies; he appeared to read little and almost never wrote anything. Nevertheless, he had a menacing presence, one reinforced by that of his large dog, a cross-bred Staffordshire terrier who lay at his feet. It stank from time to time, but no one complained. Some visitors would try to pat it, no doubt as a symbolic act of obeisance to Gifford, but it would reject such advances with a low snarl. Geezer would then laugh. 'See him?' he would say, 'If he can't eat it or screw it, he isn't interested. A great dog. Almost human, so he is.'

Like dog, like master.

Gifford had supporters right across the city and in East Antrim, by virtue of his reputation for sheer toughness and recklessness. Yet, somewhat strangely, he was a devoted follower of McVeigh, whom he trusted implicitly to lead the organisation in the right direction.

No doubt about it, Geezer was the danger.

Blitzer brooded on these thoughts as he left the house without a word of farewell and approached the Land Cruiser in the drive. As he opened the door, his mood darkened even more as he recalled his daughter's words of reproach. He kicked the white-walled front tyre and said aloud,

'And fuck the polar bears anyway.'

Chapter 21

Granville was still tired, despite having had a good night's sleep in the Landsdowne Club, and despite his early morning swim there, which he looked on as one of the luxuries of his London life. The club was just round the corner from the office from which he had operated for years and was an oasis of calm, whatever the excitements of his official day.

Now he was set to enjoy another facet of which he looked on as the quintessential English pleasure: lunch at a riverside restaurant at Richmond, with Penny. George Orwell could keep his idyllic vision of an England where old maids cycled to Holy Communion. He had his own version, which featured a smart, freshly coiffured Penny in a summer dress, seated at a table in a wayside pub, overlooking a lazily flowing Thames. He wasn't sure what the Irish equivalent would be, but he could not suppress the image of the willowy Noleen which flooded into his mind. Perhaps on the shores of Lough Erne.

'I think we need the second bottle of Sancerre,' he said, coming back to Richmond.

'You don't seem very relaxed,' said Penny. He was lighting his third Gauloise of the afternoon.

'I'm probably not. It takes a couple of days to de-compress after Ireland.'

'Is it that bad? I thought from the newspapers that things were calming down.'

'On the surface, yes, but underneath it's bubbling away like a witch's cauldron. It could either change to politics or blow up in our faces.'

'What about danger?'

'For me, or generally?'

'For you, of course, I have my priorities ...' She touched his forearm lightly.

'For me, no danger at all worth talking about. Probably less than the average citizen. Of course one can always be unlucky – wrong place at wrong time and all that – but mathematically, safer than London.'

'But psychologically very different?'

'True, but you have to look at it rationally. The real strain is that everything changes constantly. People hesitate and vacillate and go off at tangents. Contradict themselves. No one is reliable.'

'Except you!' she laughed. Seeing his face darken – I meant that as a joke – but you *are* a reliable person.'

'Am I?'

Another cigarette.

The day had clouded over suddenly. They walked hand in hand back to her flat on the lower slopes of Richmond Hill, but with a partial view of the Thames.

Must give up the fags. Bad taste..

As though reading his thoughts, 'Your toothbrush is in the holder by the wash-hand basin, the blue one. But I'll taste you as you are.' She laughed happily, then kissed him long and hard, as they headed to the bedroom.

Their love-making was urgent rather than passionate. Granville would have loved another Gauloise, but the earlier conversation ruled that out.

Out of the blue: 'When are you coming back to London?'

She means back to me. She feels I am 'away'.

'Impossible to say. I'm plugged into an ongoing process and while no one is indispensable, I have a key role to play in it. So it could be anything for up to a year.'

'A year?'

She stiffened.

'It doesn't have a timetable, it's not a bus company you know,' said he, rather sharply.

Penny grew more reproachful.

'Couldn't I have a nice long holiday out there with you?'

'No, 'fraid not,' said he hurriedly. 'Too dangerous.'

'But you said it wasn't dangerous.'

Shit, walked into that one.

'It's not, if one goes about with a whole team of protectors – which you wouldn't have. And you'd stick out like a sore thumb amongst the locals. Accent, style and (*regaining his footing*) far too elegant, even when slumming about.'

'Now you're being facetious.'

'I thought that was part of my irresistible charm.'

She hit him in the face with a pillow, but playfully.

But no doubt there are more conversations like this on the horizon.

'Tell you what. How about coming with me when I do my next rehab of the old pins in Archena?'

'Yes yes! Oh yes *please!*'

Do I really want her there? Too late, I've exposed flank. The dangers of bedroom promises.

They were still in bed at six o'clock. Granville reached for the TV remote control and switched on. No picture. He sprang out of bed and thumped the set hard twice with his right hand. The BBC news came to life.

'*Vorsprung durch Technik,*' said he, proudly.

The second headline was 'The Secretary of State for Northern Ireland holds out an olive branch to Republicans'.

Wheeler had done his job in talking up the importance of this 'historic' speech, which Granville had drafted almost a week before. It had taken him three days to pass, almost in its entirety, the scrutiny of the Foreign Office and Number 10, before being delivered at a businessmen's lunch in Belfast. More importantly, it had been given the green light by Bunny; and its release time facilitated the Andersonstown News.

The kernel of the speech contained three main themes:

'Republicanism is a perfectly legitimate political concept. It is not one I personally hold to, but I respect it nonetheless, as every democrat should.

When we add to that concept the adjective "Irish" we must also respect that tradition and acknowledge that its followers have had honourable aspirations and have often suffered in its cause. But the goals of Irish Republicanism – like the goals of Unionism – must in modern society be pursued by totally peaceful means.

It is not the policy of Her Majesty's government to favour either of the two political groups in Northern Ireland, far less to impose a philosophy of our own. It is our goal to work for a lasting peace which will allow both traditions to safeguard their own identity and to work together for the good of all the people of Northern Ireland. I sense that our goal is shared by the overwhelming majority of the electorate. The time has come to bring conflict to an end.'

The BBC had done a reasonable job of summary, as had ITN, the latter half of whose coverage Granville caught as he switched channels.

'So far, so good,' said Granville, repressing the urge to light another cigarette, 'Let's see if Bunny can reciprocate.'

'It's all so much hot air. I don't see how that's such a Big Deal,' said Penny.

'Believe me, it is,' replied Granville, curtly.

Chapter 22

As in life, so in death: Blitzer McCann's end came suddenly, brutally and without his having even contemplated the possibility of it.

He knew, of course, that in the 'Council', McVeigh's so-called 'new thinking' had appeared to make an impression on the leadership. On the other hand, he felt that he had himself mounted a good contrary case, warning of the dangers of 'going soft' and of being absorbed by the mainstream party politicians, who didn't give a toss about Loyalist areas, but who would exploit them as soon as they could access them, just the way they had done for decades in the past.

He hadn't paid enough attention to the body language of Geezer Gifford, (the only language in which Gifford expressed himself to any significant degree). Gifford had nodded briefly, but positively, at various points in McVeigh's exposition, but had looked steadfastly at his Rolex Seamaster, during his, McCann's, interventions. The meeting agreed that it would be premature to take decisions that day on such important issues; and a new date was fixed for the next 'Council'.

There was time to muster support; but political talk was such a waste of time and effort.

Blitzer usually had the services of a UDA driver, one Andrew 'Gabby' Hayes, on his evening excursions into the fleshpots of East Belfast. The exceptions to this rule were the nights McCann intended to be at the King Arthur around closing time, to collect some 'insurance money' from various 'clients' and to offer a lift home to the Braniel Estate to the pretty Tracey Hewitt. 'I like fat cheques and thin chicks' was one of his oft-repeated quips. Gabby's presence on such occasions would have been indelicate and, besides, he was not technically needed as a 'designated driver', since Blitzer did not over-imbibe on such occasions. Brewer's droop could not be allowed to spoil the fun. But no harm in a 'wee one' now and then.

'What'll it be?' asked the barman, respectfully.

'A Tina Turner, as usual,' was the reply.

As always on a Friday night, the two big rooms of the ground floor bar were crowded with enthusiastic punters, sinking pints of Guinness and joshing with one another. Football and horse racing were the main topics of conversation; several were spectators at a needle darts match in the corner. Occasionally the cry of 'one hundred and eighty' would resound and the proud thrower of this maximum score would bow ironically to the onlookers. Towards the back of the premises stood two pool tables and Blitzer, sipping his Black Bush liqueur, played, and lost, a couple of games with some old friends. His mind was on other things; and he kept his eye on them, in her tight-fitting blouse, as she worked efficiently behind the bar, flirting with the drinkers, but keeping up with the steady stream of orders as, metaphorically speaking, pay packets and Giro cheques passed from pocket to till.

'Last orders' were finally, thankfully, called and half an hour later Blitzer walked out of the main door, followed at a discreet few paces, by the lovely Tracey. A lack of attention to detail was his downfall. He had not noticed that the four bulky figures on the pavement were facing inwards, towards the pub, towards him, instead of away from it, as the last of the drinkers were on their way home. It was all over in seconds. Tracey was grabbed from behind and bundled back into the pub without a sound. Blitzer was hit once on the head – his raised forearm failed to deflect the full-on blow, and he was dragged into a side alley where more blows rained on his now defenceless head. He never had the slightest chance of deploying his famed street-fighting skills; he had been taken totally by surprise, by overwhelming numbers who had serious weapons and no inhibitions.

Within the hour, the switchboard of the Belfast *Newsletters* received a coded call indicating where McCann's body was to be found. The fact that the call was UVF-coded meant that this was 'official'. So was there a split in the Loyalist paramilitary ranks? The media immediately began pumping out stories about a feud, but Granville and his colleagues were not so sure. Blitzer, whilst a powerful individual feared by many, was not the leader of a discernible faction, was the initial reasoning. He had been too lazy for that; he was basically a thug on the make. Nevertheless, his murder could have a significance beyond its own circumstances; it could be a signal, particularly to the Loyalist paramilitaries as a whole, that dissent would not be tolerated by those in authority in the 'Council'.

The pathologist's report would later conclude that death was due to severe cerebral injuries, sustained as a result of multiple blows to the head, inflicted with a heavy blunt instrument or instruments, possibly baseball bats.

'Funny thing that about baseball bats,' mused HSB at the JSC. 'They're now more numerous than either hockey or hurling sticks.'

'Perhaps they're better for hitting home runs,' chipped in the GOC. 'Apparently they swing more comfortably.'

'Any specific suspects so far?' asked Granville, from the chair.

'The word from within is that it was Gifford's hoods who carried it out, to his orders, and with McVeigh's approval. That's as clear as the balls on a bulldog.'

'Not Gifford himself?'

'Dear me, no. But he is *so* crass, it's unbelievable. Listen to this: he not only constructed a cast-iron alibi by being seen at the rock concert in the King's Hall, he even had the gall to go into Queen Street police station at the material time, in order to report the alleged loss of his wallet.'

'That about clinches it. He did it,' laughed Granville. 'Well, I'll let you get on with the investigation.'

He confided to Wheeler afterwards, 'I wouldn't put too many resources into finding out who killed friend McCann, if I were the RUC. I look on that lot as a horrible sideshow. The IRA/Sinn Fein are the main act in our circus ring.'

Chapter 23

County Kildare looks its best on a sunny June morning. The grass on the meadows of the many stud and training farms for racehorses is still lush from the generous rains in April and May; the sun is high in an almost completely blue sky, and only a few puffy white clouds drift slowly over the hills to the east. The further one travels away from Dublin, heading west across the county, the thinner the traffic becomes, so that a leisurely drive becomes an idyllic antidote to the stresses of everyday life.

Ireland as it ought to be.

As he sat in the back of his green VW Passat, immediately behind Donny his driver, Bunny's thoughts were more on the everyday stresses than on the restfulness of the landscape as it slipped by. He was on his way to deliver the most important speech of his life – a speech on which his own life could indeed literally depend. In the small town of Bodenstown, which is scarcely more than a village, there is to be found, in the little graveyard, the last resting place of one of Irish Republicanism's iconic figures, the eighteenth-century revolutionary, Theobald Wolfe Tone. Every year in June, on or about the anniversary of his birth on the 20th of the month, his heroic struggle for Ireland's freedom is commemorated by a series of ceremonies organised by various strands of republicanism – Sinn Fein, the Worker's Party, the Irish Socialist Party *et al* – all of whom have their own 'take' on the man himself, what they think he stood for, and how their own positions are in a direct line from his. As an Irish revolutionary hero, Tone ticked most of the necessary boxes: a romantic who had sought French military support for rebellions against England; a great orator of high-flown, stirring speeches – even from the dock in which he knew he would be sentenced to death; a non-sectarian egalitarian; a persecuted prisoner of England and, above all, a martyr for the cause, in the best Irish tradition, having died of self-inflicted wounds, following a botched attempt at cutting his own throat with a pen knife, while awaiting execution in the Provost's prison. There was enough in that life – and death – to inspire and justify a whole range of political attitudes and actions, so that a wide spectrum of party leaders could ritually advance their own position 'in the spirit of Wolfe Tone'.

Bunny had often delivered the Sinn Fein speech at the annual Bodenstown ceremony. Media interest was always intense in what were perceived to be such 'keynote' speeches. At party headquarters on the Falls Road he had often joked to his colleagues that he was working on his 'State of the Dissolution of the Union address.'

Today's speech was 'make or break' on several levels. In party terms, he had to face down opposition from those who were wedded to the idea of the armed struggle all the way to victory. He had to prepare public opinion, especially in the nationalist and republican community, for a radical change of tack. And he had to fulfil an undertaking to Jeremy Granville that he would respond to the Secretary of State's 'olive branch speech' with his own public 'confidence-building measure'. Failure on any of those fronts would spell disaster – disaster for the policies he had personally developed, for his community, for relations with Britain. Failure would also empower his opponents within SF/IRA, who would certainly look on his 'removal' as inevitable.

On the road approaching the graveyard it was obvious that the party's well oiled PR machine had succeeded in arousing great media interest in what they billed as his 'wide-ranging policy statement'. Amongst the many cars lining the road were several communication trucks, bristling with antennae and satellite dishes fully a metre in diameter. In the crowd, which was still outside the churchyard, he recognised Paul Devlin, from the Dublin office and organiser of the ceremony, who came forward to greet him as he opened the car door. Donny extracted the obligatory wreath from the boot of the car and, accompanied now by a posse of party officials, they moved through the entrance gate. Set into the three metre high wall at the entrance was a larger-than-life bust of Tone, looking streamlined with his aquiline nose and swept back hair. (Or was it a wig, or a trendy eighteenth-century hat?).

Bunny waited patiently while the cameramen from TV and the print media manoeuvred and jostled themselves into position to record his act of wreath laying. He looked around the crowd: party members from North and South; political correspondents; one or two influential feature writers; even some plain-clothes Garda Síochána Special Branch men. The wreath laying he carried out in almost slow motion, so that it could not be missed. Handshakes could always be repeated for the benefit of the paparazzi but wreath laying was a one-shot operation.

Bunny stepped back from the bust and bowed his head respectfully.

'Prince Charles couldn't have done it better,' Granville would later tease him.

No one appeared to take any notice of the card clipped to the wreath, which read 'In memory of Theobald Wolfe Tone, an Irish Patriot, who struggled for justice'. No doubt Danny, the PR man, would later draw that to the attention of appropriate reporters.

On a paved area between the outer wall and the first of the gravestones stood a temporary wooden lectern, surrounded by four flag poles, on which fluttered two Irish tricolours and two Sinn Fein flags showing the party logo superimposed on a green map of All-Ireland.

There were two introductory, and thankfully brief, speeches by party officials. As Bunny listened he was pleased to note that they contained no political meat worth talking about – nothing to detract from his own. He now wished that he had remembered to drink some water before leaving the car; his mouth was caked and dry and he feared that his voice when he came to speak, would croak embarrassingly.

At last he was at the podium. His voice was OK and without too much stumbling, he had got through the opening paragraph of pious praise for Tone which young Eamonn Hughes, his nephew, had written for him in Irish. He was into his stride and could feel confidence flowing into himself. He had the text before him on the lectern, on A5 paper sheets, in enormous print, but he knew it by heart, so long had he laboured over it and so often had he recited it to himself. The main thrust of it had come to him as he walked alone on an Atlantic beach near his holiday home in Donegal. Sometimes he wished he could stay on that beach forever, listening to the ocean breakers as they came crashing in, and to the cry of the seagulls and the gannets, as they wheeled and dived for fish out beyond the surf. But he knew that was self- delusion. What made him tick was the adrenalin rush of the multiple struggles he was involved in – struggles within the party, in the Army Council, with the security forces, with the two sovereign governments, and with hostile elements in the media. They wore him down, but they were his lifeblood. For the foreseeable future Donegal could not compete.

He knew that the theme of his Bodenstown speech would have to be peace. But it worried him. In the outside world 'peace' ranked with motherhood and apple pie as an unassailable positive. But not in Ireland, not in Republican circles. It could too easily be linked to such negatives as 'suing for peace', and 'the peace of the grave', in other words, defeat.

Then it had come to him: 'Peace – with – justice!'
You can't have one without the other.

He had tried that out on Danny, who was one of the most media-astute operators imaginable. He had joked, 'You mean a fixed expression, like "love 'n' marriage" or "fish 'n' chips"? But had nevertheless given the slogan his approval.

'It provides a link back to the injustices of the past and, if endlessly repeated, will pass into the public's consciousness as a single concept.'

'Thank you, Sigmund Freud,' laughed Bunny, but the endorsement from such an expert settled his nerves.

The Sinn Fein Bodenstown speech invariably contained certain traditional passages, which Bunny proceeded to deliver. Beginning with an encomium to all frontline freedom fighters engaged in 'the struggle', there were expressions of thanks to all Volunteers, and condolences to the families of named victims of the 'British war machine' or 'unionist death squads'. This year there was even a passage of thanks to the media, whose more informed reporting in recent weeks had helped alert world opinion to the real issues of social, economic and political injustices in the 'occupied Six County Statelet'.

Then came the real theme: Peace – with – justice.

'The IRA, with the support of the nationalist community, has fought a long and hard battle for Irish freedom and for the rights of the Irish people, North and South. Together we have shown the world that no longer can Britain hope to suppress us by force, as she has done so often in the past. As I predicted at successive Ard Fheisanna, we have been able to answer vicious military attack with heroic military defence. We have suffered as a people, but we have prevailed.'

Danny at this point sparked off a sustained round of thunderous applause.

'Now the time has come to profit from our sacrifices. The British government knows – and in its more honest moments admits – that a political solution has to be found. They and their unionist allies cannot defeat us. That political solution must acknowledge us as equals.'

More thunderous applause.

'The Secretary of State now says he recognises the legitimacy of our republicanism and he talks of peace. But I say to him, peace yes – but only peace – with - justice. Justice for our prisoners, justice for our party and justice for our community.'

This tertiary rhythm carried the audience up to another burst of noisy approval.

'We are prepared to negotiate peace – with – justice. We have earned the right to do so. But I warn the British government: if you don't deal fairly with us, I have no doubt the IRA will punish you severely. Remember this: recent operations have shown that the British heartlands are not immune to the righteous vengeance of the awakened Irish people.'

Was this reference to a renewed bombing campaign in 'Great Britain' a big enough bone to throw to the hardliners from South Armagh and East Tyrone? On the other hand, was his expressed wish for peace negotiations positive enough to satisfy Granville's political masters? It had just about satisfied Granville himself a few days before, when they had together reviewed the text of the final draft in the visitors' reception room of the Clonard Monastery. Only time would tell, and in the meantime he would have to continue to ride two horses at once: One called Peace – with – Justice, the other called War. He deliberately turned to his left to observe the reaction of a group of those he knew to be hardliners. Their faces showed no emotion but they did not enthusiastically join in the general applause.

'So I say to the IRA,' (at this point there were smiles and nudges from many, at this barefaced repetition of the fiction that the leadership of Sinn Fein and that of the IRA were two separate entities), 'let's call London's bluff. A total ceasefire will create extra space for the necessary political negotiations at the highest level. You have fought a truly magnificent fight for Ireland. Your armed struggle has obliged the enemy to acknowledge the legitimacy of our cause. Now it is up to all of us to pursue that struggle in politics at the negotiating table. We do so with your strength behind us. We do so with confidence in your continuing presence. We do so in the knowledge that were the British Establishment to attempt to stall the progress towards peace – with – justice, you stand ready to resume hostilities. Tiocfaidh ar la!'

As he left the lectern, a group of his supporters, in a well-rehearsed move, rushed forward, cheering and slapping him on the back, like *aficionados* congratulating a triumphant *torero*. If they didn't carry him shoulder high from the ring, they were, metaphorically speaking, nevertheless awarding him both ears and the tail. The bull of the eternal armed struggle appeared to have been dispatched.

Chapter 24

Blitzer's funeral was a grand affair, well stage managed by the newly confident leadership. Not since the state funeral of Feldmarschall Erwin Rommel had hypocrisy and pomp combined in such a spectacular extravaganza. For public consumption there was a show of Loyalist unity, which attempted, with little success, to gloss over two ugly facts: that McCann had been a criminal; and that some of his fellows had savagely murdered him. He was to be buried something of a flawed hero, with an underlying message that whilst his direct action style had had its uses, it was really time to move on. That would be into politics – *Realpolitik* – with comprehensive policies, vote-getting, majorities and a recognised representational role. In a word, respectability, which is what McVeigh began to crave above everything else

Yes, respectability, properly financed, of course. One couldn't be too scrupulous about that; we live in the real world, after all.

The funeral service was held in the Belfast Mission Church on the Lower Newtownards Road, with a PA system relaying the service for the benefit of mourners who could not get into the church buildings and who stood outside in the rain. Despite the weather, the crowds were so big that the police had to close the main road and set up traffic diversions via neighbouring side streets. RUC 'snappers' were positioned in the upper floors of the shops on the opposite side of the street, photographing all and sundry, the passing rubbernecks as well as the numerous big-named hoodlums in attendance.

The latter sat, resplendent in Armani suits and conspicuous bling, in reserved seats at the front of the wreath-bedecked church, immediately behind the widow and daughter, both of whom wept softly into their black veils. Maureen's lips trembled in prayer, something which surprised her daughter when she glanced sidewards. The family considered themselves to be 'Protestant', but clearly of a non-practising variety. As McVeigh, himself no great theologian, once said of Maureen, 'she probably thinks the road to Damascus is a Bob Hope movie'.

The service was taken by the Rev. Roy Meharg, a Presbyterian minister who no longer had his own congregation but who had made a name for himself through a 'calling' to serve in what were euphemistically called 'difficult areas'. In these he maintained daily contact with the local powers that were, that is to say the UDA, UVF and Red Hand Commandos, on behalf of the ordinary Loyalist community. He was forever putting himself forward as a mediator in any confrontational situation, and the news media tended to indulge his personal fantasy that he was 'making a real difference for peace and reconciliation'.

Obviously, the obsequies for a thug such as McCann, posed more than usual difficulties for the officiating clergymen – Catholic priests faced the same dilemma when dealing with the passing of well known murderers, but they could more easily fall back on a lengthy recital of the appropriate liturgy to fill out a respectable three quarters of an hour.

For the Rev. Meharg, the choice of hymns posed no problem – the family had readily approved of 'The day thou gavest Lord, hath ended', (which was chronologically incontrovertible), and 'Abide with me', with its resonance from another solemn community occasion, namely, the FA Cup Final. Everybody knew the words and the singing was, as the Rev. Meharg said, inspirational. The content of his prayers was also no great challenge – comfort for the family; an end to violence and suffering; and wisdom for the decision makers in these perilous times. These petitions to the Almighty wrote themselves. But what to say about Blitzer himself? 'A man with a zest for life', while undoubtedly ambiguous, nevertheless sounded positive, as did 'he persevered tirelessly in everything he put his hand to', though to those shopkeepers from whom he had regularly extracted protection money, the phrase had a more chilling meaning, as the hand in question had never been far from their throats. Financial generosity was often a virtue ascribed to deceased villains, but it would have been stretching things a little too far, even in these circumstances, to refer to any eleemosynary activities on Blitzer's part. Instead, Meharg restricted himself to a vague reference to his 'numerous acts of kindness'.

At last the grisly ceremony was over, and the solid oak coffin was carried by six moustachioed gorillas from Blitzer's own 'battalion', out into the main road, where the *pièce de résistance* awaited – an enormous hearse, drawn by four plumed, black horses – the first appearance of such an *attelage* in Belfast since the 1940s.

Along one side of the hearse, an array of white roses spelt out 'B.L.I.T.Z.E.R.' It was a work of art, but the florist may have been rushed, for the final 'R' listed somewhat to the left, thereby partially ruining the effect. On the other side of the hearse was a row of red roses, this time spelling out 'DADDY'. The widow's personal contribution was a simple wreath on top of the Ulster flag draped coffin, with a card attached, bearing the ambiguous, but possibly sincere message: 'I will never forget you, Maureen'.

Behind the hearse came two ancient, but well maintained, Austin Princess limousines, the sole purpose of which was to convey the mountains of floral tributes which had arrived from all parts of the Loyalist low life world. It had been arranged that the coffin would be carried up the Lower

Newtownards Road to the junction with the Albert Bridge Road, in five 'lifts', the changeover of pall-bearers each time causing some anxiety until the new 'lifters' got comfortably into step. The horses were made nervous by the sounds of the big crowd swirling about them. The coachman had difficulty in controlling them and when two of them simultaneously defecated, the pall-bearing unit was forced to zig-zag gingerly in order to keep their shoes clean.

At the top of the road, at what the locals still called the 'Ropeworks Corner', despite the fact that the works had been demolished over twenty years before, the coffin was slotted into the hearse and the horses set off at a trot in the direction of Roselawn Cemetery, nonetheless causing traffic chaos in half the city for the next forty minutes.

Chapter 25

HSB looked on his monthly meetings with his opposite number in the Garda Síochána as amongst his most challenging duties.

The Joint North-South Co-ordinating Committee on which he took the lead for the RUC, was sandwiched below the Baldonnel Committee at political level and above the Border Superintendents' Committee, which handled most of the on-the-ground co-operation between the two police services. In the view of the security community in Northern Ireland it would have been more useful if the Irish army, which had the more appropriate equipment and training, had been the South's main anti-terrorist force . However, that had been, from the beginning of the 'Troubles', ruled out at ministerial level in the Republic, for quasi-philosophical reasons. The Dublin politicians of all the political parties believed that to have the army in the lead would give the whole co-operative exercise a state-to-state character, whereas the national myth – not yet relinquished – was that the six Northern counties were de jure, if not de facto, part of the Irish state, a proposition which argued in favour of police-to-police security co-operation.

That strange reasoning sometimes also coloured the stance taken by HSB's opposite number and his colleagues on the Co-ordinating Committee. The atmosphere at their meetings was invariably friendly and the hospitality offered to RUC visitors in Dublin, in the Ashling Hotel, near the Garda HQ on the edge of Phoenix Park, was unfailingly generous. Those attending were all policemen together, facing similar problems day-by-day. They were men who understood one another better than any outsider group could, and as the bottles of

Jamieson's followed bottles of Jamieson's, their professional talk became increasingly in-house and brotherly in character. Yet two things always bothered him. The appointment of the Garda Commissioner, the highest ranking officer, was always a politically charged one and the relationships upwards to the minister and downwards to the ranks of the Garda, were heavily influenced by political considerations. Close co-operation with the RUC could either be looked upon favourably as helping to safeguard public safety throughout the island, or as a necessary evil to be kept to a minimum. Fortunately, the recent change in both minister and Commissioner had tilted the balance in favour of deeper co-operation.

HSB's second worry was about the integrity of some of the individual Gardai involved in anti-terrorist work, especially in border areas. It was widely believed within the RUC that the murder by the IRA of two officers in 1989 near the village of Jonesborough in South Armagh had been facilitated by a tip-off from the Garda station in Dundalk, where they had attended a cross-border meeting. The danger came not from Garda officers being active IRA militants – that would have been too obvious within the force – but from the so-called 'sneaking regarders', that is to say from those who had a sneaking regard for the terrorists' actions.

HSB's opposite number was a large, bluff man, called Finbar Flannigan, a renowned Cork hurler in his youth, who had carved out a distinguished career for himself from the age of eighteen. HSB genuinely felt he could trust him and he had gone so far as to give Flannigan the name of the Garda officer in Dundalk who was the RUC's main suspect as the murderer of their colleagues. At their next meeting, HSB raised the matter again. 'It's very difficult, as you can imagine,' said Flannigan rather awkwardly.

'There's no proof of collusion. Certainly nothing that a case could be based on. And of course, politically … dynamite.'

Was the matter to rest there? Flannigan then said very firmly, holding out his hands as though to emphasize his innocence, 'The individual concerned has been transferred to duties which would give you no further grounds for concern. That's the best I can do.'

Things had moved on from those days, to the point where at each meeting detailed lists of individuals and their activities were exchanged routinely. Acts of violence had tapered off considerably for several months, but the two big money-making rackets, namely contraband fuel and cigarettes, had greatly increased. So-called 'fuel laundering' involved a crude industrial process to remove red marker British dyes and green Irish dyes from diesel which had been marked in that way in order to identify it as being for agricultural purposes and therefore subject to a much reduced excise duty. The new, illegal fuel, transformed by being filtered through certain cheap acids or even clay or cat litter, could then be sold on, usually in Northern Ireland, to customers who were either innocent of the fraud, or to those 'in the know', who enjoyed the sweetener of a discount on the full price they would otherwise have paid for legitimate fuel. This racket naturally required secluded premises and an investment of several thousand pounds in the equipment, but the financial rewards were so high, because of the difference between the cost price of the carburant and the price at the pump with the notional addition of duty, was so great, that the smugglers could afford to lose one or two laundering units every month. For every thousand pound invested the racketeers reckoned to gain fifty thousand in four weeks. Inevitably, the farmer on whose premises such installations were discovered, would plead that he had been forced to co-operate with the terrorists under pain of death. That was even sometimes true, but usually the said farmer was found to have militant republican family links.

Some months the meetings contained little more than the exchange of statistics and of impressions as to how the battle against the terrorist was going, but today there were meatier items on the agenda. HSB told his counterpart that he had intelligence from a normally reliable source (in reality, from a recent recruit to the Protected Witness Scheme), according to which one of the main technical brains behind the bombing campaign was an academic 'in', or it could it have been 'from' – Dundalk. Either way it should be easy for the Gardai to pinpoint a small number of likely suspects, as there couldn't be hundreds of them. And since the security forces in Northern Ireland believed that the total number of 'bomb-brains' was not more than half a dozen, to have one of them taken out of circulation would be a major victory.

Another 'goodie' which HSB brought to the meeting was a file on the Israeli detection equipment with which his American friend Miller had supplied him. Links with what was euphemistically called an 'intermediary' had already been established and the RUC hoped to deploy the device within weeks.

In return, Flannigan had a present for his visitor: his technical men had managed to place a listening device in the home of a well known Republican leader in Dun Laoghaire. He was perhaps the most influential of the Southern Command. Being of an earlier generation, and indeed now virtually house- bound due to a severe arthritic condition, he had been gradually sidelined, but his voice still carried weight throughout the movement. He had been visited only ten days before by Bunny and one other, unidentified man. The quality of the sound on the tape was poor, but the Garda had succeeded in piecing together a transcript of a full evening's conversation which captured about eighty percent of what had been said. It made fascinating reading.

Clearly there was a North-South divide amongst the Republican leadership. Bunny argued in favour of, as he put it, 'cashing in our chips' now rather than risk being in a weaker position in a year's time. That was the firm view of his colleagues. The Southerner disagreed: the armed struggle had gone further than ever before, and could go further yet. British public opinion was sick, sore and tired of the North and that opinion would eventually force the politicians to disregard the hardline 'securocrats'. Besides it was a moral issue – could the leadership now betray the Republican dead, the hunger strikers, the imprisoned and the maimed, for some hoped-for electoral gain?

'It's all right for you down here, talking,' said Bunny, genuine anger sounding in his voice. 'Your people can watch from afar and put a punt in the collection tin and philosophise about war and peace. Our people are under the cosh day and daily. There is a risk our support in the community could crumble. And at the same time the Brits have shown they are willing to talk turkey. It's the moment to pursue that.' He then added, in a calmer, almost inaudible voice, 'We don't need to turn everything off operationally, quite the reverse. Especially as regards the England Department. That's our most secure one and the one which can do most damage and thus concentrate London's mind wonderfully.'

The conversation did not appear to have a decisive conclusion and there were many gaps in the transcript, as the participants appeared to leave the room, perhaps to have something to eat in the kitchen. When the transcript resumed there were two priceless items of intelligence: firstly that the receipt of 'goods' would be the responsibility of Eamon Hogan, a senior Custom's official known to the Garda as a Republican sympathiser.

HSB at once thought he knew of the operation Hogan would be involved in, and the nature of the 'goods'. He put Flannigan in the picture about the next instalment of the 'arms from Libya' story.

The second piece of news was an unfortunately garbled reference to a 'forthcoming event', which appeared to be a planned bank raid. A reference to Seamus McLoughlin helped HSB surmise that the raid would be in East Tyrone, McLoughlin's sphere of operations.

Bunny had been uncharacteristically explicit about these 'coming attractions' as he described them. But that showed that he needed to convince the older man that he and his comrades in the North had not gone soft.

HSB gratefully took these 'treats' on board. It had been an unusually productive meeting from his point of view, even though it had ended sooner than he had expected. His driver was just arriving back at the hotel car park from his lunch when HSB emerged.

'Okay Billy. On our way. And I think we'll take the Slane road home. It's longer, but a change of plan is always safer.'

Chapter 26

Cassidy's visit to Paris weighed heavily upon him. Normally he liked to concentrate on one thing at a time, preferably horse racing, now that Colette was history, but apart from pleasures his instinct was to think about each problem in life separately. Multi-tasking had never been his strong point, yet his need to master it had increased dramatically. His double life as a businessman and IRA operative had become a triple one, with his enforced recruitment by the security forces. Had he the temperament to maintain such complexity, he often asked himself, or would he simply crumble at some point and be exposed as a despicable sham? Noleen was both a help and yet another complication. She seemed happier recently and even her father, old McManus, had said to him, 'You must be looking after my wee girl quare an' well. She's just radiant, so she is.'

But he had never taken the risk of telling her about the full extent of his involvement with the 'Government'. Would she out of devotion to him take that in her stride also, or would she denounce him to the IRA? His very life depended on that relationship not going wrong. He was not entirely convinced that Granville's protection could save him from the vengeance of his alleged 'comrades-in-arms', since their arm was a long one and their patience unlimited, as the execution of several deserters in Great Britain over the years had dramatically shown.

Cassidy pondered on these things as his Air France flight from London came into land at Charles de Gaulle airport. The next three days were going to be complicated, reflecting the complications of his life. The official, public reason for his visit was as a board member of the West Belfast Growth group, on a study visit to see how the French authorities were tackling the social and economic problems of *'les cités'*, the vast high-rise housing estates on the outskirts of Paris, where unemployment, crime and 'alienation from authority' were endemic and, so far, intractable. Costly programmes, devised by special task forces had been put in place to combat these deep-seated and interlocked problems, such as the provision of small factory and warehousing units near to the housing; travel-to-work subsidies for the employed seeking jobs in Paris itself; and detox centres in the housing silos themselves. It was worth examining which measures might be applicable in Belfast.

That is how governments imitate one another in wasting taxpayers' money.

It had been Granville's idea that West Belfast could learn some lessons from this experience and, through his contacts with the British embassy, had laid on the visit programme for Cassidy. Indeed, since Barlow, the MI5 official, alias NIO Economics adviser, had 'taken ill', ('Adenauer flu' as it was known in the service) Granville himself, travelling separately, would join Cassidy in Paris and be part of the study visit, providing liaison with the embassy and French authorities. Granville would also play a backup role in the second part of Cassidy's visit, which was to rendezvous with Verhagen and McGiolla in order to inspect the 'merchandise' and effect the next instalment of payment.

The third aspect of the visit would be no easier for Cassidy: he had persuaded Noleen to accompany him, as it would be their wedding anniversary in a few days' time. What better way to celebrate than to do so in Paris, city of light and romance And, of course, the celebration was another layer of cover for his activities. Would he take her on one of the river cruises and, over dinner, come clean with her about every fact of his life, throwing himself on her mercy and love and hoping to be free from at least one burden. He had not yet decided; it remained an option.

Granville always had mixed feelings whenever he was back in Paris. There was, of course, the sadness of his loss of

Helena, with whom he had spent such a splendid time in the city, working out of the embassy. They had been a glittering couple on the diplomatic circuit, at a time when Foreign Ministries all over the world had had the upper hand over their respective Finance Ministries and vied with each other, in prestige capitals such as Paris, in the lavishness of their style and hospitality. But his memories of the city went back further than that, to his student days at the Sorbonne and the exquisite excesses of youth. He had been spoiled, he admitted, by an uncle, his father's brother, who lived in great style in a magnificent apartment on the Ile St Louis – a *style de vie* he could afford, as a senior executive of an Anglo-French bank. Uncle Damien, a widower with no children, seemed to live vicariously through nephew Jeremy and was delighted when Granville came to study at the Sorbonne. Neither admitted to Granville's parents the extent of Damien's avuncular support. 'I just give the boy a saucer of milk and a biscuit every now and then', but it even ran to a secret monthly allowance which Granville 'put to good use', as he euphemistically described it. Granville did not stay with his uncle, preferring to lead the full student life on the Left Bank. His accommodation was, however, well above the average student quarters, being in a hotel – albeit a modest one – in the Rue Vernueil, close to St Germain. Nostalgia always brought him back to that district; even to that hotel, which over the years had moved steadily upmarket to become what was now known as a 'boutique hotel'.

Discretion had decreed that he had arranged for the Cassidys to be booked into the Lutetia on the Boulevard Raspail, which was large, international and anonymous. It was quite near, but far enough away to sustain the pretence of 'distance', as far as Noleen was concerned. Mr Michael Lushby, First Secretary at the embassy, took them there in an embassy car and as they checked in, Aidan became the unwitting protégé of the DST, the French equivalent of MI5, who would tail him during his stay in France. That was a goodwill service on Granville's behalf, but also, for the

French, an investment as regards possible intelligence gains about arms trafficking on French soil.

The 'study visits' to the cités were a chore as far as Granville was concerned. Apart from cover, they served no purpose in his terms. But he had better stay awake and scoop up whatever documentation was available, in case Cassidy needed 'administrative support' in writing his report for his West Belfast Growth responsibilities. Granville suddenly realised that he had never seen a word written by Cassidy: was he up to writing such a report or would he, Granville, have to undertake that chore himself? The thought put him in a bad mood. He thought instead of Noleen – off shopping, for clothes and for nineteenth-century prints – and he wished the day away. That evening the Cassidys were to dine alone, while Granville visited and had a meal with Uncle Damien, who was still spry in old age and enjoyed his food. 'Only pleasure left in life' he would say with conviction at every meal. He had been a good cook in his day, but nowadays his *gouvernante* (house-keeper) who conveniently lived just across the river, cooked for him three times a week. He and Granville spent the evening chatting about family news.

The Cassidys did not chat about much. The *bateau mouche* scenario, which in Aidan's mind had been the possible setting for his confession to Noleen, disintegrated when the city was lashed by a prolonged rainstorm which reduced visibility to a few metres and drove the temperature down by almost ten degrees. Aidan, more relieved than disappointed, grasped at this turn of events as 'a sign' that the time was not propitious for his disclosures'. At Lushby's suggestion, they dined in the Boeuf Mode in rue de l'Université The meal was mediocre, the service poor and their conversation rather flat for wedding anniversary celebrants. In all, not a successful evening.

The following morning was one of those autumn days in Paris that the songwriters write songs about. Everything seemed to sparkle like new after the rain, the sky was a deep,

deep blue and the warm sunshine, forecast to last all day, had brought out summer outfits once more, for a last glorious fling.

When they met over breakfast in the Lutetia, Granville disclosed that he was going to play truant from the day's (alleged) study visit. This visit existed only on the typed 'Programme of Visit', which would be appended to Cassidy's report. In reality, he too, was going to be a truant, off on IRA business, to meet Verhagen and McGiolla in an industrial warehouse near the markets at Rungis, on the southern outskirts of the city.

'And what are your plans?' said Granville, turning to Noleen. Then he risked adding, 'Perhaps we could play truant together?'

'Oh, I don't think so,' replied Noleen, but with a slight giggle which betrayed her attraction to the idea. 'You see, I'm going gallery-crawling. I want to revisit both the Jeu de Paume and the Quai d'Orsay collections.'

'Well, I could endure that, especially the Impressionists,' countered Granville. 'And perhaps a spot of lunch somewhere nice this fine day.'

'That's a great idea,' said Aidan, apparently without suspicion. 'Why don't you do that?'

'OK,' said Noleen, cheerfully, 'that's the programme decided.'

When Cassidy got out of the taxi, carrying his Gladstone-type briefcase, at the address he had been given, he found himself in an ugly commercial/industrial estate, made up of small factories and large warehouses, no doubt built there because the site lay in the fork between the A6 motorway and the N7, *Route nationale* .

Verhagen was already waiting for him at the door to the reception area of a warehouse. Cassidy's DST shadows were parked in the customers' car park of the building on the other side of the street. The photographer prepared to take shots of anyone who entered or left the warehouse.

Inside the warehouse itself, a gloomy cavern of a place, McGiolla was talking in careful airport English, to two men of North African appearance. The two Irishmen grunted statutory greetings and nodded to the *Maghrébiens*.

'OK, *allons-y*,' said Verhagen briskly, 'we've got a lot of checking to do and financial matters to attend to, so let's make a start. Fast.'

He led the group towards the back of the warehousing space, where long corridors of shelves reached almost to the ceiling.

'Lot 162, here it is.' A stencil on the side read *"équipments agricoles"*, and the *destinataire* was shown as 'Mommens en Zoon, stevedores at Antwerp'. McGiolla drew a sheaf of paper from the depths of his pockets while the two Algerians began deftly to open the packing cases for inspection.

'This could take some time,' said Verhagen to Cassidy, 'you like a coffee in the office while we work?' Cassidy nodded assent. He needed something to steady his nerves and he preferred not to be looking over McGiolla's shoulder during the latter's professional work. In fact, he never felt comfortable in McGiolla's's presence. There was something chilling about that man, despite his 'hail fellow well met' bonhomie, when drinking in pubs in Crossmaglen, singing Republican songs till the rafters rang. He had the focused personality of the true zealot, who never for a moment lost his concentration on 'the cause'. The two men shared a keen interest in horse racing, but Cassidy could never generate a relaxed conversation even on that topic.

That's what this armed struggle does to a man. It sucks the humanity out of him. God, I wish it was all over.

When the others joined them in the tiny, anonymous upstairs office there were a few adjustments to be made to accounts, in the light of minor discrepancies in the number of assault rifles ordered and now 'semi-delivered'. Agreement was swiftly reached on the amounts to be paid to the Algerians and a further interim payment to Verhagen. Cassidy made the payments by way of banker's drafts, drawn on a bank in Zurich, plus a small amount in US dollars.

'We're all weighed and all paid,' said McGiolla, as though he were at a point-to-point race meeting.

Within minutes the five men had departed in different directions.

In central Paris, Granville and Noleen were having a very different day, one which Granville had taken great pains to stage manage as much as possible. The visits to the Jeu de Paume and the Quai d'Orsay galleries had gone well. Noleen was particularly excited by a special exhibition of Pisarros made up of many paintings borrowed from other museums and private collections. In her enthusiasm, her eyes, Granville thought, seemed to dance with that gaiety which many Irish women possess but all too frequently have little cause to display.

Once, when they were crossing the traffic on the Pont Neuf, Granville took her by the hand, protectively. It was not, however, the grasp of a boy scout helping an old lady across the road; rather it was in the manner of would-be lovers. She did not immediately pull her hand free when they had safely reached the opposite pavement, but waited until he, reluctantly, released her.

Their lunch venue had been carefully chosen – a long-established brasserie on the corner of the Rue d'Epéron and St. André des Arts. Granville had known it for years and had always enjoyed its delights. Whenever he was feeling he deserved a real treat he indulged in a raid on its extensive cellar. He had hoped she would be enchanted at its atmosphere of Parisian chic, and it appeared he had hit his target: Noleen talked volubly and laughed a lot, a high tinkling laugh which encouraged Granville to both tease her and make flattering remarks about her appearance.

'Oh look, I didn't know poussin was a baby chicken,' she cried.

'You thought it was a seventeenth-century painter!'

'Yes! That's right.'

'My godfather wrote the definitive book about him. I must dig you out a copy.'

'How lovely. I'll hold you to that.'

Noleen started with mussels soup; Granville with a plate of *fruits de mer*, sent on its way with a flinty Muscadet. Then, on his recommendation, they both had *faisan farci aux marrons* and a bottle of *Echezeaux, Domaine de la Romanee-Conti*, which the sommelier poured with a care bordering on reverence. *Ruinously expensive, but look on it as an investment.*

'Oh, if only Ireland could be like this,' Noleen said wistfully.

'Do you mean politically or personally?' He tried his best to load the word 'personally' with intimate meaning.

'I suppose I mean both,' she said seriously. 'I mean, my life is partly ruined by the situation (she made quote marks in the air) and I don't know if it will ever be anything different. That's the depressing thing.'

'Well, I'm an optimist. Some day – please God, soon – there will be some sort of settlement. Everybody's tired of it.'

'Tired of it, yes, but there are still two big obstacles in the long run.'

'Which are....?'

'For a start,' she said with sudden passion, 'you Brits don't seem capable of calling the unionists' bluff and of telling them to get on with living with the rest of us in a united Ireland. And then the unionists themselves – all of them, not just their fascist leaders – can't see how much better off they'd be in a united Ireland. Look at the Republic's economy, roaring ahead. And all the social benefits far superior to those in the North.'

'I hear what you're saying,' he said, falling back on his automatic soft-soap FCO vocabulary, 'but I think you're wrong on your first point. The UK won't force the unionists into a united Ireland, but we won't hold on to Northern Ireland as though we were all in a colonial context. We want to see all sides on the island settle down together and fit into the modern world.'

He lit the first cigarette of the day – progress was slow on that point, but steady.

'And as for the unionists, I think they're pushed into their defensive mode precisely by the Irish pressure. The Irish should be courting them, not bombing them. And as for the economy, I share the unionists' suspicion that the Celtic tiger – which, incidentally, I thought Sinn Fein didn't like, as a bourgeois creation – may one day have to limp to the vets.'

She shook her head, but nevertheless smiled at him. 'I see you are teasing me because you think I'm not a very good republican. It's true I don't go along with all the party's hairshirt economics, but when it comes to Irish freedom, I'm a Republican all the way.'

'Anyway,' said Granville in a tone which indicated he was keen to leave the swampy ground of Irish politics, 'I'm still an optimist and meantime "gather ye rosebuds while ye may".'

He touched her hand across the table and she touched his with her other hand. They lapsed into silence.

After lunch they strolled down to the Seine, by way of St. Michel and across the Pont de Sully to the Ile Saint Louis. When they reached the ornate iron outer door of Uncle Damien's apartment building on the Quai d'Orléans, he put his arm round her and said, 'Now I have a surprise for you. I want to show you how the French bourgeoisie live,' and punching in the code, he opened the door. In the broad passage inside, as though by automatic mechanism, the concierge popped out of her loge, like a figure on a weather chalet. *'Ah, Monsieur Jeremy, bonjour. Desolée, votre oncle n'est pas là, il est à Londres.'*

'Ca va, that's alright, Madame Lagrange,' replied Granville, 'I knew that. He gave me a key.'

Madame gave Noleen an up-and-down look, which was at once aesthetically approving and morally disapproving, as the couple got into the lift.

Inside the vast apartment, with its double doors over three metres high, Louis XVI furniture, ormolu clocks, gilded mirrors and Goblin tapestries, Noleen observed the scene with obvious delight.

'And the view!' she exclaimed, opening French windows to a balcony off the salon, which looked south across the river. It was much cooler now and the sun shone weakly as it began to set over the rooftops of the Quai de la Tournelle, on the Left Bank opposite.

'I never tire of it,' said Granville, 'Now let's see – I know where Uncle keeps his brandy.' Opening a lacquered cabinet he took out a decanter and two balloon glasses.

'Here's our digestif,' he said, handing her a glass with a generous measure of the tawny liqueur. When their drinks were almost finished they were sitting side-by-side on a green chaise longue. With the calculation of a matador choosing the moment of truth, he asked, 'Would you like to see the master bedroom?'

Noleen smiled knowingly and blushed. She hesitated. Then she touched his arm again. 'No, please, no. Not ....'

Did she mean definitely no, not ever, or merely not yet, or possibly even yes, if you coax me some more?

Granville, quadrilingual though he was, could not definitively interpret this response. Deciding not to take any risks, he accepted it with a light remark about the pity it was not to see the whole apartment, but as they were in the lift on their way out, he leant forward and kissed her full on the lips. She did not pull back or protest, but he nevertheless at once said, 'I'm sorry. I shouldn't have. But I couldn't resist.'

Noleen said nothing.

Chapter 27

PANORAMA had been a massive step forward in anti-terrorist equipment, used and praised by all its users in the various intelligence agencies. 'The greatest thing since the sliced panacea' was HSB's description. But one thing which bothered the analysts of PANORAMA was that they could not glean, even from that system, the slightest indication of who 'the Sniper' was. They were pretty sure that they were looking for one individual, but one whose identity was unknown to all but the top of the Belfast command structure and one who was ultra-careful about covering his tracks. No threats, no offers of money could extract from 'the customers' at Castlereagh even a hint of who the sniper might be. Granville eventually concluded that this was a genuine secret within PIRA and its supporters – one that could not be betrayed by more than a very restricted number of top people.

It became ever more important that 'the Sniper' be caught. He was becoming an all-too-important instrument of terror in the hands of the IRA. Looked at objectively and statistically, the number of his victims – eleven so far, all of them either soldiers or policemen in uniform – was not in itself a major factor in the conflict which had already cost over three thousand lives. But the fact that this man could, with impunity, instantaneously snuff out lives, even at a great distance, struck a fear in the public out of all proportion to the mathematical threat to life which he posed. And on the other hand, the mystery surrounding him and the one hundred per cent death rate of his attacks, were used as propaganda by the Republican movement as a whole. At a time when reports of arrests and court appearances of IRA men and women were multiplying weekly, *An Poblacht* could cheer up its readers with stories about the daring deeds of a fictional *An Claiomh derg* (the red sword), which was set in a vague period of the past but which they could easily place in the context of everyday reality.

Another man in Byrne's position might have been tempted into indiscretions – boasting in a safe shebeen, or giving dark hints to his friends – but his best defence was his own secretive nature. He loved reading of his own exploits in the newspapers, as he relived those exquisite moments of primeval excitement. But he was careful never to cut out the articles – and when occasionally he heard trusted relatives gossip about who *An Claiomh derg* might be based on, he never itched to enlighten them. His secret reinforced his role. He was happy in the perverted way a drug addict can be for the duration of his 'high' – he was outside and above mundane reality. But he was forever discontented with the technical aspects of his job – the maintenance of the gun, the choice of target, the getaway arrangements – most of which were outside his control.

He didn't like the sound of his next assignment. It was attractively ambitious, but geographically out of his comfort zone and due to take place at a moment of maximum security alertness. It was outlined to him by the OC of his battalion, as they stood side by side at Casement Park, ostensibly watching an inter-county Gaelic Athletic Association football match. From sources within Belfast City Hall, the IRA had learnt that the Unionist mayor had brought off what in his mind was a brilliant propaganda coup: he had had a positive response to his invitation to the Lord Mayor of the City of London, Sir Peter Gooding, whom he had met at a 'solidarity lunch' organised in London by the Secretary of State. The invitation was not only to visit Belfast but to switch on the Christmas lights.

What a target! The personification of British imperialist capitalism killed by Irish Republican freedom fighters.

Byrne's concerns were, in reality, focused on the likely practicalities of such a hit, but he ventured a political reservation: 'Would the Americans not be turned off by the anti-capitalist bit?'

'Fuck the Americans! They're going soft on us anyway and their money's drying up. Gaddafi will love it. And he's the guy sending the big guns and possibly the big bucks.'

The OC lowered his voice, although there was no one within earshot on the windswept terrace, and said with emphasis, 'I'll look after the politics, Sean. You just take out yer man.'

The chosen stage for the assassination could not have been more public. The IRA insider in the City Hall knew that the scenario for the mayoral visit was that Sir Peter should arrive outside the main gates of the City Hall, in Donegal Square North, to be met by the Town Clerk, who would escort him to the portico at the main entrance to the building; an entrance which had long been closed for security reasons but which would, symbolically, be opened for the great occasion. There he would be officially welcomed by the Lord Mayor and brought indoors to have drinks with those aldermen and councillors who would have not heeded the nationalists' call to boycott the event. The official party would, some twenty minutes later, emerge from the City Hall and mount a platform at the gates, where the switch was located for the ceremony.

The chosen moment for the 'hit' was the initial meeting between the two Lord Mayors at the portico, on the grounds that the security detail would not yet have settled down with the newcomer, and that the risk of 'collaterals' was lower at that point than when large numbers of the Belfast public, always an unpredictable and unruly lot, would be involved. Furthermore, if something were to crop up at the 'portico moment' – and life rarely ran to schedule – there would be another, unfortunately riskier, moment of opportunity when Sir Peter would be on the platform to switch on the lights.

The sniper's position was not ideal, as Byrne muttered to himself, when setting up his equipment. Admittedly, the distance-to-target, at just over a hundred metres, was very much shorter than his usual operating range. Of course, the downside to that was that his eventual pursuers would also be closer to him. He had to be ahead, and out of sight of the inevitable chase, until he reached the designated 'safe house' in Joy Street, where he would be 'cleansed' of all forensic evidence by a nurse with relevant experience, and be provided with a cast-iron alibi, playing cards with three 'friends.' Exceptionally, the AK-47 would this time be sacrificed as he retreated. It would not hold any forensic clues. His providers had secured for him a second floor office window in a red sandstone building on the corner of Donegal Square North and Chichester Street. The usual occupant of the office, a manufacturer's agent and Sinn Fein sympathiser, was conveniently in Las Palmas with his wife, for a week's sunshine break, all expenses paid.

What irked Byrne about this position was that the windowsill was at the wrong height. He could not get comfortable, no matter which way he approached the problem. He had, in advance, requested a tripod, to be delivered by his 'caddy', but he had found that did not really help in setting up a shooting position which combined steadiness, good visibility and comfort. He pulled over a chair, knelt on it and rested the rifle on the window ledge. He was now six inches lower than before. That would have to do. Now for the wait, always a strain on the nerves.

The whirling blue lights on the police motorbike outriders heralded the arrival of Sir Peter's hired limousine. Already flashes from the paparazzi were lighting up the gloomy November night.

Sir Peter was wearing his long red and gold robes of office, with a broad ermine collar, and around his neck and across his chest hung the heavy, glittering chain of office. Byrne took in this scene as a whole, but his concentration was reserved for the portico, at which the Belfast Lord Mayor had now appeared. God, there were an awful lot of people milling about, but the formal handshake at the portico for the benefit of the photographers, would isolate the two principals and slow up the game. A wild thought crossed his mind: could he take out both? He almost laughed at the enormity of the thought, then put himself back into his hunter's trance.

Miraculously, the golden moment arrived exactly as planned: the two gaudily accoutred principals stood motionless, vigorously shaking hands and beaming for the photographers. Byrne had Sir Peter in his sights. But in the nanosecond it took him to squeeze the trigger, the Lord Mayor's head turned and he looked to the left. The movement could not have been more than half an inch, but it saved his life. In the same second a chunk of white stone masonry flew outwards from the portico's pillar.

'Shit !'

Byrne could scarcely believe he had missed. There was no sudden movement amongst the people at the City Hall entrance – it always takes seconds for the mind to take in a sudden and unexpected development. Byrne fired off another round hurriedly and without taking precise aim. Another plume of white dust sprang out of a pillar. Heads were now turned in his direction and some people were diving for cover into the portico.

Byrne's first failure was followed by panic and suddenly everything started to go wrong for him. He lost precious seconds fumbling with the key on the inside of the lock on the office door, then on the ground floor he couldn't remember whether to turn to the left or right at the end of the back corridor in order to get to the door into the alleyway beyond. He went left; he should have gone right. When he finally reached the alleyway he headed east, in the direction of the Law Courts. There were people about in Montgomery Street, but not a big enough crowd into which he could easily melt. And he could hear the sound of running feet from behind him. What if the police already knew what he looked like. And what about the revolver in his pocket – should he dump it now, or hold on to it in case of a shoot-out. He decided to keep it and to run for it.

As he ran down another alley, the length of a multi-storey car park, he heard someone running towards him, police reinforcements called up by radio, he supposed. He ran into the ground floor of the car park – his only way out – and made for the stairs. If he could get to the roof, he might be able to penetrate another building in the street and make his getaway from there. He could hear the pounding of his pursuers' feet – he had obviously been seen, but at least there only seemed to be one policeman close to him. If he could hide from him until he had passed to higher floors, or if he shot him, he would still have a sporting chance of escaping.

At the third floor he pushed open the door and dived into the area in which cars were parked. Could he hide there? He crouched behind two cars but could not hear whether his pursuer had gone past the door and up to the next floor, as cars moved down the exit ramp, drowning out any footfall. Then he saw the door open and a tall figure enter, a revolver in hand. He reached for his own weapon, took aim and with both hands out in front of him fired. And missed. The other immediately went to ground, rolling between parked cars. Now it was cat and mouse, except that, no doubt, other cats would be on their way. He must get out now. Another car moved down the exit ramp, then silence. He crept nearer to the door opposite the one he and his adversary had come in by. As he crept along the side of a large 4X4he did not see that another driver had come through the first door, behind him. The newcomer pulled his keys from his pocket and pressed the remote, as he approached his own car, thus triggering the flash-back response from the vehicle. Byrne reacted instantly, in an automatic reflex, to this sudden noise and flash of light, firing off two rounds at the source of his surprise. In the gloom, this revealed where he was and Sgt. Derek McQuillan earned his Police Commendation Medal by hitting him once in the neck and once in the shoulder with two rapid rounds from his Koch and Heckler 'with little thought for his own safety and with great efficiency' as the citation would read.

Byrne knew he had been hit, the impact crashed through him like a double mule kick, yet he felt no great pain – at first. As he lay on the cold concrete floor he was conscious only of a deep numbness in his upper body and of the damp seepage into his shirt of his own blood. The next half hour passed in a blur. Increasing pain, shortness of breath, then more policemen, some in uniform. Then the agony of being carried on a stretcher down to an ambulance. The last thing he heard was the cacophony of emergency service vehicles. Then an injection, then sleep.

When he awoke, it was in the guarded wing of the Musgrave Park Hospital. An intravenous drip was fastened to his right forearm, an oxygen supply tube was fixed below his nose and, above his bed, a monitor screen beeped from time to time.

It had been a bad day at the office.

Chapter 28

Early morning mists in the western English Channel were beginning to lift, blown by a stiffening wind from the south-west, which turned the sea choppy, with white horses appearing on the crests of the waves. The St Lucia came butting along, heading for Land's End and the last stretch of the voyage to Dublin. It was, for the captain and crew, a routine trip, no different to the dozens they had made over the years between Antwerp and Dublin.

Suddenly that calm routine was broken. Out of the retreating mist to the north came the grey shape of a Royal Navy minesweeper and, simultaneously, a radio order to heave to. St Lucia's captain, with the clear conscience which comes from ignorance, complied immediately, wondering whether, in the early misty morning light, his vessel had been mistaken for a Spanish fishing pirate or mother ship. He could now see Royal Navy sailors on the deck of the minesweeper, preparing to come aboard.

Half an hour later, when the crates of 'agricultural equipment' had been jemmied open, to reveal rows of rifles, boxes of ammunition and cartons of explosives, he was both shocked and fearful. The lieutenant leading the boarding party was not interested in his protestations of ignorance.

'We are escorting you back the way you've come. You are to put into Portsmouth at a berth we'll direct you to. After that, it's a police matter.'

He paused, 'Is that clear?' It was less a question, more a command.

'Alright,' said the captain weakly.

News of the arms seizure at sea was carefully 'packaged' in Belfast. In contrast to many events, about which the media had immediate access and therefore the liberty to choose the sort of presentation to be given to the facts, the government machine had several hours start, and had control over all the witnesses, either under lock and key or in Her Majesty's Senior Service.

Granville briefed Wheeler on the essentials: the official announcement to be timed to receive maximum coverage on television; emphasis to be placed on the fact that the operation (given the codename WALRUS) had been mounted following specific information gathered in Northern Ireland; and that the Garda Síochána had co-operated closely in the preparation of the operation. Still photographs of the minesweeper, the St Lucia and part of the haul of armaments and explosives should help sell the story. Like hot cakes.

'And another thing, James. I assume you'll have a tête-à-tête with your friend Vincent Glass on this one. May I suggest that *in vino* part of your privileged *veritas* you should point him vaguely, but firmly, in the direction of South Armagh as the source of our information. No names, of course, but season your tale with measured indiscretion.'

Wheela-Deala was in luck: the day turned out to be otherwise a slack news day – no cabinet crisis, no sex scandal, no sporting highlights, no competition to the lead story, wall-to-wall, of the drama at sea. The euphoria which the news released throughout the security forces found a happy channel as the background mood to the RUC's Senior Officers Christmas Ball, held in the hastily decorated canteen of their Headquarters at Brooklyn. It was nowadays one of the few major official occasions for the top of the force to come together in a festive mood. Too often ceremonial turnouts were related to funerals or memorial occasions and sports day had long since been abandoned because of security considerations. So the officers, and more particularly their wives and sweethearts, made the most of the opportunity to celebrate. The urge to 'dress up' was undeniable and local fashion houses, from as far away as Cloughmills, rubbed their hands at the prospect of providing ball gowns for the women folk of a well paid police force.

Niblock and his young apprentice, Det. Constable Glenn Addy, watched the arrivals from his office on the fourth floor, overlooking the entrance hall.

'Some style, eh?' said he, as another couple of revellers stepped into the pool of light at the main door. 'Nice piece of curtain material there.'

Addy laughed. 'Did you see Mrs Richardson a few minutes ago. God, what a cleavage!'

'That's not a cleavage, son,' replied Niblock, 'that's a ravine. Get your head stuck down there and it'll take the Swiss Mountain Rescue Team to get you out.'

'I hope Assistant Chief Constable Richardson doesn't hear you make remarks like that,' chuckled Addy.

'And I hope the Chief can keep his hands off her. Remember last year? He played her like a cello. I thought we were in for a full-blown scandal all over the papers. "Top cop in wife swap" would have been the headline, according to Wheela.'

'I heard he managed to put a muzzle on the press boys on that. He must be good, friend Wheela.'

Niblock's eyes narrowed. 'Baldy little weasel. Take my advice: if you sup with him take a 40-foot spoon with you.'

'I didn't know you disliked him to that extent.'

'It's not a question of like or dislike. I respect him as being good at his job. But his interests aren't always our interests. He would shaft us as quick as wink.'

Looking at his watch, Niblock continued, 'But enough of this spectator sport. It's time to get down and dirty. You can have the first dance with Mrs Richardson.'

The mood at the ball was more upbeat and celebratory than it had been for years, influenced by the general belief that the war was being won, and heightened still further by the triumph of the arrest of the St Lucia. Everyone talked about it. Those not in the know speculated about the background; those few in the know merely waffled.

To the dulcet saxophone-toned music of the Zenith Jazz Octet, dancers swirled round the floor, watched from the peripheral tables by those catching their breath or sipping their drinks. Mrs Richardson was outshone by only one other wife, a much younger woman it had to be said, who , in conformity with that year's fashion imperative, dazzled in a long, multi-frilled dress in pink, à *la Sevilliana,* which would have delighted Danny LaRue.

One of the spectators taking in this scene – and he would remain a spectator all evening – was Bill Austin, reflective rather than festive, as he peered at the proceedings through his thick glasses. As a non-participant at such events, which he attended only out of a sense of organisational duty, he was used to being teased by Ben Niblock, who now sidled up to him.

'Well, Bill, what do you think of Mrs Richardson's outfit?'

Austin appeared to reflect seriously on the question, before replying,

'A beautiful woman without discretion is like a jewel in a pig's snout.'

'Sorry I asked. Can I get you a drink?'

Austin rose to the provocation. 'Ben, you know very well I don't drink.'

'I know, because you've told me often enough, that in your lifetime you haven't yet had a drink, but there's always the first time.'

'My first drink, in your sense, will be a chalice of wine at the marriage supper of the Lamb,' replied Austin, looking upwards to the ceiling, from which, unpromisingly, dangled paper Chinese lanterns, alternating with miniature plastic Christmas trees.

Niblock pulled a chastened face.

'Well in the meantime, I think I'll have another one myself, I feel like celebrating tonight. Don't you?'

The RUC officers were not the only ones to celebrate that night. When the last edition of *Le Soir* came out in Brussels, it contained a quite detailed account of the St Lucia's seizure. Emile Verhagen smiled a contented smile. Reaching for the 'phone, he dialled a UK number. There was no reply but the call went on to the 'ansa-phone' recording.

'Good evening. Just to remind you that VAT is now payable on your purchase. You have the numbers. And if you need more goods, don't hesitate to contact me at any time. It's been a pleasure doing business with you. Bye bye.'

As he hung up he muttered, 'A pleasure indeed,' and poured himself a generous cognac.

Chapter 29

Helicopters were no novelty in the skies above South Armagh. Indeed the security forces' headquarters there, originally housed in the reinforced RUC station in Crossmaglen, incongruously situated cheek-by-jowl with the local chemist's, were supplied exclusively by choppers. The nearby Gaelic Athletic Association football pitch – controversially requisitioned for the purpose – served as their landing strip. So many police and army vehicles had in the past been ambushed close to the fiercely nationalist and republican town, that even routine patrols sent out from the base used helicopters to get out of, and back into, the town, as they did their best to maintain a security presence in what the newspapers called 'the Bad Lands of South Armagh'. General Chesham had an ever gloomier view of the place: whilst he referred to the area around Armagh City and Craigavon as 'Armagh North', he dubbed the south of the county 'Armagh-Geddon.'

And it was true that, along with East Tyrone, this area contained the greatest numbers of Republican die-in-the-ditch hardliners, many of whom regarded Bunny's Bodenstown speech with the gravest of reservations. Those areas had provided the IRA with some of the organisation's very best ASUs, in terms of their daring, competence and ruthlessness. They had basked in the admiration of the wider Republican family, who looked on their 'hard men' as the epitome of what an Irish freedom fighter should be. But now, their uncompromising devotion to the 'armed struggle' was somewhat of a potential embarrassment to a growing majority of the overall leadership. However, their continuing existence as a sort of kamikasi strike force, ready to be deployed with maximum effect, was still a valuable asset, to be used sparingly, 'in the right circumstances', as Bunny would say to those close to him.

The helicopter swung low over the town, on an unusual trajectory designed to draw attention to its flight path, then veered in a north-easterly direction, still at low altitude. The fact that it did not follow the usual flight path in and out of the base meant that there was no real threat from mortar or RPG fire, so it could be as visible as the pilot chose. He was under orders to be seen as much as possible, so that the lifting of McGiolla would be public knowledge.

McGiolla was, of course, well known in the town's Republican circles and in the community at large. He had briefly been interned, which established his credentials, and he always appeared at Sinn Fein public events, such as protest marches, commemorations, parades and so on. It was assumed – rightly – that he had a special role to play in 'the struggle', which kept him away from ASUs and their risk of being captured or wounded. Some even guessed that his army past was being used in the service of *their* army, the Provisional Irish Republican Army, but not many questions were openly asked about him in the locality. It was safer that way.

A last minute check with VELLUM had confirmed that McGiolla's bugged vehicle, a rather battered diesel 4 x 4, had not moved from the vicinity of his small farm. He was, in fact, less than a hundred metres from the whitewashed house, in a field, inspecting his store cattle. He watched the touchdown with equanimity: he had been 'detained for questioning' too often to be fazed by the procedures; and as for incriminating material in his house – he supposed the police and army would have a search warrant – he would enjoy the fruitlessness of their efforts, as all his 'stuff', such as details of arms purchases, arms dumps, deployment etc. were in papers he kept in the attic of his ancient aunt's, in town.

'Remember,' said HSB with emphasis, 'the important thing from our point of view is that an interrogation takes place. Other outcomes might be a bonus, but that is unlikely.

But your work has to look normal to friend McG.' He was preparing Niblock and Austin for their encounter with McGiolla, at present on board the helicopter en route to the Castlereagh Holding Centre, where he was being brought, instead of Geogh Barracks in Armagh, for the convenience of HSB, who was playing this one so close to his chest that even his regional deputy was not 'in' on the details.

They were joined by Granville, who would sit in with HSB in the observation room, in order to follow the interrogation next door.

'He may well give us the usual "I am saying nothing",, which would not be a tragedy, but we will still, in that case, have to spin things out for say a few hours, maybe even days if we're lucky, in order to be credible in his eyes.'

'Isn't that the most likely result?' said Austin, 'The real hardliners have clammed up successfully for quite some time. As I'd do in their shoes. "A man who guards his mouth and his tongue keeps his soul from troubles."'b

'How very wise,' laughed HSB, 'Who said that? Friend Stiletto?'

'No, it was the wisest man who ever lived: King Solomon himself.'

'I'm not so sure I'd take lessons in wisdom from a guy with three thousand wives, or whatever the number was. But I take your point about the senior Provos being better prepared nowadays to resist interrogation, unless they're looking for a way out, and / or for serious dosh.'

'It's only the volunteer amateurs we can get going with nowadays,' said Austin. 'Mind you, we do hear a lot of evil things from them.'

'I think we might have more of a reaction from McG,' replied HSB. 'He'll be pretty confident about his Brussels trip, but he'll want to sound us out about how much we know. Besides, he's an arrogant bastard, who thinks he can play cat and mouse with us.'

'*Fáilte, cara Tomas, fáilte go Caisleanreagh*,' said Niblock with a grin, as McGiolla was shown into the interrogation room.

'Welcome, but is it "*go Caisleanreagh*" or is it "*na*"?– the prepositions in Irish always fox me.'

'You can go and fuck yourself,' growled McGiolla.

'Now that's not very friendly, Tomas. And here's me trying to learn Irish – for all our futures, together.'

'Your future, you Orange bastard, will be up against a wall.'

Niblock, well satisfied that he had provoked his quarry out of careful passivity, moved straight to business. 'We'd very much like to hear what you were doing, and where, between the 17th and the 23rd of last month, inclusive. Crossmaglen and even Tullyhanna felt bereft at your absence.'

'I was enjoying myself.'

Austin intervened. 'Now, Tomas, I think it was Wilde who said everything truly enjoyable is either illegal, immoral or fattening. Let's leave morality and nutritional values out of it. What about illegal?'

'No, and you have no right to harass me on my movements. That's an abuse of my human rights.'

'A wee birdie told me,' said Niblock, 'that you were out of the jurisdiction during that period.'

'That's not yet a crime, even in this police state.'

'True, but withholding information is. If – I mean when – I find out the truth we can come back to you on that … In the meantime we can hold you until Saturday to see if your co-operative spirit revives in the meantime.'

'You can't hold me for that.'

'Oh yes, we can,' said Austin, in pantomime fashion.

McGiolla put his hand to his forehead. So they knew he had been away. Probably no more than that. Better to shut the game down as early as possible.

'Since when has going to the races been a crime?' he said.

'Oh, the geegees? And where – Punchestown, the Curragh?'

'No. France, Longchamps.'

'Longchamps, no less. Wow! With your Louis Vuitton suitcases no doubt. And I take it you can prove that?'

'Yes, I flew from Dublin and stayed with friends outside Paris. The boarding passes are possibly at home if your goons haven't lifted them. But anyway, Air France should have a record. And as for my friends, they work at the racecourse. Francis Murphy and Paul Wheatfield. I can give you their addresses if I can have my address book.'

'Now there's something you don't see every day,' said Niblock, 'a terrorist with an address book. No doubt with the details of the members of the Army Council. A likely story. But don't worry, we'll have your racing friends checked out.'

'And you can stay here while we do so,' added Austin. 'That will give you time to reflect on your past deeds. You could help us – and yourself – so much if you made a clean breast of things. It's never too late to repent.'

'We could help you get out of your dangerous lifestyle. See you were protected. Help you financially,' said Niblock, more out of habit than with any expectation of success.

'Fuck off!'

Both sides lapsed into a sullen boredom: McGiolla now determined not to utter another word and wondering how long they would hold him, as he was now convinced they had nothing specific on him; his interrogators wondering how long they could credibly spin out this non-interrogation.

The next day, early in the morning, Granville rang from his office on his secure 'Goliath' telephone and asked for Niblock.

'Anything new?'

'No. He's back in his shell.'

'I think the time has come to return dear Tomas to the wild. Make sure every last parishioner in and around the 'glen' see him delivered.'

'OK, understood. But hold on a minute. I'm getting an urgent report on the other line...this is interesting. About South Armagh. I'll ring you back when I get a clear picture.'

Gransha Farm, Tullycreevy, South Armagh was the scene of two helicopter visitations that day. Firstly, a police chopper, which had been criss-crossing the fields nearby, came to hover, at only ten metres above the lane leading up to the farm, about one hundred metres from the house. On board was a crew of three: the pilot, an observer/lookout and a sergeant, who operated the 'Goodlight' detector equipment recently acquired by the RUC from an Israeli provider. The advance represented by the 'Goodlight MR 5' machine over its predecessors was that it combined an indicator of recently disturbed earth with a remote metal detection capability. The lenses of two cameras, like the barrels of a cannon on a galleon, protruded beneath the middle of the helicopter. Inside, the operator could monitor two display screens, each projecting a coloured image of the area covered by the camera. If there was no obvious innocent explanation for a change of colour there was frequently the suspicion that something was amiss. The operator could also fuse the two images on to a larger monitor screen. And where there was a sizeable overlap between them, that suspicion would harden into near certainty.

'Bingo!' said the sergeant excitedly, 'I think we've struck gold.' His companion checked his GPS reading against the co-ordinates on an Ordnance Survey map of the area folded on his knee and handed the pilot a scribbled note, on the basis of which he radioed a coded message to his base.

A second helicopter, this time an army Wessex, containing a patrol of soldiers, arrived within minutes, like the Fifth Cavalry, from the 'fort' at Crossmaglen close by,. As it arrived, the police chopper flew off in a southerly direction. The Wessex came in low over the designated area, but as the ground on both sides of the farm lane rose up in uneven mounds, the pilot did not attempt to land there. Instead, he swung round behind the house and carefully landed in an open field. Immediately the patrol sprang out, rifles in their hands, and fanned out in a well-rehearsed movement as they approached the farmyard through a gap between two outhouses, moving swiftly in a semi-crouched position. In the farm close stood an elderly man and as the patrol entered the yard a younger man emerged from the house. Both put their hands up. Though the lieutenant did not recall the fact at that moment, the older man's photograph had featured for some time on the 'villains' mug shot gallery' which, behind a curtain, was attached to the wall of the Humintel room back at the 'fort'. He was Barney Keefe, a tall, raggedly-dressed man, with all the habits and social graces of a grizzly bear. As regards politics and 'the situation' a baddie, for sure.

'Who else is here?' said the patrol leader, as his men adopted the three hundred and sixty degree defensive formation.

'Just my visitor, my neighbour from over there.' He pointed in a northerly direction. 'Just what the hell do you want, comin' in with all that racket, scarin' the shit outta my cattle. I'm goin' to complain to Armagh.'

'And no doubt claim compensation. I'll leave you the application form ...when we've finished.'

Three squaddies moved cautiously into the house and emerged after a few minutes, giving a thumbs-up sign. In the helicopter the radio crackled. 'New order: secure all approaches to premises. Await further orders. Over.'

'Goodlight' had trebled the discovery rate for arms dumps within six weeks of its introduction and it remained one of the security forces best kept secrets. It served two useful purposes for the RUC: firstly, it helped detect any arms cache in open country, so that only arms and explosives hidden in a place which did not contain soil, such as the bottom of a silage silo, were sheltered from its searching vision; secondly, once a cache was suspected, one of the local 'evil persons', as Austin quaintly called them – that is to say a conveniently based individual who featured in the PANORAMA database – could be implicated in a later 'discovery', thus causing 'useful disarray in the ranks of the wicked'.

Granville now went to see for himself such a ploy put into practice. He sat in the back of a car with blacked out windows, following the RUC squad car which was taking McGiolla back to 'the wild'. In front of it drove an army Land Rover, in which rode six heavily armed soldiers.

When they reached the farmyard at Tullcreevy, McGiolla was brought out of the car and, flanked by two SB men, was brought down the lane on foot. Granville's car slowly followed them. His eyes were on the house and, to his great satisfaction, he saw three faces at the window of the front room of the farmhouse. If the occupants knew McGiolla – and the chances were heavily in favour of that in the tightly knit local community – they could not have failed to recognise him at that distance in good light.

With perfect timing, a giant army JCB digger arrived along the narrow road in front of the farm. McGiolla's escorts stopped him gently in the laneway beside the mound which was to be excavated. He showed neither surprise nor apprehension. The JCB had trouble swinging into the narrow lane, but after a dozen turns the driver managed to bring the vehicle into position and immediately manoeuvred it at right angles to the hedge which divided lane from field. Then, like a hungry dinosaur, the machine began to demolish the hedge and to break into the earth in the rising ground behind it. The scoop of the digger deposited the excavated soil to the right of the 'target' area and oscillated to and fro between the ever widening hole and the heap of spoil a few metres to the right of it. Within minutes the monster's probing scoop hit wooden planks which were the protective casing of the arms cache.

In the event, the 'find' was of considerable military significance – four AK-47s, a small amount of explosives, but, more importantly, a Soviet-made Dushka heavy machine gun. But the real value of the operation was the brief announcement, written by Wheeler, put out via the RUC's information office that night, and carried, unedited, by the BBC: 'Acting on local information, the security forces have made a significant arms find on a farm at Tullycreevy, in South Armagh.'

In St Oswald's, Granville switched off his bedside radio and smiled to himself. He hadn't had a G and T, or even a

194

Gauloise, all day. He turned up the volume on his hi-fi system and settled back to savour a Chopin nocturne.

Chapter 30

At three o'clock in the morning all was quiet in the so-called
military wing of the Musgrave Park Hospital, in the southern
Belfast suburb of Balmoral. That wing housed two very
different – and yet similar – categories of patients: seriously
wounded soldiers and some policemen, suffering from life-
threatening bullet wounds and blast injuries from bomb and
mortar attacks; and a small number of Republican prisoners,
under arrest and treated for their injuries until they were well
enough to be discharged from hospital and then to be charged
with their crimes before the courts. Security was provided by
units of the Military Police and by the RUC (mostly Reserve
Officers). The security goals were to protect the one from
outside attack and to ensure that the other would remain in
custody. 'Indoor baddies in; outdoor baddies out' was the
policy slogan.

The Republican wounded prisoners were accommodated
in a separate unit, accessed by a single corridor, running north
to south, which was blocked off by a security door guarded by
two policemen. At the northern end of the corridor, twenty
yards beyond the security door, was another long passage,
leading to the wards in which lay the wounded soldiers. It was
similarly approached via two military police posts.

Sean Byrne detached himself from his monitoring
equipment and, slipping out of bed in his single room, he
listened at the door. The night nurse had just left him sleeping,
as she thought, and he heard the slap, slap of her trainers on
the corridor floor, then the sounds of the security door
opening. But not closing. The routine breach of security was
running to schedule. Byrne had built up a knowledge of the
usual movements of his nocturnal carers and gaolers. In the

middle of the night the ward office outside his door was closed down and the nurses would check on him every half hour, coming from the military wing corridor to do so. *A second-class system for us even in here, he chuckled to himself.* The nurse was supposed to open the security door by both PIN pad and heavy key, and to secure it each time she went through. Over-security is as dangerous as inadequate security: the procedure was too cumbersome and in that middle-of-the-night tiredness which comes upon even the most practiced of shift workers, nearly all the nurses would neglect to lock the security door until the end of their shift, at eight in the morning. Sometimes the attendant policeman would do it for them; sometimes not.

Byrne had three immediate police guards, two at the door closest to him and one in the corridor beyond that, with its ever-open door giving out to a metal fire escape. He knew that when the night nurse passed at three or thereabouts, those policemen took it in turns to go to the main military ward for a cup of tea. He could only hope that tonight two might go together, thus massively improving the odds in his favour. Though he had been in dangerous situations before, this was the first time that thoughts of his own possible, or even probable, death flooded his mind. Yet he was strangely elated. Better seize the one chance he was likely to have than face life imprisonment.

He returned to his locker and from two Kleenex boxes extracted a small Savage Striker .22 bolt action pistol and a specially adapted four-inch long tubular SWR Warlock II silencer. Screwing the two together he went back to the door. His heart thumped in his chest, his mouth was dry as dust and his wounded shoulder hurt as never before. He crept towards the security door, which was ajar. On the other side of it, slumped lazily on a chair, was an RUC Reserve man. So far, so good – only one to contend with then. The policeman stretched, yawned and closed his eyes. Was he going to nod off? Could Byrne tiptoe past him? No, the dangers were too great, for if he were past the policeman who then awoke, the risk of being shot in the back was high – too high.

So Byrne, at a range of barely six feet, killed his man. The pistol jumped with surprising violence in his hand, but the sound was no louder than the closing of a door on an expensive car. The policeman's head jerked sideways and a spurt of blood streamed down his face.

That's for Uncle Bernie.

Byrne moved swiftly to where the two corridors met and, peering round the corner, could not believe his luck. There was no one there. Turning down the third corridor, he half ran to the end of it and pushed the emergency door out into the night. The cold air hit him in the face and he felt his head beginning to swim with the effort of moving. He took his bearings and headed west, looking for the Meadowbank Geriatric Unit, beyond which lay an internal perimeter road and, more importantly, a perimeter fence along which, at regular intervals, were planted pine trees. He searched behind several of them, growing more frustrated by the second, until he found what he was looking for – a small gap in the high fence made by wire cutters; a neat and unobtrusive job by his 'supporters'.

He wriggled through and some fifty yards further on he found himself at the top of a slope on the side of the M1 motorway. Below, on the hard shoulder, sat a small Volkswagen Golf, behind which was positioned a breakdown triangle at a distance of some 40 metres. Traffic at that hour was light, but he waited until there was a 'black' interlude in it before half-sliding, half-running down the gentle slope to the car. He fumbled for the ignition key which he knew would be secreted by sticking plaster below the off-side wheel arch, and got into the car. He reached over into the back seat, to a holdall and took out a tracksuit which he pulled on over his hospital- issue pyjamas. The car started first time and he drove off, at speed.

Chapter 31

'Morning Prayers' in the Chief Constable's office was usually a routine affair. Twenty minutes in which the various strands of policing could be reviewed by the Chief and his Belfast-based Assistant Chief Constables, who could each bring a member of staff for administrative backup. A low-key ritual before the real business of the day commenced. Today was different.

'What the hell went wrong at Musgrave?' roared the CC. 'One of our biggest fish, all packaged for us, in bandages and tubes, allowed to get hold of a firearm, shoot the guard and apparently stroll off to a waiting car. We're a bloody laughing stock.'

'There is a massive manhunt under way, though the trail is very cold at the moment; I've set up an inquiry right away,' said a flustered Assistant C C McMinn, 'and we already have a picture of at least some of the things that happened.'

'And?'

'There was certainly a breach in security through the non-observance of the control procedures.'

'I'll say there was,' snarled the Chief.

'According to the two other officers on duty there, they had both gone to investigate a suspicious noise outside Corridor B of the Military Wing – here, you can understand it better if you look at this plan of the layout.'

He spread a neat architect's plan on the table.

'When one of them got back, only a few minutes later, to Control Point A – here – he found Reserve Constable Robinson slumped on the floor, shot through the front of the face. And of course, Byrne gone.'

'And the weapon?'

'We won't know until the pathologist and the forensic and ballistic boys have compared notes. But it's almost certainly a small pistol, which must have been silenced, otherwise a shot would have been heard at that time of night.'

'Yes, but how the blazes did he get hold of a weapon? I thought all the nurses on the Military Wing at Musgrave were Vestal Virgins or something, way above suspicion. The doctors, ditto.'

McMinn shifted uncomfortably. 'There must have been a leak there, it stands to reason. Our people will review all the security profiles of every single person who could possibly have had access to Byrne.'

'What about the visitors we do know about?'

'None. He wasn't allowed any.'

'Not a single one, like his dear old mum?'

'None, only his priest, on two occasions.'

Silence fell on the group for a moment: this was delicate ground.

'Are we sure about him?' asked the Chief quietly.

'Yes, the log book shows that he was given a grade A1 search both going in and coming out on both occasions. There is even a note in the log to say that he objected to the searches. Thought he was exempted as a member of the clergy.'

The Chief Constable sighed and tapped his biro on the pad in front of him.

HSB intervened: 'Presumably we know who this priest is, he must have applied for admission. Why did we grant it?'

'Well, you know, these religious points are very sensitive. If we turn down a request for permission to administer the last rites, or to say Mass, we'd be portrayed as the rapists of Mother Teresa.'

'The Eucharist – that's it,' cried McAteer, the HSB's assistant and the only Roman Catholic in the room. 'He's smuggled the shooter in his pyx.'

Baffled looks all round.

'Picks, as in shovels?' queried the C.C.

'No, p – y – x, it's the container priests sometimes carry the sacraments in, hung round their necks in a pouch.'

'Do we pull this priest in?' asked ACC McMinn.

'Not really worth it just yet,' said the C.C. 'There'd be no "forensic" on him. He'd deny everything we put to him and the Church would kick up a stink about "harassment". But put a shadow on his movements. He could lead us to some interesting parishioners.'

'Meantime, Chief,' said McMinn, plaintively, 'what is McGuigan to tell the press corps at the eleven o'clock briefing?'

'How about: "We are actively pursuing several lines of inquiry", or perhaps, more believably, "Here's my ass. Kick it?" said the Chief, provoking the laughter necessary to relieve the tension.

HSB raised his index finger.

'I can't offer any crumbs of comfort about the Byrne escape, but there is potentially very good news coming out of VELLUM'.

'Do tell us,' said the Chief. 'I need somehow cheering up this morning.'

'I know many of you have been sceptical about our heavy investment in the manpower needed to monitor the movement of "customers" identified as important by PANORAMA. But there are dividends. In the Coalisland area, last Sunday night, no fewer than seven bugged vehicles had a rendezvous at the farm of a high-grade suspect. We assume they weren't there for a *ceilhe.*'

'An ASU?' asked the Chief.

'Probably. Certainly a PIRA occasion. So we can target more precisely now that we have established the link between these individuals. I'll introduce surveillance measures on all of them and try to bug their houses.'

'Have you the capacity to do that?'

'Yes, that is to say at one remove. The army have been very good in offering their "logistical support". They've got some super new listening equipment and the means of deploying it. The GOC is keen to be in on the act.'

'And friend Granville?' asked the Chief, with a smile.

'Probably too early to inform him. Later. That's the general's opinion.'

'I'll bet it is. But this is dangerous. Proceed with care.'

'As always.'

'So where the fuck is he then?' rasped Stiletto.

He was walking alongside McGiolla, in a field in which the latter's store cattle were grazing. Nowadays, even in Cullyhanna, security was only guaranteed in the open air – and even then ...

'I've told you. I've no idea. He just didn't show up at Mick O'Toole's house, as agreed. So how could we take him over the border to the safe one at Lisderg? At nine o'clock I sent the message to Belfast. We thought he must have been taken near the hospital. On the news I heard the police are looking too.'

'That could be a diversionary tactic. They may have turned him.'

'They'd hardly let him shoot one of their own,' replied McGiolla with a laugh.

'True. Though I wouldn't put it past them. But they may have captured him, without announcing it. Just to make us jumpy.'

'I'm not jumpy,' said McGiolla, defensively, 'and I don't know why you have to come down from bloody Belfast to investigate me.'

'Take it easy, it's not an investigation. I mean it's only for information. The top dogs just need to be re-assured that nothing went wrong at this end.'

'Well it didn't. Look at it from my point of view: Belfast didn't deliver their man. And that's that.'

'Had Byrne any contacts down here?'

Stiletto made "down here" sound like Alabama.

'None that I know of. I thought he was the complete "townie". And I hear on the radio that a burnt out car has been found near Larne. Was that ours? I mean a "borrowed" one? If so, yer man may have been on the ferry to Scotland. Doesn't it look that way, or is that too obvious?'

'I don't know about the car yet. If he has gone to Scotland, without Brit support, he won't last long. And if he does come back he'll have some answering to do, I'll tell you.'

The wind sharpened and the two men walked closer to the hedge for cover.

'Let's go in,' said Stiletto, 'I don't like those cattle. The way they look at you.'

McGiolla guffawed. 'There's a helluva lot of people don't like the way *you* look at them.'

Chapter 32

PIRA lost no time in investigating the causes of the St Lucia disaster, which had been a heavy blow to morale and prestige, and a corresponding boost for the security forces. Orders came from the Army Council for Stiletto to 'interview' any suspected informers. Because of the way the whole operation had been handled, from a security point of view, and because the Royal Navy had obviously been acting on precise information relating to a specific vessel, the list of prime suspects was a limited one. It boiled down to four: McGiolla, Cassidy, Hogan, the IRA sympathiser in the customs office in the port of Dublin, and Verhagen, the Belgian arms dealer.

Hogan had not been told in advance on which vessel the arms were to arrive. He only knew the date and would be informed of the ship's details on the day. The dispersal team waiting for his tip-off and help in getting to the lethal cargo was to have been kept in the dark about the ship's identity until the day of arrival. It was theoretically possible that Hogan could have had access to information relating to expected arrivals in the port and to have made an educated guess as to which one the goods were on, but that was a long shot.

Hogan had several times acted as 'facilitator' for a cell in Dublin. He was very security conscious and content to be a small cog in a big machine. Furthermore, as he sat flanked by the OC of two Dublin-based PIRA cells, he stood up well to the habitually hostile questioning of Stiletto, who interviewed him in the back downstairs room of a small terraced house in the shadow of Dublin's Croke Park sporting stadium.

'Look, I know you have your job to do – and good luck with it. But if you think I had anything to do with it and this feckin' shipload, you're barking up the wrong tree,' he said with real anger in his voice.

'I've acted on your behalf in the docks for twelve years now and if you suddenly think I might not be trustworthy, you can go jump in the Liffey.'

'Take it easy,' said Stiletto, soothingly, 'nobody's accusing you of anything. We just need to get to the bottom of the matter – who knew, and who did what, when. You've no suspicions yourself?'

'None whatsoever,' came the instant reply, 'none that is that I could put facts to. The leak, I feel, must have been in the North. Nobody down here was really in the loop.' The other two Dubliners nodded in agreement and in encouragement of Hogan.

'Why don't you look at the other end of the chain,' said the elder of the two, 'are you sure of your supplier?'

That was an awkward one for Stiletto. Verhagen was to all intents and purposes out of reach and control. But he had benefited several times in the past from IRA shipments and in the normal course of events, thought Stiletto, he could hope for more orders in the future. Why would he wish to betray them? That didn't make sense.

Except, of course, that Verhagen had made the calculation that the military phase of PIRA's war was approaching its end, so, despite its impressive size, this order was more than likely the last one which would come his way. Orders for another arms shipment were not a good bet. This was more the moment to cuddle up to the intelligence community. He knew that the security authorities in Belgium, the UK and France had a lot of 'material' on him as regards both the Balkans and the Middle East and the deal he had been offered, namely to 'co-operate' in return for a certain administrative amnesia as regards his recent past, was simply too good to refuse.

For Stiletto, that left the choice as one between McGiolla and Cassidy. In his mind it simply had to be one or the other. Both had impeccable credentials as long-term Republican activists. This was not a case of some eighteen year old Volunteer either taking fright when apprehended by the police, or succumbing to greed when offered the 'thirty pieces of silver' to inform. Neither suspect betrayed the slightest ambiguity in their passionate denials of any sort of involvement with the fatal leak. But there was a difference in the circumstances: McGiolla had been at Castlereagh for a long interrogation; Cassidy had not. Furthermore, there seemed to be a lot of credibility attached to the South Armagh rumours that McGiolla had been seen at Tullycreevy, in the company of police and soldiers the day of the arms find there. McGiolla had been summoned to a house in Dungannon to be de-briefed by Stiletto personally. His story was that he had gone through a long interrogation at Castlereagh but had refused to say anything. Stiletto waited for him to mention his visit to Tullycreevy. He did not, preferring to keep his story as simple as possible. Such reticence was instinctive for a Provo, whoever the interrogator might be. It was a bad mistake on McGiolla's part; it was a bad sign from Stiletto's point of view.

Stiletto knew that he would come under increasing pressure from the Army Council to make his report, yet he hesitated over a weekend to do so. Unusually, he was not free to have either suspect tortured (referred to in the trade as 'interrogated in depth') – they were both too senior for that. Eventually, having received two urgent messages requesting his report 'as soon as possible', he briefly put on paper his analysis, narrowing the field of definitive suspicion to McGiolla and Cassidy. He could not, he reluctantly confessed, easily decide between the two, but pointing out the fact of McGiolla's interrogation by the RUC and the rumours about Tullycreevy, he decided on McGiolla and requested further orders.

The reply which he received was a surprise to him, but not to Granville when he heard the details. Acting on instructions, Stiletto sent a trusted runner to consult the oracle of the Derryman, in order to have Army Council cover. It was a cold winter's day, with a weak sun nonetheless peeping through the grey clouds from time to time. A small group of worshippers stood around outside the Catholic church of St

Mary's on Fanad Drive, in theCreggan, gossiping and greeting one another after twelve o'clock mass. The Derryman stood in the middle of a little sub-group of admirers. He knew all these people, his supporters to a man (and woman), and he was relaxed and even jovial in their presence. That was especially true today, as he was putting in a special appearance with his mother, a daily Mass-goer, whose birthday it was. He exchanged 'how are ye doin?' greetings with all and sundry and waved cheerily to some passers-by who called out to him in friendly fashion from across the street. He was still waving to them when the runner, seizing his opportunity, whispered his password and asked 'What's the answer?' Still smiling and waving, looking into the distance, Butch said, out of the corner of his mouth, 'Stiff 'im.'

It was just before dawn when they came for McGiolla. The front door of the old farmhouse yielded in seconds with a crash, which wakened McGiolla, alone in the house. As he sprang out of bed, instantly wide awake, he cursed himself for leaving his pistol in its hiding place in the old dairy room, instead of taking it to his bedside, as was his wont at night. Three of the intruders quickly overpowered him, pinning his arms behind his back.

'No, no,' he cried, as a fourth man came behind him and tried to push a tampon into his mouth. He managed to shake his head free for long enough to shout, 'A priest!'

'Not for you. Traitor. Bastard.'

His head was forced down towards his knees. He almost got his left arm free, but it was seized again and pinned back.

'Now!' shouted one of them. The fourth man pressed a revolver against the back of McGiolla's head and pulled the trigger. The report was a crisp thud and McGiolla rolled forward on to the floor without the slightest twitch.

Ten minutes later, having carried out a perfunctory 'ransacking' of the farmhouse, the hit squad set out in the two cars they had arrived in, to take the unapproved road some five miles away, which would take them over the border. After two days of 'Rest and Relaxation' – in plain terms drinking in the pubs of Dundalk – they made their separate ways back to Belfast. Mission accomplished.

McGiolla rendered one final, posthumous, service to Republicanism: P.J. O'Neill, the clandestine mouthpiece of the IRA, in a communiqué to all media outlets, condemned 'the cynical murder of this patriot by the security forces.' MPs at Westminster sympathetic to the Republican cause, put down Parliamentary Questions about 'the alleged deployment of SAS troops in the Province' and the 'shoot-to- kill' policy of the security forces; and about the possible collusion between those forces and Loyalist paramilitaries. Even the Irish government expressed deep concern about the death and called, with others, for a thorough, independent inquiry into the circumstances surrounding the violent death of this man.

Four days later Stiletto had one of his regular contact meetings with his army handler, sitting in a car in the car park at Shaw's Bridge, beside the river Lagan. The death of McGiolla, whose large funeral in his native Crossmaglen, with all the usual paramilitary trimmings, had featured prominently on the national and regional news, and was a natural topic of professional conversation. Something in the dark recesses of Stiletto's psyche, where normally a conscience would have resided, prompted him to seek re-assurance, in oblique terms, about McGiolla's guilt.

'I hope to Jasus we got the right man,' he said.

'No doubt about that,' was the immediate and confident reply, 'I hear he let the cat out of the bag when they had him at Castlereagh. Apparently they had something else on him. Maybe that's why he opened up.' This lie was told with the nonchalance of a footballer scything down an opponent in a 'professional foul.' It had to be done for the team's sake. Nothing personal.

Stiletto seemed re-assured.

Then it was back to elementary business, namely the exchange of information about the activities of certain members of ASUs in the Belfast area, against a traditional brown paper envelope containing used banknotes.

Stiletto had the delicatesse not to count them, before tucking the envelope into an inside pocket of his leather jacket.

His information was fed into the PANORAMA database the next morning, in conformity with the inter-agency agreement on intelligence sharing.

Chapter 33

Granville's visits to the Clonard Monastery began to take on a routine. He always arrived before Bunny and Butch. The priest – or was he a monk? – he was always in mufti – who showed him into the first room along the dark corridor which led off the reception room, now greeted him each time as a 'regular'. Parking had been a problem, as well as a security risk in that area, but his welcoming friend had solved that for him, by giving him access to a side courtyard. He had chuckled loudly when telling Granville the code to punch into the keypad in order to lift the barrier: 1690.

'It's the last number anyone would think of in relation to this house,' he said, referring to the Ulster Protestants' fixation with the Battle of the Boyne in that year. Granville's plain clothes Military Police driver was invariably siphoned off and given tea and scones while he waited for his charge.

The cleric now stayed with Granville each time until the others arrived, as though he were a guest to be entertained. He talked easily about Premier League football, the weather or whatever was in that day's news headlines (except items related to the 'the situation'). Today he was full of the busy time the monastery had had, with that year's noventa – a sort of marathon pray –in for which the Clonard Monastery was famous, with Masses following on one another all day long, every hour on the hour. 'Biggest crowds ever,' he said, 'I think the theme of "peace with justice" brought the people out, from all walks of life.'

Granville, in reluctant admiration of Bunny's subliminal propaganda coup which that opinion represented, was about to say 'I'm glad to hear that,' but, suddenly conscious that such a curt reply would be impolite, and not being able to think of anything appropriate, he decided to remain silent. He was saved from embarrassment by the arrival of Bunny and Butch, both of whom greeted him with a loud 'How's about you Jeremy?' and a bear's hug. He answered, somewhat self-consciously, in the Belfast vernacular, 'stickin' out' ('excellent'), which greatly amused the others. The Secret Service was not one in which one got to choose one's friends, or even acquaintances, but an ability to manufacture familiarity was a professional asset.

Jeremy prolonged the small talk by enquiring after the health of Butch's mother.

'Much better, thanks,' he replied. 'It was a scare. We thought a heart attack, but it's only an increased atrial fibrillation, a sort of heart flutter – which she has had for years. There's life in the oul' doll yet.'

When they got down to business, it was to mutual recriminations. Granville expressed his disappointment that IRA attacks on 'non-military targets' had not decreased. 'How can I believe you about political and constitutional matters when you tell me lies – there is no other word for it – about your operations?'

'Listen, Jeremy, we have always told you up front that we may from time to time, under the pressure of events, have to lie to you about operational matters, but in our real negotiations about the end of the conflict, we have always spoken the truth. And we always will.'

'That's a fine point,' said Granville, 'worthy of Ignatius Loyola himself, but I need to know where I am with you, all of the time, otherwise our negotiations will run into the ground.'

'But that can't be one-sided,' countered Bunny. 'Out there, despite our genuine gestures for peace, your lot are stepping up the pressure on us, pursuing our lot by fair means, but mostly foul.'

'Foul?'

'Don't sound like a molested schoolgirl, all innocence. You know what I mean – our sympathisers brought in, in increasing numbers, for alleged "questioning" are being blackmailed by the RUC.'

Bunny put on a stern face and a growly voice, to imitate a policeman, 'Tell us about the big IRA men in your district or we'll tell your missus about you and Mary Moffett.'

'Really?' said Granville, raising his eyebrows exaggeratedly and struggling to keep his face straight at the thought of Bill and Ben the Statements men putting their customers "through the wringer" as the RUC slang had it. 'Surely not!'

'Before we go any further,' said Granville, tapping the table, 'I must tell you very clearly that last week's bomb outrages in GB, which could well have had more victims, are in danger of turning political opinion on our side against any sort of a settlement. You are sabotaging your own strategy.'

'No,' said Butch, with a determined shake of the head.

'GB operations are our banker. You are powerless to stop them – they can be mounted by our best and most secure units. And, as you have just confirmed, they hurt like hell. If you were tempted to backslide from agreements with us, GB operations would be – what's the word? – significant.'

'That brings us to the nub of the matter.' said Granville. 'We have to get down to the outline of the specifics of our agreement.'

'With respect to you and your mandate, Jeremy, our detailed negotiations have to be with the Prime Minister and they have to be known about publicly, in order to carry the necessary weight here in Ireland.'

'Take it easy. There are risks on both sides when you go public. You will not negotiate with the PM in the normal sense. We need – you and I – to come to an agreement, in a pretty advanced level of detail, before things get into the public glare. You can then "top and tail" the agreements with the PM. That way both you and we are covered. And we need to know in advance that agreement over the whole range of items is possible before we embark publicly on the negotiations. In other words, the entire pie has to be precooked confidentially, then merely microwaved politically in public. It's a process. A peace process.'

'A peace with justice process,' said Bunny.

'Let's not complicate things. Everybody understands "peace". Let's leave it at that.'

'So how do you see this "Peace Agreement"?'

'Well, obviously on your side a complete cessation of violence, including disarmament, and a commitment to pursue your political goals – now publicly recognised by HMG as legitimate – by peaceful, democratic means.'

'And what are you offering?'

'A phased release of all IRA acknowledged prisoners, the closure of the Maze prison, and a revisited constitutional convention, to ensure equality between the communities here.'

'I'm very disappointed, Jeremy, because you know, and I know, that what you have said is not fair, by anybody's standards. We haven't been fighting for thirty years just to be able to stop fighting. We want to see profound changes to the Six Counties and, above all, we demand guarantees.'

'Guarantees?'

'Yes. What am I to say to the leader of an ASU when he asks "do you trust the Brits?" It's no use saying " yes" – even if that were true,' he added with a smirk. 'I've got to be able to show proof, not just of bona fides, but of copper bottomed guarantees, as John Major promised the unionists.'

Granville pulled his cigarette case from his pocket, tapped it tentatively, then thought better of it, in view of his surroundings, and put it back in his pocket.

'You see,' said Bunny, 'we have a list of legitimate demands which go far beyond what you have been talking about. You are not Field Marshal Montgomery, receiving the unconditional surrender of the enemy on Luneberg Heath, you know.'

'Of course not,' said Granville, 'but I need to see the detail of what you are talking about, in a document. It needn't be one that is attributable, but we have to …'

'Be bureaucratic' completed Butch, with a grin.

'Don't forget, I work for a bureaucracy, not a …'

'Peace organisation,' completed Butch again. They all laughed.

'Right,' said Bunny. 'You shall have your document, my dear. But here is the first instalment: the immediate release of all our prisoners and an amnesty for those on the run and for past actions, by our members.'

'Hold on a second,' interjected Granville, 'prisoners can't be just let out like that or past crimes swept under the carpet. Even at the end of World War II, it took eighteen to twenty-four months to phase out the prisoners, and there was no generalised pardon covering the past.'

'You're trying to play politics with our POWs' said Bunny angrily. 'They are central to our considerations and if you only knew the details, they are the best "dove" friends you have. So don't knock them. But that's just the start. We are demanding the disbandment of the RUC and the creation of a two-tier police service, with local police working at district level. There must be a withdrawal of troops, not just to barracks, but to GB, where they belong. And we want a reform of the judicial system and the removal of British insignia from court houses and other public buildings. It goes without saying that we need a constitutional settlement which strengthens Sunningdale, so that one community can never again rule over the other. The path to a united Ireland must be clear and unobstructed. And the Irish language must be fostered.'

'The Irish language? You must be joking?'

'It's not just an educational, linguistic matter – it's about putting a cultural identity on an equal footing with the neighbours.'

'That's quite a list you have there,' remarked Granville, 'I noticed you did not say much about disarmament.'

'That's true – for a very good reason. This isn't a surrender, in which a defeated army lays down its arms. It's a negotiated settlement. Obviously, some agreement will have to be devised about our arms not being used again, but you must understand that in Irish political lore the concept of "a pike under the thatch" still has a powerful resonance.'

'I foresee difficulties with that. The world will need to be convinced that the cessation of violence is complete and for keeps. We'll need to work hard on how to express that to the satisfaction of both sides. You have first go in your document.'

The others nodded in agreement.

'And remember,' added Granville, 'we have to sell what we're doing as a process, avoiding, for your purposes, the idea of "victory" or "defeat", but emphasising it is a peace process which is irreversible and that the war is well and truly over. Even before the public meeting with the Prime Minister we need to agree on choreography and timing, so that the wall which exists between us today is seen to be dismantled brick by brick, in an even-handed way. That will gradually lead supporters on both sides to embrace the concept of peace.'

In a back room of Tolan's Bar in a side street off the main Falls Road, Bunny met Stiletto to be briefed about Sean Byrne. Stiletto, head of the disciplinary 'nutter' squad, as the locals called it, had carried out an extensive inquiry, along with Duffy, the Belfast 'security officer' of PIRA into Byrne's mysterious disappearance. The venue for the meeting had been chosen only the day before, and would be used only once, so great had become the paranoia of the 'leadership' about the bugging of their usual haunts. This was a well-founded fear, in the light of the Logistical Support Group's increasing successes. Transmitter bugs smaller than a drawing pin and shielded electronically against the best sweeping devices available to SF/IRA could be inserted into so many places that although the occasional one was spotted, their sheer numbers were overwhelming. Attempts to use such bugs to relay false information to the listeners had usually failed, because if the bug was approached within ten centimetres its transmitter automatically shut down. The growing problem for the security forces was to provide enough listeners and analysts to process the material thus collected.

'Well, any news?' asked Bunny, sipping his sparkling mineral water.

How Stiletto hated teetotallers. So bloody smug and dry in every sense of the word.

'Nothing concrete. Only speculation everywhere, including amongst our own people. Mostly fevered imagination stuff.'

'But why not a shred of hard facts?' asked Bunny, with obvious frustration.

'You and Duffy are supposed to keep us all watertight and now you have come up with damn all, after all this time. It's very unsettling for all levels in the movement.'

'I know it is. But you've got to take into account the exceptional circumstances. It wasn't like your average break-out, say like the mass escape from the Maze. Byrne was alone throughout his escape, so there's nobody else to get a grip of.'

Bunny looked at the other's large frame and steady gaze and could not help imagining what such getting to grips with would entail.

'Well, why the hell was he alone? Who organised that?'

'O'Hare,' said Stiletto with alacrity, glad to have the focus shift to someone else. 'He authorised it as a solo operation, because of the risk factor.'

'What was so different about Byrne?'

'To shoot your way out of a military hospital and drive off down a motorway was thought to be a madcap idea, but it was Byrne's own idea and he insisted he wanted to try it. The chances of success were, let's face it, minimal, so we couldn't risk others being involved. They'd stood to go to clink for fifteen years if things didn't work out. So, O'Hare laid on the shooter, through our friend the priest, and the getaway car and left Byrne to it. And the bugger pulled it off. Fuckin' amazing.'

'Are you sure our guys in South Armagh or Dundalk aren't hiding anything?'

'Sure I'm sure. He never showed up there. If he had, there would be bound to be reports, or at least rumours, about that. But no, nothing from that quarter at all. '

Stiletto allowed himself a pause, as he quaffed his Guinness for the first time.

'I know this sounds far-fetched, but we have to think of all possibilities,' resumed Bunny. 'What are the chances the Brits have him? Could they have turned him, like a few bastards you and I can think of, with money, a new life and all that shit?'

'No chance whatsoever. They were very much shat upon by the whole story, so to put Byrne on trial for murder, especially of a policeman, would in their eyes be sweet revenge.'

'Any problems with missing money?'

'None. He did not have access to any dough. Apart from expenses and his bounties for knocking off Brits and Rozzers. There was no kitty for him to make off with.'

'How about women?'

'Lots of them. Sean put himself about quite a bit. He's been round more curves than a Monte Carlo Rally. But I couldn't get any news of a special favourite. He just shagged whatever was available at any one time. I don't think he's in the arms of some dolly bird. He was never out of Belfast for any length of time and there is no local lovely missing from her usual whereabouts.'

'Could he have topped himself, in some remote location, like a forest?'

'Don't think so. He's not the type. I think a guy who shoots his way out of custody doesn't suddenly go soft in the head.'

'An accident then?'

'The car was found burnt out near Larne, but he wasn't in it. And no unexplained corpse has shown up, like after a hit-and-run or a drowning.'

'I've always thought the Larne location was a red herring, to make us all think he'd taken the ferry to Stranraer,' mused Bunny.

'Too obvious. But let's suppose he did. It would be very difficult for him to disappear in Britain, without a lot of help from others. Has he relatives there, or supporters of ours who might mistakenly protect him?'

'We've checked that out. Didn't lead anywhere. No known relatives or contacts. And he never had anything to do with the England Department.'

'Jazus, what a Houdini! Let's assume the worst: the Brits get him. What could they get out of him by way of info?'

'I've been concentrating on that, with Duffy. The answer is "not much". The training camps he knew at first hand down south haven't been used for years. He could, of course, tell them about sniper techniques – but those are based on British Army manuals. Therefore, no big deal there. He knows next to nothing about our structures or who's who. He only knows some Volunteers, and Duffy himself, of course. But then Duffy isn't exactly a secret to the enemy and since he gave up active personal participation in his crazy three-times-a-day operations, the Brits are unlikely to pin anything on him on the basis of what Byrne might tell them.'

'So,' sighed Bunny, 'we're no further on. It's a deep fucking mystery, so it is. We scored a PR goal with the escape, but I am still a bit nervous about not knowing what happened – in case the mystery jumps up and bites us in the arse one day.'

Chapter 34

Before the 'troubles' Drumphoe had been a medium-sized, relatively prosperous market town, serving the surrounding farmlands by providing the usual range of services, such as a variety of shops, schools, churches and even a cinema. It had an almost equally divided nationalist–unionist population, the sort of ratio most likely to encourage extremism, as the two sides squared up to one another in a balance of prejudice and grievance. The IRA was strong in the locality; as against that, the town and its hinterland provided a large number of UDR and RUC Reserve personnel, larger, proportionally, than the Northern Ireland average. Several local members of the security forces had been assassinated in horrific circumstances: an off-duty policeman shot in the back as he sat on his brother's tractor, ploughing an isolated field; a UDR volunteer, a part-time school bus driver, had been killed in front of a class of school children he was picking up at the school gates in the afternoon. On the other hand, the nationalist community complained of discrimination in the job market and of harassment, through frequent and roughly handled body searches, the disruption of very frequent vehicle checkpoints and, overall, the occasional oppressive police and army presence in and around the town.

Drumphoe had suffered two major explosions, which destroyed several Protestant-owned businesses in the main street. Only some of these had been rebuilt, leaving several premises either as derelict shells, or boarded up, waiting for peace and business confidence to be restored. Halfway along the main street there ran off at almost right angles the second most important in the town, Sperrin Street. Barely fifty metres along it stood the solid building of the Ulster Bank, one of only three banks in the town, if one discounted the rash of new building society premises.

General Chesham stood at a table in his office at Thiepval Barracks, Lisburn, poring over an enlarged street plan of Drumphoe. He was being briefed by a senior military Intelligence Officer, Eric Hammond and by Major Philip Fitzwilliam, the operational head of the SAS in Northern Ireland.

'RUC SB are pretty sure that an ASU, with local support, is planning to hit this bank some time in the near future,' said Hammond, producing photographs from his briefcase.

'Why so sure?'

'Because there have been several meetings between the top people recently in a known activist's house. Our bugs in this house have not been as efficient as we would like – nothing is ever perfect – but we have picked up 'bank' as a frequently used key word. The police tell us that two of the people identified by VELLUM and PANORAMA have been seen near the Ulster Bank on at least three occasions, behaving in a way which would suggest that they were "casing the joint".'

Chesham picked up the photograph again and peered at it, narrowing his eyes, then, tapping the street plan with his index finger, said, 'The building marked "A" you propose as an observation point and hide, overlooks the back of the bank building. Is that practical, or is that the best we can get?'

'In fact it's ideal,' interjected Hammond. 'Building "A" is empty and we can get a team in there without too much difficulty. And they should be able to remain undetected. Most importantly, it is the rear of the bank which will be the business end of the operation.'

'How come?'

Major Fitzwilliam took up the running. 'You see, sir, recent security measures introduced in most banks make it harder than ever for a conventional ambush or "hold-up" type bank raid. The delivery vans now have armed escorts, which make an ambush a risky business from the terrorist's point of view. And within the bank's premises, the strong room is time locked, so no joy there. The weak spot is the back room, behind the vault. It is not alarm-wired.'

'Why should it be worth penetrating?'

'It's used for the counting and recording of monies placed in the night safe, which is used by customers to place their day's takings in. That happens every morning. Anything between one hundred and two hundred thousand pounds can be processed in that way.'

The GOC reflected for a moment.

'But surely the risk to our robber is great, going through the bank to get to the back room. Every panic button in the place would be pressed. And I assume that standing orders for this counting house must include an instruction to lock the door during the operation.'

'That's true,' said Hammond, 'but we think the ASU will prepare a way into the back room, by sawing the iron bars on the window in advance, allowing them to swiftly break in on the day. That's what we would do in their shoes. The great advantage from our point of view is that we can strike with full surprise. Another Loughall.'

'Another Loughall, maybe,' reflected Chesham, 'but remember the controversy about that one. We killed the baddies, right outside the police station, but there was all hell to pay from the tender hearts brigade. We'll have to be careful.'

'Who's going to involve MI5 in the detailed planning?' asked Hammond, perhaps innocently. There was an awkward silence. Chesham smiled a thin smile. 'Oh, I don't think any of us needs to do that just now. Do you? On the day, our patrol could come upon a bank robbery and act accordingly.'

'But with SAS involvement is that credible? I mean who is going to believe that "they just happened to be in the neighbourhood"?'

'They were led there by RUC Special Branch in an emergency situation,' suggested Fitzwilliam.

'OK,' said the GOC, crisply, 'let's run with it. I'll take the flack afterwards if necessary, and there will probably be flack, whether the operation is a success or failure.'

As usual, Granville arrived on time and was therefore first for the next Clonard meeting. It was bitterly cold, with sleet being driven by an easterly wind that seemed to be coming directly from the Russian Steppes. The Falls Road, miserable enough at the best of times, was dreary and bleak. To add to the midwinter discomfort, he had caught a severe head cold, which blocked his sinuses and made his eyes stream. The gloom of the echoing monastery added to his feeling of misery. And yet his mission with the IRA seemed to be flourishing, as one contentious issue after the other had been identified and calmly examined, instead of the traditional uncompromising rantings of Republican representatives.

The man who greeted him, whom he had christened to himself as 'the cheerful monk', showed him into yet another sparsely furnished room down the familiar corridor.

'That's a bad dose you've got there,' he said, 'would you like a wee hot toddy to make you feel better? I'll have it made for you in no time.'

'Thanks, I could do with that.'

Having whiskey forced upon me is obviously one of the hazards of the job. Still, medicinal purposes, as Mother used to say ...

A quarter of an hour later, which in the under-heated monastery seemed a great deal longer, despite the burning comfort of the bumper toddy, Bunny and Butch arrived, full of effusive greetings and without apology. When they were all seated at the table, Bunny was the first to move on from meteorological small talk.

'Well, where are we now? Have you an invitation for us to a televised meeting with the Prime Minister in Downing Street, to kick off publicly the negotiations we have already concluded?'

'Not so fast,' replied Granville, 'there are still a few i's to dot and t's to cross before we go public. For example, what can be said about the extent of the amnesty – I mean, in principle it's covering the on-the-runs, as you have requested, but we have to work out the details of how that will work in practice. Not to mention disarmament. Your so-called assurances about 'putting beyond use' are nowhere near enough. We will need proof of arms laid down.'

Bunny sighed. 'You Brits don't seem to be able to put yourselves in our shoes. We have a debt to our own history, to our traditions, and to our martyrs. If we can't pay that debt in the eyes of our community, any agreement we would enter into with you would not be worth a wet Woodbine.'

'Talk me through it, I'll be your student.'

'For starters, you have accepted that the end of the war should lead quickly to the release of all political prisoners. Right?'

'OK.'

'For us that must cover the on-the-runs, who are held in great respect by our people. And for us, it's logical, and indeed necessary, to wipe the slate clean for those on the run, as well as letting the POWs out – I know you don't like the term POW, but it is *our* description. And I can tell you this: those two categories will be overwhelmingly in favour of the peace process. We greatly strengthen the chances of success for all of us if we can carry them with us.'

'HMG will concede that, but you must remember we, too, have a public which needs to be satisfied as much as possible that what we are doing is both equitable and free from danger. The compromise, as I see it, is that the concessions for you can't happen all at once, but should be spread out over a period of, let's say two years, during which time you will demonstrate your good faith by closing down all military activity. That will re-assure *our* public.'

'Interesting,' said Butch with a smile, 'We can't go nap on that today, but there is, I believe, a basis for agreement there.' He did not look for support from Bunny, but the latter nevertheless nodded vigorously in agreement.

'Now for what you call "disarmament",' said Bunny, 'As we said before, we are not talking here of a defeated Germany after the First or Second World War. We haven't lost. Both you and we seek peace on the basis of equality. I would remind you of the traditional "pike under the thatch". It's not just a deep-rooted tradition, we need to be able to keep some arms in case we need them at some point in the future.' 'Yes,' chimed in Butch, 'we don't want another 1969 on our hands, with Loyalist gangs burning down streets of houses.'

'With respect,' said Granville, 'we can understand your so-called tradition, but we cannot be bound by it. The arms, explosives and ammunition will have to go – and in a visible and verifiable way.'

'Then we're stuck,' said Bunny. 'It will be an unforgivable tragedy if the peace process should founder on this issue.'

'Again, I think the process can survive with another compromise, by phasing action on this point. First, you declare that the arms will be given up and, given the logistical problems, that action will be spread over two years. That period can be linked to *our* action on the release of prisoners and your on-the-runs etc. Balanced, fair, careful and transparent.'

'I'm glad to see you are already drafting the Secretary of State's speech for him,' teased Bunny. 'Perhaps we could help improve it for you ...But we'll have to think about your proposal. It's a very difficult one with our community. Any feeling that our leadership is being suckered and it's goodbye the agreement – not to mention, goodbye, us. You must understand, failure for you means a career disappointment – maybe not even that; but for us it would mean curtains.'

Granville smiled and changed the subject slightly, 'I see you have one fewer possible opponents to worry about. In South Armagh that is. '

Butch could not suppress a chuckle as he replied, 'We now know McGiolla was a traitor. It's a bad thing to be thought of as a traitor. That's my point.'

'As a matter of interest,' said Granville nonchalantly, 'why did you try to put the blame on to the security forces?'

'At first, we didn't know who had done it. So it might well have been the SAS. We later learned he had betrayed his trust, so punishment was inevitable and was carried out by his peers locally. We stuck with the ongoing story which had been put out in good faith, in order not to increase the distress to his family, who have served the cause in South Armagh for generations.'

Butch delivered this explanation at the speed of a newsreader, in a rather flat voice.

Does he really expect to be believed? Does he care whether he is or not? One thing is certain: the removal of a leading hardliner like McGiolla, from South Armagh, the most hard-line 'stick with the armed struggle' sections of the republican movement makes the task of Bunny and Butch that little bit easier and the chances of agreement with HMG that little bit better.

Granville consoled himself with that thought.

Chapter 35

A white Ford Transit van moved slowly up Drumphoe's' rainswept main street. It was the middle of the night and no insomniacs or dog walkers were abroad. The van stopped just before the junction with Sperrin Street and five dark figures soundlessly alighted. One jemmied the front door of the chosen derelict shop in seconds. The unit slipped inside. The door was fastened closed again from the inside and the van drove off. A good start: getting into places unnoticed was often one of the most hazardous aspects of a deep surveillance operation.

On the upstairs storey to the back of the building, the SAS men quickly and quietly established their 'lie' and set up their glasses and night vision equipment, focused on the back wall of the Ulster Bank building, across a narrow strip of backyard and a delivery entry which ran behind the bank and the adjoining shops.

It was Thursday. Intelligence reports had forecast a raid 'within the next few days'. How many made a 'few'? Each day, each night, spent almost entirely in silence and with the minimum of movement, could feel like a week. At least they had a roof over their head, however leaky, which was better by far than some of the hides they had experienced, literally in a ditch, watching the movements of suspect farmers in rural areas. Field rations were nutritionally nourishing, but scarcely a culinary treat, consisting largely of cereal bar type 'energy biscuits'. Food also meant waste disposal and they had the necessary containers for that, along with a specially developed air freshener. Odours could be one of the worst giveaways for such an operation. The team operated a rota for the task of 100% observation of the target area, namely the back of the bank building. Those not on watch dozed fitfully in their sleeping bags, or quietly did press-ups on the floor. Reading was not allowed and their radio was only to be switched on in an emergency.

One sudden alarm the next morning was the constant barking of what sounded like a very large dog, just outside the boarded up shop. What had sparked that off – and would someone connected to it try to enter the building to see what had animated the dog? It was always some random, unforeseen circumstance – curious dogs were a classic menace – which could suddenly endanger a surveillance operation. The team prepared to move on, with their gear, into their fall back position, which was to pull themselves and equipment up into the roof space. The small square hole which gave access to it was just outside the room they were occupying. It had no built-in ladder, but the SAS men were fit enough to pull themselves up into the roof space within seconds, should the need arise.

Finally the barking ceased, and in the minutes which followed, there was no sound of an attempted break-in. The team relaxed; the binoculars, night-sights and tripod were returned to their former position at the window.

It was in the early hours of Sunday morning that their quarry turned up. It was raining again – did Drumphoe ever have a non-monsoon season? – and the shadowy figure who appeared on foot down the service alley, was wearing a vast parka with hood and waterproof peak. He was carrying a long sports bag, of the type used by Wimbledon tennis players, and this he slung over the back wall of the bank's perimeter fence, before nimbly pulling himself up and over after it. He approached the single window on the back wall, which was six feet off the ground, protected by five vertical, two inch thick metal bars.

'Here we go,' whispered the SAS observer to his team-mates, who crowded behind him in the darkness.

Burglar unzipped his bag and took out a small fold-up mini stepladder, like those used by shoe shop salesmen or librarians in order to gain a foot or two in height for retrieving shoes or books from higher shelves. The next object to emerge from the bag was a hand-held Black and Decker circular saw. The noise of the sawing reached the watchers, but would not have been heard in either Sperrin Street or Main Street. It took the IRA man some twenty minutes to complete his work, then he quickly withdrew, packing his equipment, slinging his bag over the wall before heaving himself over after it, then walking briskly away in the direction from which he had come.

As Granville packed his travelling case he wished he had never invited Penny to join him. He was due to take his annual 'cure' in the physiotherapy department of the thermal resort of Archena, near Murcia in the south-east corner of Spain. He owed a lot to the rehabilitation treatment he had received there in the months following the car accident. The hot mud treatment and the expert physiotherapy in the medical section of the resort had not only enabled him, post-operation, to walk again more or less normally, but had given him the confidence to suppress, if not entirely to eliminate, in his mind, the trauma he had endured on the motorway and in hospital.

He had gone back to Archena every year, for what he called 'a week's top-up', repeating the exercises he had first learned there in the 'Torture Chamber', relaxing in the hot thermal pools, and enjoying good food and the calming, quasi-monastic separation from everyday life. Normally, he looked on this week as a self-indulgent treat, but today his heart wasn't in it. Perhaps he was too tired – and his persistent cold didn't help – and perhaps the mounting tension in his work, as things moved towards what he called the 'Endgame', was taking a greater toll on his nerves than he had imagined. But there were other factors which weighed more heavily on him. He had invited Penny on the spur of the moment, out of a sense of guilt towards her – he had certainly been neglecting her and she was bound to have felt that. Now she would either be reproachful for a full week, or put him under pressure to marry her. Or perhaps both. Marriage was bound to become an issue sooner or later, he acknowledged to himself. And he admitted to himself also, that until recently he would have drifted comfortably, even happily, into that stage of his relationship with Penny. But had she ever affected him in the way that Noleen now did?

As he checked the contents of his toilet bag he noticed several sachets of nicotine patches. These had been urged upon him by Penny but he had only occasionally applied them and didn't really believe in their efficacy. Perversely, the sight of these packages now reminded him of his Gauloises.

'Bugger it,' he said out loud and mechanically lit one. It was going to be a difficult week.

Chapter 36

The operational silence was broken by a whispered question: 'Isn't Monday a Bank Holiday?'

'Yes, but not a public holiday.'

'That's it! It has just occurred to me: the buggers plan to come back on Tuesday morning. You see, the night safe will then contain what local businesses have deposited on Friday, the weekend, and Monday evening. A double or even triple catch compared to a normal day. Could be hundreds of thousands.'

'That's a thought. You're probably right. But we'll have to be on full alert in the meantime.'

Silence and a bored vigilance re-descended, like dusk, on the SAS unit. Tuesday morning was still a long way off.

Granville had treated himself to hiring a Cherokee Jeep from Herz at Alicante airport. As they bowled along the Alicante-Murcia motorway, through the green olive, orange and lemon groves, irrigated by the waters of the River Segura, he was conscious that Penny's thoughts were probably elsewhere, possibly on what she would say to him in a show-down.

'Look out for the turn-off to Albacete,' he said. 'It's a tricky exit and easily missed.'

'Will do. Can you turn up the air conditioning please, it's getting awfully hot.'

'Yeah, OK.'

She's never comfortable in a car. It's either too hot or too cold, the seats are either too hard or too wallowy. Always something. Is that the sort of irritating detail which drives couples apart?

Once the switch to the Albacete road had been successfully manoeuvred and, ten minutes further on, the equally tricky turn-off to Archena, Granville's mood lightened. The landscape was a striking mixture of lush orange groves, with a rising background of cactus-strewn scrubland and, above that, jagged bare hills, reminiscent of Arizona. On the far side of the town of Archena lay the *balneario*, the spa resort, nestling in a bend of the Segura River, protected on three sides by hills, which rose up dramatically from the narrow valley. The spa village consisted exclusively of three hotels. In the bowels of the most expensive one was the source of the spa, gushing hot water and mud, both of which were used in the medical and recreational aspects of the resort. The thermal waters had been exploited since Roman times. Between the three hotel buildings a luxurious garden blossomed and in its paths there wandered, at a cloistered pace, small groups of guests/patients in their standard issue long, white *albornozes*. A very faint whiff of sulphur hung in the air. The atmosphere was one of profound, languorous calm and other-worldliness. A luxurious, secular equivalent of Clonard Monastery, a place of reflection, far from the preoccupations of everyday life, but with all mod. cons. Leading European industrialists, investment bankers and media personalities could always be found amongst the guests in the five star hotel, which, *noblesse oblige*, had the best position of the three.

Granville knew from experience that this blissful calm was in stark contrast to the forthcoming pain to be endured in the physiotherapy department, especially in the gymnasium. There he would be submitted to excruciating stretchings and twistings, which felt as though they were pulling his legs free from his body. All in the name of 'annual maintenance'. This treatment, punctuated with mud baths and rigorous massages, lasted every day from breakfast time to lunch. The afternoon was more comfortably spent in and around the heated swimming pool, in which, given its heavy mineral content and its steady temperature of 37C, one could not really swim, but instead wallow like a contented hippopotamus in the Zambesi. Evenings could be spent in a rota of visits to bar-restaurants in the town, where the riches of the local Murcian cuisine were enthusiastically sampled by all visitors. Granville, whose inherited work ethic gave him a slightly guilty conscience about all this *'luxe, calme et volupté'* eased only by the thought that his lotus-eating was only for a week. And, of course, the suffering at the hands of the physiotherapists had a compensatory, redemptive effect, at least in his own mind.

In any event, his lotus-eating days were to be numbered. His improved mood was briefly shared by Penny when they were installed in their de luxesuite on the top floor, overlooking the garden. They felt and acted like lovers again, but as Granville pulled on a post-coital Gauloise, he was conscious that there was little he wanted to talk to Penny about. She seldom asked him about his passion in life, namely his work in Ireland, except every so often to pose *la question clé* – how long? To which there could be no definitive answer. Her life had ceased to inspire his curiosity, let alone the sort of interest which one lover naturally has about the object of his or her love. Moreover, he could sense that she, knowing him so well for so long, had detected his gradual change of attitude towards her

Was this also what 'drifting apart' meant?

He both relished and dreaded the week ahead.

Chapter 37

Seamus Toner, alias 'Harry-the-hound', was feeling upbeat, despite the fact that his kidney condition disrupted his sleep at frequent, painful intervals every night of his life and complicated his life during every day, with equally painful side effects. The reason for his good humour was that he felt his personal importance was at last increasing, in both of his 'lives', that is to say, as an IRA Volunteer and as an RUC 'Secret Agent', (a title skilfully bestowed upon him by Det. Sgt. Bob McKinney, which sounded so much better than 'tout'). It was a strange thing, he reflected, as he unwisely sipped a Guinness at the bar in Central Station ... strange that he should like McKinney, whom he knew as 'Macintosh', much more than his IRA superiors. He felt that the RUC man genuinely 'cared'. He went to enormous lengths to protect Toner's security and a bond of friendship had gradually been established between them. Macintosh never failed to ask after his health and family and would chat about his everyday life – his worries, his sporting interests and his hobby of model aircraft building. As time went by, the handler showed a growing appreciation of Toner's value as a 'Secret Agent', which was reflected in the increasing amounts of money he was slipped every month. By contrast, he had never felt that his superiors in his local battalion of the IRA gave him the recognition which he believed he deserved. He was part of the machine alright, but was always acutely conscious of how small a cog he was in that machine. His local OC treated him as though he were a not very bright schoolboy and the tasks he was given, as a runner, were basically those of a message boy.

However, things were beginning to look up, even on that front, to his great satisfaction. He had been detailed to 'look after' two VIP visitors from the South, who were due to arrive off the Dublin to Belfast Enterprise express in fifteen minutes time. He had not been told, of course, who they were. Externally, one was an academic, a senior lecturer in Electrical Engineering at a Dublin university; the other was a trade union official. Internally, one was a bomb-brain, the other a security officer of the IRA and liaison man with Belfast.

The reason for their visit north was the growing problem of bomb production. Bombs nowadays had to be ever more sophisticated, the bomb makers complained. Sinn Fein/IRA policy, in the twilight zone of transition to politics, now required that civilian casualties had to be kept to the minimum. That meant warnings had to be given, in order that all civilians could be evacuated from the scene of the coming explosion. That in turn meant that the mechanism of the bomb had to outwit the disposal experts in the relatively short interval between warning and timed detonation. As Major Tomkins and his men grew ever more efficient in their job, the challenge to the bomb makers – and behind them the bomb-brains – similarly increased. In this situation the pressure on the small number of bomb-brains was becoming critical, since only they could be counted on to design the necessary technical traps for the bomb makers to incorporate in their devices. And on top of that, within a month, the services of two key designers had been lost to the organisation, due to the successes of PANORAMA. It was unlikely that the police would be able to gather enough evidence against them to have them charged. However, since they would themselves know, by the very fact of their arrests, that they had been 'rumbled', it would be very difficult for the IRA leadership to rely on their future help, which had always been given at one remove. Now that they were compromised they both wanted to keep out of the 'game', as they brutally described their activities.

The visitors from Dublin were therefore on a mission to co-ordinate with Belfast how best to meet the problem of shrinking top-level expertise and how to improve security.

Toner had been given no information whatsoever about his charges, beyond their status as VIPs. He merely positioned himself with the small knot of meeters and greeters near the ticket collectors, as the passengers streamed from the Enterprise Express into the station concourse. He carried a small, yellow holdall with, along one side, an unusual logo of a green snake. It was a conspicuous enough identification marker, but Toner nevertheless was momentarily startled when a man stopped in his stride as he reached him and used the clichéd password, 'Excuse me, I am from Tipperary. Could you tell me where the taxis are?'

'Yes. Just come with me,' he replied. As they walked towards the exit, they were joined by another man, who was obviously known to the first.

'Mind if I share a taxi with you if you're going to the city centre?'

'Sure.'

Before they got into the last black taxi on the rank outside the station, Toner, mindful of the Dublin accents of his charges, said, 'Listen fellas. Don't say a word in the taxi. Let me do all the talking.'

'To the Europa Hotel,' he said to the driver. Five minutes later they alighted there, and when the taxi had driven off into the busy traffic of Great Victoria Street, Toner led the trio across the road and into another taxi from the row waiting for customers in nearby Amelia Street. This time they set off for their real destination, Lenadoon Drive, in the suburbs of West Belfast. Toner chatted to the driver almost non-stop, to deflect attention from his companions, and instructed him to drop them at the corner of the street, from where they walked the hundred yards or so to where Stiletto and Charlie Ryan, an experienced bomb maker, awaited them. The tenant of the house was an old-timer in the Republican cause, whose only service now was to make his home available as a 'safe house'. No longer the tearaway gunman of PIRA lore, he spent most of his days lolling on the sofa in his front room, like a panda in a Chinese zoo – bamboo shoots, that is to say tins of lager, courtesy of the generosity of the local Benefits Office of the Department of Health and Social Services, ranged on a low table before him.

Toner was sent away and told to return with a taxi in time for the visitors to catch the evening Enterprise back to Dublin.

HSB was still at his desk in RUC Headquarters when he received an urgent call from his opposite number in the Garda Síochána in Dublin.

'Afternoon my friend. A titbit for you. I've just heard that two of the local rowdies here are supposed to be up with you today on big business. I'm told they took the train, so they may well come back that way.'

'Many thanks. Any other details – names, descriptions etc?'

'I'll fax that to you right away, on secure. Plus two mug shots. Not very good quality, I'm afraid, but it should help.'

'Thanks a million. I'll action at once when I have your fax.'

As he hung up, he shouted to his PA in the adjoining office, 'Maggie, this is urgent. Get me the timetable for the evening Enterprise.'

'I don't need to. I was on it last Friday. It leaves at ten past six.'

'Damn, we're going to be too late. But we can still get them off at Portadown, or better still at Newry. That gives us nearly an hour. Get me Chief Superintendent Ellison down there, then forward to him the fax that's coming in from Dublin.'

Passengers on the Enterprise began to look at their watches, as the train sat on in the station above Newry town, well beyond its scheduled three minutes.

'Not another bloody "bomb on the line" story,' muttered someone. 'They'll have us off on a bus to Dundalk and we'll be at least an hour late in Dublin.'

Three groups of policemen, some in uniform, some in civvies, moved systematically through the carriages, scrutinising faces as they went. It took them ten minutes to find the Dublin two, who had been sitting separately and they were led off, without protest or struggle, and bundled unceremoniously into waiting police cars.

At Castlereagh neither Niblock nor Austin made any headway with the two detainees. Confident that there could be no forensic or ballistic evidence against them – the great advantage of 'clean skins' – they both stuck to the simple story that they had spent the day as tourists. Their superficial knowledge of the city allowed each of them – they denied having been together – to outline a sort of tourist board day out: visits to Parliament Buildings, the City Hall and Queen's University, a pub lunch, (one mentioned the Crown Bar, the other couldn't remember the name of the hostelry in the university area), then window shopping in Donegal Place and Royal Avenue. It was clear to their experienced interrogators that not only were their stories lies, but that they knew that they would be seen as such. Obviously they didn't care, confident that nothing could be pinned on them. The fact that they had been pulled off the train showed their cover had somehow been blown, which was a great pity, but what else could the police do to them?

Electrical Engineer felt confident enough to taunt Niblock.

'Since when has it been a crime in this fascist statelet to spend a day sightseeing? I'd heard about your police methods and all that, but I never thought I'd see it at close hand myself.'

Niblock refused to rise to the bait. He merely smiled and said, 'Well, when we've compared your fingerprints with our prize collection we'll have a better idea of what you've put your hand to up here.'

He did not, of course, believe that, for he was pretty sure that these two men would never be 'hands-on' operators.

When he rang HSB to report on the state of play, or more accurately non-play, his boss said, 'I'm not surprised. We could do a CCTV check on them, but that's hardly worth the time and bother. Life's too short to iron the gusset of your boxer shorts. But keep them there for the max. I'll have an Order prepared for the Secretary of State's signature. Just to sow a bit of doubt and confusion amongst the opposition. Make sure McGuigan tells the press of the dramatic arrest on the train. That should stir things up a bit. Thinking about who knew and who told will keep a few baddies out of trouble for a while. And it's good for morale elsewhere, even though it's a damp squib.'

Chapter 38

Howard Kerr, manager of the Drumphoe Ulster Bank, arrived at the front door, in the half-light, at 8.25am, with the keys to open up. Within five minutes, all the members of his staff had arrived, and began going about their routine business before opening to the public at 9.30am. Having consulted the work rota, Kerr detailed two clerks to clear the night safe, count the cash and cheques and do the necessary follow-up records, acknowledgements etc. They took two large sacks with them to the back of the night safe and it took two runs each for them to effect the transfer into the bank 'counting house', the door of which stood to the side of the vast steel vault. Once inside the room, they locked the door and set about their tasks.

Five minutes later the watcher on duty at the window in their hide, prepared for action. He did not take his eyes off his binoculars; the others checked their weapons, not just as an automatic routine, but with concentrated serious intent. No one even whispered. Ten minutes later the watcher suddenly stirred.

'They've arrived!' he hissed.

Below, in the alleyway behind the bank, a narrow Toyota van pulled up. Three figures swiftly alighted. One stood in front of the van, dressed in jeans and a green parka, a woollen mask covering most of his face. The other two jointly heaved, with some difficulty, a large sack over the wall then followed it with considerable agility. A fourth member of the team appeared from the rear of the van, carrying a small, collapsible stepladder. Then he joined the others below the barred window. Mounting the stepladder, he took the large bag from the others and swung it against the bars, which immediately caved in with a large crash of metal and glass which was clearly audible in the SAS hide. The other two men replaced him on the platform of the steps and produced handguns from their jackets. The watchers could not hear what the raiders were shouting but clearly they were threatening the bank staff within, then one after the other, through the window, they disappeared from view.

'Right, let's go. Go! go! go!' The SAS team descended the stairs, slipped through the neglected backyard and through a gap in the slats in the fence, emerging into the alleyway just yards from the Toyota. The sentry spotted them at once and reached into his jacket for his weapon. It never appeared: there was the dull thud of a silenced Uzi and he slumped forward without a sound, a red dot, the size of a 10p coin, in the middle of his forehead. The unit swept on, over the wall and, cautiously now, up to the platform in front of the window. No one looked out and from outside they could hear the murmur of voices, betraying no alarm inside the target area. The problem which they had debated beforehand – 'how to determine who is who' – did not arise: three occupants of the room wore parkas, the other two were in indoor civvies. In an instant, the pent-up tension of the SAS men exploded, as a fusillade of shots rang out, followed by screams of pain and terror. Then only low moans from one of the bank tellers and hyperventilation gasps from the other. Three parka clad bodies lay askew over the upturned table, envelopes and bundles of banknotes and cheques littered the room. In the bank beyond the 'counting house', pandemonium reigned ...

Granville had not felt well all morning. He was sorry now that he had drunk most of the bottle of Ricoti red the night before, on top of three sharp 'finos'. The local red was all very well as an accompaniment to a barbecue, but at 15 degrees, in large quantities, it claimed many a victim. Penny had been moody, bordering on sulky, all evening; had refused more than a half glass of wine, and had insisted, patronisingly he thought, on taking over the driving on the way back to the hotel. Breakfast had been a rather sombre affair; and the morning's physiotherapy was particularly painful, as a big brutal nurse bent his legs to what he felt must be near breaking point. Things had somewhat improved in the hot mud session. He lay on a bed covered in brown viscous mud and wrapped in a linen shroud-like garment. He could feel his body relax after the rigours of the 'Torture Chamber' and had fallen into a light sleep before the attendant roused him. His shroud was unwrapped and the jet of hot water from a hose scattered the mud from his body in seconds.

He tried to observe his own gait as he walked at the patient's pace, back to his room. His slight limp seemed to have improved over the last year. He must come here for longer periods and more frequently, he decided.

In his room the red button for 'messages' was blinking on the telephone. He lifted the receiver, to be connected to Pablo, a jovial youth who doubled as concierge and telephone exchange operator.

'*Buenas dias, señor*. Very urgent call from your friend Mr Oui-la. He want you for TV programme. I no know where you are. You get his numbers? Right? *Vale.*'

'Yes, I have. That's OK. Thanks.'

As he dialled the number of his PA, Elspeth, his eye took in a significant detail he should have noticed on entering the room: no 'Penny clutter', no clothes on the floor and through the open bathroom door he could see no array of bottles of lotions on the shelves above the left-hand basin.

Elspeth answered. 'Thank goodness you have surfaced,' *(en clair: where the hell have you been?).* 'I'll get James to ring you right away. He's somewhere with the main press boys. God, it's mad here. Have you seen the news? About the SAS shoot-out?'

'No.'

'Well, it's on BBC 1 now, can you get that?'

'Yes.'

'Hang up and James will ring you back.'

As he hung up, he reached for the TV remote control. On it (she knew where he was likely to find it) was an envelope marked 'J. Granville Esq. Personal.'

The TV picture and sound came on. It showed a shot of what he was later to learn was the back of the Ulster Bank building in Drumphoe, with a zoom into the gaping hole of the window, followed by shots of bloodstains on the ground in the alleyway. The voice over was saying 'Nationalist politicians are calling for an immediate inquiry into the incident and at Westminster there have been requests for an urgent debate this afternoon.'

At the bottom of the picture the 'ticker-tape' flashing from left to right read, 'Army kill four in bank raid ambush. One bank employee seriously injured.'

'Yes, James. Sorry. I was having treatment and they didn't come for me. Yes, I have just this minute seen the BBC story. Is this SAS stuff?'

'We've been holding the line so far that we don't comment on army or regimental movements. But the Secretary of State will eventually have to tell Parliament, through parliamentary questions or in debate.'

'Hold the line for as long as possible. It could soon blow over, even with four dead and an innocent injured!'

'It's worse than that. Seems another IRA man, maybe a lookout, scorched out of town in his car and a mile down the road hit an oncoming car head on. He died on the spot and the driver of the other car, a thirty year old mother of two, died on her way to hospital.'

'Jesus. There'll be hell to pay about this!'

'We've managed to reel in the General a bit, but the media are bound to play his initial gung-ho reaction. You'd think he'd won World War III.'

'I can imagine.'

'I hear Bunny and Butch are looking for you, urgently.'

'Not surprised. Tell Elspeth to get me out of here and back to Belfast *prontissimo*. See you tonight.'

'Jesus,' repeated Granville as he replaced the receiver. He said it with such feeling that a theologian would have been hard put to decide whether his exclamation was blasphemy or pious invocation.

He knew what would be in the letter. It was just a matter of how it was expressed.

'Dear Jeremy,

You have always prided yourself on being a realist. I have been more of a romantic, but I have now realised that I, too, should be a realist.

As I'm sure you know, I hoped that our relationship would continue to progress. Clearly that is not the case. You once said that the place a relationship can best be evaluated is over the cornflakes at breakfast. I think you're right. And judging by this morning, would either of us want that to be our future?

I am sorry about the suddenness of this, but I'm sure it's better this way.

I hope we can nevertheless remain friends.

With genuinely best wishes,

Penny.'

Granville's thoughts were of Noleen as he tore up the letter.

It's simpler now, but it's not that simple. In fact it could be even more complicated.

An hour later, Granville was loading his luggage into the back of the jeep. The *mozo* helped him in a way which required no great effort on his own part, springing the back door of the vehicle open, lifting the smaller of the two cases, and opening the driver's door for Granville. As he trousered Granville's tip he said, with gusto, '*Gracias, señor y buen viaje.* 'Ave a good day now.'

Unlikely.

Chapter 39

Reaction to the events at Drumphoe polarised press, politicians and public opinion as no other topic had done for years. 'At last, SAS in action!' screamed the headline in the *Newsletter*, reflecting broad unionist opinion. 'Horror killings by British troops' was the headline in the *Irish News*, followed by reports of condemnation by Sinn Fein, the SDLP and the local Catholic clergy.

'Bloody Chesham throws the crockery at the wall and I've got to pick up the pieces. *And* put it together again,' said Granville to Wheeler. 'I don't buy the line that the SAS were called in at short notice because the police couldn't handle things themselves, once the scale of the IRA operation became clear. I'll want a detailed timeline established for the whole affair, as a matter of urgency.'

'Well I can tell you right away that our man up there and your office weren't put in the picture until it was far too late to do anything about it.'

'I'm not surprised. I'd bet the farm on it having been cooked up personally by the GOC and HSB. They are sometimes far too cosy together, those two, for my liking. And in some ways one is as bad as the other. Chesham is upfront and obvious, but Campbell is a dark horse.'

'Do you really think he's all that clever?' asked Wheeler, doubtfully.

'Well, he'd be unlikely to solve the Riemann hypothesis, but he's a crafty bugger all the same. Not to be underestimated. Or always trusted, as this episode illustrates.'

'You will never really know the full story, I suspect. My guess is that there will be no paper trail on this. More likely a conversation on a green at Knock Golf Club one fine Saturday morning.'

'If this is the GOC's interpretation of his orders to "cool it" and "hold the ring", I shudder to think what he'd have done if we had given him martial law when he was calling for it eighteen months ago.'

'By the way,' said Wheeler apologetically, 'Vincent Glass tells me that Bunny and Butch are genuinely very upset. They'll accuse you of bad faith – and mean it this time. It's not just a ploy.'

'Of course, of course. What else are they to think? Fortunately I think the timing is right for a ploy I can use to bring them back on board.'

'Am I allowed to know?' asked Wheeler, with just a hint of anticipated reproach in his voice.

'I think you can guess,' replied Granville with a smile, 'I am confident that if we have a reasonable amount of time to move away from this incident, we can save our overall game plan. But the immediate problem is to get them back into play, before everything drifts away from us. A vacuum in our dealings with them would be bound to play into the hands of the PIRA hawks.'

'Does the way back pass through your favourite canon?' asked Wheeler.

'Indeed it does. Which does not fill me with unalloyed joy. But business is business. I'll just have to eat humble pie AND flatter him. AND promise his chums the moon, and, if necessary, the earth.'

Meetings of the Joint Security Committee, Granville reflected, were now becoming as difficult as his Clonard encounters, if not more so. But he was nevertheless pleased that in the overall scheme of things in London and Belfast, this committee, *his* committee, had been gradually taking on the role of the most important forum in the whole politico-administrative scene.

He called the meeting to order and introduced the first item on the agenda, "Follow up to the Drumphoe Incident".

He deliberately did so in flat, factual terms as though he were a neutral observer. Not a word of praise crossed his lips.

The General was first to demand the floor. 'I should have thought, Mr Chairman, that the success of this mission would engender a somewhat greater enthusiasm from you. My men were working under very difficult, and indeed dangerous, conditions and they managed to inflict an obvious defeat on the enemy, which should deter other misguided young hooligans from indulging in such activities. I would have thought ...' Granville interrupted him with a manual stop sign. 'General, your operation, quite apart from drawing on to HMG international criticism at the UN, no less, caused the death of an innocent motorist and severe injuries to an innocent bank clerk. It may have been a success as viewed through military eyes, but frankly it was against the policy of the peace process.'

'What is this policy? Can you please explain to us what it is,' said a reddening and angry General.

'I thought I had made that clear many times; the process *is* the policy. We're reeling them in. Into a post-war situation. We are agreeing to things that would happen at the end of any such conflict, in return for their acceptance that the war is over.'

'The war is over, is it?' demanded the General, 'Well if it is, can you please tell me who has won?'

'The population at large has won. That is to say, they will reap the peace dividend when all the loose ends are tied up.'

'Well, where is the surrender?' demanded Chesham, still very *agitato*.

'The sort of surrender you have in mind, General, would only mark a pause in hostilities. Another generation would take up arms, as they have done before. This time we must have a settled settlement.'

'This is all very confusing. What am I expected to do?'

'For as long as you are GOC NI,' said Granville – the threat was obvious – 'you should confine your forces' activities to peace-keeping. Keep up the intelligence gathering by all means, which we all do and which is our greatest weapon, and react to any acts of overt violence. That's all.'

'If you're saying my Secretary of State will sack me for success I'll be very surprised.'

'No question of sacking. On the contrary I look forward to congratulating you on a further promotion ... when it comes.'

HSB kept his head down, metaphorically and almost physically, during these exchanges. He was glad that the heat which they generated helped divert others from posing questions about the role of his branch in the Drumphoe incident. Not that Granville had forgotten about that aspect. HSB's silence told him all he needed to know; he didn't need any written report, a report which would, he knew in his bones, be a fudged account of what had taken place between police and army and why MI5 could not be put in the picture at an earlier moment. But there was no point in pushing those two into a permanent alliance against himself. In the long run, the police would be needed more than the army.

Canon Murray's green VW Beetle crunched to a halt on the gravel drive in front of St Oswald's. As he emerged from the car, he took in the splendour of the magnificent sweep of lawns and, beyond them, the pine trees which marked the boundaries of the property and hid it from sight from the roadway.

Such a change from the cramped concrete jungle of the Lower Falls.

He took a deep, deep breath of the slightly sea-tangy air and would have liked to stay where he was for a refreshing pause, but a young official hurried down the flight of steps at the entrance to greet him and show him into a spacious drawing room, where Granville awaited him.

'Thanks for coming,' began Granville, gripping him firmly by the hand.

'I thought it was time we renewed our acquaintance and took up the threads of our first meeting. Which was, of course, both interesting and, as you know, fruitful.'

'That's not quite true,' said Murray, unsmilingly.

'Oh? How come?' replied Granville, raising his eyebrows in mild – and feigned – astonishment.

'Let's be frank. You invited me here because you are in deep trouble and you think I might be able to get you out of the mess you have made for yourself.'

Granville reflected for half a second.

Should he prolong an argument about the motives for his invitation? Was it not an argument he would almost certainly lose?

He chose, instead, the opposite tack.

'Rumbled again,' he cried, smiling broadly, 'But surely you won't hold that against me. After all, I'm only taking you up on your own self-definition of "peacemaker"?'

A girl appeared with drinks on a tray. Murray lifted a glass of Bushmills, which he swirled for a few seconds before returning to the charge.

'That was a limited role, to help the two sides to come together. But we're long past that stage now. You Brits have had your chance. You've completely destroyed any trust that was building up. And without trust there is no way forward.' He was now into his hectoring mode, as though he was chiding his flock for the paucity of their Easter offerings.

'The massacre at Drumphoe was a huge political mistake.'

'Let's not exaggerate, Father,' interrupted Granville. 'I can assure you it was not a political mistake. It was an accident.'

'Accident?' snapped Murray in indignation. 'Accidents just happen, in the twinkling of an eye. Drumphoe required planning, organisation, co-ordination. That was no accident. That was a deliberate and reckless decision by the British Establishment.'

Granville poured him another generous Bushmills, before replying,

'Now, you are a fair and balanced man. I take it you would not deny that from time to time things go wrong for the IRA. They have even publicly admitted that themselves. And when I say"v go wrong" I don't just mean a technical detail, like a bomb going off prematurely, but "go wrong" because someone down the line misinterprets the leadership's general directions and embarks on a course of action which is actually against those policies.'

'Are you trying to tell me,' retorted Murray, with some force, 'that you are putting the British army on the same organisational level as what you otherwise call a clandestine paramilitary gang?'

'No, I'm not. But equally, you mustn't assume that the Establishment, as you like to call it, is a perfectly organised, monolithic structure, in which everybody knows what everybody else is doing, minute by minute, and why. I would never, ever, guarantee that elements in the security forces will not occasionally act in a way for which their training has prepared them, but which is not helpful to overall policy.'

'Are you saying that the powers that be were unaware in advance of the Drumphoe operation?'

Summoning up his most sincere demeanour, Granville said in a low, confidential tone, 'I can personally give you that assurance.'

'What has happened to those who stepped out of line? Have they been put on a charge? Disciplined?'

This is awkward. Kick for touch.

'As you know, the incident is being fully investigated. It would be wrong of me to comment until the results of that inquiry are known. But I can tell you, strictly off the record, that the government greatly regrets what has happened.'

Murray was silent for several moments.

'Even if I were to take what you say at face value – which I must frankly tell you I find hard to do – what do you think I could do to help the situation? Surely it's a matter between you and the representatives of the IRA.'

Granville thought he sensed that the atmosphere was thawing. Now was the moment to make his play.

'Father, I think you know. I don't have to spell it out. The interlocutors you kindly introduced me to are, how shall I put it, not returning my calls. Neither metaphorically nor practically. So, in view of what you told me at our first meeting about your vocation as a peace maker, I thought you might be prepared to act as what I believe you in the Church would call an "intercessory saint" and one with great influence over some key individuals.'

He paused before adding in lighter vein, 'I take it that you still believe in intercessory saints?'

'Yes, but I'm not one of them,' said Murray firmly, but with a twinkle in his eye.

'Oh, give it time, give it time. I'm sure some heavenly power is working on your promotion.'

Murray, now apparently drawn into the spirit of the tease, replied, 'You should know that to be a saint you have not only to have two miracles attributed to you, but you must also be dead.'

'Well in that case we'll allow the celestial and ecclesiastical authorities a long, long time before a final decision is taken; we don't want to lose you,' said Granville with a flourish. 'However, as practice for the long term future and to enrich your spiritual CV in the meantime, you could in the short term render not only me but the entire peace process a great service by helping to restore relations to their pre-Drumphoe status.'

'By doing what?' said the canon, now serious once more.

'By convincing your friends of the sincerity of my regrets. And of my good faith. And of my desire to move forward once more, with them, in our confidence-building measures. I have some proposals for that which I am sure will be of considerable interest to them.'

Would he take the bait ...and pass it on?

Murray was silent for several seconds, pursing his lips, then swallowing a mouthful of whiskey, with an audible gulp.

'I don't think I, or anybody else, can do anything at this moment. It will take months, and a lot of patience, to get back to where you were.'

'But we haven't got that sort of time. If the momentum for peace is lost because of a continuing stand-off, a great opportunity will be missed. In that case history will not be kind to any of us.'

'You should have thought of that – not that I believe you Brits spend much time thinking about our history here – before allowing a bunch of SAS thugs over here in the first place. Let alone turning them loose in an area like Drumphoe with a licence to kill.'

With that, Murray rose from his chair.

'Sorry, but that's the way I see it today. Thanks for the whiskey anyhow.'

'I'm sorry, too; very sorry that you can't see your way to help just now. Perhaps another time. Soon, I hope.'

'Perhaps, but unlikely.'

Later that afternoon Wheeler rang.

'Any progress?'

'No great enthusiasm or optimism, I'm afraid. He may go back to them with what I said, but I have my doubts.'

'Shit!'

'And not a word to friend Glass or anyone else.'

'Course not.'

Chapter 40

HSB was with his various counterparts at a meeting of the Joint Security Committee when he was called to the telephone to take an urgent call from Bill Austin.

'This had better be important,' he said.

'It may well be; it's for you to judge. I've had a call from CID to say we are holding Canon Murray for questioning in the barracks in Andersonstown.' (Austin always preferred the word 'barracks' over the, to him, weak PC modern term 'station', which, as he would say, 'is where you go to take a train'.)

'They thought it was a delicate matter.'

In his most sepulchral 'What's the world coming to' voice he went on, 'There has been a complaint from a minor, a boy ... about a sexual assault.'

'Good God! I'm pretty sure our clerical friend is a customer of you know who. Tell Andersonstown to hold him there in the meantime. No action, no charge. No need to explain. I'll deal with Andytown direct. Thanks for the tip-off.'

Before setting off for West Belfast, Granville, having been briefed by HSB, put Wheeler in the picture.

'If any hint of this gets out, the 'Camoo' (camouflage) story is that Murray is in there to complain about army activity in the area. Complaints about the army are nothing out of the ordinary in those parts. Totally believable, I'd say. But better still if no explanations are needed.'

Andersonstown RUC station had the outer appearance of a modern version of a 'Beau Geste' fort. Its already high outer wall, defaced by elaborate 'RUC SS' and 'Brits out' graffiti which the personnel inside had long since given up painting out, was topped by a wire fence of almost equal height. Over the years the station had been attacked by gunfire, bomb and mortars; even now entry by car had to be co-ordinated by radio.

Once inside, Granville and HSB were shown into a starkly furnished room at the back of the building, in which Canon Murray sat at a plain deal table, opposite a Detective Constable. The handshakes were slightly awkward, but Granville, left alone with Murray, adopted a relaxed tone.

'Sorry you have had to stay here for such a long time, but the delay was unavoidable. When I heard you were here, I had to look at all the material in the file, to see if I could help in any way. To be honest, the police are keen to prosecute, on the basis of the available evidence, but, as I say, I would like to help, if you could help me ...if you understand.' He paused in order to judge whether Murray did indeed understand. He appeared to.

'What evidence? You have no evidence. I'm totally innocent. This is a frame-up. It's a scandal. I'll sue you all and expose this RUC plot.'

'Take it easy,' said Granville, calmly. 'Let's not talk about your exposing anything, shall we?'

Shouldn't have said that. Concentrate on the deal.

'You ask about evidence. Well, young Michael Doyle has provided a very detailed account –an all too detailed in fact – of what has happened in the sacristy of St Martin's and elsewhere apparently, since he was eleven. That's seven years, a long time. Now he wants to face up to all of that and he is prepared to give evidence in court against you.'

Murray showed no emotion.

He really is a hard nut. Or is it possible that he can turn denial and autodenial into a solid defence mechanism?

Granville changed tone again and spoke in a friendly, almost cajoling manner.

'From where I'm sitting, things look bad for you, Father. Why don't you plead my cause – you know how to do it – and

I promise to help you. Only you and I will know anything about our agreement.'

'No, I won't be blackmailed,' he almost shouted.

'I will not be blackmailed. I'm innocent, I tell you. That young Doyle is a well known scamp and teller of tales.'

His defiance grew ever more strident.

'And an ungrateful little blighter, after all I've done for him and his family over the years. Go ahead and charge me. No judge or jury would take his word against mine.'

'They might if they listened to the tape.'

'What tape?'

The first hint of anxiety in his voice.

'The one Michael Doyle made the very last time you ...saw him. At Easter, after Mass, in your house.'

'I don't believe you!'

But you're not so sure. Worth going for the jugular.

'Are you going to force me to play it to you? I don't think you or I want that, do we? The sound quality is exceptionally good for an amateur recording. Every endearing word, every little sound, can be clearly heard ...'

'Are you going to have me charged?' said Murray defiantly, but in a voice which Granville was convinced was now very far from confident.

'I hope not. But that now depends on you.'

At that moment Granville slightly lost his nerve and decided not to risk anything more for the moment.

'I'll give you to the end of the week to decide. You can send me a message, to say the channels with our mutual friends are open again. If not ...' His voice trailed off. 'By the way, in case there are any questions anywhere about what you were doing here, we can agree that you were complaining on behalf of the local community about army harassment. I've read about such complaints in the *Andersonstown News* this week, so they must be well founded.'

Murray did not react to this sarcasm.

'Tell you what: I'll arrange for the General to meet you and a small delegation – say half a dozen councillors or community workers – at your house. Look on that as a small bonus for your co-operation.'

Murray, his head slightly bowed, declined to shake Granville's outstretched hand as they parted.

That evening Granville was in festive mood, as he recounted the day's events to Wheeler.

'I take it from what you say that the police don't have an incriminating tape?'

With a loud chuckle Granville replied, 'As the good – or perhaps not so good – canon would say: what tape? He had his doubts, strong doubts, but he didn't dare put my assertion to the test. He didn't pay to see my hand, as we poker players say. He was afraid to. Which indicates two things. Firstly, that he is as guilty as hell. And, secondly, that he WILL deliver the message to Bunny, as politely requested by me. Buggers can't be choosers. He will even preach a peace process sermon to PIRA, in order to cover his own, rather muddy, tracks.'

'What's more, they will listen to him. I have a strong feeling that he is more of a guide on tactics than either they or he would admit. Goes back to childhood, obedience to authority and all that.'

'But what about the boy?'

'We can tell the RUC to tell him that his complaint is still being investigated. We can spin that out for quite a while. Long enough for us not to need the canon any more.'

'But if his family get impatient and kick up a stink?'

'Provided Murray plays ball with us, we can tell the Doyles that there is not enough evidence to justify a prosecution.'

'And if they run to the media?'

Wheeler could always be counted on to think of his customers, and to judge whether there were any juicy scraps to feed to them.

'Hardly likely, it's a one-parent outfit, but if they do, same reply.'

'You would be nicely scuppered if it transpired that a tape DID exist,' said Wheeler, laughing loudly at the thought of it.

'No chance. If it did, Doyle would have produced it right at the beginning. No, it's a matter of his word against Murray's. I believe the boy, of course. He is taking a big risk in pointing the finger at such a pillar of the church. He would only do that if fired up with genuine indignation. It's a classic case, I would say.'

'Aren't you setting aside questions of justice here?'

'Justice is all very fine and dandy, but I've got more important things to worry about right now than some kiddy-fiddling cleric and a complaining choirboy. Justice can wait.'

'And what will the General say about your committing him to a meeting with a bunch of malcontents ?'

It was Granville's turn to laugh mischievously.

'I think you will agree that Chesham merits some sort of sanction for the Drumphoe balls-up. Don't forget, I'm what Sir Julian calls the Lord High Security Co-ordinator. Arranging security meetings is a vital part of that co-ordination. And I must admit, it will be fun to drop old GOC into the slurry. He richly deserves it.'

Granville poured both of them a stiff nightcap.

The meeting the GOC reluctantly attended, was held in what the canon's housekeeper called 'the front parlour' of his house near St. Peter's Pro-cathedral in the Lower Falls. Murray presided with some formality, sitting in a vast armchair in front of an ornate, inactive fireplace, flanked by a local councillor and two 'community workers'. The GOC had asked for their names in advance and was not surprised to find that they all featured in the PANORAMA database, classed as 'SF militants/PIRA sympathisers/no confirmed direct terrorist activities/not priority status for surveillance'. General Chesham, dressed down in his khaki 'woolly pullie', sat somewhat uncomfortably on a low sofa, accompanied only by his young ADC (although outside a heavily armed protection squad surrounded the house).

Having introduced the others, Murray outlined the substance of the complaints.

'It's an overall problem, but seems to have become particularly bad in Lenadoon, which is where my friends here work and represent the local community. It's at its worst at night and seems to be deliberate. Army patrols make a lot of unnecessary noise, revving engines, slamming vehicle doors, shouting obscenities and so on. And when they are sent to carry out searches, they time such harassment for the middle of the night.'

'It's worse than that,' interrupted one of the community workers. 'The soldiers urinate, even defecate, in the front gardens.'

'And when they arrive at three in the morning to carry out searches they don't give the householder more than a minute to open the door before breaking it open with a battering ram,' added the other.

The councillor was keen to have his say: 'People come to me just about every day, to complain that their houses have been ransacked during these raids, with furniture ruined, such as settees ripped open.'

'Such damage is, of course, regrettable, but there are procedures for compensation,' said the General, defensively.

'Yes, but the reception we get when we try to lodge a complaint is always hostile. The people who are supposed to take our complaints on board treat us like dirt and mutter things like "fuckin' bogtrotters".'

Chesham took a deep breath, put down his teacup, and leaned forward stiffly in a stance which was well known to his colleagues on the JSC.

'Naturally, I'm disappointed to hear all this, and I am grateful to you, Canon Murray, for having given all of us the opportunity to air our views. Let me give you the other side of the story. My men have a rough time of it. They are insulted and even spat upon at every street corner, reviled at every turn. So is it any wonder that some of them, some of the time – not all of them, all the time – indulge in what you and I would see as unimaginative acts? They are, after all, only human.'

'Does that mean you are not going to do anything about it?' asked Murray.

'No, emphatically not. I will speak clearly to my men. It would help enormously if you could also speak to your parishioners and constituents, to encourage them to be more civilised towards my men, who are only trying to protect them.'

'Protect? Who from?' shot back one of the community workers.

'From anyone who acts against them outside the law – paramilitaries of every stripe. Orange or Green, they're all the same to me.'

'That's something I'd find hard to believe, General,' intervened Murray.

'You should face up to it: you are an occupying force. You must expect the natives, as you would call them, to resist in whatever way they can. Your actions are actually holding up the reforms which are necessary to end discrimination against the Catholic population.'

'Now you are straying outside my bailiwick. I'm a simple soldier. Politics and – with apologies to you, Canon – religion are not in my remit. Not to mention above my pay rate. But I am happy about that. To come back to your complaints, I've taken them on board and will take action. I only ask that you do the same. Thanks for the hospitality; those scones are delicious.'

As the visitors moved down the dark hallway on their way out, Murray plucked Chesham's sleeve and held him back.

'Tell your man Granville I have delivered and endorsed his message,' he whispered. 'He can expect a phone call anytime now.'

Uncharacteristically, they were waiting for him – *lying in wait for him, more likely* – when he arrived at Clonard

Monastery. Greetings were barely grunted and palpable resentment added to the chill of the gloomy room.

'I knew nothing about it.'

He did not need to mention context.

'We don't bloody well believe you,' said Bunny. Then echoing the Murray line, 'An operation like that just doesn't happen – it takes not just organisation but a series of approvals.'

Should I ask whether he is speaking from experience? Perhaps not, remember today's objective.

'As you know, I was out of the country and I've made my investigations. None of my staff was in on the operation in any way. Any organisation, including yours, if I may say so,(*is that too sarcastic and counter -productive?)* is liable to be taken by surprise by the unauthorised actions of a rogue element.'

'Are you telling me,' said Butch, red of face, 'that you view a regiment of the British Army as a rogue element. Whose fault is it, if the SAS is out of control?'

'You've seen the Secretary of State's statement. There will be a full inquiry.'

'And another whitewash, no doubt, months or years from now. But it is *now* that we are in the shit.'

Bunny took up the running, 'You don't seem to understand what this does to us. Here we are, at your prompting, putting out a line that a just peace is obtainable and that the war effort on both sides is being scaled down. That's a position under great strain throughout the Republican movement and community. Then your rogue elements come crashing in.'

Granville could not hold back from saying, 'Let's not forget that your activists crashed in first of all.'

I must stop sounding like Chesham.

'Do you realise,' interjected an increasingly agitated Butch, side-stepping that uncomfortable fact, 'that you have created five more martyrs?'

'I thought martyrs, like the hunger strikers, were all good propaganda fodder for you,' Granville shot back, unable to resist this unwise return of serve.

'Up to a point,' conceded Butch, 'but we can all become subject to the tyranny of the martyrs. Did Bobby Sands – or all the others – die in vain? That is the sort of sentiment which gets in the way of a negotiated peace. Do you guys not get it?'

'That's only true if you've nothing to show for it. But I have no doubt that the two proposals I want to put to you will be not only compensation, but a real bonus.'

The others looked at him, sceptically and in silence.

'Firstly, the SAS. Let me say frankly, my own view is that they should never have been deployed here in the first instance. I'm not knocking their expertise, which is acknowledged worldwide, but they're not suitable for use in a civil setting. They always, always cause collateral damage. And here they have too many people cheering them on.'

'You're telling me,' said Bunny, hostility still in his voice.

'Look at it from the point of view of ministers. They simply cannot reply positively to your demands that the SAS be withdrawn. The price of doing that is far too high, not only here but in GB and you must take that on board.'

'So you're saying no move on the SAS?'

'No, I'm saying no *announcement*. We have already announced an inquiry into Drumphoe and we've stuck to our policy of never commenting on troop movements. But – and this is the important point – we can soon feed out, under the table, to certain journalists, your friend Glass being one of them, that the SAS will soon be on their way. And in a few weeks they will be, without an official announcement. You have my word for it.'

'Your word, Jeremy, has lost a lot of its value, lately. The government will have to do better than that.'

'Well, I think we can. I'm authorised to tell you that the Prime Minister is now willing, on the basis of what we'd already agreed, to invite you to Downing Street and for the meeting to be publicly seen as an important part of the peace process.'

He could see the impact this had on them, temporarily throwing them off balance.

'When?'

'As soon as it suits you. You choose the date.'

'We'll consider it,' said Bunny cautiously.

'You have until the weekend to phone me. You know you'd be crazy to pass this up. It will be the first fruits of the process you can show to your people.'

'We'll see.'

That is as good as a 'yes'.

Granville wondered who else could take such a decision. Possibly the current ex-leader of the Republican prisoners, a man known in security circles by his code name Mungo. If that were the case, no problem. Mungo had already been encouraged in the paths of peace by his RUC handlers, who held over him some undeniable evidence of most unorthodox sexual activities, the public disclosure of which would blow Mungo out of the water, probably by his own relatives.

Was there any normal, legitimate sex life in these parts?

Chapter 41

Sir Julian Beardsley's suite of offices in the Foreign and Commonwealth Office reminded the visitor of the past glories of empire – not to mention the glory of the present incumbent. His own room, with its extraordinarily high ceiling, its gilt and plush furniture was, he believed, with some justification, the most sumptuous in Whitehall. A massive desk, which sat in a pool of bright light from two ornate table lamps, and a gleamingly polished conference table which was longer and broader than any other outside the Cabinet Room, reflected his importance as Head of the Diplomatic Corps and one of the Prime Minister's closest and most valued advisers, on matters both within and, more importantly beyond, his official job description. His climb to the top of the greasy pole had been thanks not only to his strictly diplomatic expertise, but to his secret service background and his ability to influence national policies over a wide spectrum. He had taken over the FCO from his ailing predecessor in late spring. And the fact that the head of the Home Civil Service was a rather lacklustre character by recent Whitehall standards and one who did not get on particularly well with the PM, further enhanced Beardsley's role as the most important *éminence grise* in government. He was enjoying it immensely, in his own double-breasted, pompous way.

A large clock ticked imperiously on the mantelpiece.

'I thought I should convene a meeting of the civil powers exclusively,' he began. The others smiled at this dig at the army and police. There were just three of them, plus Beardsley's note taker: Sir Richard Pickford,(PUS/NIO), Granville and Crispin Myles from the Prime Minister's office.

Crispin had never liked his name, which he thought was a burden in modern Britain. At Marlborough, a classics master had christened him Cincinnatus and he was prepared to accept, indeed embrace, the abbreviated nickname of 'Sin-Sin', by which he was now universally known, even by his mother, who had initially protested, saying, 'It sounds like an immoral panda'. His earlier career had been in the FCO, so he was yet another of Beardsley's protégés. It is through such networks that mandarins protect themselves in their old age. Within the PM's Private Office Myles had been given a special role as liaison man on all things relating to Northern Ireland and he spent a great deal of his time shuttling to and fro, in the interests of, as he put it, 'keeping up with a fast moving game'. There was, however, another, personal, reason for the frequency of his visits to the province: for several years he had been the live-in partner of a senior Home Office official, Maurice Hobson, who, on promotion, had been seconded to the NIO in Belfast. Thus, weekends 'out there' were no great hardship. Nor were the reasons for them a big secret, as his lover was the soul of indiscretion, telling his PA, who was every bit as indiscreet, how much he was looking forward to his every weekend, when Crispin would be over again. This partnership was more than frowned upon by Austin, with whom Hobson had to do business every so often; Niblock merely laughed and made ribald remarks about Myles, whom he dubbed 'the London Derrière'.

'As Jeremy and Sin-Sin know,' Beardsley went on, thus somewhat isolating PUS/NI, 'the Foreign Secretary and the Prime Minister are looking to us to bring finality to our Irish project asap. We can't hope to put together a package which will please everybody and which will not slightly unravel from time to time. But Ireland is no place for perfectionists. The much sought-after 'Solution to the Irish Question' will inevitably be a frail barque which may well need to be bailed out from time to time. But if we can keep all the motley crew on board *that* will constitute success.'

He paused to sip his morning coffee.

'Frankly, both my man and the PM are anxious about certain aspects of how things seem recently to have slipped back, after the excellent progress achieved these past few months. Lurid descriptions of SAS ambushes are all very well as fodder for the popular press and comfort to the unionists. But there are downsides, as you are especially aware, Jeremy.'

Granville nodded in agreement. He was relieved that Beardsley had phrased his displeasure about the Drumphoe incident, and his own failure to have averted it, in such mild terms. On that fateful day, when Beardsley had at last made contact with him in Archena, he, uncharacteristically, had been roaring expletives down the telephone, to such an extent that Granville feared for his posting, indeed his future career.

'Anything that appears to be "shoot-to-kill", or sounds like we are striving for "victory", stirs up a hornet's nest, in Parliament and elsewhere.'

'Yes, worldwide even,' chipped in Sin-Sin.

'Our American cousins are particularly restive at present, precisely at a time when we need their support on various items, like extradition and visas, not to mention non-Irish ones, such as Zimbabwe.'

'I agree,' said Sin-Sin loudly. It would have been hard to imagine many things about which he would not agree with Sir Julian.

'As I say, all talk of "victory" is unhelpful. We're not after victory, we are after an honourable draw. What's the speed of progress on the political front, Richard, with the so-called "constitutional" parties?'

PUS/NI took a deep, audible breath. 'Of course I can only speak about my dealings, in support of my S of S, with them, but I have the distinct feeling that everybody is watching and waiting for what will come out of Jeremy's side of things, which we all hope will subserve our purely political goals within the framework of overall strategy.'

'And I should at once say that dealing with those parties is like herding the proverbial cats at the crossroads.'

He nodded to Granville, as though to acknowledge that he had the more important role in all of this. He ploughed on.

'The SDLP are holding back, trying to put together a pan-Hibernian front, which they think will carry more weight. But it seems to me that Dublin is no longer so keen on them.'

'That's right,' chimed in Granville, 'they now think, having thought the opposite for decades, that Sinn Fein are the better bet in the longer term.'

'I agree with that,' echoed Sin-Sin.

'As for the unionists,' continued PUS doggedly, 'all their varieties are still thrashing around. Publicly the two main unionist parties are in competition as to who is the stronger advocate for military victory and the least likely to make concessions to the minority. But privately both of them are making noises that clearly suggest to me that they would welcome an agreement imposed by us, which would get them back into some sort of Stormont. Even their ultras will, at the end of the day, settle for half a loaf. They're now hungry for power, – for a new and solid role, not to mention salaries, cars, perks and all the baubles.'

'It's clear to me,' said Beardsley, with the air of the Lord Chief Justice summing up a challenging case, 'that everything turns on whether we can get Sinn Fein publicly and irreversibly on board the Good Ship Settlement, not just with us, but with all the other parties. We are almost there with them – barring further "unforeseens", such as Drumphoe – as regards an outline settlement between them and ourselves. But that will not be enough in the longer term; we have to get them to be prepared to sit down with the other players and work out an overall agreement. How do you see it, Jeremy?'

'We are making good progress and I think Drumphoe, whilst still a sore point, is decreasing in importance. I think we can say that, privately, there is now little between Sinn Fein and ourselves. The problem is that we can't advertise the fact, not even by leaks. We are at the most delicate stage and we must keep the army quiet.'

'Yes, but we mustn't muzzle them altogether,' interjected PUS, 'otherwise they'll go public and play into the hands of the more bloodthirsty, gung-ho tabloids.'

Granville said, in measured terms, 'We've been around this one before, without very much success, but I say it again: it would help enormously if the PM were to issue instructions, rather than vague suggestions, to SoS/MOD to rein in the troops, especially the General and the top brass. By all means the army should go on gathering intelligence and contributing to PANORAMA. Naturally they should prevent paramilitary operations whenever they find out about them. Incidentally, I think it's fair to say that there have been very few of such operations recently, as the IRA move towards us. That is why the army shouldn't go around arresting people – how shall I put it? – unnecessarily, particularly the known doves.'

'Doves?'

'Yes, PUS. All these terms are relative. I'm more and more convinced that we need them, and can use them to great effect right now. And we must acknowledge that the 'doves' have by and large ensured that the ceasefire has been almost complete. The IRA leadership have shown that to a large extent they can turn off the violence. That's going to be of extreme importance in the future. All now depends on whether we can get Sinn Fein / IRA to the wider conference table with the others in one piece. They are almost ready. And if they come, without any significant splits, all the other parties, whatever may be said or written, will be a pushover. But if the Provos split, it's back to the drawing board for everybody.'

Sin-Sin said, with a gravitas of which Beardsley himself would have been proud, 'I'll see what the PM can do. He's very keen to be seen publicly to have had detailed substantive talks with Sinn Fein and to be able to call a definitive peace conference, just as soon as you have secured the way. It's a make or break risk and he can only take it if he is just about 100% satisfied about the outcome. When the moment is right he's ready to move fast and imaginatively.'

Granville replied with urgency, 'I'd hope that is only a very few weeks away, at the latest. So, with respect, I would urge you to make haste. We must not miss high water. The moderates – pardon the expression, PUS, I suppose "moderates" is no better to your ears than "doves" – are still in charge, but if they can't show results soon the tide will go out and they will be left high and dry, with disastrous consequences for us.'

'Point taken,' said Sin-Sin, consolingly. 'Could you let me have some draft paragraphs for use in a prime ministerial statement in the Commons and some material for use in an eventual press conference with Sinn Fein on that doorstep of Number 10?'

'Certainly.'

Beardsley intervened, teasingly, 'I'm sure Jeremy can ensure that neither speech will upset his contacts.'

The others smiled at this little jibe.

What's so funny? It's my bloody job.

Sir Julian went on, 'If we can get Sinn Fein into publicly agreeing to substantive negotiations with the other parties as a follow-up to their negotiations with the two sovereign governments, I'm sure all the others involved will quickly agree to attend a round table conference. I think Jeremy is right: we must now go for broke. I'd say we should aim at getting to the crunch by Easter.'

'What about the Irish?' asked Granville.

'The embassy in Dublin has kept them up-to-date on progress, but I'll now go over myself and take them over this ground. It's in their interest that we move on and I detect the *taoiseach* is very keen to notch up a success on this one. The Northern Ireland issue has fouled up politics in the South for so long the government there is willing, for the first time ever, to help us get a solution.'

Back in St Oswald's, Granville briefed Wheeler over a nightcap of a good brandy.

'It was the usual Beardsley performance – a record number of mixed metaphors: packages, ships, tides going out, victory at the games – I lost count, but it was mostly a pulling together of his admin. resources in preparation for a final push.'

'The others mostly listened, or sucked up to him, especially Master Sin-Sin, who kissed his every orifice.'

'Aren't you just showing a prejudice against him, because he has the special role on NI in the PM's office?' challenged Wheeler, emboldened by a second bumper of cognac.

'Not at all. I don't mind Sin-Sin. Somebody has to look after NI affairs in Number Ten and he doesn't bother me. He's both lazy and biddable, so he'll take my line on things back to Whitehall. As you know, he was far too pretty at Eton and I think he somewhat fears what I might have on him, from my previous incarnations, about *his* previous incarnations. Something Positive Vetting DON'T know about. That's the way to keep it.'

'As for Julian, you have to hand it to him, he has played a long game and brought the big beasts of Westminster, as well as his Whitehall colleagues, with him all the way to the endgame. I agree entirely with his primary goal, which, incidentally, I have never heard him express – but it's obvious to me – which is to have HMG's political policies in Ireland driven by intelligence, rather than by so-called democratic theory.'

'Don't be modest, Jeremy,' said Wheeler. 'Beardsley couldn't have got this far without your input. But you're right: he steams ahead and ministers and Perm. Secs. follow in his wake. It always strikes me as a bit strange that they all go along with him without protest, despite the fact that his Jehovah complex must get up their noses from time to time,' said Wheeler.

'That's true,' replied Granville with a smile, 'but at the same time one must admit that his sheer arrogance and single-mindedness help get things done. It's not quite done yet, of course and it's all a bit hairy, now that we are so close. The biggest threat to success is our own side in the field and in NIO. The security forces are still to some extent playing "goodies versus baddies" and any reckless operation by them could scare away the very people who matter in Sinn Fein / IRA. And as for the NIO, they still concentrate on what Hume or Trimble say about this or that, whereas you and I know, James, that a few years from now Hume and Trimble won't matter a damn. Our dear colleagues don't really take on board – I mean in their heart of hearts – that the co-operation of yesterday's "baddies" is not only a *sine qua non* for getting the big peace conference off the ground; the "baddies" are , in fact, our best bet for the future, on the far side of the conference.'

'That's going to be a hard sell, everywhere,' said Wheeler, doubtfully. 'Who is going to forget the acts of terrorism – the bombs, the murders, the mayhem?'

'We have to close our minds to the things they have done in the past – we don't have to love them – and, above all, we in the service of HMG must see where our long-term interests lie and try to influence things accordingly.'

'And I'll tell you something else,' he went on, swirling his balloon glass and slurring his words ever so slightly, 'The memories of all but those directly affected by the violence will be surprisingly short. Peace, real peace, will be precious and the last thirty years will be as a bad dream; there will be what Gladstone called "a blessed act of oblivion".'

'I hope you're right.'

'Aren't I always right?' he laughed, then added, 'That's enough philosophy for one night. I'm off to my pit.'

'Sleep well.'

But it was an hour later before Granville closed the door of his office and headed at last for his bedroom, his 'homework' done.

Chapter 42

Bunny was in the chair at a full meeting of the IRA Army Council, in a safe house near Letterkenny, Co. Donegal. The location had been chosen only two days previously, to minimise the danger of Garda Síochána surveillance and all the participants had taken great care to ensure that their movements were not observed. Only one of their cars, fitted with a locational device, appeared on VELLUM and as its owner was from Fermanagh, a crossing into Donegal was an uneventful occurrence.

'We are at a critical stage in our strategy,' began Bunny. 'A public meeting with the British Prime Minister is now being lined up and the bulk of our demands agreed upon in advance. Once that next stage is underway, we'll be the only show in town!'

The others smiled and nodded.

'However, the price for that is a complete ceasefire, and the lowest of low profiles. I know that will not, initially at least, be popular or rightly understood by our supporters.'

'You can say that again,' said McCarthy from East Tyrone in a fairly hostile tone of voice. Bunny ignored the comment and went on, 'On the other hand, I am sure that in the meantime, and I'm talking about a very few weeks, we've got to keep the pressure on the Brits, in England. For two reasons: to keep them in accommodating mode, and to re-assure our own people that we haven't gone soft or that we are no longer up to waging the armed struggle.'

No one challenged this analysis, but the silence in which it was received did indicate an important element of doubt. Conscious that Bunny needed support urgently, Butch intervened, 'You're absolutely right. It's crucial that we can keep on goin' in the final furlong, despite recent setbacks.'

The word 'setbacks' clearly focused the attention of the other Council members. They were all painfully aware of the details – the increasing number of key personnel arrested and charged; the disaster of Drumphoe; the foiled post office hold-ups; the loss of bomb-brains. All of which added up to a paramilitary organisation in crisis. And one in which the cancer of collaboration was spreading at an ever faster rate.

Butch rather needlessly took them through the list of weaknesses, before concluding, 'I think it's obvious to all of us that our greatest weakness is treachery within. It's hard for me to say that, after thirty years in the movement, but it's an inescapable, nasty fact. And we have to face up to it. That is why Seamus Tolan here and I brought in Bobby Duffy from outward intelligence, to examine how things – and people – have gone wrong.'

'Why didn't we know about this?' asked McCarthy, sharply.

'There wasn't time. After the Enterprise fiasco, we had to act quickly to identify the source of the leak, before all the details evaporated with time. And to examine other big failures – who was involved, who knew what and whose behaviour, whose spending, gave rise to suspicion, and so on.'

'I think that's an insult to our rank and file,' said McCarthy angrily, looking round the room for support. But none came.

'Unfortunately,' continued Butch, 'it wasn't only Volunteers who showed up as suspects when we looked at the probabilities of who was touting. For example,' – here he paused and involuntarily lowered his voice, – 'our Enforcer's name cropped up several times in the context of who knew what at critical moments.' A stunned silence followed.

'And we're no longer as sure as we were about the Treasurer at the time of the St Lucia. McGarrity has had suspicions about how kosher the books and funds are. He can't always get sight of them when he wants to. So Bobby is looking into a few cases like that.'

Those present could guess what 'looking into' might entail. Duffy versus Stiletto would be quite a match, but of course Duffy would be accompanied by some 'assessors', to give weight to his enquiries.

Bunny was anxious to steady nerves around the table.

'I know this state of affairs is a disappointment to all of us. Touts in my view deserve to die.'

Mungo stared at the table.

'But we mustn't be deflected from our main goals, which are now within reach. It's not surprising that after more than thirty years our organisation should have acquired a few "bad 'uns". No revolutionary movement in history has been free from Judas Iscariots. We are no different. But we are facing up to the challenges and will do what we have to do.'

He hoped he had steadied the ship, but only time would tell.

The following week a parallel crisis meeting took place within the JSC. The GOC reported that Stiletto was in a state of near panic, because of the investigation which had come upon him, from Duffy and Tolan. He was not worried about financial matters, since he had always been careful to salt away his payments offshore, as he had long-term plans to live in the sun in his retirement. But for the moment questioning had concentrated on the ill-fated 'Enterprise' episode, as very few people had known about it in advance. He hoped he could survive that – after all, he was 'innocent', (a rare case), but what earlier cases would be scrutinised? Once the investigators stood back and took a look at the big picture, his name would be associated with all too many security failures that he was bound to be in big trouble.

'We can't allow this to happen,' said the GOC with great emphasis, 'Stiletto is by far my best – our best – ever informant. There must be a way to save him and his lines of communication to us.'

'To save his skin, I'm sure the RUC would, *in extremis*, shelter him as a Protected Witness, even though he has not witnessed in court. Isn't that so?' said Granville.

'I suppose so,' said HSB, thoughtfully, sucking on his ballpoint. The GOC intervened, 'I'm not just talking about his skin. I'm not interested in saving his wretched skin as such. When all's said and done, he's a bloody terrorist and once he's no longer of use, I hope he gets the chop, as he probably will. No, what I'm interested in is maintaining the flow of 'information' from him. He's the goose that lays the golden eggs and I want to preserve the rate of ovulation.'

'The only way we can do that,' said Granville, 'is to create a diversion, by pushing someone else into the limelight, or more accurately, into the wilderness, as a scapegoat.'

'What do you have in mind?' asked HSB, cautiously.

'Well, if they are starting with the train arrests another potential suspect is bound to be your tout, since I recall he was involved in the operation from the IRA's perspective.'

'You mean sacrifice my man?'

'Regrettably, it is sometimes necessary to sacrifice a pawn to protect a king. And don't get too possessive and sentimental about "your man", as you call him. Like Stiletto, as the GOC rightly says, he is a terrorist, only one of less value to us.'

'I know we're in a very difficult situation with this one. But can we really be happy about the moral aspects of such a decision?'

'HSB,' said Granville with some impatience, 'Happiness and morality don't come into it. This is the Joint Security Committee, not the Synod of the Church of England – or Ireland. Let's not lose sight of our moral responsibility towards the other, completely innocent humans, namely the population of the United Kingdom of Great Britain and Northern Ireland. Besides, we don't know for sure what will happen to your man when he is exposed.'

'We've a pretty shrewd idea, though,' countered HSB. 'He'd be very lucky to get away with only the loss of his kneecaps, or his testicles. More likely he'll lose his neck.'

HSB was as hard-nosed a policeman as a Head of Special Branch could be expected to be, but he sometimes wondered about the morality of his British colleagues. He had always been brought up to believe in the purity of British governmental intentions, but he had been shocked to the core some years before, when a fatal bomb outrage in the town of Claudy had been traced to the activities of a local Catholic priest, who was then simply transferred to a parish in Donegal by Cardinal Conway (who knew of the man's guilt), with the connivance of the Secretary of State for Northern Ireland, William Whitelaw. Now here was another case, albeit in a very different context, which showed how fickle the needle on London's moral compass could be. Despite the new Prime Minister's religious-sounding pleas to the population, his honesty levels did not impress him or indeed his colleagues. When he had said to Austin, who should know about such things, 'What do you make of the PM's piety?' he had replied, 'Given the lies he's telling, it's more like porkpiety'.

HSB himself was confronted in his daily job by the problem of whether the end justified the means, but this was the first time that the issue was one of life or death and one in which he was, willy-nilly, obliged to make a choice. His professional inner voice told him he would have to go along with the sacrifice of the scapegoat, but he would do so with a heavy heart. It was necessary, he told himself, and at least it would make him that little bit more tolerant of his colleagues' 'pragmatism' in other fields.

Granville was not to be diverted from his theme and the decision which would flow from it.

'We mustn't get hung up on the nasty details of the everyday brutish, and perhaps brief, life of our customers. We can't worry about whether they've passed their go-to-hell-by date. There's a war on.'

'And we should make sure we'll win it at all costs,' said the GOC, scoring his little point over Granville.

'Well, if that's the decision of the Committee – and I trust our discussion will be carefully minuted, if at all – I will look into the possibilities,' said HSB.

'Urgently,' said Granville.
'Of course.'

The unlikely solution to HSB's quandary turned out to be
Constable Eric Snowdon, from Traffic Branch, based in the
Musgrave Street police station, just over the Queen's Bridge
from East Belfast. Snowdon had wanted to be a policeman
from the age of seven, and once he had become one he wanted
to be a detective or Special Branch officer. In this latter
ambition he had been disappointed, largely because his
superiors in the RUC came to regard him as 'a bit of a lig',
meaning an unserious person, indeed something of a Walter
Mitty character. His 'Mittyism' and frustration with what
appeared to him to be an eternal posting to Traffic Branch had
led him, a few years beforehand, into a dangerous flirtation
with the world of security. If the police force wouldn't let him
into that sphere, he determined, he would make his own way
in. This he did by drinking in pubs up the Falls, or other
Republican strongholds, and talking to all and sundry. A
perilous game for a policeman. But he had been lucky –
although originally suspected by the local IRA of being a
police undercover man, his offer to them to be their agent had
been accepted, after a great deal of hesitation on the part of
the battalion's security officer. Snowdon agreed to work for
the Provos for a small fee, but his real motivation was the
thrill of being part of the world he had dreamt of for so long.

He would have been devastated to know that within a
month of 'joining' the ranks of IRA supporters he had been
'shopped' to the RUC by a police informer in the Lower Falls.
That informer had always given material which checked out
as one hundred per cent accurate, so although Special Branch
were surprised at the revelation, Snowdon was not
interrogated, but closely monitored and, above all, kept well
away from sensitive information.

Snowdon had been in the same recruitment squad as Ben
Niblock at the RUC Training Depot in Enniskillen, and he
now envied Niblock his life in SB. Putting personal sentiment
aside, Niblock now built on their shared past to befriend

Snowdon again, to the extent of going with him to watch Linfield FC play at Windsor Park and to share a mild bout of drinking afterwards in a pub on the Lisburn Road.

Niblock never had to raise the topic of his work, as Snowdon invariably raised it in conversation, then hung on his friend's every word, vicariously savouring every detail of the ideal world revealed to him. Niblock let him have, in measured dosages, pieces of information which would be of interest, but ultimately of little use, to the Provos – just enough to string Snowdon and them along. Early on the temptation had been to give Snowdon important false information which could mislead the IRA on some crucial issue. That temptation had been revisited, on the decision of HSB himself.

'Look on Snowdon as a conduit for a really "big one". Keep him in reserve for the crucial moment.'

That moment had arrived.

Niblock was tasked accordingly by HSB. He was not overjoyed with that task and was not comforted by Austin, who commented, as he often did, with a biblical quotation: 'Confidence in an unfaithful man in time of trouble is like a broken tooth and a foot out of joint.'

'If you see me walking with a limp and holding my jaw tomorrow morning, you'll know what's happened,' said Niblock, ruefully.

Bobby Duffy was surprised when he received the news, through Snowdon's contact, that Toner was the villain of the piece.

'Didn't think he had it in him. Always thought he was as useful as a nun's nipple. Certainly not the brightest, but when you think of it – the information he had access to as a runner, and presumably he has been opening and reading the "scripts" for ages. No wonder so many ops. have gone up the spout.'

He turned to Bunny, 'Shall we take him out right away and waste the little bastard?'

Bunny thought for a moment, his lower jaw twitching in concentration. 'I'd like to see where he can lead us. No use stiffing him straight out. And there's a risk, I think, in putting the squeeze on him. In his state of health – God, I saw him a few days ago and hardly knew him – I fear he'd croak on us before we got anything out of him. Better to play him along a bit, nice and slow. In fact, the play's probably the very thing.'

Chapter 43

At last, Seamus Toner, alias Harry-the-hound, felt he was getting some recognition of his true value and talents. He had arrived punctually at Unity Flats, a bleak new-build block at Peter's Hill at the city end of the Falls, to meet the local OC, Declan Shields, and receive his running orders for the day; he found his PIRA boss in jovial and friendly mood.

'How'd you like a run out of town, Seamus?' asked the OC. 'I mean you go about the town here like a fuckin' yo-yo every bloody day of the week. A change will do you good.'

'What sort of change?' asked Toner, somewhat anxiously.

'To tell you the truth, Seamus, we need your help – the help of a resourceful man like yourself. One that we can rely on for an important mission.'

'Oh,' was the only reply Toner could make, but his mind began racing.

Flattery is rarely unproductive.

'You see, it's getting harder and harder to keep our supply lines going. Too many of our men who used to do runs from the South have either been lifted or their faces and vehicles are too well known.'

'Yeah, I read about new arrests the other day. Awful.'

'We don't know exactly what those fuckers in the army observation towers in the border area are up to. You know, what they can do, what technical gizmos they have and so on. It may not be them, but something is causing havoc with our regulars down there.'

'How do I fit into all of this?'

'Well, Seamus I won't bullshit you. I've known you now – for how many years? – and I want you to continue with the cause with your eyes wide open, on a mission which, I'm telling you now, is dangerous but very important.'

The surge of excitement which Toner felt at these words overwhelmed all other sensations.

Adrenalin over apprehension.

'What you have to do is drive a van, which has a secret compartment fitted, down to near Ardee in County Louth. You pick up the goods and drive back to a garage in Whiterock. Easy at one level – but as I say, not without its dangers. Get caught with that lot and it's five to twelve years in the slammer.'

Toner looked pensive, as he took that in, but said nothing.

'So, you're up for it?'

'Just one thing ... I mean two. I don't know my way around down there. Been to Dublin a few times but in the train.'

'No problem,' interrupted Feeney, 'you'll be given a very clear, sure-fire map. And the route in the border area will give you the best chance of missing police or the Brits. You know what UAR stands for?'

'Not really. Ulster Association something or other. Who the fuck are they anyway? Sound like Loyalists.'

'Oh, for Christ's sake, Seamus, it's an unapproved road – gets you over the border without passing checkpoints at the main crossings. There are so many of them snaking about in Armagh and Fermanagh that the fuzz can't keep tabs on them all round the clock.'

'OK, but then there's the other thing. With my kidney problem I need a piss every hour or so.'

'Sure you can find a ditch or two along the way. Or take a bottle. But don't use it while stopped at the traffic lights,' chuckled the other.

Jesus, what a piss artist in every way.

'Can you do the day after tomorrow. There and back in the day?'

'Right.'

'Stickin' out. The van is at Lannon's garage on the Whiterock road. You know it?'

'Yeah.'

'Be there at nine o'clock. And no fuckin' sleepin' in. Right? You'll get all you need there.'

'Thanks.'

The health of Toner's van, which carried the markings 'D. R. Cruise + Co. Builders' Merchants, Belfast' on its side, was adding to his cartographical and urinary worries. He had noticed the clutch slipping slightly as he had changed through the gears when coming off the M1 motorway at Sprucefield and turning on to the A1 dual carriageway, which went south in the direction of the border and Dublin. This was the easiest part of the journey, but what if the van broke down in some godforsaken townland in the arsehole of nowhere in South Armagh? Better not think about that just now. Toner tensed momentarily when a police car overtook him, but it went on its way at a much greater speed.

That reminded him of his RUC handler, 'Macintosh'. Should he have contacted him to tip him off about the new type of mission? He recalled Macintosh's oft repeated pep-talk: 'Always keep me right up to date, at the earliest possible moment, about everything that is happening. Every little detail, no matter how small, can be important.' He could have rung on the secret number yesterday, or even this morning at the shopping centre he passed at Sprucefield, but something had held him back. Might his handler impose some additional task on him, or tell him to abort the mission? He always found conversations with Macintosh re-assuring and full of good advice, but this time his sense of adventure overcame his instinct to confide in, and be guided by, his handler. He decided he would wait until the job was done, then pass on details of what he had learnt, but in a way that ensured the information could not be traced back to him as the source by 'the battalion'. You had to watch your back ever so carefully these days. A lot of informing was going on, that was clear, and quite a number of informers were having tougher and tougher punishments dealt out to them. Putting such thoughts out of his mind, he fumbled the radio into life for the first time and allowed himself to be diverted from the problems in hand by the pop music which he found, and the intermittent chatter of the DJs.

The first half of the mission went smoothly, barring continuing clutch trouble, once Toner had turned off the good roads in the Republic on to the N52, towards his destination, which was a farmhouse set well back off the road at Mandistown. His directions were indeed, sure-fire, as the OC had promised, and he found without difficulty the pair of large white pillars which marked the end of the farm's laneway. He was well received by two men – father and son by the look of them – who were standing in the yard behind the house when he drove in. No names were exchanged, but the men offered their hands in greeting.

'Now you come on in and have a cup of tea and a bite to eat while we load her up,' said the older man, showing him in through the back door, into a large, modern kitchen. A middle-aged woman was putting a pot on to a giant Aga stove. She shook hands with Toner, with a warm smile.

'Tea or coffee? And would you like a bowl of vegetable broth?'

'Oh yes, please. I could do with that.'

The men withdrew and it was clear he was meant to stay indoors, away from the action. He was not told what his cargo was. It could have been Semtex, or guns. He only hoped it wouldn't rattle. He had enough to think about without that. He need not have worried: sandbags don't rattle. When the farmer's wife left the kitchen to answer the telephone, Toner took out his map and tried to memorise the six different road changes he would have to make before he was back on the A1 across the border.

'There you are. All ready for delivery,' said the farmer, wiping his boots before coming back into the kitchen. 'So I'll wish you a safe journey home. And tell your fellas up there to keep goin'. No feckin' cold feet at this stage.'

'I'll do that,' said Toner and thanked the farmer's wife for her hospitality. He tooted the horn as he drove out of the yard.

'Well, there he goes,' said the farmer to his wife and son as they waved him off, 'I hope for his sake he's shite at map reading.'

His wife crossed herself and went inside.

Without an Ordnance Survey map and excellent carto-interpretive skills it was almost impossible to know on these side roads, where one had crossed from the Republic into South Armagh. The border was not marked by any sign; indeed, even on the main roads the old placards announcing, 'You are now entering Northern Ireland' had been blown up so many times that the Roads Service had given up replacing them.

Toner judged that he was probably across and a change in the road surface – it improved – argued in favour of his now being in County Armagh. The fact that he could scarcely force a gear change into top did not yet handicap him much, as the twisting road was one on which he could only rarely reach forty miles per hour in any case.

He rounded a blind bend and exclaimed 'Fuck!'; the gears seemed to be stuck in third and, more ominously, there was a police checkpoint immediately ahead, which, along with a green Land Rover Defender and a chicane, blocked the narrow roadway. He had no option but to glide to a halt at the chicane. He could see three RUC men and when he looked to his left he noticed another man, in army battledress, sitting behind the ditch, a rifle across his knee.

Hope he's Brit and not UDR. Better be co-operative either way.

He wound down the window.

'Could I see your driving licence please?'

'Certainly. There it is.'

The constable took a hard look at it and pointed at the Belfast address painted on the side of the van.

'You're a long way from base, Mr Toner. Where have you been?'

'Near Ardee, visiting relatives.'

'And you came back over unapproved roads.'

'Yes. Sorry about that, but it's a short cut from where I was coming from.'

'Is that so now? Have you papers for this vehicle, or an authorising letter from your employer?'

'No officer, I haven't. The boss gave me permission, but no papers. You see, my own car broke down.'

'Would you mind stepping out of your vehicle, sir,' said the policeman, firmly but politely.

Toner could only stand by and watch as the other two policemen began to search the van. He opened the bonnet at their request and they peered inside, then tapped the hubcaps on all four wheels, but did not remove them.

'Where do you keep your spare wheel?' asked one of them.

'It's in a compartment below the back tray.'

'Well let's see it.'

Toner, his heart now pounding, found the catch with his fingers and released a lid, beneath which lay the spare wheel.

'That tread's a bit dodgy. You should get it seen to,' said the policeman, who then tapped the inside wall of the compartment.

'Hello, that's a funny sound. We'll have to see what's behind there. Maybe cigarettes or something like that. Eh?'

'No. Nothing at all,' said Toner, a little too quickly.

'You wait over there with my colleague, Mr Toner, while we have a good look at what you might have here.'

Toner did as he was told – there was no point in trying to run away. That would only give the UDR man the excuse to shoot him in the back. He had heard about such cases.

'Jesus, look at this!' he heard one of the policemen shout.

The first policeman drew his pistol from its holster.

'You're under arrest, Seamus Toner, for possession of arms and explosives.'

'But it's not what you think. That's not the whole story. I mean, I'm on your side,' gabbled Toner.

'Oh really?'

'Yes, I'm working undercover as an …as an agent. My contact, that is to say, my RUC handler, is in Belfast. He can tell you and explain everything.'

'How interesting. We'll have to check this out right away. In fact we'll do that right now on the blower. What is your contact's name?'

'Macintosh.'

'You'll have a telephone number for him. Right?'

'Yes, I know it by heart.'

'Write it down here,' said the policeman, handing him a small notepad.

'And is there an ID code for you?'

'Yes, I'm ELM107.'

At this, the policeman, Toner thought, seemed to be more relaxed about the situation.

Thank God for Macintosh.

'You'll have to wait over there, and talk to my colleague about your Mr Macintosh while I find out whether this is true or a load of baloney. You realise that if it's baloney you'll go down for fifteen years.'

He climbed into the cab of the Land Rover, in which a radio crackled.

Number two policeman chatted to Toner about his life and work, breaking off only to stop, then wave on, another stray car, the first to have been on that road since Toner had himself been stopped.

'I've often wondered how you guys operate. Tell me about your contact procedures. Must be a fascinating job.'

Toner, now almost fully relaxed, was only too pleased to oblige. After several minutes number one policeman returned and said to his colleague, 'I think we've probably got as much as we're likely to get. Agreed?'

'Yeah.'

'OK, Mr Toner, You're coming with us for a little walk in the woods. Get in.'

Mother of God, a set-up. These guys are Provos.

The Land Rover went back down the road he had come, then over the border, turned off to the east, towards

Ravensdale Forest. Then a service road took them deep into a dark tunnel of mature pine trees. When they all got out of the vehicle, Toner was marched a hundred metres or so off the track. Only when they halted did Toner notice that one of the men had taken a long-handled spade from the back of the Land Rover.

'Right, this'll do,' said the leader. He threw the spade at Toner.

'Start diggin', you miserable little shit!'

Toner took the spade in both hands, but he could suddenly feel both nausea and weakness sweeping over him. He staggered to his left, then collapsed in a heap.

'Fuckin' hell, we'll have to dig the grave ourselves.'

'First things first,' said one of his companions, who pressed a pistol into the left side of Toner's temple, thought better of it, stood back and at almost point-blank range, fired three rapid shots into the prone man.

Thus ended Harry-the-hound, one more of 'the disappeared'.

Chapter 44

'Too many coincidences. Too many bloody coincidences,' said Bobby Duffy, thoughtfully. He was sitting at a long table in the dining room of a large country house in Quoile Road near Downpatrick, County Down. It belonged to a doctor with a practice in the town – and a willingness to help the IRA in any struggle. 'It's the duty of the middle class to play their part in the liberation of our country', was one of his usual sayings within his large family. He was honoured to provide protected accommodation to two important guests, namely Duffy and Bunny. Here they could work in peace, without the risk of the proverbial knock at the door.

Duffy had laid out on the table a series of small rectangles of paper, each one bearing the name of a PIRA operative in the Greater Belfast area, whether Volunteer or Officer. Across the middle of the table were the names of those who had, in the previous six months, been convicted in the courts for offences ranging from membership of the IRA to the possession of firearms, to attempted murder, or who had been arrested on suspicion and later released. Beside each name Duffy had assembled as large a number as he could remember – and his underlings had helped supplement the list – of those who could possibly have known about the operations concerned and who therefore could, theoretically, have been in a position to tout for the police or army.

'Just look at the pattern,' Duffy went on. Bunny whistled softly.

'Yes, when you see it like that it fairly jumps out at you.'

'The two names with by far the biggest ... the greatest degree of commonality, are Toner and Cassidy.'

'That only leaves Cassidy above the daisies, now that Toner has been dealt with.'

'Couldn't have happened to a better person, the little gobshite,' added Duffy, with considerable venom. Duffy was well known as a cool, ruthless operative. He had served two years in the Maze and was deputy leader of the PIRA prisoners during that time. He had suffered the humiliation of discovering, as had everyone in his circle, that his wife had given birth to a daughter during his second year in the prison. The joke in the shebeens, told ever so furtively, was that 'somebody has had it in for him'. He was no longer the butt of such banter when, on his release, he beat his wife black and blue, threw her and her daughter out of the house, tracked down the man who had cuckolded him and put a bullet behind both of his knees, crippling him for life.

'What I can't understand is why FF, our favourite Enforcer, has never taken a grip of the situation.'

'My view is that FF is an excellent enforcer and an even better interrogator, once he is pointed at a doubtful customer. God, the things he has extracted! And I don't just mean teeth. Wonderful. But his weakness is that he can't stand back and see the big picture, whereas it's only the big picture that can tell you where to look.'

'I know.'

'That's why the Council brought you in. Internal intelligence is going to be more important now that we're virtually on ceasefire, with operations winding down, in order to keep things going in negotiations. I can't devote as much time as I would like to that side of things. This politicking, not to mention media interviews and appearances, take up a helluva lot of time.'

'I hope it will all be worth it. And that we don't lose sight of the ultimate goal,' Duffy said, rather doubtfully.

'It is worth it alright. Just look at the political profile we have built from virtually nothing. I see that our ratings in the public opinion polls are climbing fast. We could overtake the SDLP in a matter of months. Of course, that doesn't remove the need for our own internal security to be watertight. Which brings us back to friend Cassidy. We may have made a mistake in allowing him to get close to the Brits.'

'I take it that it seemed to be a good idea at the time?'

'Something like that. He was left too much on his own. I also wonder whether he has been in cahoots with Toner. They had a lot of contact, nearly every day in recent months, after Doyle got lifted. And another thing. McGarrity has complained that he can't have sight of all the books when he wants to. Cassidy deals with him piecemeal. Always has a reason for not giving him full and immediate access.'

'Put all those factors together and it doesn't look good for Cassidy.'

'We should bring him in – to give an overview of our finances, or something like that. Line up the Enforcer and a few of the lads and we can put all these circumstantial indications to him, and see what he says. If need be, we can stimulate his memory – via his short and curlies.'

'OK. Leave it with me.'

Aidan Cassidy was not taken in for a second by the 'invitation' which arrived, via a new runner, to bring the Army Council up to date with financial details, at their meeting to be held in Co. Donegal the following Sunday. He thought it best to reply, by return of runner: 'OK. Certainly.' As he wrote the words on a scrap of paper, he was aware that his handwriting was wobbling slightly. He hoped none of his readers would notice. When the runner had left the office, Cassidy slumped over his desk.

Sweet Jesus, get me out of this!

He waited for half an hour, in case he was being watched for signs of panic, then walked slowly to the car park situated on waste ground near the Great Victoria Street bus and rail station. He climbed into the Jaguar and set off for Myrtlefield Park, almost felling a traffic bollard at the exit. He let himself into an empty house and made straight for the cocktail cabinet. He had just poured himself a stiff Scotch when Noleen arrived back from her morning equestrian outing at

Purdysburn. She took one look at him and knew that something was wrong. Badly wrong.

'Terrible news,' said Cassidy. 'There's a feud in the Belfast 'RA. And I think …I'm pretty sure …that one lot have it in for me. But I don't even know who they are.'

He flung his arms round Noleen and held her tightly. He could feel that she was sobbing, silently.

'What do we do?' she cried.

'I'd better contact Granville. There's nowhere else to go.'

'If that gets out in these circumstances, we're finished, regardless of who's who.'

'But if I just stay here we're finished anyway. They have sent for me.'

'Do you know who "they" are?'

'Members of the Army Council … some of them.'

After a pause Noleen said, 'You haven't told me everything, have you?'

'No, but that was to protect you from …well, to protect you.'

'Do you think Granville will protect us now? Can he protect us now?'

'He has good contacts. He's our only hope.'

'I've asked James Wheeler to sit in on this. When the solids hit the fan we'll need careful news management, or the story could spiral out of control.'

Granville was chairing an emergency meeting of the JSC at Stormont Castle, following a frantic phone call from Cassidy.

'We have some time – a day or two at most – before the rumour mill goes into overdrive.'

'You're absolutely right,' said a confident Wheeler, delighted to be at the top table, instead of having to hang around waiting for the post-meeting guidance Granville would normally give him.

'There will be mega-interest from the media. "Pinstripe terrorist suspect disappears", – all that sort of hype. We'll be under pressure to say what we know and flat denials may not be sustainable in the long run.'

'It comes at a delicate time,' said HSB. 'Things have settled down a great deal since Sinn Fein have been openly in the political game and this sort of thing could disrupt the equilibrium, if it appears we have been running traitors to their cause. The concept of "mutual trust" will take a bit of a knock.'

'Could upset your peace process,' said the General, with more than a hint of sarcasm.

'There's another aspect to this,' resumed Granville, not rising to the bait. 'We have other protégés right now and we don't know how many more we might need in the future, if the politics go pear-shaped. There is merit in letting it be known that we look after our own agents all the way.'

HSB frowned deeply.

'I agree,' said the GOC, patting the table.

'That's all very well,' said HSB, 'but I assume you will be asking us in the RUC to take over responsibility for the protection – and we could be talking about lifelong protection – of Cassidy and probably his wife.'

HSB tried not to look at either Chesham or Granville at the mention of Noleen (though he did say to the GOC the next day on the golf course, 'I do hope his balls don't run away with his brains').

'You will recall,' continued HSB, 'that at the beginning of the HERMES operation, you in MI5 undertook to finance it. I believe that should continue to be the case, even if the RUC have to protect by re-housing and relocating customers under the Protection of Witnesses.'

'My dear HSB,' said Granville mockingly, but in a friendly fashion. 'I never thought of you as a bean counter. I suggest we get our plans in place and worry about the financial aspects later. It's up to ministers to decide that sort of thing. That's what they're there for. Isn't it?'

'I'd still like it minuted that I raised the question of cost. These people will be a high maintenance job – it's not like re-settling some run of the mill hoodlum in Bolton. They'll need to be far away and set up in some style.'

'First,' said Granville firmly, anxious to move on, 'we need to decide on our protective action, both in the short and long term. Short term: have we a suitable safe house available?'

'We will have in a week to ten days. We have that police family lodged in Cherryvalley after being attacked in their home in Onslow Parade, near the Ravenhill rugby grounds. They are being permanently re-housed in Bangor, but they don't get possession of their new house until the thirteenth of the month. So there is that short-term problem.'

A long pause ensued.

'In view of the exceptional circumstances, I think I could put them up at St Oswald's,' ventured Granville, hoping he wouldn't blush. He was, nevertheless, conscious of raised eyebrows.

'You're assuming that these people will be willing to have their lives re-organised in this way?' queried the GOC.

'Oh, I think so, to judge by Cassidy's phone call to me. Better to have one's life organised, than one's death.'

'How very true,' remarked HSB, apparently now resigned to Granville's proposals.

The exodus from Myrtlefield Park was chaotic. The fact that it happened at night made the operation even more difficult. Cassidy wandered about from room to room in a daze, muttering to himself. Noleen had a book of coloured markers in her hand, which she used to mark furniture and other items which were due to be put into long-term storage; those which were to be stored with easy access; and those personal effects which they would need in the immediate future – their future *exile,* she thought to herself, as she stuck markers on some family photographs, having decided they should be in the short-term category. One was of their wedding day. How young they all looked, even her father and mother. When would she be able to see her father again?

Would he even want to see her? There was already a certain frostiness between them, since McManus had begun to take his housekeeper, the Widow Bradley, to social functions, giving the appearance – or was it confirming the reality? – that they were 'an item'. The thought of Mrs Bradley replacing her mother in the McManus household and family was a repugnant one. Noleen shook off the depressing thought and went on with the markings, as a large team of removal men loaded up two vast lorries parked in the driveway.

'Welcome to St Oswald's,' said Granville, trying, not completely successfully, to sound cheerful, as he stood in the elegant hallway of his house-cum-alternative HQ.

'Sorry that your visit should be in such disagreeable circumstances. But make yourselves comfortable.' It was four o'clock in the morning and the rain was almost horizontal. The interior of the house was warm and indeed welcoming. A Military Policeman appeared as if by magic, bearing a large tray with mugs of tea. A woman in uniform led them up the broad staircase and showed them into a bedroom which was at once old-fashioned, elegant and comfortingly cosy.

During the night Cassidy disappeared several times into the en suite bathroom to be physically sick. Despite that and the upheavals of the past thirty-six hours, Noleen fell into a deep sleep, feeling strangely safe.

Chapter 45

One of the many things which Granville's colleagues in other services did not know about him was what he called his *Mashreg – Maghreb* (sunrise – sunset in Arabic) daily routine which had been his since his days in North Africa and the Middle East. It involved his personal study time early in the morning and last thing at night and in St Oswald's that took place exclusively in an office just down the corridor from his bedroom. There he received, through the media of papers and secure telephone calls, on a system modestly called UNIVERSE, reports from his five deputies, only two of whom were known to the other security agencies. They supplied him with information and intelligence gleaned through each of his networks, which greatly supplemented the flow of allegedly 'shared' information in the context of the Joint Security Committee.

MI5 had, disgracefully in his professional view, been entirely absent from the 'field' in Northern Ireland until 1986, when OPERATION CHIFFON had been launched. It was only then that ministers had given the green light to start operations. Ironically it was the growing success of the IRA's bombing campaign in Great Britain in the late 1980s which was to prompt ministers to authorise MI5 involvement – an involvement which brought the greatest pressure to bear upon the terrorist organisations on both sides of the community. Since the beginning of CHIFFON, its penetration of the paramilitary organisations had grown exponentially and, combined with the work of police and army, had sown confusion and wreaked havoc amongst the paramilitaries.

Even to those who watched him closely – and quite a few policemen and soldiers did – Granville seemed to spend most

293

of his day moving around the HQs of the other members of the Joint Security Committee, asking questions, offering advice and generally 'sticking his nose in', as HSB was often heard to remark. His colleagues on the JSC were often surprised, at a nine o'clock meeting under his chairmanship, how up to date he was with developments in their own fields, even those which had taken place overnight. They did not know that he would have had an hour in private, at St Oswald's, before breakfast, 'digesting his info. before his porridge', as James Wheeler put it. And when he said 'Good night' after dinner his hosts, or his guests, did not suspect that another hour's work lay ahead of him before bedtime. His sunrise and sunset sessions at St Oswald's were when he mostly ran his own organisation, rather than from his official office on the second floor of Stormont Castle, isolated by a grille on the landing at the top of the stairs. It was true that by day he tried to run as much as possible of the other organisations under his umbrella.

The candle at both ends – but it's not for ever, thank God.

The morning after the arrival at St Oswald's of the Cassidys, Granville thought it discreet to have breakfast in his bedroom, leaving his guests to be looked after by the staff in the large, airy kitchen, which opened out on to an equally large conservatory, beyond which lay the well-kept garden, with its rolling lawns. The early morning hoar frost had almost retreated from the grass before the weak warmth of the spring sunshine. The deciduous trees in the garden had already sprouted half their green and burgeoning foliage.

Granville, entering the kitchen from the hallway, took in this scene, but focused on, to him, a more interesting sight: standing in the conservatory was Noleen, motionless, watching Aidan pace up and down, between the giant rhododendron bushes which grew halfway to the trees. His head was bowed and his shoulders slumped, giving him the appearance of a convict circling the exercise yard of a prison. Noleen was startled when Granville, having watched the scene for several seconds, finally said 'Good morning'. He could see that she had tears in her eyes.

'Isn't it awful?' she said, turning to look again into the garden. 'He'll be a prisoner for life. With no remission!'

If he's bloody lucky.

'But he's not a prisoner. He's being protected. As you both are. And I will make sure you and he will go on being protected for as long as necessary. It's just difficult at the moment, before everything's sorted out.'

'You say "as long as necessary" – but how long is that?'

'As I've told you before, this war is not going to last for ever.'

'Maybe so, but the end of the conflict will not protect us from the revenge and punishment of the Army! You have no idea how a ... a situation like ours is looked on in our community. There will be no mercy, no forgetting and no forgiveness.'

She shook her head slowly and the tears now streamed down her cheeks, as her gaze never left the forlorn figure shuffling to and fro in the garden.

'Remember what you Brits did to traitors in your war with Germany. Executed them. And with public support. Our community is the same.'

How could he find words to comfort her and at the same time drive her away from Cassidy?

'This is the blackest time for you. Things can get better, believe me.'

'How can you say that?' she snapped back. 'We're facing exile – exile! Either here or elsewhere. Never to be safe from the past ... from this. How could Aidan have got us into this?'

Granville waited a few moments before saying, 'You don't have to go with him, you know. There is nothing pointing at you that your community would think of as guilt.'

He almost added, 'and both of you would be much safer if separate,' but instead asked, 'why do you feel that you can't look after your own interests. After all, it's Aidan's fault, and his alone, that you are in this difficulty.'

'You mean to abandon him? When he needs me the most? I could never do that.' Thoughts flooded in of the initial crisis of her own life – of England, Florence and a disgrace avoided only at the last moment.

'He was there when I needed someone. Whatever else he has done – and I'm still trying to understand that – he has always been a good faithful husband to me.'

Should I tell her about Colette, the gambling debts, the embezzlements?

The temptation was great, but the consequences of such revelations too unpredictable. Another time ... His frustration at her naivety was overshadowed by his admiration of her character. And, God, she looked lovely, even – perhaps especially – in her early morning un-made up state. That shining hair, that porcelain complexion, that willowy body.

'You know, you don't have to take definitive decisions just yet. You will be safely – and well – housed near police headquarters at Knock, where nobody knows you. There will be not only complete protection, but expert help in building a new life either here, or somewhere else.'

He paused and his voice lowered. 'I'm sorry, truly sorry, Noleen, to see you suffer in this way. None of this is your fault. You are the victim of tragic circumstances. My job often revolves around such circumstances – it has to – but that doesn't make it any the easier to see someone like you caught up in them.'

He had moved very close to her and she now did not look directly at him, but rested her head on his shoulder.

'I know,' she said softly.

Det. Sgt. McKinney sat in HSB's office at RUC Headquarters, his head bowed, gazing at the mug of tea on the desk in front of him.

'Bob, I know it's difficult,' the older man began, 'It's hard on you, harder than on anybody else outside his family. But we've got to be realistic – and sensible.'

'Are you sure there's no hope?'

'None. You checked out most of the hospitals yourself – which was itself a bit iffy in the circs. Since I called you off the detail, Section D has been beavering away, looking for clues. Absolutely none to date, except the inevitable rumours.'

'You can't rely on them.'

'I know, but in this case I think we've got to assume that the basic rumour is true. Most probably the Provos rumbled him, bumped him off and buried him somewhere where he won't show up for a long time, if ever.'

'Poor Seamus. He never had a chance in life.'

'Now snap out of that, Bob. Poor Seamus was up to his ears in terrorism and was then one of our paid touts. That doesn't exactly make him Boy Scout of the Year, does it?'

'But he wasn't a bad lad, deep down. Might have made it on to the straight and narrow when this thing's over.'

'No use dwelling on the might-have-beens.'

'But I can't help it. He was so brave about his health problems which had always held him back. I wanted to give...' His voice trailed off.

'You wanted to give what?'

McKinney sobbed before blurting out the killer words: 'a kidney.'

'A kidney? For God's sake, Bob, are you out of your mind?'

'We talked about it. I was to be checked to see if I was a suitable donor.'

'Well,' said HSB with more firmness than sensitivity, 'look on the bright side, some fucking IRA hit squad has saved your spare parts. I've never heard the like of it.'

McKinney blew his nose and held his head in his hands.

'Now Bob, we've got a job to do. And it's one we've got to do well, to protect our operations, and, not least, protect you, you daft bugger.'

'I've put all the data in my report.'

'That's good. But we have to go over it all again, in case we've missed anything. Let's assume the worst: they got him and he sang – sang the whole fucking song, all the verses. They'll have gone through all the contact procedures, magic numbers, codes, all that crap. I know you were always careful to keep each of your customers walled in from one another

297

and it's just as well you were. But there are other dangerous details, such as a good description of yourself. Bear that in mind – and get a shave and your bloody hair cut. No more West Belfast for you, Bob. We're putting you on the analysis team in PANORAMA.'

'But I'm a field man, not a backroom Johnny.'

'You're a backroom Johnny as of Monday. I expect you to put your heart and soul – not to mention both your kidneys – into the work. Now let's look at this report from the beginning... '

The next phase of the Cassidy future was what the Soviets would have called 'internal exile', that is to say they were accommodated in a safe house, far from their usual haunts and surroundings and insulated as much as possible from neighbours and anyone who might recognise them. Their life was protected, but restricted.

The house was in Cherryvalley, a road almost opposite the main gates of Brooklyn RUC HQ and which snaked along, following the contours of the quiet-flowing Knock River. On one side of the road were large detached houses, set well back, and on the other, the safe house was approached through a wooded area which sloped down to the river, and could not be seen from the road. Of much more recent construction than the other houses in the area, it was a large chalet-bungalow with dormer windows. Inside it was tastefully but sparsely furnished. It was not Myrtlefield Park, but was even more secluded and – more to the point – its garage contained a round-the-clock police protection unit.

In the days following their arrival there the Cassidys were systematically prepared for their new life. Aidan grew a beard (which itched) and acquired a pair of tinted glasses and a flat cap; Noleen had a makeover by a policewoman with amateur dramatic connections. They were instructed never to go out together. A Mini was at their disposal, the number plate of which was changed once a month and an RUC graduate of the police special academy in Ashford, Kent, passed on his knowledge about 'tailing' and what to do about it. The only bright spot in Noleen's life during the first week in Cherryvalley was an excursion, with a stylish policewoman in civvies, to a good dress shop in Newtownards, some eight miles away, to buy several new outfits in keeping with her makeover. But she had never imagined herself as a brunette.

Another bright spot appeared soon after, in the form of Granville, who 'just dropped by to see how you were doing'. He brought with him a present.

Better not call it a house-warming present, that's bound to be the sorest possible point.

'This is to cheer you up. And deepen still further your expert knowledge of the impressionists,' said he with mock ceremonial seriousness. It was a copy of Michael Palmer's recently published glossy work, entitled 'Magritte and the Belgian Impressionists'.

'Isn't that just lovely!' cried Noleen, with evident pleasure.

'And I haven't forgotten the Poussin book. It's at my parents' in England. I'll pick it up next time I'm there. I tried to get a copy here, but apparently it's out of print.'

The first few times that Noleen went out in her new persona she felt that every passer-by was looking at her. Aidan rarely went out; he watched horse racing on television, and drank ever-increasingly large amounts of vodka. He often spent entire mornings mooching about the house in his dressing gown and pyjamas. Both began to get used to their new life, but not to like it, or even psychologically to accept it. Compared to what life would really be like on the run, under their own steam, it was a gilded existence, but it was in a gilded cage. Without discussing it – they only rarely discussed anything nowadays – both knew that things could not go on like this.

Chapter 46

At her initial view of Wellington, Noleen's spirits lifted for the first time in months, if not years. She was standing on the Skyline Terrace, at the top of the cable car which brought commuters and visitors up from the city to the entrance of Victoria University and, further still, to the suburb of Kelburn. The harbour below, as big as Belfast Lough, gleamed in the spring sunshine, which was already warmer than she was used to in summer. To the south, beyond the green bush-clothed hills rose the Aorangi mountains, still topped with their winter snow. To the east lay the Hutt River Valley and beyond that another snow-capped range of mountains, the Akatarawas. The inter-island ferryboat entered the harbour, completing its voyage from Picton on the South Island and a flotilla of small craft moved out of its way. The sound of traffic from the city below reached her as only a distant rumble. Louder were the noises from the university cricket ground, immediately below her; and louder still was the intermittent, frenetic buzz of the cicadas in the foliage in the nearby well-watered gardens.

Perhaps they had been right, after all, to decide on New Zealand. Life had become intolerable for both of them in Cherryvalley, despite its safety and advantages. From this minor exile they had had to choose a place of permanent exile, where they could resume something approaching normal life. The choice was between 'lives' that could be offered by the police, through their contacts with friendly colleagues elsewhere in the world, usually where an Ulsterman, preferably an ex-RUC man, could be of influence. The very thought of leaving Ireland was repugnant to both of them and no amount of talk about 'fresh starts' could kindle an enthusiasm for the English Midlands, Toronto, upstate New

York or Wellington. Granville had argued, a little too obviously, in favour of England. His 'vested interest' was clear to Noleen, who was perhaps relieved, when the decision was made in favour of Wellington, to be free from the temptations that would certainly have otherwise presented themselves. The clincher was that the RUC's main contact man there could handle all the usual protective measures, but also an appropriate job for Aidan, in a private accountancy firm on a long-term contract with the police service of New Zealand. Ironically, it was in the context of detecting and preventing insurance fraud. Poachers often do make the best gamekeepers.

It took several weeks of careful preparation to equip the Cassidys for their new identities and lives. 'Brown' became their surname, as seen on all their documents, including Aidan's degree certificate and professional qualification diplomas, expertly forged by a vaguely referred to 'Special technical branch'. Equally important, they were rehearsed repeatedly on their personal background stories, to ensure their credibility and to avoid contradictions. Both were offered a means of communication with close family members. This would involve an elaborate roundabout procedure, whereby they could use Canadian airmail letters, which would be sent in the diplomatic bag to Ottawa, for posting to Northern Ireland. Family replies would come through the same channels in reverse. Both Aidan and Noleen, after much agonising, declined this offer. Aidan was sure that his family would have nothing to do with him – and what could he offer by way of excuse for his betrayal? It was more difficult for Noleen, as she was sure her father would put the blame for the whole situation on her husband; but what made it easier to say 'no' was the thought of Mrs Bradley in her mother's bed.

Noleen did not know whether to be relieved or disappointed that Granville had not shown up to say goodbye on their last day in Belfast. However, a small packet was passed to her, which contained the book on Poussin. On the fly page Granville had written:

As promised, the baby chicken. Enjoy it.

Yours ever,
Jeremy.

Would she remember the lunch in Paris – in the way he did? He hoped he had struck just the right degree of intimacy without compromise.

John Walker, a senior New Zealand policeman (ex-RUC) had personally welcomed them and seen them installed in their temporary safe house in Kowhai Road, just five minutes' walk from the top of the cable car. He ensured that there were no other Ulster people on the New Immigrants courses which they attended in order to familiarise themselves with their new surroundings. He encouraged them to avoid social contact as much as possible until they had 'built up enough local identity to fly free', as he put it.

Aidan started work within a few days, in a tall building on 'The Terrace', which ran in parallel with the waterfront and from which he looked out over the downtown area of the city and the harbour beyond. He was relieved to find the work was comprehensible to him, and that his new colleagues were both congenial and seemingly uninterested in his past.

A pleasant surprise for the Cassidys was that, at long last, their housing finance from the sale of Myrtlefield Park, had been sorted out in Belfast by the police. They could now purchase a home in New Zealand.

After much research and on-the-spot viewing, their choice fell on an out of town location, Waikanae Beach, a mostly residential settlement some thirty miles due north of Wellington, off the main road towards Wanganui and the centre of the North Island. The principal advantages were that they could afford a smallish clapboard house right on the beachfront, in Williams Street; and that Aidan could easily commute to the city on the suburban electric train, 'the unit', as it was known in the local vocabulary.

Had their pasts been different, they could well have been happy there. Aidan almost enjoyed his work, at first, and they could afford it that Noleen stayed at home. She joined the Pony Club in nearby Otaki and took up painting again. In that she gradually became fascinated with the view out over the water to Kapiti Island, in which light and colour seemed to change from one minute to the next. She painted that same view so many times she came to calling it 'my water lilies'.

Gradually they made friends with some of their new neighbours and the inevitable invitations to beach barbecues followed – the true mark of Kiwi acceptance. Their 'history' never presented any embarrassing problems and an outside observer would have thought of them as being well adjusted, well integrated new immigrants.

However, both knew, without sharing the dark thought with the other, that all was not well. Not for nothing was 'Exile' historically thought of as a harsh punishment; and in their case was the added torture of the fear of being exposed. Aidan was possibly the one more at risk, coming into contact with far more people every day. He certainly felt the greater strain, which, after the excitements of the first few months, began to show in several ways. His drinking increased and he would waken in the night several times a week screaming, as he emerged from yet another nightmare. More worrying still, at home he would spend hours silently staring out to sea, rocking to and fro in his chair like a distressed animal. Neither of them talked about this situation. Both knew there was nothing either of them could say which would ease the suffering of the other. They could read one another's thoughts but they had become intimate strangers.

A new level of crisis was suddenly reached one evening when Aidan burst into the living room, eyes blazing, on his arrival home from work. 'I've seen him! I've seen him!' he cried.

'What? Who? Calm yourself. What are you talking about?' replied Noleen, instantly anxious.

'I've seen him – Sean Byrne. I'm sure it was him. Looking at me from behind a pillar in the station in Wellington. He's come to get us.'

'Nonsense,' said Noleen firmly, but without conviction that her husband's ramblings were delusional. One could never tell.

'I tell you, he looked straight at me, then ducked out of sight. He must have recognised me. I ran like hell along the platform and, thank God, the unit pulled out right away. But what are we to do?' he added plaintively.

'Aidan, you must be mistaken. Your imagination is playing tricks with you. Look at it rationally: if Sean Byrne is another 'Protected Witness' like us, they would never have sent him to the same place as us. And if he got here by himself he would want to go to ground. Why would he want to bother us?'

She said this soothingly, holding Aidan's hand, but in reality she could think of one or two reasons why he might be looking for them: for Aidan as a traitor; for her as ...prey. Memories of Portstewart Strand. But she knew that the IRA had also been looking for Byrne, so it was not in his interest to show himself to anybody in this way. No, it didn't make sense, the more she thought about it. Aidan was sinking into paranoia. There was no use, she felt, in suggesting a doctor; instead she suggested they contact John Walker. But Aidan would have none of it. He was locked in his own frightening mental world.

In the days ahead Cassidy's behaviour became even more worrying for Noleen. He became obsessed with personal security procedures – looking under his car twice or three times a day with a mirror, and varying his route home. The only thing which changed was that he spoke of no more sightings of Byrne. Was that a good sign – that his original had been an imaginary episode? Or could it mean that he was not after all delusional and had really seen Byrne? Neither thought was reassuring.

Chapter 47

Operation GILLESPIE had not produced anything of note for several months. McCune was eager, no doubt, to stay the right side of his handler and equally keen to stay on the payroll, to the fruits of which he had become financially accustomed, if not indeed addicted. He therefore kept up a flow of documents almost on a weekly basis, but their content revealed little of interest to RUC HQ. Then came a copy of a memorandum from PUS to Secretary of State which read:

'S of S NI

This is a summary of my assessment of where we have got to, post GFA. Detailed papers will be in your weekend box.

The biggest gain has undoubtedly been the sharp decrease in all the indicators of violence (Cf. Appendices 1 and 2 of Paper A) and the concomitant switch of public interest from armed conflict to politics. That switch has been the basis of the generalised euphoria of the media and outside observers.

I believe that euphoria to be somewhat premature. You will recall how shaky the Ulster Unionists were when trying to get internal consensus on participation in the Executive; there are signs that their instability has increased in office and there have been some significant deserters from the party.

The SDLP has not managed to win the credit which they feel is their due in winning improvements and concessions for the broad nationalist community. They are an ageing party and for some time have been out-organised on the ground by Sinn Fein.

To quote Yeats out of context, 'the centre cannot hold' and I predict that sooner or later they will be outvoted by the ultras on both sides.

In the meantime we will have to face many alarms and excursions, with perhaps even the re-imposition of Direct Rule. If that happens, we shall have to grin and bear it – and make clear from the outset that such a development can only be temporary. The public must get used to the thought that devolution is here to stay. They cannot hope to run home to nurse every time there is a crisis.

The unionists of both stripes – and the media – are fixated on the 'de-commissioning of arms' issue, which is proving to be a serious acnestis on the body politic. I cannot see this issue being resolved in the near future. Interestingly, our 'friends' in intelligence are sanguine about that, indeed believe it could ultimately be the catalyst which brings about a power-sharing arrangement which accurately reflects the division of real power between the parties.

We, of course, have our preferences as regards which parties run the place, but I believe we should now let nature take its course.

Suggested paragraphs for your speech in the Commons on Thursday are attached. They are much more upbeat than what I have said above, but I trust leave you enough room to brachiate on to another policy position, if need be, in the months ahead.

PUS'

'Bloody 'ell,' said HSB, 'we're not going to get HMG's support on de-commissioning. I always knew friend Granville wasn't sound on that, but I thought the NIO looked on it as a necessity, if the settlement achieved is to be a lasting one.'

'Now they are taking a back seat to MI5,' agreed Niblock. 'I suppose that's the logical consequence of the way the Secretary of State got pushed aside at the Good Friday negotiations. One of my chums was there and he told me that Granville actually sat in the government team and was constantly in cahoots with the Number 10 and FCO wallahs. And he would wander off and call into the Sinn Fein office for a cosy chat. We think of intelligence as being a tool for government. Granville and Co. have gone far beyond that.'

'I think you are right. It's now a case of the tail wagging the dog.'

'It's all right for him to be blasé about IRA and UVF arms. When we have to deal with them – again! – he'll be over the hills and far away, on the champagne and caviar circuit, in a warm climate somewhere.'

'Yeah, can't you just see him in tropical whites on the veranda of the 'Residency', sipping his aperitif and telling his luncheon guests about his adventures in Paddyland?'

'Talking of embassies, must tell you some bad news,' said Niblock with a grimace. Our man 'Gillespie' is being transferred to the embassy in Rome. Leaves next month.'

'Shit!' said HSB.

'Should I try to find a way of keeping our talons in him? Like copy to us what goes out from London about NI to embassies abroad?'

HSB thought for a moment. 'Naw. Too complicated, too risky and probably the game wouldn't be worth the candle. Cut him loose.'

Chapter 48

During the first few months in New Zealand, Noleen had been more interested in 'the Situation' in Ireland than she had ever been at home. But that phase passed when politics then took so many amazing twists and turns that it was impossible at a distance – and what a distance – to follow the complexities of what was going on. The Good Friday Agreement had not, of course, solved all aspects of the community problem at a stroke, but it did shift public attention, even in nationalist areas, on to party politics. Bunny and Butch succeeded, by a slimmer margin than was generally realised, in bringing the IRA and Sinn Fein into the constitutional arena – an arena which had taken new shapes, all of them in their favour. They had at first been in overall public difficulty on the de-commissioning of arms issue, but Granville, confidentially, encouraged them to play a long game on this.

'There will, of course, come a time when total, visible, verifiable disarmament becomes absolutely essential, even in your own interests. But at the moment your political commitment is only to use your best endeavours in that direction. HMG will not accuse you of bad faith or of breaching the Agreement. The longer you can string it along, the more you will weaken the Official Unionists, surpass the SDLP as the real show in town as all the media attention will be on you. And at the same time, that will build up Paisley, which will be essential in the long term.

'Build up Paisley? Why?'

'Because the only agreement worth having here is between you and him. Together you can make it stick for keeps this time. Nobody else can do that.'

They didn't quite believe him about that – or when he told them that, methods apart, British interests in the future of Ireland were closest to theirs. Nevertheless, they had gone along with his advice *faute de mieux* and were even poised to reap the harvest from it. Not that they would tell him that in so many words. But when they heard he was to leave Northern Ireland for a new, ambassadorial posting, they asked to see him one more time.

The meeting took place in the familiar, if gloomy, surroundings of Clonard Monastery. They were in fine spirits.

'Well, Jeremy, where's it to be next, now that you've solved the Irish question – Palestine, Iran, Chechnya?'

Granville had to smile, then in mock imitation of the old Bing Crosby film, he burst into song: 'Like Webster's Dictionary, I'm Morocco bound'. But don't tell anyone. It hasn't been announced yet.'

'We can keep a secret,' said Butch, apparently without irony.

'Jeremy,' said Bunny, solemnly, 'you and me haven't always seen eye to eye, but I think we can both be pleased at how far we have travelled. And to remind you of all that, as you wallow disgracefully in the colonial luxury of your next appointment, here is,' – he opened his briefcase, the first time Granville had ever seen him carry one – 'a genuine blackthorn shillelagh.' It's engraved " Oglaigh na Eireann!" Granville put out his hand then hesitated.

'It's alright,' encouraged Butch, 'It's a de-commissioned one. It's not quite a pike, but you can keep it under the thatch.'

As Granville thanked them, with something he feared was almost approaching sincerity, the door opened and a shock of snow-white hair preceded the bulky form of Canon Murray, bold as brass and without the slightest sign of embarrassment. Butch and Bunny went to stand up – pupil-master relationships can last a lifetime – but he motioned with a wave of his hand that they were to stay seated. Not for the first time, Granville wondered, but more seriously, whether the relationship between Murray and Bunny might have gone beyond that of teacher-pupil and priest-altar boy.

That could explain a lot.

'Ah, here's the man who doesn't believe in the afterlife,' said Murray jovially, slapping Granville on the shoulder, as though Andersonstown police station, not to mention St Martin's, had never happened.

'Sometimes I find it hard to believe in *this* life,' was his rejoinder. They knew what he meant, politically, and laughed.

'But in our little theological debate I have a big advantage,' said the canon, 'for when we both die, you will never know if you have been right. But I, on the other hand, will never know that I've been wrong.'

Typically Irish – always complicating things.

'Touché,' said Granville.

'Now we'll have a wee drink for the road – the road of peace and enlightenment,' said Murray, heading for the cabinet. Bunny and Butch had, as usual, a soft drink each, the canon, an enormous whiskey and Granville, who had long since admitted in this sort of company where his beverage preferences lay, had an equally enormous gin and tonic.

'To Peace,' said Canon Murray, raising his glass ceremonially.

'To Peace with Justice,' replied Bunny.

They never give up, do they?

Chapter 49

Cassidy decided he would go home early from the office. His mind had been wandering all day from his files, as was increasingly the case nowadays. He still managed, on his better days, to keep on top of the job, but his boss was beginning to think that he wasn't quite the gifted grafter he had at first seemed to be. Drink certainly appeared to be part of the problem. Whilst he was never seen to be drunk on the job, he did often reek of alcohol first thing in the morning.

Cassidy had enough self-awareness to know his problem was increasing. He was also lucid enough to know where the source of this problem lay. But he could see no way of solving it. No one could help him fight his demons of guilt, a guilt which intensified rather than diminished with time. Noleen had stood by him all these months and would no doubt try to comfort him if he fully confided in her. But his guilt towards her prevented him from doing so. Indeed, whenever she tried to approach him in any serious way he would snap at her and leave the room saying, 'I don't need your bloody help' in the gruffest possible way.

Why sit here staring unproductively out the window for the next hour and a half, only to get stuck in the northbound traffic during the rush? Since his scare about the possible sighting of Byrne, he had given up travelling by train.

He drove out of the underground car park and five minutes later suddenly decided not to take the shortest way home, up the Ngauranga Gorge out of the city, but followed the sea level motorway towards the Hutt Valley. He would then have to take the mountain road which twisted over the hills before descending to Plimmerton harbour on the north-south coast, where he could resume his northerly journey home.

The journey would take anything up to half an hour longer, but, that consideration aside, it was part of his paranoiac policy of varying his travelling routes. Lessons from Belfast still had their effect, however misplaced. Besides, he normally enjoyed the scenery: the crumpled green hills where the sheep grazed in enormous flocks, the inaccessible valleys still under their lush primeval bush, and finally, the glorious views from the highest point on the road, out over Kapiti to the mountains of the South Island to the west. The narrow road down from the summit fell very steeply, through twenty or more hairpin bends. A driver's nightmare.

As Cassidy turned off the Hutt Valley motorway and veered past the vast electricity substation at Haywards, his thoughts wandered back to Myrtlefield Park. What if it were possible to benefit from the general amnesties declared by all sides back in Northern Ireland as part of what had been known as the Peace, Justice and Reconciliation Programme? He had toyed with the idea but news of the fate of one of the IRA Army Council drivers, who had been known to him, was not in the least encouraging. The unfortunate had been unmasked as an MI5 agent and soon after his flight to the wilds of Donegal he had been executed in the cottage in which he had holed up some months before.

'Christ, if they do that to a driver, what wouldn't they do to me?'

Besides, even if that sort of revenge was not taken, the fear of it would still haunt him – always. Furthermore, he suspected the Brits had betrayed the driver for reasons he could not fathom, but might a day not come when he, too, would be 'surplus' to the government's policy requirements? And, quite apart from security considerations, how could he hold up his head ever again in Belfast? Exile was to be his punishment, wherever he was. He was exiled even in his own mind.

Instinctively, Noleen knew at once when she opened the front door to a policeman and woman. Aidan was no more. Her husband's Holden estate car had been found in a crashed state, at one of the hairpin bends on the hill above Plimmerton. It had failed to take the bend. No other vehicle was involved. Cassidy had been pronounced dead at the scene. As she took in these facts Noleen swayed slightly and the policewoman put her arm round her shoulder.

'I'm dreadfully sorry,' said the policeman, as he always did on such occasions.

You couldn't really train for it.

The wheels of justice and the law do not turn any faster in New Zealand than anywhere else and it was several months before the inquest was held, in the Coroner's Court, housed in the regional courthouse in Porirua. The hearing was a simple affair, with few participants and no sense of occasion. The facts of the case were outlined by a policeman reading from his notebook in a monotone voice. No witnesses to the crash. Nothing vitally wrong with the vehicle, for example brakes. Pathologist's report showed nothing out of the ordinary. Blood alcohol level had been registered, but below the legal maximum. Cause of death: shock; crushed diaphragm. In summary, a straightforward, tragic accident.

The coroner, a kindly man, thanked the Inspector and expressed his condolences to the widow. He was privately pleased that no suspicions of suicide had arisen – that was always a painful and unproductive element for the family – and he guided the proceedings to a swift conclusion. A verdict of 'death by misadventure'.

The only face which Noleen recognised in the courtroom was that of John Walker, who had arrived late, having torn himself away from an important seminar, to give her a few minutes of support. Outside the courthouse he apologised for not having been on time; and further apologised for having to leave her again so soon to get back to the office.

313

'That's the worst over, Mrs Brown. I'll go over the bureaucratic bits of business with you in a few days. Don't worry, you'll be alright. And don't take any rash decisions about the house and so on; wait till things settle down!'

As he got into his car he said once more, 'Catch up with you next week, take care.'

Noleen looked around her. Not a face that she knew. But self-pity was not in her character.

The first day of the rest of my life.

She smiled to herself, remembering how she had often mocked that cliché, but now it had come true for her. As she walked towards her car, past the park in front of the courthouse, she had what she at first thought was a delusional moment. Was she also falling prey to her own imagination? For there, coming towards her was a man who looked remarkably like Granville. It *was* Granville.

Neither of them greeted the other: they simply embraced. It was not the polite embrace of old friends meeting, rather it was a long, tight, animal-like embrace, in which emotion surged to and fro between them.

That night, in Waikanae, they talked and talked, and laughed and cried. The next day Noleen would have found it difficult to recount precisely all that they had talked about. Except what Granville had said when they finally parted – words which really would change her life forever.

'You'll love it in Rabat.'

THE END

POST SCRIPTUM

In order to satisfy the reader's curiosity, the following notes outline what has happened since the above was written:

Sir Julian Beardsley – got his 'G', so is now a Knight Grand Cross of the Order of St Michael and St George (GCMG). He looks forward to his automatic seat in the Lords on his retirement from the FCO in two years' time. He is already sketching his personal coat of arms; he has decided that he will be known as Lord Beardsley of Plymouth.

Granville – got his 'K' and is therefore now a Knight Commander of the Order of St Michael and St George (KCMG). He is also one of Her Britannic Majesty's Ambassadors. He and Lady Granville (née McManus, but a.k.a. née Brown), are renowned embassy hosts and patrons of the arts. He is a non-smoker at last.

Sin-Sin (Crispin) Myles – left Whitehall and joined his uncle's firm in the City, as a special adviser on governmental affairs. His former colleagues said he had always been a 'merchant banker' at heart.

Bunny and Butch – are both in Government. They travel extensively to receive Peace Prizes and honorary university degrees for their successful policies of 'inclusiveness'.

Mungo – his treachery has so far escaped detection, as his secret is still safe, for the moment, with the security services. He is a major party figure.

Stiletto – gives many interviews to pundits and authors, for a fee. He takes frequent holidays 'overseas'. His immunity from IRA retribution is believed to be due to a cache of documents about Bunny and Butch which he has lodged with his solicitors.

Bobby Duffy – his health, ruined by a hunger strike in which he had participated in the Maze in the 1980s, deteriorated rapidly. An uncompromising 'armed struggle' man, he came to feel betrayed by Bunny and the 'politicos' on his own side. He died a disillusioned man.

General Chesham – is an international security consultant. He advises governments in the Middle East on weapons procurement and law and order issues. The new AA719 dye-spraying water cannon, manufactured by Anglican Armaments, features prominently in his work, under both headings.

HSB – has retired after thirty-five years in the RUC. He plays golf three times a week at Knock and in the winter often travels with Chesham to play in Dubai.

The Chief Constable – has moved on to higher things within the police 'Establishment'.

Ben Niblock – is now Assistant Chief Constable PSNI (Finance and Human Resources). He is seriously bored.

Bill Austin – is, in his retirement, a lay preacher, whose hell-fire sermons put the fear of God into Congregational congregations up and down the country.

Canon Murray – has recently been vilified in the press for an alleged cover-up of cases of sexual abuse by Catholic priests (including, it is rumoured, himself). It is also rumoured that he may soon be transferred to the Philippines by the Vatican.

PUS/NI – has been replaced, in the fullness of time, by another PUS/NI. Few have noticed the difference.

McCune – is still in Rome. He has changed his tipple to Campari soda (also, he claims, a favourite of the present Pope); he secretly supports Lazio Football Club (ditto His Holiness, he says).

Major Tomkins (retired) – was tragically knocked down by a motorcyclist when crossing the street in Keswick, Cumbria, and died of his injuries in hospital.

Penny – runs a Cancer Research charity shop in Richmond, Surrey, and plays bridge three nights a week. She remains a widow.

Rev. Meharg – published a book entitled 'Riots and Reconciliation'. Few read past page twenty, but he was awarded an MBE in last year's Honours List, 'for services to the community'.

James Wheeler – was seconded to the BBC World Service to head a project called 'Presentation without Propaganda'. As he told his colleagues, 'It should make a change.'

McVeigh – got a six month suspended sentence and a fine of £1500 for the illegal importation of a dangerous dog, to wit a pit bull terrier, from Finland. The finances of his association and minor political party are under police review.

Geezer Gifford– is currently in prison, convicted of assault and battery following a brawl in a pub on the Newtownards Road.

Det. Sgt. McKinney – suffered a nervous breakdown. Now recovered, he works on the Community Relations side of policing.

McManus – has diversified into the hotel and catering industry. He drives an antique Bentley and he and the new Mrs McManus often go cruising in the Caribbean.

Sean Byrne – has never been seen or heard of again – by anyone.

The British Army – is back in barracks, in diminished numbers.

The RUC – was simultaneously awarded a collective George Cross for bravery, and disbanded, in order to placate Sinn Fein. It has been replaced by

The Police Service of Northern Ireland (PSNI) – which is greatly admired by the foreign media.

Special Branch – has been replaced by a Criminal Investigations Department and (in the background) MI5. Crime detection rates have never been lower.

The 'Loyalist' paramilitaries – and some stragglers from the PIRA – have abandoned politically related activities and concentrate on rackets. In terms of their grip on deprived areas, they are, by and large, left alone by the PSNI.

MI5 – for inadequately explained reasons, have erected their biggest building outside London inside the army base at

Palace Barracks, Holywood, Co. Down. It is perhaps Sir Jeremy's professional legacy.